IDENTITY CRISIS

IDENTITY CRISIS

PETER CARROLL

The manufacturer's authorised representative in the EU for product
safety is Authorised Rep Compliance Ltd, 71 Lower Baggot Street,
Dublin D02 P593 Ireland (www.arccompliance.com).

This is a work of fiction. Names, characters, businesses, places, events
and incidents are either the products of the author's imagination
or used in a fictitious manner.

Troubador Publishing Ltd
Unit E2 Airfield Business Park,
Harrison Road, Market Harborough,
Leicestershire LE16 7UL
Tel: 0116 279 2299
Email: books@troubador.co.uk
Web: www.troubador.co.uk

ISBN 978-1-83628-203-7

British Library Cataloguing in Publication Data.
A catalogue record for this book is available from the British Library.

Printed and bound in Great Britain by 4edge Limited
Typeset in 11pt Minion Pro by Troubador Publishing Ltd, Leicester, UK

DEDICATIONS

To all those deeply scarred, physically and mentally, by the unimaginable brutal events at Omarska, Trnopolje and Visegrad (1992), and at Srebrenica (1995).

I will open my mouth with a parable; I will utter hidden things, things from of old
– Psalm 78:2

CHAPTER 1

July 2012

The agitated soldier grabbed a man with a straggly grey beard by his shirt from the crowd of condemned men, and pushed him forward onto the muddy ground under the shadow of an ancient oak tree. A second soldier in the line facing the great oak raised his Heckler & Koch assault rifle, aligning the sights on the chest of the bearded man.

The commander gave the order. 'Fire!'

Bang-bang-bang.

The man slumped silently forward, face down, his shirt flapping in the wind, leaking blood. Dozens of clothed bodies lay sprawled in the hastily dug open grave in the once-green meadow, bordered by a pine forest beyond the great oak.

A line of soldiers with cold-blooded intent in camouflage battle dress stood in front of the heaps of culled men with cold indifference. A third soldier pushed forward the next civilian man into the firing line.

With a resigned expression, the man looked up to the sky and exclaimed, '*Allahu Akbar!*'

Bang-bang-bang.

He fell; dead.

Once again I heard the distinctive sound of the Heckler & Koch magazine clicking into position in readiness for the next victim. A bird squawked above, and I glanced up at the high branches of the oak tree. My eyes panned across to a large white-tailed eagle perched halfway along a branch. The bird of prey looked intently down at me and then at the warm human flesh piling up beneath its perch. I considered if the bird had been there by chance from the beginning, or whether it had been attracted by the scent of death permeating into the forest. The oak tree would probably be crowded with vultures before too long.

Three more rapid gunshots echoed back from the forest. I looked down to catch sight of a blond-haired man wearing a loose checked shirt as he slumped down on top of the corpse of a man with a dirty sweatshirt – a new addition to the macabre matrix of clothed bodies with limbs intertwined. A dark thought entered my mind, *Once you've killed one, why not them all? Would any amount of good in the world ever be enough to account for the sin of this day?*

I was the last one standing in the line. I stepped forward, a fear gripping me like I'd never known before. The oak tree beckoned me into the dark forest beyond like a gatekeeper of this malevolent twilight zone. The sun appeared from behind a cloud. The shadow of a rifle barrel being lifted horizontally by the soldier facing the deathly pit came into view. I stood still for what seemed a lifetime. I cast my eyes down to the soil under my feet to evade the glare of the demons bearing down on me. It was beyond my grasp how I had got to be standing here, staring down the barrel of my fate. The sharp-beaked eagle was now pacing from side to side, its long talons gripping the high branch, waiting for the next victim to fall.

But the eager bird was disappointed, as at that moment I was handed a shovel and directed to cover the bodies with soil from the fresh earth mound taken from the excavation.

As ordered, I threw the earth over the great expanse of clothed corpses, taking it in turns with two other men to load up our shovels from the soil pile. I threw the loose soil from my shovel in the direction of the vast open grave, not looking where it fell. I glanced up only once, to see a shirt sleeve with a drooped hand sticking out above the layer of scattered brown earth. Exhausted, I wanted to rest, but we were ordered to carry on until we had levelled the soil mound, and then to return the shovels onto the back of an open army truck.

I feared that in completing my task I had outlived my usefulness, but I was lined up with the soldiers and forced to march along a track, under the command of a captain rank. We marched past a solitary soldier standing along the way who fixed my eyes with a fierce gaze as he handed me a half-full hessian sack. As I continued to march I eased open the neck of the sack to reveal a folded army uniform inside. Further down the track a faded road sign came into view – Srebrenica. My pace slowed as I passed, transfixed by the sign, which got me thinking, *I know this place. I've been here many times before, but I can't remember when.*

An eagle hovered high above, screeching down at us. I couldn't be sure if it was the same bird that had been perched high in the oak tree. It circled above, taunting us. I marched on in step with the soldiers. The marching squad was halfway around a bend in the road when the ambush came. Bullets cut through the air, hitting flesh and bone, shattering pine branches in the adjacent forest. The soldiers collapsed down onto the road, some screaming out in pain. The captain lay fatally wounded on his own a few metres ahead of the squad. I threw myself down onto the road but slipped sideways, falling through a gap between two bushes at the edge of the forest on the opposite side of the road to the incoming fire. The ground beneath me fell away, and I rolled down the slope, coming to rest at the base of the trunk of a large pine tree.

I gathered myself, inspecting my body for exuding blood. There was none, just some sharp thorns in my thigh where I'd rolled down the incline. Lying flat under the low branches of the pine tree I was out of sight from the higher road level. Keeping low, I twisted my neck to focus on the bushes that I'd just fallen through, when one of our squad stumbled through the same gap. He'd nearly made it to safety, when multiple shots thudded into his back. His legs stalled from their stride; he fell forward, choking on the blood filling his lungs. He was beyond saving.

The hail of bullets suddenly ceased. I could hear voices approaching as the ambushers emerged from their concealed positions in a shallow ditch and crossed the adjacent field. A dozen uniformed Bosnian soldiers with semi-automatic rifles walked down the sloped field towards the road just above me. Judging by their unhurried manner they were confident that there were no survivors.

Keeping low, I edged back slowly into the forest, sliding on a layer of damp leaves, the hessian sack still in my grasp. I negotiated my way through the dense forest, being careful not to snap any twigs that would announce my presence. The soldier's voices suddenly grew louder as they approached, and I froze in position. Two soldiers appeared in the gap in the bushes, scanning down the slope into the forest with their rifles. They bent over the dead soldier, his back red with blood, kicking him for a reaction. I held still, desperately hoping they hadn't noticed my fresh footprints leading into the woods.

One of the soldiers looked up into the forest as if straight at me. I stooped down behind the cover of a low branch, kneeling as if to pray, controlling my breathing, my heart pounding. The soldiers then turned away, exchanged a few words, and left the way they came through the gap in the bushes. I remained on my knees and shuffled backwards. The voices tapered off into the distance, which was my cue to make my way deeper into the forest.

I was soon confronted with an unearthly pungent odour. The colourless gas filled my lungs, causing my legs to fail beneath me. I was paralysed as my senses became dumb and I descended into a lifeless darkness, my consciousness fading. My inmost being was shutting down; memories being lost one by one as if my identity was draining away like sand through the hourglass. My time was nearly out when I sensed a ray of light flickering from within the forest. I strained my mind's eye onto its source, and I saw a bright light shining through what looked like an open door between the trees in the far distance. The door offered me a reason to turn over the hourglass, and my senses slowly began to return.

I can't remember how long I was out for, but some

time later I gained sufficient strength to continue into the forest, albeit at a snail's pace, crawling on my hands and knees, my eyes watering and my head throbbing. Still crawling, I reached the edge of the forest, into the bright sunlight. A green oasis of meadow opened up before me. On the far side of the meadow, I could just make out through my squinted eyes a dilapidated wooden shack. Judging from the holes in its sagging timber roof and the single broken window, it had been deserted for decades. I remembered the instruction given to me to change into the uniform in the hessian sack, and the shack would be ideal cover. As my coordination returned, I got up off my knees and stumbled on my feet across the meadow, gambling that a sniper wasn't lying in wait for me. Halfway across the meadow I looked upwards at the clear blue sky. There was no sign of the eagle; a good omen, perhaps.

I approached the hut and jolted the door open, ripping the rusted lock from the rotted wooden frame. Inside the shack was a warped wooden bench. I sat down on the warped bench and untied my left boot, and then the right, loosening the laces further to get them off my swollen feet. I removed my shirt and trousers, still not knowing if the folded uniform would fit me.

Above the thrill of birdsong a strange new sound intensified from across the meadow. *What is that noise?* I peered upwards through the shack window towards the approaching throbbing vibrations. *A helicopter!* It was descending onto the meadow. I grabbed the uniform trousers from the bottom of the sack and pushed one leg through, then the other, trying not to be seen through the broken window. The trousers were loose around the waist, so I fumbled to tighten the leather belt. The roar of the helicopter blades was now almost deafening as it descended into view just above the tree line. I grabbed the uniform shirt from the sack, left arm first, then the right. The fit was good enough. I started with the top button, the second, then the third. The helicopter was now hovering a few feet above the ground, the powerful downdraft flattening the long meadow grass beneath and kicking into the air the thick layer of leaves from the floor of the hut. I felt the weight of something still in the hessian sack, so I reached in and pulled out a decorated army cap and silver ID chain. I put them on briskly, both askew.

I slid my feet into my army boots, and as I bent down to tie up the laces, beads of my sweat and blood dripped onto the rotten wooden floor. Out of the corner of my eye, I saw four armed men jump out of the helicopter as it landed on the meadow. I gave up tying the boot laces and made my escape from the hut through the side door, but tripped over the threshold onto the ground outside. Dazed, I lifted my head to see two sets of black army boots pointing towards me.

'Stay down, soldier, hands on your head,' said one of them in a loud assertive American tone.

I turned as I heard heavy boots approaching from behind me. I caught a brief glimpse of the rifle butt just before it hit my skull.

'Aaagghh!'

Tariq Markovic awoke with a start from his nightmare in his bed in Beckenham, south London, as he had done many times before. Unsurprisingly, his wife, Alice, had long since banished him to the spare room. Awoken by his exclamation, she walked, half asleep, across from the master bedroom and poked her head around his bedroom door. He mopped the sweat off his brow with a tissue from the box he kept by his bed, his thick mane of long brown hair (he dyed it) spread over the damp pillow. She had become accustomed to her husband's bad dreams, but wanted to reassure herself it was nothing more than the routine.

Tariq looked up at her and muttered an apology. 'Sorry.'

His wife grunted incoherently and returned to her bedroom, shutting the door firmly behind her. He got up from his bed and stepped gingerly along the landing to the bathroom.

***

A week after being picked up by helicopter a few miles south of Srebrenica, Tariq regained consciousness in a United Nations (UN) hospital in Eastern Cyprus. He was eventually diagnosed as suffering from Post Traumatic Stress Disorder (PTSD) with selective memory loss. Despite rigorous questioning by the UN in Cyprus and by the immigration authorities in the UK, he was unable to provide any details of his life in Bosnia or of his involvement in the 1995 Bosnian War. He was fortunate to be granted asylum in the UK, as the Home Office refused most applications.

In the UK, he demonstrated his security planning skills, somehow acquired from his previous life in Bosnia, to gain employment by government agencies and high-profile companies to carry out security audits on their physical and cyber documentation storage and retrieval systems.

His discretion could be relied on to address potentially embarrassing security breaches. He then successfully applied for the role of a junior case officer at the Serious Fraud Office (SFO). After three years at the SFO, he was promoted to senior disclosure officer.

CHAPTER 2

'Will you hurry up, darling!' Alice shouted from the bottom of the stairs. 'The appointment is at 9:30. We can't be late!'

'Nathan's brushing his teeth. You can't rush Nathan!' Tariq shouted back down the stairs. 'Do ya hear that, Nathan?' he shouted at him through the bathroom door. 'We're waiting for you as usual.'

Millie, Nathan's younger sister, came to his defence. 'Leave him alone, Dad. You're just winding him up on purpose when he needs to stay calm.'

'Bloody hell!' Tariq complained to all who could hear him. 'Someone's got to hurry him up.'

'Five minutes!' Alice reminded them, the stress in her voice rising.

As Tariq walked across the landing to his bedroom to retrieve his watch, Millie leaned close in to the bathroom door to ask Nathan if he was alright.

'The timer says one minute to go,' Nathan responded in monotone.

Satisfied that Nathan wasn't panicking, Millie went downstairs to the kitchen.

'How are you feeling, Millie?' her mother asked, her

face contorted with concern. 'Have you had a drink? I've just made some tea; can I pour you some?'

'Just a small cup, please. Thanks, Mum,' Millie replied.

Millie finished her tea just as Nathan could be heard unbolting the bathroom door upstairs. His mother encouraged him to come downstairs and get in the car as soon as he could, then said, 'Tariq, everyone, we need to go!'

'Coming,' Tariq responded as he made his way down the stairs, securing his watch on his left wrist. Alice pushed a cup of tea towards him as he entered the kitchen.

'Drink it! Then get in the car,' she commanded.

'OK, OK.' He gulped it down and put the empty mug in the sink. He passed the line of coat hangers in the hallway, bulging with coats. He thought to himself, *No need for a coat today. It's going to be a warm July day.*

Alice was in the dining room just off the hallway, explaining to Nathan, 'You know where we're going, don't you, Nathan?'

'Yes, we're going to the family therapy session with Charlotte, the child psychologist,' Nathan replied in an instant.

Mother smiled. 'You like Charlotte, don't you? I know she likes you.'

'Yes, I do. Why can't Dad be like Charlotte? She understands everything. Dad is just so stupid.'

Unfortunately, his father was in earshot down the hallway.

'I heard that, Nathan. I'm just being straight with you, that's all. It's a badass world out there, and the sooner you realise that, the better!'

'Don't take any notice of him,' his wife said, glaring back at him, as she often did. She told her husband to get in the car and added, 'I'll come out with Nathan in a minute.'

Millie was already in the car when Tariq opened the door and sat in the front passenger seat. He turned around to Millie to ask her, 'You OK? Feeling any better?'

'About the same, thanks, Dad. When will we get the test results?'

'Should be Thursday; they said two weeks, didn't they?'

The car doors opened in unison as Alice and Nathan let themselves in.

Nathan's expression froze with worry. He blurted out with loud urgency, 'We can't go, we can't go! I haven't got my wordsearch book.'

His father reacted, 'For God's sake, Nathan, we'll only be in the car for half an hour. Can we please go?'

In defiance, Nathan opened the car door, saying, 'I'm not going! I'm not going!' He repeated with increased intensity.

'Bloody hell, Nathan!'

'Tariq!' Alice cut in. 'Let him get the book.'

'I'll go with him,' Millie offered.

'You sure, Millie? You should rest,' her mother advised. It was too late as Millie was already walking down the garden path with Nathan with the door keys jingling in her hand.

The silence in the car was palpable. Alice turned to her husband. 'Remember what I told you, that I'm in the middle of a project audit at work, and I need to get to an important meeting straight after the session, so *you'll* have to drive Nathan home, as we agreed.'

'So, where does that leave me?' Tariq complained. 'I've got a big case on. It's the final stage of logging the documents for the court hearing; there are deadlines, you know, which I have to meet, or I'm in the shit. I am already on notice since losing my last case, which wasn't my fault, as you know.'

Alice repeated her earlier point. 'We talked about this. Why can't you work from home?'

Before he could answer, Millie and Nathan returned to the car, Millie with the novel *The Hunger Games*, and Nathan with his wordsearch book and two pens, one black, one blue. Alice released the electronic handbrake on the silver Renault Grand Scenic car dashboard and drove away.

'I like Mum's driving best,' Nathan declared in a comic tone, 'It may be a bit boring, but you get there safely, and she doesn't shout at other drivers.'

Dad retorted, 'That's because there are so many idiots on the road, Nathan, and someone needs to tell them, and that person is me; otherwise, they'll never learn.'

'That's very noble of you, but please, not this morning; I don't want an idiot *in* the car,' his wife said bluntly, staring ahead.

The journey continued in silence, with Nathan ringing words with his black biro at breakneck speed in his wordsearch book, and using the blue biro to cross off each word from the list at the bottom of the page as he found them. With one puzzle finished, he put the book away to focus on the passing urban landscape.

A red Mini came out of a side street, causing Alice to brake.

'Bloody dickhead!' Tariq shouted as he lowered his window, having already forgotten his wife's earlier chastisement.

Alice glared across at him. 'It doesn't matter,' she replied, stifling her anger.

'That's rude. You shouldn't say that word,' Nathan added.

Tariq, realising that he was outnumbered and that he'd lost the moral high ground, pushed the window close button, followed by a final mutter of 'Twat!' as he composed himself.

Nathan's keen sense of hearing picked up his father's utterance and he informed him, 'That's a rude word as well because…'

'Alright Nathan, that's enough,' his mother interjected. Millie smiled across at Nathan, which helped to put him at ease. Nathan smiled back. The backseat comradery was interrupted by Alice instructing her husband in a serious tone.

'Now Tariq, can you please engage and be helpful? These sessions are as much for you as they are for Nathan.'

Tariq replied defensively, 'Why is it always my fault? It seems to me that I always take the blame when it comes to Nathan?'

'Because it would be so much better if you could just have a little patience now and again, and didn't lose your rag with him when he doesn't do things your way. You should know by now that as Nathan is on the autistic spectrum, so he does things differently, that's all. Surely you should understand that by now? You are the man of the house, and you should set an example. How many times do I…' Alice

14

tailed off her lecture, taking into account that winding her husband up could backfire on her strategy to keep him in a positive mood for the family therapy session.

Tariq was wounded at his fatherhood being undermined. 'Real men get things sorted. They face things directly and say what has to be said. You're a woman, so I don't expect you to understand.'

'Don't talk nonsense,' Alice said in a lowered tone so as not to create a scene. 'Face things directly?' she quoted back at him. 'That's rich coming from you, considering you still can't bear to remember what happened to you during or before the Bosnian War. That's a closed book, isn't it? We can't talk about that, can we? If you can't talk to *me* about it, you should talk to someone else, but you won't let anyone talk about it, will you?' After a slight pause, she added, 'If you don't mention the nightmares, I will.'

They approached the high metal gate of the Melanie Klein Child Psychology Centre, part of King's College Hospital in Camberwell, South London. Alice pressed the intercom button and announced that they were the Markovic family to see Charlotte Hardy. The gate opened, and she parked the car in the private car park adjacent to the building. Nathan and Millie had to be coaxed away from their conversation in the back seat by their mother. She spoke into the building intercom; the main door buzzed, and she pushed it inwards, with her family following behind. After completing a short registration form in the reception foyer, they were directed to take a seat in the wide carpeted hallway, which was a soothing pastel turquoise colour. Nathan read the wall posters promoting good mental health, some of which had interesting pictures and diagrams. Alice squeezed her husband's hand as a peace offering and a thank you for joining the family for the session, especially as this was only the second time that he'd attended out of five sessions. Tariq returned the gesture, despite already feeling irritable at the extended wait. After fifteen minutes, his patience was wearing thin.

A gamut of voices projected down the corridor towards them, and a family appeared with Charlotte escorting them behind. A girl, about thirteen years old, looked gaunt and thin. Alice noticed the anorexia nervosa poster facing her, and surmised why the girl was there. Tariq continued to stare ahead, oblivious of the family walking past down the corridor. Charlotte bid the family farewell and the security door clicked shut behind them. She then turned around to face Nathan and Millie, taking a second to recall their names.

'Nathan and Millie, so good to see you again,' she said with a genuine smile. She then twisted around towards Alice and Tariq, pausing slightly as she tried to remember their first names. 'And good to see you, Mr and Mrs Markovic. How are you both?' A platitude of positive responses came back, and she asked them to bear with her for five minutes while she retrieved some paperwork.

Nathan looked across at his mother. 'I like Charlotte; she's nice.' Alice concurred. Tariq was getting more agitated with the further delay, seeing through the therapist's honed professional tone, and recalling the negative comments made about him in the car. He was not looking forward to a potential all-against-him scenario at the family meeting with Charlotte. Alice squeezed his hand again.

Charlotte reappeared a few minutes later. She was of short stature with a friendly, well-balanced face and medium-length ginger hair. She led them into the consulting room, furnished with a comfortable red sofa, some black armchairs, and a fresh yellow décor. Nathan made sure that he sat in one of the black armchairs.

'Millie, there's something different about you,' Charlotte observed.

'Yes, I've curled my hair and had some highlights done. My friend at church helped me.'

'Very pretty; it suits you.'

'Thanks.'

Looking down at her notes, Charlotte said, 'Before we start I need to fill in some missing details? I hope you don't mind. Alice, what is your profession?

'Accountant; Associate Partner at Butterworth and Wheeler.'

'OK, good. Tariq, what about you?'

'Senior disclosure officer at the Serious Fraud Office.'

'Oh yes, of course, I remember now.'

Nathan intervened, 'When I ask Dad if he has caught anybody in the office doing fraud, he says he's not allowed to tell anyone.'

Charlotte continued. 'And I've got down here that, Alice, you are fifty-two, and Tariq, you are fifty-six? Sorry to have to ask; it helps us with our family profiling, which is completely anonymous.'

'Yes, that's alright,' Alice confirmed. 'We understand.'

Charlotte completed the data entry sheet. 'OK then. So, good to see you all again. It's always great to see the whole family together, as it doesn't always happen. How are you all?'

Nathan explained that he wasn't always happy, but he was feeling quite relaxed now that he was in the room sitting on the black chair. He said it wasn't always Dad's fault when he was unhappy, like Mum said it was.

Tariq interjected, 'Thanks, Nathan. I think there's a compliment in there somewhere.'

Nathan replied innocently, 'That's alright, Dad. Charlotte says that it is good to be honest.'

'You're too honest, Nathan; don't worry about that,' replied his father.

Charlotte, well-practised at leading discussions, kept on topic and referred to the notes she'd collected from her office. She looked up and asked, 'So, Nathan, do you remember what we talked about last time you were here?' Nathan's eyes darted around the room, searching for an answer, but nothing came to him. 'Well, Nathan, you'll be eighteen in September, and that's when you're an adult in medical terms.'

'So what does that mean?' Nathan asked.

'It means, Nathan, that I can't see you here anymore after our final September therapy session, as this is a children's and adolescents' centre.'

Nathan was distressed at the news, rocking his head slightly backwards and forwards. He responded, 'That's not fair. I like it here, and I like you.'

His mother interceded, 'Charlotte likes you as well, Nathan. We all like her, but she can't change the rules.'

'The rules are stupid then!' Nathan retorted.

'I agree, Nathan, they are stupid,' said his dad.

'That doesn't help,' said Alice to Tariq.

'On the positive side, Nathan,' Charlotte continued, 'you're making good progress, and we can talk about you getting extra help after that.' Charlotte paused to allow

Nathan to settle himself. 'Your mum tells me that you're learning to calm yourself when you get overloaded, so you're having fewer meltdowns. Is that right Nathan?'

'Yes. It helps if Mum is around,' Nathan responded.

His mother explained. 'Nathan is now good at seeking out a private place, usually a toilet that he can lock. He puts the lid down and sits on it with his head between his lifted knees and his hands clasped around his ankles. It helps if he has a pillow which he can rest his head on, so I bought him an inflatable fabric ball that he can carry around with him.'

Nathan's eyes lit up as he removed the scrunched ball from his pocket. His father looked on indignantly.

Charlotte said, 'That's so good, Nathan, well done, really well done. We talked about this last time, didn't we? As soon as you feel you're getting over-stimulated and anxious, you should find a quiet spot where you can go to calm yourself to avoid a meltdown.'

'Yes, if I can find a quiet place,' Nathan said.

Charlotte changed tack. 'And how about the speech therapy? How is that going?'

'The speech therapist says that I am doing really well,' Nathan responded.

'Hey, that sounds better than last time. Can you repeat what you just said again, making the good-feeling words sound more upbeat?'

Nathan didn't hesitate. 'The speech therapist says that I'm doing *really well.*'

'Excellent, *really good,*' Charlotte replied.

'I've noticed the difference,' Alice was pleased to report. 'It has helped him interact better with the other boys in his class, and he notices so much more how others vary their tone.

Nathan said, 'I know now that my friends' tone usually goes down when they are not happy, and it goes higher when they want to say something that they are happy with; and when Dad is sarcastic he thinks it's funny to say it with an up tone when he doesn't like something.'

Tariq's attempt to conjure up a sarcastic remark was stopped in its tracks by a piercing glare from his wife.

Charlotte explained. 'So if something that you think is bad is said with an upbeat, you can always ask, "Are you being sarcastic?" and say it with a smile to show you aren't judging them. If you don't understand something, you can ask them if they can explain it again in smaller steps. People would rather you say you don't understand than pretend you do and get it wrong.'

Nathan nodded.

She continued, 'You have the advantage, Nathan, that you look normal...' She corrected herself; 'You look neurotypical. You are a good-looking young man. The only downside of that is that people can have higher expectations of you.'

Nathan smiled gleefully at the compliment as he pushed his fingers through his long brown curly hair. Millie gave him a sisterly smile.

Charlotte sipped a glass of water and turned over her notes.

Something caught her eye on the page, which focused her attention. She looked up at Tariq with a measured expression and asked him how he was.

Tariq replied, with a deliberate deadpan tone, that he was OK.

'No he isn't!' his wife butted in. 'Tell her about the nightmares.'

'I had a flashback last night, that's all,' Tariq stated as a matter of fact.

Alice added, 'One of many! His flashbacks have been getting worse since the trial of Ratko Mladic, the Bosnian General, for war crimes has been on television, which started at The Hague a few weeks ago. It's obvious that it's affecting him, especially when they show archive film footage. He gets all tense and paces around the garden until his dark emotions have subsided, and then he usually disappears into the study, probably to have a—'

Nathan interjected, 'Mum says when she first met Dad, he looked like a soldier, but she now wishes that he didn't still behave like one, and Dad told me once that he doesn't remember which side he was on in the Bosnian War. It was seventeen years ago, and he doesn't even want to remember cause only bad things happened.'

Tariq was keen to clarify. 'I was an officer in the Bosnian army, and my name is Tariq Markovic, so that speaks for itself, alright? What more is there to say?'

Alice grimaced, as she often did at her husband's refusal to face his demons of war, which was the reason for his ongoing nightmares, as she saw it.

Charlotte said in a trained professional voice, 'Interesting. So it says that you have two recurring dreams, one when you're being interrogated in a dark, damp concrete room, and the other…' she read on, paraphrasing, eyebrows raised, 'a mass shooting event.'

'It was the second one,' Tariq said curtly.

'We have specialists in PTSD at King's College, you know, that I could refer you to.'

Alice explained, as she had done at nearly every session.

'That is the problem; he refuses to get help; he refuses to let anyone understand what happened to him, and when it gets too bad, he just gets drunk.' Tariq looked back at her, formulating his defence, but she added, 'Don't lie as you usually do; I know you do, when I'm in bed asleep.'

Nathan backed up his mother. 'Yes, and I found a bottle of Jack Daniels whiskey behind the sofa once.'

Millie, too tired to contribute to this long, repeated subject of discussion, nodded at Charlotte in confirmation.

Tariq, in defensive mode, folded his arms and stated, 'Please! I'm alright most of the time, and if I need any extra help, I'll ask for it, OK?'

The stress in her voice rising, Alice repeated her assertion, 'But you never do, and you never will!'

Charlotte judged that the self-fulfilling prophecy touted by his wife wasn't the best approach to making progress. Her training informed her that the person living with PTSD had to make the decision to seek help; they had to *want* to be helped. The same went for alcoholics and drug users. 'Please come back to me if you like, Tariq. If you change your mind, my door is always open.'

Before Alice could pile further condemnation onto her husband, Charlotte turned and said, 'Millie, my dear, you aren't your usual chirpy self. I hear that you've had some blood tests done recently. Was that here at King's College Trust?'

Millie brushed her light-brown locks across her pale face, 'Yes it was, and we're expecting the results...'

'Thursday.' Her father finished the sentence, relieved that he was no longer the topic of conversation.

Charlotte said to the whole family, 'I hope that the tests confirm that it isn't anything too serious.'

'Yes, I hope so,' Millie rallied, her tiredness showing in her green eyes.

Charlotte concluded, 'Oh, I mustn't forget to give you this. It is an official letter from the hospital explaining that Nathan qualifies for the government *Work for All* scheme. You can give it to any employer who can then claim a subsidy from the Department for Health if they were to employ Nathan. Most government agencies have been given targets to achieve, which are for a six-week minimum placement. The scheme has been running for a couple of years now, but hasn't yet been widely taken up by employers.'

Alice thanked her and took the envelope. Charlotte reached into the top drawer of the small chest behind her. 'Nathan, this is for you. It's a two-player game called *Guess Who*. You have to work out who the other person has chosen by guessing if they're male or female, what their hair colour is, if they wear glasses, and stuff like that. You'll have to read the instructions. It is an excellent social interaction game.'

Nathan was impatient to take the sealed square box from her and mumbled a thank you, then returned to his seat to study the instructions on the back of the box. Alice also thanked Charlotte for the game. Charlotte looked up at the wall clock and announced that their time was up, and guided them back down the corridor. Tariq and his family said their goodbyes and signed out in the visitors' book. The security door clunked shut behind them.

CHAPTER 3

The newly appointed Serious Fraud Office Managing Director (MD), Sir Peter Brownley QC, approached the gathered staff from the seventh-floor lift lobby, flanked by two stern-faced senior executives in dark pinstripe suits. Brownley was wearing a plain grey style suit without a tie, with his top button undone. He smiled at the assembled staff sitting at a variety of round and oval-shaped white tables. As an experienced Queen's Counsel (QC) he was adept at holding the attention of a captive audience. His two senior colleagues sat down cross-legged behind him while Brownley stood with a dignified calm, scanning the faces of the numerous SFO employees. The room quickly became silent as the seated staff keenly awaited his announcement. He only did important announcements.

Tariq sat at one of the small round tables at the back, next to the window, occasionally glancing up sideways at the summer sky, which was a comforting deep blue. Sir Peter's delivery was expertly crafted and engaging. Tariq figured that a successful QC such as Brownley was skilled at appealing to the sentiment of his audience; in this case, the full complement of junior and senior SFO staff. He had a reputation for knowing his brief, which enabled him to win several well-publicised high-stakes business-related High Court cases.

Brownley spoke. 'Thank you for making time in your busy schedules for this briefing; I won't keep you any longer than necessary, but I should take this opportunity to respond to the recent statements made by the Home Secretary, Teresa May. Most of you have probably read in the papers and seen reports in the media recently in regard to her proposal for a National Crime Agency (NCA) to be launched some time next year, 2013. She has also made – I think unhelpful – comments about the SFO here at Elm Street being subsumed into the NCA. What I am eager to communicate to all SFO personnel is that this is *not* government policy, and these were informal comments made subsequently at a private function, the details of which are not relevant, to a well-known unscrupulous journalist hack. I have it on good authority that her standpoint on this matter is *not* shared by several of her senior ministers, or other government departments, for that matter. As you know, the SFO reports to the Attorney General's Office, whereas the NCA would be supervised directly by the Home Office. The Attorney General himself has confirmed to me in person that he would object to such a misguided proposal. It has been said in some quarters that this manoeuvre is merely a power grab, and a feeble one at that, by the Home Secretary.'

Tariq's concentration was broken by a firm hand on his shoulder. 'Hi Tariq,' said the man, who sat down next to him at the table.

Tariq responded quietly. 'Stephen, how are you? Not too stressed, I hope?'

'I'm alright, mate. I'm still working on the Nadir case,' he whispered back.

Sir Peter, in full flow, glanced across in their direction, prompting Tariq to curtail their conversation.

Sir Peter continued his briefing. 'And you've also probably got wind of the fact that our budget is under threat, due to monies potentially being redirected to the new National Crime Agency, which incidentally will also house the proposed Serious Organised Crime Agency and the long-awaited National Cyber Crime Unit. All I can tell you right now is that negotiations with ministers are ongoing and we hope to be able to make an announcement in the next week or two. If we don't get what we're asking for then we'll need to cut our cloth accordingly.'

Stephen whispered in Tariq's ear, 'So he'll be buying his suits from Marks and Spencer instead of Savile Row, will he?'

Tariq sniggered.

Sir Peter went on, 'I can assure you that SFO staff will be informed of the agreed budget as soon as it is finalised… and all the indications are that we'll win the Asil Nadir case; the judge is due to pronounce his verdict early next month. Whatever happens, I want to give a big thank you to all those on the Nadir Case Team for their sterling efforts over the last three years, and especially to the disclosure officers for compiling, collating and indexing some fourteen hundred boxes of evidence – a tremendous achievement.' He concluded on a lighter note. 'As you all know, the Olympics will be kicking off in London in just over two weeks' time on 27th July. The SFO have five Olympic Stadium tickets on offer, no less, in a VIP executive box. Staff members will be selected at random; there's no charge, but please donate as much as you can to one of our charities.'

Sir Peter left as quickly as he'd arrived, exiting the same way he came, in a lift with his two smart-suited sidekicks.

Stephen Hardacre was near retirement age. He had a mischievous lined face, and a reddish complexion as a result of a lifetime of binge drinking. He recounted to Tariq, 'Do you know what? The last time I saw you was at the Christmas party, and it looks like you haven't cut your hair since!'

Tariq, embarrassed, pushed back his long, wavy brown hair from his square-profiled Slavic face. 'Ha! I could probably do with a trim.'

'Anyway, who can forget the Christmas party? You and Cheryl were getting close and personal, as I recall.'

'Yeah, well, I was drunk. I don't remember much about it, to be honest.'

'Let me remind you: you both left in a taxi. What we all want to know is - what happened next?'

'Bloody hell, Steve, nothing happened. We both went to the station to catch our trains home; there's nothing more to say.'

'Tariq, mate, we're only jealous that you got to look into those sexy brown eyes of hers and—'

'Look,' Tariq responded, trying to keep his composure, 'we're just good friends.'

'As she's head of Quality Assurance, you could argue that she has a conflict of interest. She's supposed to check up on you, isn't she? That you are following process?'

'Drop it, would you? Anyway, I bet you're relieved that the Nadir case is coming to an end soon, and looking good for a favourable verdict. I've seen so many cases where the judge has thrown them out at the last minute on some stupid technicality.'

'You're right, it's a relief.' Stephen then asked Tariq, 'So what's the case you're working on now? Sorry, you may have told me; I can't remember.'

'The Magnus Conan-Whittaker case, the Serbian investment banker. We've got to submit the ledger of disclosure documents by September, and the sensitive material by January, but we're struggling. We're behind schedule and need to speed up the document reviews. The Case Controller is Lawrence Bashford, which doesn't help. He's more interested in sucking up to Burton; I think he's after his job. I guess you can't blame him for that.'

'Yes, I heard that the job's his if he wants it,' said Stephen.

Tariq got off his chair to make a move back to his desk, 'Anyway, I'm looking forward to going down the pub with you and the team to celebrate the Nadir verdict.'

'Not so fast. But I hope so.'

Tariq's mobile rang.

'Sorry Steve, it's my wife. I'll catch up with you later.' Stephen smiled back and walked away.

'Hello darling, what's up?'

She sounded distraught. 'It's Millie. The test results are back. The consultant's just phoned me. He said... he said...' She started to sob.

'He said what?'

'She's got acute lymphoblastic leukaemia.' More sobbing.

'Oh God.'

'The consultant says that there's a bed free at King's College Hospital, and she can go in tomorrow for further tests, and then start chemotherapy a week after that if they have the right drugs in stock.'

'I see.'

'I'm sorry, Tary, I can't stay at home, it's too much,' said Alice as she blew her nose into her handkerchief. 'I'm going to stay at Mother's. Herne Hill is just down the road from the hospital so I can take Millie in in the morning and visit her after work. I can't cope with Millie and having to deal with Nathan, and I'm in the middle of an audit… That's mother; she's just arrived at the house. I'm going to stay at hers tonight, so I need to pack a few things for Millie and myself. I haven't cooked anything for tonight so you might as well get yourself a takeaway. What time will you be home?'

Tariq looked at his watch. 'Well, if I catch an earlier train from London Bridge, I'll be back around six o'clock.'

'Alright then. Get here as soon as you can.' She hung up.

Tariq returned to his desk on the fourth floor, logged off and put his empty sandwich box in his briefcase. He walked briskly down the stairs and the outside stone steps of the Elm House office, north central London, then up the incline towards Grays Inn Road, turning left towards the bus stop. A number 46 bus arrived after ten minutes, which stopped at Chancery Lane tube station on the Central Line, where he disembarked. He transferred to the Northern Line and then caught the 5:18pm southbound train from London Bridge to Eden Park.

On the train, he rested his head on the upholstered seat and stared blankly out of the window as the grim reality of his daughter's illness began to sink in. She was seriously ill, and his wife was now moving out of the house, leaving him to look after Nathan. He also contemplated that he was still under probation until October due to errors he'd been accountable for on his last SFO case.

He picked up a discarded *Daily Mail* on the seat in front of him and flipped over the pages to read the lead articles: Andy Murray was to face Wilfred Tsonga in his first attempt to reach the Wimbledon tennis final; Oscar Pistorius was proud to have been selected for the South African 4 × 400m relay team; a baby boom was predicted thanks to the success of the *Fifty Shades of Grey* book, and living alone after divorce leads to aching loneliness. He threw the paper back down onto the seat, returning his gaze through the dirty window. The train was now slowing for Elmers End station, one stop before Eden Park.

It was a ten-minute fast walk from Eden Park station to his home on Village Way. He stopped off at the Eden Park Costcutter local shop to buy a bottle of Famous Grouse whisky, a box of Hamlet cigars and a couple of pizzas. He made space for his items in his black leather briefcase with a combination lock. As he walked past St John the Baptist Church, he recalled Millie and Nathan running over from the church to the adjacent halls with excitement for the Sunday School games and activities. What he'd give now to return to those innocent times of joy and laughter. He walked past the church feeling disillusioned with the so-called promises of God he'd heard the vicar preach on. What could God promise a fallen man like him? How could he let this happen to Millie, of all people – a Christian?

He approached his front door with trepidation, noticing his mother-in-law Margaret's D-reg red Datsun

Cherry parked across the driveway. He walked up to the door, reaching for his keys, but Margaret opened the door ahead of him.

'Hello, Tariq,' she said in a subdued tone.

'Hello, Margaret.' He kissed her cheek, picking up her usual aroma of Chanel foundation and No.5 perfume. He always felt on edge in her presence due to her critical comments soon after his marriage to her daughter sixteen years ago, fuelled by disparaging remarks from his wife about his PTSD-related symptoms.

Margaret, with blonde-streaked bobbed hair, turned and walked back into the house, announcing to Alice, 'Tariq's here.'

Alice approached him and gave him a sincere hug. She didn't have anything to say.

Millie embraced her father, 'Don't worry about me, Daddy. Come and visit me soon, won't you? Mum says that I'm going in tomorrow, and I'll get the best treatment.'

'Millie, we need to go,' said Alice. 'You need to rest as much as possible. Why don't you sit down until we're ready to leave?'

'I need to put my bags in the car,' Millie said.

Margaret offered before Tariq could volunteer. 'I'll do it. Let me take your bags for you.' She gathered up two well-packed leather burgundy travel bags placed next to the front door. Millie followed close behind, turning back to smile at her father as she crossed the threshold. Nathan, who had been distracted up to now by something engulfing his attention, ran up to Millie and stopped short to rest his head on her shoulder, arms down by his side. He didn't do hugs. 'I'll miss you, Millie. Please come back.'

Millie gently put her hand across his back, 'Yes Nathan, I'll be back soon.'

'Can I bring the *Guess Who* game with me when I visit you in hospital? I need to play it with someone and Dad is rubbish at games.'

Millie replied with as much reassurance as she could. 'Of course, Nathan, bring the game. I'll look forward to playing it with you. That would be nice.'

'Millie!' shouted Alice, who was now waiting by the car. 'Please, we need to go.'

Margaret added, 'Come on, Millie, your mother's waiting.'

Tariq and Nathan stood on the pavement waving as the women drove off. Millie waved back through the rear window.

CHAPTER 4

After seeing Millie off, Nathan skulked up to his bedroom to process adjusting to the departing of his mother and sister and being left alone in the house with his father.

Tariq put a couple of pizzas in the oven, poured himself a double whisky from the bottle he'd brought home in his briefcase, and slumped down on the large light-brown sofa in the living room. After his perusal of the *Daily Mail* on the train, he decided against turning on the TV at the risk of depressing himself further. He swilled his whisky and stared at the blank TV screen. Nearly asleep, he was awoken by Mozart's Allegro blaring through the ceiling from Nathan's room above. His initial instinct was to shout up at him to turn it down, but he just sat there enjoying being lost in the music to distract him from the shock of Millie's diagnosis. Was it really Nathan playing Mozart or was he having an out-of-body experience? Maybe he could awake from this bad dream? The oven alarm was dinging; for how long, Tariq had no idea. He rushed through to the kitchen to rescue the burnt pizzas before the smoke alarm went off. He shouted up the stairs for Nathan to turn the music off and come down for dinner. With the music as loud as ever, he went upstairs towards the increasingly distinctive overtures, and knocked on his door. Nathan turned the music down.

Tariq asked through the closed door, 'Do you want some pizza, Nathan?'

'No, I had shepherd's pie earlier. Mum always makes shepherd's pie on Wednesdays.'

'Oh, I see. I didn't know that.'

'That's because you're never home on a Wednesday because you're playing cards with your friends until late.'

Tariq returned to the kitchen, wounded by Nathan's observation. He salvaged the pizza by cutting off the burnt crusts, and made a lettuce and coleslaw salad.

Tariq awoke sometime later on the same sofa in the darkness, next to a clean plate and an empty crystal-glass tumbler. Lee Child's Jack Reacher book *The Hard Way* lay on the beige carpet below him. He arose from the sofa and went into the kitchen to put the plate and glass in the dishwasher. He forced himself up the stairs to the bathroom to brush his teeth, and went to bed.

Tariq had arranged to work from home the next day, which allowed him an extra hour in bed. He was in the kitchen pouring a strong coffee from the cafetière when Nathan entered in his black pyjamas.

'Good morning, Nathan.'

'Morning, Dad,' Nathan replied as he walked across the kitchen, looking down at the floor.

'I've made a bacon sandwich. Would you like one?'

'No, I hate bacon. I've never had bacon; it's red. I don't like anything red! I always have toast in the morning with Marmite, cheese and marmalade. I don't like bacon, so why are you asking me about bacon?'

'Your loss. More bacon for me, then.'

'Where is the bread?'

'It's in the bread box, Nathan.'

Nathan opened the box with obvious disappointment. 'There's only wholemeal brown bread here. I don't eat wholemeal bread!'

'So what bread do you like?'

'Fifty-fifty bread. Mum always buys it. Why couldn't Mummy be here? When is she going to be home? I'm surrounded by an idiot!' Nathan exclaimed.

Tariq half-smiled at Nathan's comical expression, and said, 'Calm yourself down, will you? You're being ridiculous!'

'Yes, Dad, running out of the proper bread is ridiculous, which means that you are ridiculous.'

Tariq got tired of trying to reason with Nathan and reluctantly drove to the local shop to buy the specified bread. Unfortunately, the Costcutter store had sold out, so he had to go to the large Sainsbury's in Beckenham. After returning, Nathan mumbled a thank you to his father as he prepared to make a cheese sandwich, and then went upstairs to his room.

Nathan later reappeared from his bedroom, wearing black jeans and a grey top, with a black-and-white striped Newcastle United shoulder bag. From the hallway, he mumbled to his father that he was going out for school lessons. Before his father could question him Nathan slammed the front door shut. Tariq then remembered his wife telling him something about Nathan attending catch-up classes at Village Park Secondary School.

Grateful for the quiet life without Nathan, or Mozart, Tariq made a coffee and logged in to the SFO server from his laptop. He noticed the time on the bottom bar of his laptop: 8.37am. Throughout the morning he sent various emails to Lawrence Bashford, the Case Controller, including the working-from-home request form, as a concession for Millie's illness. Tariq considered that he was more likely to get sympathy from Bashford than Jack Burton, the Head of Investigations. The SFO case document collation was already behind schedule, and Burton wouldn't appreciate him slowing things down by working from home.

There was a multitude of unsorted boxes in the named Property Room No.1 at the SFO office, rammed full of random papers, record books, documents and media storage, such as CDs and memory sticks. The Property Room was the designated location for all incoming case documentation. Only selected staff working on the case were allowed access as it contained a mountain of sensitive material. There were reported occurrences in less scrupulous countries of staff working within the same office taking bribes to destroy damning evidence supporting serious fraud cases. There could be huge sums at stake in confiscated bank accounts and fines, not to mention lengthy prison sentences. It was, therefore, forbidden to take any documents out of the building once they had entered the Property Room, without a record on the Case Ledger of its destination. The disclosure officers reviewed each document to assess its relevance to the case; hence, working from home was not a viable long-term option. At the present rate of progress, Tariq's team was in danger of missing the court deadlines set by the judge, which could only be postponed following a special request from the SFO Case Director with a bona fide justification.

Late in the working day, an email appeared in Tariq's inbox from Sandra, the case administrator, asking if she could meet him soon, as she had something sensitive to discuss with him in person. Sandra was a capable, strong-willed woman, adept at putting office egos in their place, so it was unusual that she wanted to discuss an urgent matter with him. It was doubly frustrating that he was now stuck at home and couldn't see her in the office until later in the week. A subsequent email from Lawrence Bashford summoning Tariq to a priority team meeting on Monday to discuss his recent working-from-home request was even more concerning. To top off a lousy day, Tariq's work laptop crashed and wouldn't reboot, so he would, in any case, need to take it into the office to get it fixed or replaced, which was clearly problematic since he was now stuck at home with Nathan.

***

The following morning Tariq and Nathan made the trip to King's College Hospital to visit Millie at the Davidson Haematology Ward on the second floor. Neither of them was in the mood for a confrontation, and Nathan ensured that the car journey was uneventful by sitting on the back seat solving word puzzles.

At the hospital, Alice was waiting for them at the second-floor reception with her mother. Her mother was always smartly dressed in pastel colours. Tariq maintained that she dressed like the queen, and behaved like her, by means of her formal and aloof demeanour towards him. Early in his marriage, she had made it clear that she considered Tariq beneath the calibre of her daughter, especially as a foreigner with psychological baggage. What she conveniently forgot was it was her daughter who had had the baggage in the form of two young children aged two and four from her first husband who had died suddenly of a faulty heart valve. He now loved them as his own. Tariq was accustomed to her occasional condescending remarks, some veiled, some not so.

The consultant, Dr Julian Freeman, arrived twenty minutes late. Despite his rushed state, he offered them a professional and cordial welcome. Dr Freeman had short dark-brown hair with a touch of grey, and a young-looking, clean-lined face. He directed them to a private side room with a few chairs, which he arranged so to speak to them candidly.

'Has anyone explained to you the prognosis for Millie and the treatment she will receive?'

'Not really,' Alice replied anxiously.

'The blood tests have come back…' He hesitated as he thumbed through some printed sheets in an A4-sized buff folder. 'Ah yes, now that's good. The results show that it is B-cell, which is less aggressive. However, the high white blood cell count is a concern.' He presented the optimistic outlook. 'Children in this country have an excellent chance of surviving childhood cancer, and King's College is a world leader in leukaemia treatment, so she's in the right place. Survival rates are even higher at King's.' He went on to explain, 'There are three main stages to the treatment of leukaemia: induction, chemotherapy and consolidation. The immediate priority is to get her on a course of steroids for about a week. The steroids will start to neutralise the leukaemia cells, stabilise her, and give us valuable feedback on the type of chemotherapy we need to prescribe. Anyway, let's talk to Millie; I'm sure you're very keen to see her.'

Nathan rushed ahead to Millie's bed, keen to ask if she would like to play the *Guess Who* game Charlotte had given him at the family therapy session. Millie apologetically declined, saying she was too tired and could not concentrate, and explained that she'd only just had enough energy to read her book, *The Hunger Games,* a few pages at a time. Nathan suggested they go to the cinema to watch the film together when she was better.

The rest of the family joined Nathan at Millie's bedside. Margaret, Millie's grandmother, leaned over her bed and gave her a brief kiss on her forehead. Millie's mother asked, 'How are you feeling, little darling? You don't have to answer that; I can see that you're tired. The consultant told us that they're going to start you on a course of steroids to stabilise you, and after that, they can work out what the best treatment for you is.'

'Yes, they told me this morning. Don't worry, Mum, I'll be alright.'

Her mother wiped gathering tears from her eyes, 'Yes, of course you will be, darling. Just rest and let the nurses look after you. The consultant said that the steroids will knock you out a bit, so you'll need to—'

'Yes, Mum, I know; they've already explained everything.'

After about twenty minutes of chat, they said their goodbyes to Millie and left the ward. As the four of them walked down the hospital corridor towards the exit, they passed a small open area with tables and chairs. Tariq said, 'Nathan, Margaret, you go ahead; I just want to speak to my wife about something.' Tariq ushered his wife to sit down on one of the chairs. 'Look, Alice, I'm under pressure to return to the office. I have a big case on, and I need to demonstrate that I am doing all I can to clear the backlog of—'

'So what's the problem?'

Tariq checked that Nathan was out of earshot and said angrily, 'What am I supposed to do? I can't take Nathan with me to the office! Can you look after him, at least for a week or two?'

'No. No, Tary; that's out of the question. I've already told you that my audit work needs my full attention, so I must be in the office and there for Millie. I can't cope with anything more than that right now. I'm sorry, Tary, I just can't.' Alice opened her handbag, brought out the letter that Charlotte had given her on the Work for All scheme, and handed it to Tariq. 'Look, take this to the SFO and demand that they honour the scheme. That's what it's for, isn't it?'

'You're kidding! The SFO have long-winded vetting procedures. Everyone is vetted, including criminal convictions and their family connections.'

'Well, he's your son, isn't he? And you already work there, don't you? Besides, if a foreigner like you managed to get a job there, there's hope for anyone.'

'That was different; I was a unique case. The British Foreign Office gave me special clearance as I was a—'

'So is Nathan! That's a government recommendation, isn't it?' she said, pointing at Charlotte's letter.'

Alice and her mother made the short drive to the mother's home in Herne Hill, a semi-detached Victorian house backing onto Ruskin Park.

Tariq and Nathan drove home the way they'd come. Nathan wasn't in the mood for any puzzles, so he scanned the houses and streets for anything that would take his interest, especially the advertising billboards. He preferred the twilight as the colours weren't so bright and aggressive. He looked across at his father and asked him in a matter-of-fact manner, 'Do you think Millie will live, Dad?'

'I don't know, Nathan. I don't know.'

'Doctor Freeman said there's a good chance of her surviving, so that's good isn't it?'

'Yes it is, Nathan, that is good,' Tariq responded, sceptical of his optimism.

Nathan had two autistic meltdowns over the weekend. The first was the result of his father making him beans on toast with cheese, as he hated red beans in red sauce. The second was due to his father refusing to take him to St John's Church on Sunday morning, as Nathan usually went with Millie. His father made some excuse that he wasn't in the mood to meet strangers. The real reason was that he was recovering from a hangover after finishing off the bottle of Famous Grouse whisky the night before.

After lunch on Saturday, Tariq hit a hundred balls at the golf driving range with his new Wilson Ultra Gold clubs. He'd cancelled his regular round of golf at the Shortlands Golf Club as he couldn't leave Nathan on his own for five hours, and Nathan had refused to be his caddie. Having failed Nathan Sunday morning, Tariq made amends by taking him to the West Wickham diving club later in the afternoon. It was the first time Tariq had taken him, as he was usually on the golf course or in The Ship pub on Sunday afternoons.

At the pool, Tariq was taken aback to see Nathan exiting the changing rooms with full scuba diving gear strapped to his back, including large black flippers. The diving instructor checked Nathan's equipment, and Nathan then carried out a controlled backward flip into the deep end. He disappeared for three minutes, swimming the entire length of the pool and back, with only bubbles visible on the surface. Various team tasks followed, such as carrying heavy plastic bricks wrapped in thick towels. Nathan was always eager to compete with his fellow divers. At the end of the session, the camaraderie continued as they returned their equipment into the storeroom and proceeded into the changing rooms.

Still excited, Nathan exited the changing rooms ten minutes later. 'Did you see that, Dad? I could see you watching. That was my eighth lesson. Next week, I'm going to take a confined water diving test. You have to replace your scuba gear underwater and do a mini-dive, and if I pass, I'm allowed to dive in open water. Maybe you can drive me there, but I don't know where it is yet. You have to do four open water dives to get your open water badge.'

At home, Nathan asked for cheese and pickle sandwiches. To avoid being the target of Nathan's wrath, his father asked which cheese, pickle and bread his son required, and if he wanted the crusts cut off. Nathan ate his sandwiches while watching his favourite TV programme, *Phonejacker,* in which a fictitious man took on various identities in conversations with members of the general public with a variety of comical voices. Nathan loved any programme with distinctive accents and dialects, which he then mimicked with uncanny accuracy for the rest of the evening, and some of which he re-enacted weeks later.

With his supply of whisky exhausted and the shops shut, Tariq went upstairs, laid on his bed, and fell into a deep sleep.

A man in camouflage uniform stood over him, shouting, 'What are your orders? Who is your commanding officer?' Another man in the room then tipped a bucket of ice-cold water over his head. He was choking, so he turned his head sideways to face the damp concrete wall to drain the water from his throat and catch his breath.

Tariq responded, as he always did, 'I don't know. I can't tell you!'

CHAPTER 5

Monday morning, Tariq reluctantly scan copied the Work for All letter that Alice gave him at the hospital. He emailed it to Jack Burton, requesting that Nathan be allowed to work with him to get used to the work environment and help with basic tasks such as photocopying. To add weight to his request, Tariq emphasised that this arrangement would enable him to return to the office and accelerate the document reviews for the Magnus Conan-Whittaker case he was working on, which was behind schedule. Tariq reassured Burton that he would supervise Nathan throughout his time at the SFO, were this to be sanctioned.

He expected Sandra, the case administrator, to contact him to arrange a meeting, as she had requested out of the blue last week, but later noted that her status on the SFO online communicator system was *out of office*.

At mid-afternoon, Tariq was surprised by an email from Lawrence Bashford requesting that he attend a rescheduled meeting tomorrow, Tuesday, and he was to bring Nathan with him to the office. Bashford stated in his email that he had discussed the issue of work experience for Nathan with Jack Burton, who'd agreed that he be enrolled in the Work for All programme over the summer. Burton had most probably given his sanction as a means of catching up on the programme on the document sifting for the Magnus Conan-Whittaker case. Maybe he'd seen the large array of neglected boxed case files building up in the Property Room. As the investigation head, he had clearance to enter all four of the Property Rooms in the Elm Street SFO office.

At home that evening, Tariq cooked a fish pie with mashed potato and peas for dinner. Nathan was excited at the prospect of visiting his dad's office, an enigma to him throughout his childhood. Although Nathan didn't usually cope well with changes to his routine, giving him sufficient notice reduced the impact of such events. His wife had long understood her son's adverse reaction to such scenarios, but not Tariq, but he'd got lucky on this occasion. Nathan now had the time he needed to mentally process his preparations. He polished his shoes and asked his father to iron a shirt. He downloaded the train app, checked the train times for the morning, and set bedtime and wake-up alarms.

***

The following day, Tariq was upstairs putting on his fine-striped navy trousers when Nathan shouted from the kitchen, 'There's no cheese, Dad, there's no cheese! If I can't make a cheese sandwich, I'm not going!'

Tariq secured his trouser belt and descended the stairs to the kitchen. 'Nathan, calm down, will you? I'll buy you lunch at work.'

'It's Tuesday. Mum always makes me a cheese and pickle sandwich on Tuesday. Otherwise, I'm not going. Don't change things around, Dad. Not today!'

Tariq whispered to himself under his breath, 'This is bloody ridiculous.' He said aloud, 'I'll tell you what, Nathan, we'll stop off at the Costcutter shop on the way to the station, and I'll buy you a cheese and pickle sandwich, OK?'

Nathan went into the sitting room and sat on one of the upholstered armchairs. He put his hands behind his head and leaned forward so his elbows touched his knees. Tariq soon found him but thought better of disturbing him. He looked at the clock in the hall; they needed to leave in eight minutes if they were going to catch the 7:38am train.

After four minutes, Tariq repeated his offer. 'Nathan, I'm sorry about the cheese. If we leave now we can buy a sandwich from the shop, yes?'

Nathan abruptly lifted himself up from the chair. 'Yes, alright then. Alright then, we'll go to the shop.'

Tariq was getting increasingly impatient when they left the house a few minutes later. They needed to walk at a brisk pace. Nathan suddenly stopped in his tracks and announced, 'Puzzle book! I've forgotten my puzzle book! I want my puzzle book. I need to go back.'

'Fucking hell, Nathan, there are free puzzles in the London Metro paper. Why don't you do one of those?'

'Dad, don't swear! It makes you sound stupid. Millie says let your "yes" be "yes", and your "no" be "no", and don't swear by anything else. That's in the Bible.'

'Sorry, Nathan. No more swearing.'

'And no, I don't want one of those puzzles in the Metro, I want *my* puzzle book. I'm not going on the train without my book.'

Tariq resigned himself to getting the next train and took Nathan back home to collect his book. He was relieved that there was a cheese and pickle sandwich in the Costcutter shop. Nathan was mildly excited at the novelty of buying the pre-wrapped sandwich.

Tariq and Nathan were a few minutes early for the 7:58am train, so they sat down on the Edwardian mahogany-style wooden benches in the station waiting room. Tariq read the free London Metro paper and Nathan started a new page of his puzzle book. There was an announcement over the tannoy that the train operator was sorry that the 7:58 train to Charing Cross had been delayed due to signalling problems.

'Is that *our* train, Dad?'

Tariq just shook his head in disbelief. It was later announced that the train had been cancelled. Tariq put his head in his hands and muttered, 'For God's sake.' Others in the waiting room had similar expressions of disdain. Nathan picked up on the restless atmosphere and buried his head in his puzzle book in an attempt to calm his increasingly nervous state, aggravated by the ongoing unscheduled events.

There was a sudden flurry of activity as people in the now-full waiting room pushed through the narrow door towards the approaching train. Nathan was alarmed at the commotion and looked around for sanctuary, for a safe place to hide, but all he saw were four walls closing in. His father said in an exacerbated tone, 'Nathan, we need to go. We need to catch this train. Come on!'

Still in the waiting room Nathan froze as he was confronted by the hostile crowd outside. Nathan went into meltdown mode, 'Bah, bah, bah, not going there. Bah, bah, bah, not going there.'

'Come on, Nathan. Please!'

Nathan pushed himself a few steps forward towards his father, as he urged him onto the train. Nathan looked through the window at the tightly crammed passengers, and said in a panic, 'Nooh, nooh, nooh, not doing it, can't do it, going home, I'm going home!'

Tariq stepped onto the train and shouted back, 'Nathan, this is your last chance!' but he had to jump out again onto the platform as the doors shut behind him. Nathan had now retreated into the empty waiting room with his feet raised on the wooden bench and his head between his elbows saying, 'Nooh, nooh, nooh, bah, bah, bah.'

'Nathan, sorry. I get it, that train was too crowded. I'd rather not travel with all those people either. Look, let's just calm down and we'll catch the next train, OK?' His father's request didn't register with him.

'Nooh, nooh, bah, bah, not going. I need to go home now.'

Tariq had to remember his promise not to swear.

After returning home with Nathan, Tariq texted Lawrence Bashford his apologies for being unable to attend the office meeting because Nathan needed another day to get ready for the office. He attempted to log in from his laptop, but it wouldn't boot up. 'Stupid thing!'

After pacing around the house like a cat on a hot tin roof for most of the morning, Tariq went upstairs to check on Nathan. He knocked on his bedroom door. The soothing sounds of the violin from Ave Maria, based on Bach's Prelude No.1, went quiet. Nathan enquired through the door, 'Who is it?'

'Who do you think it is? It's ya dad.'

'What do you want?'

'Can I come in?'

Nathan opened the door and sat back down on his bed, with a pillow between his knees in anticipation of further emotional trauma. Dad sat down on the desk chair to face Nathan, and looked around at the room decor. 'I haven't been in your bedroom for weeks, Nathan. Everything's still black and white, I see.'

'I know. It's my calm place. It's more relaxing without colours.'

Tariq went across the room to examine a football team poster on the wall.

'I didn't know you supported Newcastle United.'

'Yes, I started supporting them two years ago. They are a good team, and I like their black-and-white strip.'

'Of course.'

'They were fourth in the league last season. Their manager is Alan Pardew. The top scorer last year was Demba Ba. He was on a free transfer from West Ham, which is really good. He scored sixteen goals last season. Papiss Cissé scored thirteen goals.'

Tariq listened and paused, before asking. 'How are you feeling, Nathan?'

'I'm sorry, Dad, I wanted to go to your office. Can we try again tomorrow? Mum said once that the earlier trains aren't so busy, so can we catch the earlier train?'

'Yes, let's do that. Now, if you're hungry, I'll make some pasta with green pesto, and we'll get everything ready for tomorrow, OK?'

'Alright then. I'll come down when I'm ready.'

Alice phoned after lunch to update Tariq on Millie's

condition. She explained that Millie was very tired and would start the steroid pre-phase medication tomorrow after she'd been seen by the consultant. They discussed visiting her again that evening, but Alice agreed that Nathan shouldn't have to make a second trip out after the morning's tribulations at the train station. He needed some chill-out time to recover and try again in the morning.

***

The following morning, Tariq said as few words as possible to his son so not to risk winding him up. A minor panic was averted when Nathan finally managed to find a pair of grey socks in the clean clothes wash basket. They had to be grey. Tariq's patience was tested on the walk to the station when Nathan crossed the road three times to avoid approaching groups of school kids and a barking dog; but was later relieved that the earlier train was on time and less crowded, as Alice had predicted. Tariq boarded the train first, followed by an anxious Nathan. Nathan walked the length of the train to find the least crowded carriage. As the train started filling up at each station, he became increasingly uncomfortable with the restricted personal space, and so swapped seats with his father to be next to the window. Nathan could then distract himself from the crowded carriage by studying the tower block balconies as the train approached London Bridge station.

Nathan observed that on the second floor down from the top row, on the third balcony along, there was a set of two red plastic chairs and a matching table. They were bright red, so were probably quite new. He had read somewhere that red fades quicker than other colours as it absorbs more light. Plant leaves are green as they absorb the red light and reflect the green light. *This is probably why red is such a bad colour,* he thought, *as it's the opposite of nature.* Most red things on plants were poisonous anyway, like red berries and toadstools; and tomatoes tasted horrible.

On the third floor down, fifth balcony along, was a giant palm tree in a huge grey pot. It had been put near the edge, central to the open balcony railings, so it could get more sunlight. This meant that it was in front of the sliding glass doors onto the balcony, partially blocking the exit. This person must both understand and love plants, otherwise they wouldn't have bothered. The pot looked very big and heavy. Had the balcony been designed for the weight? Only a strong man would been able to move such a weight, unless they had used a crane, because there was room for a crane from ground level. The stem of the palm was quite long so it had probably grown in the pot, but not for that long, as by now it would have bent more towards the light. *It is a stem, and not a trunk, as it is not made of wood, which makes it impossible to age because it doesn't have rings, so the—*

'Nathan! Snap out of it, will you? This is our stop.'

Nathan was relieved to exit the cramped train at London Bridge station, but only after all the other passengers had disembarked. As they walked along the platform, Tariq turned around to locate Nathan, only to find him with his back to the wall, waiting for the platform to clear. The next challenge for him was the walk through the long, dark, sloping pedestrian tunnel down to the tube station. Another train on the adjacent platform had just arrived, resulting in a near stampede of impatient commuters. Tariq forced himself to wait yet again for Nathan until the tunnel started to clear of people. Another train approached.

'Nathan!' Tariq tried to softened his tone, and said with urgency, 'If we don't go now, we'll be stuck here all day. Nathan, please, I need to get to work today or I'm in the shit! Get it?'

'Nooh, nooh, nooh, not going down there, not down there,' Nathan responded, firmly lodged in the same spot, as commuters dodged around him.

'OK, Nathan, you win! We'll get the bus. Follow me.'

Tariq guided Nathan back along the platform, up onto a pedestrian overbridge across the tracks, then along the platform on the other side and through a lesser-used side exit. The noise of competing traffic greeted them at street level. Under duress, Nathan followed his father further down the road to the bus stop. There was a queue for the bus. Tariq said, 'We can wait here until the number seventeen bus comes.'

'How long does it take to get there? Will the bus be crowded?'

'I don't know. Let's wait and see when it comes.'

The bus arrived late, which resulted in the now long queue of passengers all trying to squeeze onboard. Seeing the crammed bus, Nathan involuntarily shook his head. Tariq told him, 'We'll get the next one, OK? It won't be long. As we caught the earlier train we're not late yet.'

By the time Nathan refused to board the third bus, Tariq was getting desperate. Adjacent to the mainline London Bridge station, he noticed a taxi rank. 'Nathan, follow me. We'll get a taxi.' After joining a short queue, they jumped into a black cab. Tariq directed the taxi driver. 'Elm House please, Serious Fraud Office, Elm Street, just off Grays Inn Road.'

'Yeah, thanks mate, I know where it is.' said the taxi driver as they drove past the still-crowded bus stop.

'This is great, Dad. Why don't you always get a black taxi?'

'Because, Nathan, it's expensive if you use a taxi every day.'

'Go on, treat yourself!' said the driver. 'It's worth it for having less stress in your life. There's no need to splash out for an expensive holiday – just get a taxi every day and enjoy the ride. That's if the taxi driver doesn't give you an ear-bashing all the way. You can pay me extra, you know, to shut up.' He grinned to himself.

Nathan watched the fare meter closely at the front of the cab and noted the final price of £10.90 as they stopped at his father's office.

'Is that expensive, Dad?'

'Don't worry about it.'

As they crossed the road on the zebra crossing, Nathan looked toward the Elm Street Serious Fraud Office building. 'Wow, Dad, is that your office? It's got ten floors, you know. Which floor is your desk on?'

'The fourth floor.'

Elm House was a nondescript, modest square-plan office block, its grey cladding in keeping with the serious business of high-end fraud investigation. On the opposite side of the road were well-kept Victorian houses with high-end cars parked in private bays.

The Elm Street side road sloped away from the main

Grays Inn Road. On the approach to the office on the left was a vehicle security barrier to the SFO car park, which extended around the back of the building. A few more parking spaces were available on the lower basement parking area, accessible by means of a steep vehicle ramp. A further security barrier was present at the top of the ramp. Tariq had never driven to work so had no reason to concern himself with vehicle access arrangements. In any case, the lower basement was reserved for directors and visiting VIPs.

Tariq and Nathan walked up the ten black granite stone steps, bordered by a pair of evergreen topiary Buxus ball plants in large terracotta pots, each within raised gravel filled areas. Tariq told his son, 'I know you're excited, but please try to keep calm; don't ask everyone hundreds of questions as they're all busy doing their own work. I don't want to get into any more trouble today, please.' At the top of the steps, designated as ground-floor level, two glass sliding doors automatically parted, revealing an expansive white reception desk. A deadpan security guard was looking on, standing at the internal security gates further on.

Behind the reception desk, a formidable-looking middle-aged woman with dyed blonde hair tied up in a neat bob looked at them intently as they approached. 'Good morning, Tariq.'

'Hi, Beryl. This is Nathan, my son, who'll be working with me for a few weeks. Jack Burton has cleared it as part of the Work for All scheme.'

'Ah, yes.' She looked down at some notes in front of her. 'Hello, Nathan, welcome. It's probably a bit scary coming here, working with your dad, isn't it?'

Nathan replied, 'Yes, I didn't even want to get on the train yesterday, and we got a taxi here today.'

'There you go then. Can you both go through that side door over there? The security team will sort out a building pass for Nathan.' Through the side door they were met by a friendly-faced Indian-looking man in his late forties. He had the beginnings of bags under his eyes, probably from years of night shifts.

'Hi, I'm Ajay, head of security at the SFO. I was told you were coming, Nathan; in fact, I was expecting you yesterday. Take a seat there, please. I just need to take a mugshot for your building pass.'

Nathan looked alarmed. 'Mugshot? Will you be shooting mugs then?'

'Ha! No, Nathan. Sorry, forgive the slang. I mean take a photo of your face.'

'Oh, I see then.' Nathan was then distracted by the array of CCTV monitors in the adjacent room. He asked, 'What's through there?'

'Well Nathan, we've got thirty-seven cameras in this building, including the basement and the car park. I'll show you them some time, but not today. OK, smile into the camera, please.'

Ajay sat down at his PC and typed in various commands, and then took a white blank plastic building pass card with a red bar across the top from a small grey plastic box on the desk.

'What does the red band on the top mean?' asked Nathan.

'Oh, that's because yours is a temporary pass. So you'll be here for six weeks. Have I got that right?'

'A minimum of six weeks,' said Nathan, which surprised his father.

'OK, I'll set you up for eight weeks, and please return it if you finish earlier.' Ajay asked Tariq, 'I assume that Nathan will require access to Property Room No.1, the same as you?'

'Yes, that's right.'

He inserted the blank card into a mini printer, which churned out the completed pass in a few seconds. He clipped the pass onto a red-striped lanyard, which he handed to Nathan.

'Why is your pass green?' asked Nathan.

'Because it's an all-areas pass for people like me.'

Nathan and Tariq emerged from the security room and returned to the reception area. Nathan was keen to try out his new pass on the low-level sliding glass security gates. His father demonstrated where to hold the pass for scanning and Nathan successfully passed through the gates with a big smile on his face, the tribulations of the morning commute now forgotten.

'Are we going to your desk then, Dad, on the fourth floor?'

'In a minute, Nathan, I need to drop off my laptop to IT on the first floor. We can take the stairs.'

The IT department consisted of two rows of desks littered with various keyboards, screens, connection leads, and other PC hardware.

One of the older, more attentive IT technicians noticed Tariq approaching. 'Hi there. Is it for repair?'

'Yes, it won't boot up.'

'Yeah, looks like it's seen better days. Can you fill out

your details on the form here and leave it with us? It'll probably take about a week, as I'll have to send it off.'

'A week? Oh man. Any chance of getting it back sooner?'

'We'll see what we can do, sir. We'll contact you when it's ready.'

Tariq and Nathan walked back to the lift hallway on the first floor and caught the lift to the fourth floor. One of Tariq's long-standing work colleagues, Paul, was already in the lift. 'Morning, Tariq. Good morning young man. I'm guessing that you're Tariq's son.'

Nathan stepped forward, looking up to make the briefest of eye contact and reached out his hand to give Paul a cordial handshake. 'Hello, nice to meet you, Paul,' said Nathan, then stepping back again in an awkward fashion.

Paul asked Tariq, 'You're working on the Magnus Conan-Whittaker case, aren't you? Man, that's a big one! A billion dollars of crude oil gone missing – that takes some doing! When's it going to court?'

'January, but we've got to submit the Relevant Material documentation to the court by the end of September. As usual, the barrister wants everything as early as possible to get prepared.'

'I bet Burton's breathing down your neck to hit the deadlines?'

'Of course.'

Tariq and Nathan exited the lift onto the fourth floor.

CHAPTER 6

Tariq escorted Nathan to his desk, adjacent to the north-facing floor-to-ceiling windows. A modern office block with a yellow and green façade stood in the middle distance, two floors higher than the SFO building. To the west were two red tower cranes, one lifting and slewing a large, orange metal hopper full of concrete. Nathan tracked the hopper's traverse from the concrete lorry at road level to high up on the far side of the multi-storey block under construction. A banksman in an orange high-vis jacket was directing the crane operator above to manoeuvre the hopper into position. The concrete discharged from the hopper in a few seconds, into the large wooden shutter mould housing a grid of steel reinforcing bars. A six-foot-high blue wooden hoarding surrounded the construction site at ground level. Immediately below them was the SFO car park, where a black transit van manoeuvred slowly around the back of the office. The van halted at the automatic barrier to the lower basement, which soon lifted, then travelled out of sight down the ramp.

Tariq informed his son, 'This is my desk,' as he tidied up some loose papers and files.

Nathan asked about the next desk. 'Whose is this desk? Can I have this chair?'

'No, that's Lawrence Bashford's, the Case Controller's desk.' Tariq went across to another desk on the row behind. 'You can have this desk, no one's using this one. Now follow me, I'll show you to the kitchen.'

The open-plan kitchen had a hot drink vending machine and two large fridges with sliding glass doors. 'Nathan, why don't you put your packed lunch in the fridge?'

'Will they mind?'

'No, course not. They're for everybody. Let me show you how the coffee machine works. Look, press here for whatever you want – coffee, tea, milk…'

'Hot chocolate! Oh, cool, can I have a hot chocolate?'

'Sure you can, Nathan. Take a mug from the draining board over there, put it under here, and press.'

Nathan sat on his newly acquired office chair, pushing and pulling the adjustment levers until he was comfortable with his seating position. He swung around 360 degrees, only stopping briefly to sip his hot chocolate. His father told him to stop spinning around before he got dizzy. Tariq logged in on his PC and printed off a document titled *Office Induction* that he gave Nathan to read while he caught up with his emails.

About twenty emails in, Tariq came across the minutes of the meeting he'd missed the day before, recorded by Lawrence Bashford (LB) and attended by Jack Burton (JB). Tariq read a note stating that JB was concerned that the collation of material documents wasn't following SFO procedures. 'Shit!' he said to himself. Also noted in the minutes was that the case material schedules were not up to date, and the whole process was behind programme. Tariq sank back in his chair and sighed. As senior disclosure officer, he was responsible for selecting and correctly logging the case documents. Burton knew that he was on probation, and no doubt wanted his failings put on record to justify demoting him if the case flunked.

Mid-morning, Tariq took Nathan down to the basement in one of the service lifts at the far end of the building, then went down some steps to the lower carpark. Tariq walked up the car park ramp, out of the building, and lit a cigarette. As Nathan caught up, Tariq took a puff of his cigarette and said to Nathan, 'I'm relying on you, son, to help me out. That's why you're here, isn't it? You've come to work, not to mess things up; do you think that you can do that, Nathan? I don't need any more trouble, got it?'

Nathan looked at his father. 'Mum would say that you're in one of your moods, and you're trying to blame me for your problems, which isn't fair.'

'Mum's got me sussed, hasn't she? Jack Burton certainly has me sussed. No one's got you sussed, have they, Nathan? The world doesn't understand you; doesn't understand me neither, so we're both in the same boat, you and me.'

'What boat is that?'

'Ha! Good question, Nathan. It's probably called the *Titanic*. Have you heard of that boat?'

Nathan was already looking away, distracted by the cranes shifting around high in the air in the building site behind him. Nathan was attracted to slewing cranes because, unlike his father, they behaved in a regular fashion.

On their return to the fourth floor, Carol Hayes, Burton's PA, a smart-looking woman with soft freckles and wavy ginger hair, said in a clear, assertive tone, 'Hello,

Tariq, and hello, Nathan, I presume. Welcome to the SFO. How's it going?'

Tariq responded, 'Hi Carol. Yes, this is Nathan.'

Nathan said, 'Hello, Carol,' and extended his hand in his usual nervous fashion, which Carol shook briefly.

Carol continued, 'Just to mention that I've sorted out a log-in for Nathan. Here's the details.' She handed Nathan a square yellow sticky note with a few short lines neatly written on it.

'OK, thanks, Carol.'

'Thank you, Carol,' echoed Nathan.

Carol said to Tariq, 'Oh, Jack B was looking for you. He wants to catch up with you soon.' She added in a more sombre tone, 'He told me about Millie. Really sorry to hear that, Tariq. I hope that the treatment works and she's feeling better soon.'

Nathan chipped in. 'I miss her already and I really want her to get better so she can come home so I can play games with her. She's too ill now to play games.'

'That's sad, Nathan. I can see you're close to your sister.'

Nathan considered that he wasn't close to his sister at all right now as she was miles away in hospital, but he didn't say anything.

Nathan logged in to his PC with the details Carol had given him on the note and completed an online office health and safety questionnaire. He then perused the SFO intranet site.

At 12:30pm, Nathan retrieved his packed lunch from the fridge, sat down to eat his cheese and pickle sandwiches on one of the round tables in the shared area, and retrieved his wordsearch puzzle book from his bag. His father joined him with a reheated risotto from home he'd made a few days ago, and read the *Daily Telegraph*. There was an article on the trial of General Ratko Mladic, a Serbian army general, at The Hague, the UN's International Court of Justice in southern Holland. The General was accused of being responsible for the genocide of eight thousand Bosnian men at Srebrenica in the summer of 1995 in the Bosnian War. The hairs stood up on the back of Tariq's neck, and a single bead of sweat dripped from his forehead down the side of his face.

After lunch, Tariq went up to Jack Burton's office on the ninth floor. He considered that it was best to face him now rather than Burton thinking he was avoiding him. Nathan went to the ninth floor with his father, who directed him to wait in the breakout area. Nathan's curiosity got the better of him, and he sneaked up close to the open door of Burton's office and hid behind a partition. It was near enough to hear the conversation between his father and Burton, the Head of Investigations. He always wanted to know what his father talked about at work. Now was his chance.

Burton, a tall, stocky Texan with a thick-skinned, wrinkled sun-tanned face, stood up from behind his desk as he entered his office. Burton adopted his big welcoming smile expression and fixed his eyes on Tariq. 'Tariq, Tariq, thank ya for coming up to see me good fella. I'm guessing Carol caught up with ya earlier. Terrible business with Millie, shocking.'

Tariq was never sure if Burton had any genuine feelings behind his well-practised displays of Texan sympathy. Burton wasn't employed to be a social worker, so what did he expect? Tariq mused.

'Tariq, I'll level with ya. I'm concerned with the Magnus Conan-Whittaker case. This is the biggest case, ya know, on our books, and we need to get it right, yeah?'

'Yes, of course.'

'Look, how ya feeling, fella? Are you up for it right now, with everything goin' on an' all? Because, if ya not, then Stephen is keen to take over, ya know. Now the Nadir case is coming to the end he can step in for ya. Let me be frank with ya, Tariq. You're on probation, right? Any more screw-ups on this one and I'll have no option but to put ya down for a while.'

Tariq responded as confidently as he could. 'It's not a problem. I know what I'm doing, I'm fine. I'll get it back on track.'

'Ya sure now? Cause—'

Tariq cut in. 'Yes, I'm sure.'

Burton considered his response for a few seconds. 'Alrighty then. You'd better get down to that property room and get crack'n then.'

Tariq returned to his desk with Nathan and retrieved a green hard-backed ring binder file labelled *Master Ledger* from the bottom drawer of his desk. The file contained about a hundred indexed data sheets of all the documentation for the Conan-Whittaker case. Every sheet had numerous columns describing each document, its source, and who in the team had examined it, checked it, and when; also, the document classification reference number and whether the material was classified as Relevant, Sensitive or Unused. Each item of Relevant Material had to be filed and stored in the Property Room No.1 on the basement floor. Unused Material were documents and the like that may be relevant to the case, but were excluded from the portfolio for the prosecution case. Sensitive Material was that which could compromise public safety and stability, the contents of which were adopted as the property of the court, which was brought to bear at their discretion. Relevant Material was that deemed directly relevant and substantial to the prosecution case. Access to all these documents was restricted to the case team and senior staff, including Jack Burton and Nigel Pemberton. Burton was both the Head of Investigations and the allocated Case Director, and Pemberton the senior International Fraud Director.

As part of the investigations near two thousand boxes of documents had been seized and retrieved from various sources, about four hundred of which remained to be reviewed by the disclosure team, led by Tariq, the senior disclosure officer. Since there were only nine weeks left, it represented a review rate of about forty-five boxes a week. Collected material in bags and sacks were counted as boxes as an established legal oddity. Some boxes could be categorised in a few minutes, some hours, depending on the nature of the material. It was no wonder Burton was concerned – as the usual maximum rate of reviewing documents was forty a week if everyone pulled together. The rate depended on the complexity of the case and the range of documents to consider. In their favour, there was a higher-than-usual proportion of junk boxes which could be quickly dismissed, but disclosure officers rushed the process at their peril. It was paramount to identify every incriminating letter, email, note, or invoice, so to present the strongest possible case in court. Such evidence was often hidden within a batch of seemingly innocuous files by accident or deliberate concealment. Tariq was acutely aware that he was on probation due to what had transpired on his previous case, Frederick Rainsford Commodities. He hadn't missed any documents, as far as he was aware, but rather, he'd failed to disclose two documents to the court that the judge later considered 'as capable of undermining the case for the prosecution against the accused'. What Tariq found particularly disconcerting was that he didn't recognise either of the two documents that had been later disclosed. The master document ledger, however, showed the date he'd logged, incorrectly, the documents with his digital signature. Burton and the International Fraud Director Nigel Pemberton dismissed his protestations. As the senior disclosure officer, Tariq had to take the rap.

From his inspection of the ledger on the present Magnus Conan-Whittaker case, Tariq noted that the two deputy disclosure officers, Stuart Harper and Simon Beecham, had recently reviewed around two hundred documents that he needed to sign off as Relevant Material. Harper and Beecham were adept at picking up the obvious stuff, but subtleties could easily be missed, such as dates on correspondence being out of sync with supposedly linked documents, which was a smoking gun of a deliberate cover-up.

Tariq needed to accelerate the progress of the document review. He considered that he had no option but to take Nathan with him to the designated case Property Room No.1 on the basement floor. It wasn't unusual to employ filing clerks on large cases, and Tariq had it in mind to give Nathan some basic tasks such as photocopying. They took the same service lift they'd taken earlier down to the basement. Outside the property room, Tariq held his building pass against the electronic door sensor, which flashed green, releasing the door. Nathan couldn't resist checking that his pass also caused the sensor to flash green, despite the door already being open. In the centre of the room was a single desk with a network linked computer, screen and keyboard, and a single black padded chair. Every wall in the room had wall-to-wall shelves except half of the back wall, where there was a cleaners' storeroom on one side with its own door, with a digital push button combination lock. On the right-hand side wall there were high shelves containing an untidy array of cardboard and plastic boxes, and black bin liners of miscellaneous files and documents. These were only some of the items yet to be reviewed in the next nine weeks before the 20th September court deadline. The remainder of the case items were stored in a secure warehouse in St Albans, twenty-five miles north of central London. On the left-hand wall were tidier rows of sequentially labelled open box files, filling three-quarters of the wall space. Every box and occasional oversized item was referenced in accordance with its status recorded on the master ledger, a password-protected Excel file held on the network computer.

Tariq grabbed a tatty brown file from a box on the right-hand side wall and sat down at the desk to review its contents. Nathan asked if there was anything he could do. Not wanting to be interrupted, Tariq answered that he'd think of something. Nathan walked around the room, studying the sets of labelled files, and went to examine some half-sized A5 blue books awaiting review.

'Don't touch those, Nathan, please.' After about half

an hour, Tariq muttered to himself, 'For goodness' sake, where are my deputies?' He opened their work calendars on Microsoft Outlook on the PC on the central desk and exclaimed, 'Two days training at HQ, both of them. Unbelievable! That's all I need right now.'

Nathan looked across at his father to check that he wasn't the object of his displeasure.

'Nathan, sorry son, it's not you, it's my team.' Tariq pondered how he could make the most of the day, and said, 'Nathan, there is something that you can do for me.'

'Yes, as long as you don't shout at me if I make a mistake.'

'Yes, alright. This is a good job for you, OK? Firstly, can you photocopy all these index sheets and the ledgers and return them to me? Do you remember how to use the photocopier on the fourth floor like I showed you? All you have to do is to feed them into the copier and press "copy".'

It was 5:30pm, going-home time, and Tariq and Nathan were washing their lunch box containers in the kitchen. The last thing Tariq wanted was Nathan panicking halfway home when he realised he'd left his favourite lunch container in the work fridge. As Tariq was drying his cleaned container, a familiar voice called his name. It was Sandra. 'Tary, have you got a minute, please?'

The distressed tone of her voice surprised him. 'Sandra, are you alright? What's the matter?'

Her usual tidy hair was frayed with tangible anxiety, and her face was framed with worry lines.

'It's Cheryl, she's gone missing...' She broke down in restrained tears and wiped her eyes with her light-blue hanky. She looked around briefly to see if anyone else was around. Sandra continued, 'she was last seen going down to the lower basement room on Friday morning. No one has seen her since. No one! I've checked with her sister. She hasn't been seen all weekend or since, and she's not answering any of my calls or texts.'

'I see. You're sure she hasn't taken some leave and gone away somewhere?'

'No, I've checked. Her sister said she was supposed to meet her in the park on Sunday, but she never showed up. I'm worried, Tary, really worried, and there's something she said when I saw her last her that's been bothering me…'

'What? What did she say?'

'That she'd noticed something wasn't right with the case, but she didn't want to say anything until she was sure.'

'Like what?'

'I don't know, Tary, that's the thing – I don't know. When I asked her, she said she didn't want to talk about it. She looked scared. It's unlike her to be scared of anything. She said that she didn't want to talk about it in the office. We'd arranged to go out for a drink after work, but she never came. Look, can you come down with me to the lower basement? That's where she was last seen.'

'Oh, I hate that place, but I'll come with you, because it's you. Show me.'

The lift door opened onto the basement floor and they walked along the corridor, the opposite way to the property room, and down some concrete steps. The cold, damp smell of the concrete walls hit Tariq immediately. Even Nathan noticed the tense expression on his father's face. The scar on the left side of his forehead went redder in hue. He took deep breaths and tried to focus on the task in hand. They entered a large plant room at the bottom of the steps with banks of insulated horizontal and vertical pipes fixed along the walls. Above them was a square steel vertical ventilation duct fixed to the ceiling. Since it wasn't connected to any of the other ducts it was probably redundant. From within the duct hung a short length of orange plastic elephant trunking which extended to a few feet above a yellow skip. The skip protruded outwards into the lower basement car park through two large open industrial steel doors. Several bicycles could be seen through the doors on rows of silver metal hooped stands.

Sandra explained, 'Cheryl received a phone call from someone requesting that she collect a package from the lower basement room.'

Tariq responded, wiping the sweat off his brow, 'OK then, I've seen everything I need to. Anything else? Let's go back up.'

'Bob, one of the postmen, reckoned that he saw a man with long hair down here on Friday morning wearing a blue suit. The man had a briefcase and was looking through those doors just behind the skip. He tried to talk to him but the man just ignored him. Bob had just cycled in and was locking his bike up, when he noticed a black transit van parked up near the ramp.'

'I saw a black van going down the ramp today, about eleven o'clock,' said Nathan.

'Is that right, Nathan? Let's check if it's still there,' said Sandra.

Tariq took a few steps towards the doors and couldn't see the van so didn't feel the need to go any further, whereas Nathan and Sandra walked through the doors into the lower basement car park area but there was no sign of the van, just a black 7 Series BMW, which either belonged to Sir Peter Brownley, the Managing Director, or Nigel Pemberton, the International Fraud Director, as only they were allowed to park there. Still in the basement plant room, Tariq noticed tyre marks leading up to the skip and disappearing under it. From their width and angle, it was apparent that the marks were not from the skip lorry as it unloaded the skip.

Nathan decided to have another look around the plant room until his father shouted at him to come over to the steps. At that moment Nathan saw a small object lying on the concrete floor next to the skip. He picked it up and walked quickly across the room towards his father and Sandra, who were waiting for him at the steps.

'What have you got, Nathan?' Sandra asked.

Nathan opened his palm to reveal a woman's lipstick, with the top missing.

Sandra gasped. 'That's Cheryl's. Where did you find it?'

'Oh, by the skip next to the metal door,' replied Nathan.

'We should probably call the police,' said Tariq.

'Oh God, you're right, but I better speak to Sir Peter first. He wouldn't appreciate it if the press got hold of the story before I spoke to him. I'll talk to him in the morning,' said Sandra.

'I suggest that you ring him now or he'll be asking why you didn't call him sooner.'

Sandra didn't respond.

CHAPTER 7

Tariq and Nathan had previously arranged with Alice to visit Millie at the hospital after work at 7:30pm. Tariq worked as late as he could to catch up on the case filing. Tariq explained to Nathan over lunch that the best route to the hospital was to walk to Farringdon station and then catch a Thameslink train to Denmark Hill. Nathan, initially alarmed at the prospect of another new journey to navigate, was later relieved that the walk to Farringdon station avoided the crowds. At the station, he slotted his ticket into the automated ticket barrier and retrieved it in his now-perfected action. On the train, he also appreciated the modern, spacious Thameslink carriages. This time, the train didn't stop long enough for him to properly study the tower block balconies.

With Nathan at ease, Tariq's thoughts turned to what could have happened to Cheryl. Judging from the evidence of her leaving her lipstick behind in the basement, she'd left in a hurry, or worse still, been coerced. Why couldn't he stop thinking about her? Maybe he still loved her? What was she trying to tell Sandra about something, or somebody, being wrong with the SFO case? Had that somebody got to her first?

Upon arriving in the Davidson Haematology Ward on

the second floor, Cheyne Wing, King's College Hospital, they found Millie sitting up in her bed at the end of the ward. Nathan went ahead of his father to meet his sister and mother. Alice got up from her chair on the other side of the bed to greet her son. 'Mum, you'll never guess what. I've been with Dad on the train to his office and I'm helping him check all the files for his case. There are thousands of files, you know. Cheryl's gone missing, and I found her lipstick, and Sandra is going to call the police tomorrow.'

Before his mother could absorb all that Nathan was telling her and respond, Nathan turned to Millie, who returned a tired smile from her pale face. Alice hugged Tariq more intensely than usual, revealing her vulnerable state. She'd visited Millie several times over the last few days, witnessing her steady decline as the course of strong steroids poisoned her body. She asked her husband discreetly, 'So how are you getting on with Nathan? He seems happy, at least. I hope you're being patient with him? What was he saying about Cheryl? She's head of process, or assurance, or whatever you call it, isn't she? What did Nathan say about her going missing?'

'Yes, she's Head of Quality Assurance. It's probably nothing. She hasn't been seen recently, that's all.'

'What about the lipstick that Nathan found? What's that all about?'

'It was in the basement; she went down to collect a package, and that's the last time anyone saw her. Sandra is going to inform the MD, Sir Peter Brownley, who'll report it to the police tomorrow.'

'Tomorrow? Why wait 'til tomorrow?'

'Look, that's what I said to her. Sandra knows what

she's doing. I told you, it's probably nothing. The SFO won't want any unnecessary fuss, that's all. Brownley will probably make his own enquiries before involving the police. What evidence is there? Only that her sister doesn't know where she is; that's all.'

Alice looked even more concerned. 'God, this gets worse by the minute.'

'I don't want to talk about it, OK? I've come here to see Millie; *we've* come here to see Millie.'

Tariq sat beside Millie in her bed. Nathan had just finished describing to her all the free hot drink options available from the work vending machine Tariq leaned over her bed and said, 'Hello, darling, how are you? Sorry we couldn't come sooner. It's been—'

'That's alright, Daddy, it's good to see you, and you're doing a great job looking after Nathan because I know he can be… let's say, *different* at times, but that's why he's my special brother.'

'Because I'm the only one you've got, right?'

Millie smiled back at Nathan. 'That's right, Nathan. Aren't I lucky?'

Millie's initial excitement at seeing her father and brother dissipated with her energy levels, especially after listening to Nathan's detailed account of the day's events. After an hour, the family said their goodbyes. Tariq was about to leave the hospital with Nathan when Alice handed him something in an orange Sainsbury's carrier bag.

'What's this?'

'It's Wednesday. It's a shepherd's pie. Nathan will be expecting it.'

'Oh yes, of course. Thank you.'

***

The next morning, Nathan and Tariq were halfway walking to Eden Park train station when Nathan insisted on returning to the house to retrieve his cheese and pickle sandwich he'd left on the kitchen table. Tariq's shouted frustrations resulted in Nathan going into survival mode, leading to him refusing to board the first two trains; but he didn't return home this time, as he'd done on his first day. He embarked on the third train as it had more free seats. To Tariq's further exasperation, the train was delayed outside Catford station for ten minutes. The train driver made apologetic announcements for the delay in a heavy Scottish accent. When the train finally approached London Bridge station, Nathan pre-empted the driver's announcement in a Scottish intonation, saying loud enough for most of the carriage to hear, *'I'm sorr'a for inconveneenc'n all ya' annoyed passengas on this treen t-day. We've had a wee bi' of trouble.'* The smiles and sniggers from some of the passengers took the edge off Tariq's embarrassment. One of them added, *'I blame the blewdy Jock drevin theece fookeen treen.'*

They finally approached the office at 9:40am. Tariq hoped that Lawrence Bashford wouldn't be around to notice his late arrival. He then observed two police cars in the office car park; not an uncommon occurrence as police were often involved in raids of offices and private residences under suspicion of serious commercial fraud. Tariq considered, surely the police wouldn't already be on the premises to investigate Cheryl's disappearance, especially as the evidence was pretty scant at this stage. Perhaps she'd reappeared anyway?

Tariq's conjecture was put into doubt when Beryl assertively requested that they take a seat in reception, as the police needed to speak to him. Tariq said to himself, 'What the hell?'

Nathan asked, 'Why do we have to stay here?' and was reaching for his puzzle book from his worn black leather bag when three policemen came through the internal security gates towards them. Two of them were uniformed; the third was a silver-haired man with a well-established scowl across his face, wearing a tailored blue and grey dogtooth jacket. Tariq quickly formed the opinion that they were the serious types, as opposed to friendly patrol Bobbies. The uniformed officers took the trouble to stand on either side of Tariq to block his exits.

The more senior silver-haired officer asked, 'Mr Markovic? Mr Tariq Markovic?'

'Yes.'

'Can you come with us, please?'

'What, now?'

'Yes, now, sir. We have a car outside.'

'What's this all about? Look, I'm with my son, Nathan.'

'Hello, Nathan. He can come too; we'll explain everything down at the station.'

Nathan was becoming more agitated by the lack of explanation for why they were being detained.

The squad car doors locked as they sat together on the back seat. Tariq gave Nathan a nonchalant smile in an attempt to calm him down. He hated surprises, and this wasn't a good one.

The journey to the City of London Police Station at Bishopsgate took about twenty minutes; but felt longer.

The younger policeman engaged Nathan by asking him about his work experience with his father, which helped him relax.

At the station, a female police constable directed Nathan to take a seat on a worn cream leather sofa in an open kitchen area and to help himself to tea or coffee, whatever he wanted. She explained that following the interview of his father, he would be collected. 'It shouldn't take too long.'

Tariq was taken with the uniformed police officers down a flight of stairs to the basement level. As he was being escorted down the corridor, Tariq's stride stalled when he saw the poorly lit room they were taking him to through the metal door, with plain concrete walls. 'Do you mind, I don't want to go in there, I'm just not comfortable, I…'

The senior officer said, 'Sorry about the makeshift room; the usual interview room upstairs is being redecorated. It won't take long, just a few questions… Follow me please.' His outstretched arm directed Tariq through the open door. The dimly lit room had a plain wooden table in the centre of the room with a single plastic blue chair on one side and two identical chairs opposite. There was a musty smell of damp concrete, and the solid bare walls, ceiling and floor amplified every sound. Tariq's breathing was getting shallower, and he felt his heart beating faster. He wanted to run. The taller junior officer was already in the far corner of the room, operating a small box of switches.

Tariq sat down and took a sip from one of the glasses of water on the table.

'Is this about Cheryl?' Tariq asked. His question was ignored.

'Before we start, I'm DCI Randall; this is a recorded

interview. You don't have to say anything, but it may harm your defence if you do not mention when questioned something which you later rely on in court. Anything you do say may be given in evidence.'

Tariq's right arm quivered slightly, which he steadied with his left hand. He looked down at the ground and took more breaths, slowing now. He gripped the front of the table with both hands to compose himself and looked up at DCI Randall seated in front of him. The junior uniformed officer seated next to Randall at the corner of the table gave him a fixed stare.

Randall asked, 'Are you alright, sir? Take your time. Is there something you want to tell us? Can you confirm that you know Cheryl Bedford?'

'Yes, I work with her; she's the Head of Assurance at the SFO… Sorry, I'm claustrophobic. Can you please tell me what this is about?'

'Are you aware that she's gone missing since Friday?'

'Yes, I found out yesterday.'

'So you're aware that she went down to the basement to collect a package addressed to you?'

'Bloody hell! No, I didn't know that.'

Randall paused, eyes remaining fixed on Tariq.

Tariq wiped the sweat off his brow with his sleeve; his red scar now more pronounced.

'Mr Markovic, what is your relationship with Cheryl Bedford?'

'I told you, I know her from work. I bump into her now and again.'

The junior policeman slid an A4 brown envelope across the table towards his senior.

The DCI put his hand inside the envelope to retrieve its contents and looked back at Tariq. 'Mr Markovic, I advise you to tell us everything you know from the outset; it will be better for you in the long run.'

'Look, I've said all I want to say on this. I don't like being in this shitty room; can I go now, please?'

Randall placed five large black-and-white photos on the table, spreading them out in front of Tariq. Tariq looked at each one in turn, which showed him in various intimate poses with Cheryl. The most incriminating photo was of them standing in front of a hotel bed. He was in the process of pulling off his tie, and she was kicking off one of her high-heeled shoes. The photographs were grainy and low-quality, probably taken from a hidden CCTV camera.

'This is a joke! She's a tactile woman,' Tariq said as he grabbed the grainy hotel shot and waved it at the DCI. 'She asked me to go with her to her hotel room after the Christmas party; she needed to catch a night flight from London City Airport to Brive, Dordogne, in France, to spend Christmas with her sister. I helped her get her suitcase out of the room; that's all! We were changing out of our party clothes. There is nothing more to say, for God's sake! What has this to do with anything? Clearly, someone is trying to stitch me up!'

Randall came in at a tangent. 'What cigarettes do you smoke, Tariq?'

'Why, do you want one?' he replied, bringing out a half-full packet of Embassy Mild-Blue from his jacket pocket.

DCI Randall leaned over the hotel photo and pointed at an item next to the bed.

'Can you explain why a packet of Mild-Blue is on the

bedside table?' He showed him an enlarged black-and-white photograph. 'Do you smoke in bed, Mr Markovic? It just doesn't look good now, does it?'

Tariq looked straight back at Randall, wiping his damp forehead, across his red scar.

'This is ridiculous! This is a set-up. Anyone can see that! Who gave you these photos?'

DCI Randall paused, his rugged, lined face softening slightly with a breaking smile. He then glanced across at the junior officer to signal a new phase of the interrogation.

'So Tariq, the key to this is, therefore, *who* would want to set you up?'

'The bastards who gave you the photos – that's who.'

'Well, clearly someone wanted us to know that you have a motive...'

'Motive? A motive for what?'

DCI Randall leant forward, keeping his gaze fixed on Tariq.

'Mr Markovic, I'm going to ask you one final question, and I want you to think very carefully about your answer... because if you tell me the right answer, the truthful answer, we'll back you up one hundred percent. However, if you mess with me, then I'll personally see to it that you're locked up in a place much worse than this for a long stay, and I can see, Mr Markovic, that is something that you'd rather avoid.'

DCI Randall stopped abruptly, gauging Tariq's expression studiously for tell-tale signs of concealment in his facial expression and demeanour.

'What question? What *is* the question?' Tariq was obliged to ask.

'Mr Markovic, are these *bastards*, as you call them, blackmailing you?'

Tariq leant forward, 'No, I am not being blackmailed.'

Randall looked back without blinking.

'Are you sure about that?'

'Yes, I am sure! Why would anyone want to blackmail me?'

'I understand that you're preparing the prosecution documentation for the Magnus Conan-Whittaker fraud case – or alleged fraud, should I say? Mr Burton, your Yankee Head of Investigations, has given me a thorough briefing.'

'That's right.'

'I'm sure you know, then, the value of the alleged fraud?'

'A billion dollars.'

'Wowey. One *billion* dollars. It's amazing what you can find out before breakfast, isn't it? Do you know, Tariq, in my experience, when that kind of money is at stake, people resort to the most desperate means possible to get it – or in this case, to keep hold of it. If, say, important documents were to go missing, as happened on your previous case at the SFO, then it could change the outcome of the case, yes? You understand now why someone would want to blackmail you? Because I sure as hell do.'

'Ball-crap! The documents didn't go missing, they were just mis-filed. I know Burton's got my card marked for that case. He's got it in for me.'

'We listen to everybody, Mr Markovic, and we look at all the evidence very carefully, rest assured.' After a final pause, the DCI put on a false smile and said, 'OK, Mr Markovic, you're free to go. Thank you for your time. We'll be in touch as needed.'

Tariq was escorted back up to the ground floor, where he sought out Nathan in the station kitchen, but he wasn't there. He eventually found him assisting a young police woman at her desk with something on her computer screen, pointing at different icons. Tariq shouted across the room, 'Nathan! What are you doing? We're going back now.'

The woman said to Nathan, 'Thank you, Nathan. You're a star. You better get going.' Looking across the room at Tariq, she said, 'Your son's a whizz at spreadsheets! Can he stay here? He can sleep in the basement.' Tariq half smiled back at her as Nathan crossed the room.

They were driven back to the office as they came, in the marked police car.

CHAPTER 8

The police driver agreed to Tariq's request to drop them off in a side street, out of sight of the Elm Street SFO office. Tariq didn't want to fuel the rumour mill in the office that the police were giving him special attention. He told Beryl at the reception desk that his visit to the police station was part of the fraud investigation.

It was now early lunchtime, so Tariq suggested to Nathan that they go straight to the canteen. Tariq chose the fish pie and peas over the pork chops and mash, in a half-hearted attempt to reduce his cholesterol intake. His super health-conscious daughter Millie often lectured him on the perils of eating too much red meat and the like. Nathan, on the other hand, was beyond reason with his insistence on cheese and pickle sandwiches in white bread for his packed lunch. Millie's previous attempts to sneak in some lettuce when he wasn't looking had resulted in him sealing his sandwiches with silver foil and Sellotape once made.

Tariq paid for the fish pie and Nathan led the way to an empty table by the window. He was prising open his hermetically sealed sandwich when a man with a cheeky smile approached the table. 'Mind if I join you?' It was said more as an introduction than a question.

'Sure, sure, please do, Jason. Good to see you, mate. How are you?'

'OK thanks, mustn't grumble.'

Tariq introduced his son, 'Jason, this is my son Nathan who's here for work experience.' Nathan looked up nervously but at least managed a smile. Charlotte had told him that people like smiles.

'Pleased to meet you, Nathan; I'm an old friend of your father's. You're a brave young man. I was scared to death when I went to work at the factory with my dad. He worked for Rolls Royce in Derby, and I had no idea what was going on. I'll give you some advice, Nathan, because my dad was sick of me after three days with all my dumb questions. So, I saved up three questions before I asked him anything, and I spread my questions out to as many people as possible. People like to help a newcomer, but they'll soon resent being pestered with too many questions.'

Nathan listened intently. 'Thank you. I'll remember that.'

Jason Eastman looked like someone more at home in a jet engine factory than in an office. Judging by his thick-skinned hands and rugged face, he'd rather have a spanner in his hand than send polite emails. Similarly, Tariq's rounded Eastern European face and ungroomed wavy hair hinted at a preference for a more practical hands-on approach to life. He looked like an outsider and sounded like one due to his perceptible Russian-sounding accent. Consequently, people like Jason, who didn't feel they fit in, were drawn to him. Others, however, held Tariq in enhanced suspicion when something went wrong on a case, especially Jack Burton.

Jason added, 'If you ever want some help, Nathan, just come and find me, OK? I'm on the fifth floor.'

'Thank you, Jason. I'm good at spreadsheets, by the way. I helped the policewoman at the police station, you know. There was an error in one of the formulas. I can do formulas. She said that I was a whizz at spreadsheets.'

'Really? When was that?' Jason asked.

Tariq cut in, 'Nathan, could you go back to your desk now so I can talk to Jason about something?'

'Oh, OK then. I'll go up on my own then.'

'Thanks, I'll be up in a minute.' Nathan left, allowing Tariq to speak to Jason candidly, 'I couldn't believe it Jason – the police were asking me about Cheryl. She's been missing since Friday.'

'I didn't even know she'd gone missing.'

'And I tell you something else – Burton had already informed the police that he suspected me of sabotaging the previous case. That was Harper's doing, not mine, but I was the fall guy. Why can't Burton back me up instead of buying Harper's bullshit?'

Jason replied, 'I've never trusted Harper: he's a shifty character at the best of times. As I recall, he was on that case from start to finish, whereas you only joined for the last six months. I wouldn't worry too much about Burton though; he deals with all the police liaison stuff and loves stirring things up. He's just a brash American. Is that the time? Sorry Tariq, gotta go.' Jason left, leaving Tariq on his own at the table.

When Tariq returned to his desk, Nathan was editing a spreadsheet. Tariq looked at his Outlook calendar, reminding him to prepare for Monday's fortnightly team meeting. 'Shit,' he mouthed to himself. He hated these meetings as he was obliged to give a presentation on the progress of the case documentation, which was behind the programme in several areas, including the first stage of category checking, when documents were first assessed if relevant. Secondly, each relevant document had to be referenced to the particular case charge it applied to. In complex fraud cases, there were usually multiple breaches of finance and criminal law. To avoid tip-offs of major investigations, simultaneous coordinated raids on offices and residences were carefully organised, sometimes in different continents, when large amounts of retrieved documents were bundled into hundreds of evidence sacks and boxes. Much of this could be quickly discarded, but this case had initially retained nearly three thousand documents. Junior sifters had been brought in to weed out *junk paper*. This approach was considerably cheaper than employing a legal firm with expensive legal assistants, managed by a five-hundred-pounds-an-hour Queens Counsel (QC). However, the Magnus Conan-Whittaker (MCW) case was such a smokescreen of subterfuge that the sifters had only succeeded in removing about a third of the pile, classifying the remaining two-thirds as unconfirmed. The crutch of the case was the disappearance of a billion dollars – a staggering amount of money, but a small proportion of the twenty-two billion dollars of investments managed by MCW Holdings.

A large amount of capital had been invested in high-risk oil exploration in the Indian Ocean. Billions of dollars had been invested in four oil rigs at secret locations, designated so for commercial sensitivity reasons, for the extraction of high-grade crude oil. The oil was supposed to have been pumped into five T1 Class tankers, each longer than the Empire State Building, with a capacity of two million barrels. According to the trading accounts, the oil was fetching a high 2008 price of just under one hundred dollars a barrel. This valued the cargo of each tanker at two hundred million dollars. The rigs and the five tankers had subsequently disappeared without trace. Even David Blaine, the magician, would be stretching his talents to achieve this feat. If you're going to commit a fraud you might as well do it big, very big. MCW initially claimed that they were an innocent victim of a humongous scam.

The implicated MCW Finance Directors had run for the hills soon after the oil refineries started complaining that the tankers they'd ordered hadn't arrived. It was no coincidence that the tankers had been planned to arrive at the same time at all the ports throughout the globe. To rub salt into the wound, none of the tankers were insured for loss, and the parent company insurance bonds provided to the oil refineries were then found to be worthless as Magnus Conan-Whittaker (MCW) Oil had since gone bust. The investigators considered the failure to insure the tankers to be no accident as any insurance company would have required each tanker to be fitted with GPS trackers to ensure, among other things, that agreed low-risk pirate attack routes were adhered to. Additionally, the underwriters would have insisted upon an independent detailed inspection of the tanker's sea-worthiness; tricky if the craft didn't exist. An international web of false oil production ledgers, invoices and transactions was now being exposed. Four out of the seven directors had been tracked down and were under house arrest in the United Kingdom. The remaining three were still at large. Burton's police contacts had recently informed the SFO that the MCW Senior Managing Director, the Serbian ex-finance minister Karlo Mitchko, had been apprehended in Serbia trying to cross the border into Montenegro, the latter country being exempt from an extradition treaty with the United Kingdom. Mitchko was credited with funding the militarisation of the Bosnian Serbs in the 1992–1995 Bosnian War and was now rumoured to be supporting Ratko Mladic and other high-ranking Serb generals with expensive legal fees at The Hague war crime tribunals now in session. Any misappropriation of governmental funds during the war had been forgiven, by the Serbs at least, so had not been pursued under a criminal investigation.

Following the initial categorisation of acquired documents, Tariq needed to analyse over a hundred pages of document ledgers, with multiple columns indicating various document categories with dates and percentage progress. The classification of each document then had to be signed off by Lawrence Bashford, the Case Controller. Bashford was mandated to comply with the classifications for each document type laid out in the SFO Case Quality Assurance protocol as drafted by Cheryl, the Head of Quality Assurance. The classifications were finally signed off by the Head of Investigations, Jack Burton, who was also the designated Case Director. Documented transactions between the MCW head office and the phantom oil rigs were designated with the highest status on the case. Also, in the highest category was anything found written in Bosnian or Serbian, as these were most likely to be connected to

Karlo Mitchko, who was fluent in both languages. The fact that Tariq could read most things Bosnian was the main driver for him being assigned to the case, despite Burton's misgivings of Tariq's integrity and management abilities. One of the initial objectives in any major fraud case was to secure enough solid evidence to persuade one or more of the perpetrators to plead guilty, with plea bargaining for a reduced or even a suspended sentence. Such a plea could open the floodgates to expose the fraud, with testimony against other accused parties curtailing the ever-increasing SFO legal bill. The slick execution of the alleged fraud, however, appeared to have been matched by the systematic destruction of both electronic and hard-copy evidence. Consequently, Tariq had an increased difficult task of finding credible smoking gun evidence from the Bosnian files. Bashford had tried to procure a suitable freelance Bosnian translator to assist Tariq without success. Even if he found someone now, the rigorous vetting and security checks would take several weeks to complete; hence, Tariq had given up asking him about getting any help on this aspect. Tariq was, in a way, relieved that someone fluent in Serbian and Bosnian wouldn't come in to embarrass him by challenging his selection of key documents so far.

Relevant documents were signed and countersigned by the SFO investigating case team, depending on their seniority. Completed ledger sheets with all the stages of review completed and signed off were then scanned into a protected data file storage system. Access to the master ledger document file was security protected by the use of digital display key fobs issued to the investigating team including deputy disclosure officers such as Stuart Harper.

Failure to disclose a lost or missing fob was a disciplinary offence as it represented a security breach. However, the key fob system was recognised as archaic compared to newer more advanced security systems, and was due to be replaced in the New Year. Burton was championing their replacement with an American cyber-secure system. The best system just happened to be American. according to Burton.

Tariq was about an hour into a three-hour stint of document analysis when he broke off for a cup of tea on the fourth floor. On his return to the Property Room No. 1, he found Nathan studying the hard-copy file of completed ledger sheets and the current online ledger.

'Nathan, don't touch those, please; they're confidential master documents, for God's sake.'

Nathan was offended. 'I'm only trying to help. Why don't you give me something I'm good at, not just boring paperwork?'

'Nathan, I can't always…'

'Tariq!' boomed Jack Burton behind him with his unmistakable American Deep South accent. matching his tall, large-framed physique.

'Hello Jack,' replied Tariq as he turned around in his chair, giving him just enough time to put on a bright face. 'What can I do for you, Jack?' He liked to be called by his first name.

'Why don't ya come over t' my office, good fella, and we can have a chat.'

'Sure.' Tariq was about to wrestle the ledger sheets from Nathan but didn't want to provoke him into a scene.

'I know what I'm doing, Dad,' Nathan said calmly.

Burton had a reputation for hijacking staff in the office just as they were about to attend a meeting. It had become an in-joke that if you were late for a meeting you'd been commandeered by the American Ambassador, namely Burton. Sovereign State embassies had internationally recognised jurisdiction to administer their home nation's statutes on its premises. Burton had the same attitude to his way of doing things, blustering his way through any obstacles in his path, whether established SFO processes or persons. He got away with imposing Uncle Sam Wild-West type methods, safe, it appeared, in the knowledge that he could retreat to his mother country with immunity. This took some inner belief, considering he was surrounded by established English gentry in the form of senior barristers, QCs and knighted dignitaries. Then again, he was six feet seven, and looked dangerous enough that you expected him to be armed. Perhaps he was. The word in the office was that his appointment last year was imposed upon the SFO by the Attorney General, much to their indignation.

When they arrived at Burton's office, Burton planted himself purposely on his burgundy leather executive chair and directed Tariq to take a less grand seat. Burton glanced through the expansive office window to his left before turning back to face Tariq.

'Tariq, I want to clear the air with you on what happened this morning. I know you were summoned to the sheriff's office this morning, which must have been a shaker for ya, com'n at ya broadside. The thing is Tariq, everyone knows you an' Cheryl are close buddies, and there was no point hidin' it; and they asked me about what happened on your previous case and I just told 'em straight. I didn't say n' more than that, buddy.'

Burton got up from his chair and walked behind Tariq. He locked the door quietly and twisted the internal window Venetian blinds shut. Tariq had to fend off a claustrophobic panic attack that threatened to overwhelm him. It was a reflex action he didn't understand himself.

Burton took a detour back to his desk via an antique oak bureau. He lowered the heavy vintage hinged lid, took out a chunky lead crystal decanter of whisky and a couple of matching glasses, and handed one to Tariq. 'Don't tell anyone,' Burton said with a wink as he poured out a generous inch of liquor into Tariq's glass, then his own. Opening the lower door of the bureau, he revealed a well-stocked mini-fridge of beer with a freezer compartment. 'Ice?' he asked Tariq, with shiny steel tongs at the ready.

'Yes please.'

They both took a moment to enjoy the sound and smell of the crisp ice blocks churning the whisky in the glass. Tariq knew at that moment why Burton was so good at getting under your skin, now relaxing quickly after his initial nervousness. He could imagine Burton clinching multi-million-dollar business deals with Texas oil barons with Stetsons after a few bottles of Bourbon at an all-night high-stakes poker game.

'I hear that you were in the forces in Bosnia back in '95. Terrible business. I guess you've been following the trial of Ratko Mladic on TV?'

'Yes, I've seen some of it. I don't know what to make of it.'

'Yeah, I get ya, soldier, I get ya. No one wants to go

back to those times.' Burton took a swig of his whisky and looked seriously at Tariq. His purposeful carved facial lines told you he'd faced the world head-on all his life.

'I was in 'Nam you know; sorry, as in Vietnam. You know it means something to a vet when they say "'Nam". Do you guys have a slang word for the Bosnian War?'

'I guess we would say *rat nezavisnosti*, which means "the war of independence".'

'Rat nevisnosti – got it.' Tariq didn't bother to correct him. 'And do you mind me asking which side you were on?'

'Oh, I'm Bosnian, as in not a Bosnian Serb.'

'Yes, I got ya, you're a Bosniak.'

Tariq was impressed that Burton knew the difference. Only in his dreams did the Bosniak identity still mean anything to him.

Burton continued, 'Goddamnit, those war pictures on TV must be hard to stomach. That General Mladic arsehole is as guilty as hell, as far as I'm concerned. Where I come from, he'd go to the chair, for sure.'

After half a glass of whisky, Tariq felt he'd more in common with Burton than he expected – they were both war veterans – enough in common to tell Burton honestly, 'This is my problem, I don't have any memory of what happened in *rat nezavisnosti*, so I don't know what to make of it myself. Sometimes I wish I did, but most of the time I don't; I'd rather think about something else.'

Burton nodded his large American head with thinning brown hair. 'Tariq, let me tell you something I wouldn't say to anyone, 'cause very few would get this… When I hear one of those choppers flying overhead, I just want to dive for cover.' Tariq could see by the vulnerability in his eyes that he meant it. He hadn't seen Burton like that before and felt privileged that he'd been considered a confidant. Burton unlocked and opened the door. 'Tariq, if you ever want to talk about anything you want to get off ya chest, my door's always open, buddy, and the scotch ready!'

Tariq made his way carefully back to his desk. While he was safe breaking the zero-alcohol SFO policy in Burton's 'embassy', diplomatic immunity ended at his door.

Back at his desk, Tariq, still light-headed from Burton's hospitality, quipped to his son sitting on the desk behind, 'Nathan, Nathan, what have you got to tell me, son? Something good, I hope?'

With a big grin across his face, Nathan replied, 'Yes, Dad, I can tell you something good because I've finished your spreadsheet report.' Tariq, speechless, took the pages of completed tables in his hand and reviewed each in turn. Tariq then said, in an imitation Burton accent, 'Goddamnit, you son of a bitch, you're not wrong. You done good, son! Thank you, Nathan, *Hvala ti*."

Nathan smiled back, 'I told you, Dad. I am a whizz at this stuff.' Nathan's expression then changed as if to give less-good news. 'Oh, Dad, I printed off the original scanned ledger on the SharePoint site and compared it with the paper sheets, and they are not the same.'

'Nathan, I can assure you that they are the same; they have to be – maybe not the page numbers, though. Nothing gets past you, I know! Look, I'll test you.' Tariq took the A3 ledger master summary sheet and walked over to the photocopier, returning with the original and the copy, and placed both next to each other on the desk in front of Nathan. He asked, 'Now Nathan, are these sheets both the same?' Nathan knew his dad was in his silly game mode but innocently accepted the challenge. After ten seconds of scanning, he responded, 'No, Dad, actually, they're not the same.'

At that, Tariq scrunched up the copy and threw it at the bin in the corner, and looked at Nathan with a Clint Eastwood smirk on the side of his face. 'Nathan, I rest my case. *Idemo*, let's go home.'

CHAPTER 9

At home, for dinner, Tariq made baked potatoes with baked beans and cheese. Nathan had the same but without the beans. After dinner, Tariq drove them both to King's Hospital to see Millie, about a forty-minute journey in traffic. Tariq was honoured with Nathan's presence in the passenger seat beside him. He was driving more considerately than usual, as he'd had a couple of whiskies after dinner. Nathan enjoyed the calming bubble of the car as the urban landscape silently passed by. Looking dead ahead, Nathan said, 'Dad, I had the best day at work today. Do you know why?'

'No, why?'

'Because it was the first time I could show you I am a whizz at spreadsheets.'

'You like that word, don't you?'

'The policewoman at the station said I was a whizz, but you didn't believe her, so I'm glad you know now. So I hope you can give me super-whizz things to do because I don't want to keep doing the boring stuff.'

Tariq looked across at Nathan, noticing he wasn't obsessing with one of his puzzle books for once. Maybe the result, he thought, of Nathan having diverted his analytical skills onto work spreadsheets.

Nathan said, 'I didn't know you did accents, Dad.'

'What do you mean?'

'In the office, you did the accent of that big American man who came to see you.'

'Oh, Burton. *Ye-hah*! Everybody does Burton.'

'Why don't ya come into my office and take a seat, yah hear,' Nathan said with an uncanny resemblance to Burton, 'you know, I can speak to ya'll like this all cotton-pickin' day until I just run out a' gas, and we' got a whole lot o' that where I come from.'

'Ha! You got 'im down t'ah tee, yes shur-ee,' Tariq quipped back.

'Now looker wha' we got 'ere,' Nathan said, still in American mode, as they entered the hospital car park. A few minutes later they approached Millie at her bedside on the ward on the second floor. Alice and her mother Margaret were already there. Alice gave Tariq the routine kiss on the cheek and a fist-pump for Nathan. Cordial kisses were exchanged between Tariq and his mother-in-law. Before they could exchange any more friendlies, Julian Freeman, the hospital consultant, arrived at Millie's bed. 'Hello, Millie, how are you feeling?'

'About the same, doctor, if I'm honest.'

He then turned to Alice and Tariq and said, 'Hello again. It's good to see you. How are you both?'

'Well, OK,' replied Alice.

The consultant then paused and said in a soft, serious tone, 'We've got Millie's test results back. She's been on a course of steroids now for a few days and there's some good news... and some not so good news.' Tariq and Alice inwardly braced themselves. The consultant explained,

'The steroids have had a stabilising effect on Millie's white blood cells, but not enough to start the second phase of treatment, the chemotherapy, so we're going to increase the dose slightly for another week.' He glanced back at Millie to check if she was also listening. Alice and Tariq stood there in silence.

The consultant continued, 'This isn't that uncommon in treating leukaemia. The steroid dose will be increased starting tomorrow, and we'll review the next steps in a week's time.' He turned to Millie with a calm, reassuring manner, 'OK, Millie?' She nodded back in a tired fashion.

The consultant added a few more medical soundbites and concluded, 'Sorry, I've got to see another patient; I'll catch up with you next week.'

'Thank you. Goodbye,' said Alice, as Dr Freeman walked off down the ward.

Nathan was already telling Millie about their visit to the police station and his successes in helping the policewoman and his dad in their respective offices.

Alice asked, 'Any news on Cheryl? Is she still missing? Did the police tell you anything?'

Tariq replied, 'No, she's still missing as far as I know. The police don't know anything.'

Nathan said, 'We went to the police station in a police car. I've never been in a police car before, and they took Dad down into the basement for a chat, and I helped a police lady upstairs with her spreadsheet. She said that I was a whizz with spreadsheets.'

With a furrowed brow, Alice asked Tariq, 'What did the police want to chat with you about?'

'It was just a routine meeting about arranging a raid on

a business for the case I'm working on; that's all. I couldn't leave Nathan in the office so had to take him with me.'

Alice told her son, 'Nathan, I'm so proud of you for helping Dad at work.' Nathan looked chuffed. She said to her husband, 'And thank you, darling, for looking after Nathan.' She hugged him again, smiling sideways at Millie.

Millie added, 'Yes, Dad, you're doing better than I thought. I told you that you should trust Nathan to help out more; he wants to help.'

'Thank you, Millie, and I'm proud of you, my little darling.' He wiped a tear from his eye with an old tissue from his pocket.

On the drive back home Tariq considered how the intimate family time in the hospital had a dark cloud hanging over it, with the news of the retrograde step in Millie's treatment. Also on his mind was the escalating situation with Cheryl's disappearance; he was on his own on this one, and needed to keep it this way.

Back at home, they both watched *Escape to the Country* on the TV. Tariq commented throughout the programme on the petty complaints raised by prospective buyers, like the garden not being big enough, the stairs being too steep, or that they didn't like the view from the bedroom window.

Tariq addressed the TV, 'There's just no pleasing some people!'

Nathan enjoyed imitating the posh voice of the TV show presenter, Cambridge graduate Alistair Appleton. 'A fine pedigree of striped lawn and Greek-style fountain statue to make the gods jealous... one only has to look in the mirror to know what I'm talking about. With features like that, you have to pay extra.'

Tariq laughed and took a final swig of whisky from his cut-glass tumbler, the ice melted by now. The TV programme credits rolled, and Nathan lifted himself out of his chair. 'Goodnight, Dad, and maybe you need to pay extra for a whizz like me.' He stepped quickly through the door, dodging the cushion his father had thrown at him.

**

Monday morning, on the train to the office, Nathan moved around the carriage to find himself some personal space and then immersed himself in number-find puzzle No.61 in his book, whilst Tariq prepared some notes for the team meeting at 10:00am. Outside London Bridge station, the bus was untypically empty enough for Nathan to tolerate embarking, to Tariq's relief, who'd resigned himself to spending a small fortune on taxi fares.

The oversized clock in the SFO office reception faced them, as they climbed the black stone steps and through the large open glass doors.

'Morning, Beryl.'

'Morning, Tariq.'

'Hello, Beryl.'

'Hello, Nathan.'

The security guard fixed them out of the corner of his eye as they swiped their passes at the glass security gates. Nathan loved the futuristic design and smooth action of the glass gates, which reminded him of *Star Trek*.

In the lift, Nathan watched intently as the green techno-LED floor level numbers lit up as it rose to the fourth floor, arriving with a crisp *ding*. He found a clear spot in the fridge for his cheese and pickle sandwich and pressed the buttons on the hot drinks' dispenser for his regular hot chocolate with extra milk. Tariq placed his briefcase under his desk and joined Nathan in the kitchen. He stood behind Nathan as he delayed removing his cup from the hot drinks' dispenser until the last drop of hot chocolate had fallen. 'Want to get your money's worth then, Nathan?'

'No Dad, it's all free, so I don't need to get my money's worth.'

'Ha! You've got me there, son. What was I thinking?' Tariq replied with a smirk.

For Tariq, it was black coffee with one sugar.

They were about to return to their desks when Lawrence Bashford entered the kitchen.

'Hi Tariq, you alright?' Bashford didn't wait for his reply. 'See you at the team meeting in a bit.'

'Yeah, see you then.' Bashford's routine manner suggested to Tariq that he was ignorant of his trip to the police station. *Probably for the best,* he thought. Regardless, Bashford appeared in high spirits, which was a good sign for the team meeting. He would have been displaying a stress-induced frown if Burton had recently given him a grilling on the case's slow progress. Reflecting on the private drink Tariq had had with Burton, he felt for the first time that he understood him more than Bashford ever would, which gave him some comfort.

Nathan sat next to his father at the white oval melanin table at the team meeting. Nathan was shocked at how close together everyone was, facing each other, and talking at the same time. At least he could doodle with his pen on the notepad as a distraction from the sensory overload. As Case

Controller, Bashford sat at the head of the table to chair the meeting. He was in his mid-forties with well-groomed dark-brown hair and sharp eagle eyes. His previous employment as a senior portfolio manager at Barclays Investments had developed in him a blunt private-sector manner. His seniors respected him for it; underlings didn't.

Stuart Harper, one of the deputy disclosure officers, sat diagonally opposite Tariq at the table, wearing his usual bright purple tie. Tariq still blamed Harper for the collapse of the Frederick Rainsford Commodities case because he had failed to alert him to the sensitive documents that the court later ruled should have been declared Relevant and made available to the defence solicitors, which had led the judge to throw out the whole case. Although Harper had initially collated the material in question, Burton had deemed Tariq culpable as he was the senior supervising disclosure officer responsible for overseeing Harper's work. Consequently, Tariq, not Harper, was put on six months' probation, of which he had six weeks remaining. At the end of his probation, he would either be cleared to remain in his present position, demoted, or worse, his employment terminated.

Bashford noticed that Nathan was new to the meeting, and that Mark Cooper was also in attendance – a rare occurrence – so he asked that everyone around the table introduce themselves.

'Simon Beecham, deputy disclosure officer.'

'Mark Cooper, international liaison, just visiting.'

'Stuart Harper, also deputy disclosure officer.'

'Jim Tipton, finance controller.'

'Sandra Cole, case administrator.'

'Tariq Markovic, senior disclosure officer.'

Nathan was hyped up for his turn and said at pace, 'I am Nathan and I'm helping my dad as I am a whizz at spreadsheets, and my older sister Millie is in hospital because she has—'

'Nathan, that's enough, son. We need to get on with the meeting.'

Bashford concluded, 'Welcome all, especially Mark and Nathan.' Nathan moved his notepad closer and resumed his doodles with increased vigour. 'OK, first item on the agenda is the court update from the legal team, which I'll read out to you: *The evidence collated to date continues to support seven out of the eight lines of inquiry; unless further evidence is forthcoming the charge of bribing a foreign public official under the UK Bribery Act will not be pursued. This relates specifically to the alleged attempt of Karlo Mitchko offering bribes to Serbian finance ministers to make investments in the failed Magnus Conan-Whittaker enterprise. A decision will be taken shortly on this matter, to give disclosure officers a final opportunity to ascertain new and strong evidence to support this charge.'*

With his purple tie twisted slightly to one side, Stuart Harper said, 'I've just come across another box of foreign files. The writing looks Serbian or Bosnian, so it's worth looking at.'

Bashford said, 'Tariq, this is one for you. Can you report back by the next meeting on whether it contains any new information.'

Tariq nodded.

Cooper offered, 'I could bring someone in if you like to interpret the documents.'

Bashford replied, 'No thanks, Mark. If Tariq needs some help we'll get back to you. So, while you're here, Mark, can I ask if there are any other international lines of inquiry?'

'No, just the Bosnian-Serb angle. Let's hope that Tariq can find the Holy Grail of incriminating evidence.'

Tariq responded, 'I'll try!'

Bashford looked down at the printout of the meeting agenda on the table in front of him. 'Tariq, can you please give us the document review progress report?'

This prompted Tariq to pass around a three-page handout to everyone at the meeting.

Harper flicked through the papers. 'These are good, Tariq, the best you've done yet.'

'Glad you like them. Nathan put his IT skills to good use.'

Nathan said, 'Yes, I'm a whizz at spreadsheets and computers.'

'Unlike your dad, hey, Nathan?' Jim Tipton quipped.

'Tariq, please continue,' the chair requested.

'OK, as you can see from the summary sheet, out of the 19,443 documents that have been handed over to us, we've now processed 15,708 as of last Friday. That's a run rate of three hundred and seventy-four per week since we started at the end of September last year. Since we only have nine weeks left, we now need to increase the review rate to four hundred and fifteen a week. The second graph shows the weekly progress rate—'

Bashford looked up from the charts, 'So we've dropped to under four hundred a week for the last two weeks. Can you explain that?'

Tariq hesitated with his answer so Nathan interjected, 'Sorry to interrupt, but if you look at the graph below it, it shows the rate per page.'

'Per page?' Bashford queried.

'Yes, per page,' Nathan repeated back. 'The thing is that just counting the documents doesn't tell you how big the document is. There were five large documents in the last two weeks. The largest document had two hundred and fifty-one pages, so when you compare that with the average weekly number of pages covered, which is 8,564, then the last two weeks was 8,822 pages a week, which is actually a small increase, you see.'

Tariq looked at Nathan in surprised incredulity. Tariq said, 'Thank you, Nathan. That's right. I asked him to analyse the data.'

Nathan looked back at his father quizzically in reaction to his incorrect statement.

Bashford said in a subdued tone, 'Yes, right, well, that makes sense then. Thanks for that. So the bottom line is that we need to increase the rate to four hundred and fifteen a week, and that's assuming no new material comes in.'

Sandra chipped in in her down-to-earth Midlands accent. 'Oh, if new stuff comes in, then you should review the contents and submit a CRF, a Change Request Form, for additional time and costs. My previous Case Controller was always doing that, and if you get a lot of them, you can make a case for an extension from the court.'

'Thanks, Sandra. Yes, so make sure you do that, Tariq, if anything comes in. Submit the CRF to me for first approval.'

'Yes of course, I always do that,' Tariq bluffed.

Jim Tipton then circulated the finance report and went through it with the attendees. He was interrupted by Simon Beecham, who challenged him that one of the published figures was a series of zeros, which was nonsensical. 'I see what you mean. Sorry, something has gone wrong here. It was correct on my original.' Tipton was at a loss to explain the error.

Harper enjoyed explaining the mystery, 'Oh, I know what that is. You probably used the photocopier on the fourth floor. It has a blank spot for some reason. You don't notice it most of the time, only occasionally, like this, when a digit goes missing. I've reported it.'

Jim Tipton responded with gratitude. 'Well, that explains why the copies are not the same.'

At those words, Tariq glanced across at Nathan, and Nathan back to his father.

As people dispersed at the end of the meeting, Jim Tipton teased Tariq that the idea of counting the page-review rate had to be Nathan's idea as Tariq would never have come up with that himself. Nathan was pleased to confirm.

Tariq and Nathan had drinks in the kitchen after the meeting. 'I should say well done, Nathan, you super-whizz, but I don't want to encourage you to get too big-headed.'

Nathan beamed. 'That man who does the finance, he knows that I am the whizz, not you.'

'Yes, I noticed you enjoyed telling him that.'

Back at his desk, Tariq was still thinking about Harper's explanation that the photocopier on his floor had a tiny flaw. At the end of the day in the office, Tariq retrieved his jacket. As he leant over towards the coat stand, he saw the crumpled sheet of paper he'd thrown yesterday at the now-empty bin when Nathan had declared that the copy he'd taken of the master ledger was not the same. Since his throw had missed the bin, the ball of paper was still on the floor behind the end desk. Tariq retrieved the scrunched-up sheet and sat back at his desk, flattening it out with his fingers over the palm of his hand. He then brought up the corresponding scanned master sheet on the PC screen and compared it. He had previously explained to Nathan that the document ledgers, by definition, would be the same, as one was just a printout of the other. He was about to give up when he noticed two minimal changes in one of the table columns. Tariq whispered intently to himself, 'It can't be, it just can't be, *o moj boze*! They have to be the same; they *have* to be.' As he looked up from the screen, Stuart Harper walked past down the open corridor carrying a box of files.

CHAPTER 10

The following morning, Tariq was looking for Sandra in the office. She was the only person he could trust to back him up with the apparently doctored ledger, and he wanted a second opinion. Tariq considered that she would at least be discreet even if he'd misinterpreted the data. Also, Nathan needed to be kept out of the loop. He would inevitably say something inappropriate to compromise his investigations.

At lunch, while Nathan had his usual cheese sandwich, Tariq spotted Sandra getting something from the fridge in the kitchen. He went over to catch her. 'Sandra, have you got a minute?'

'Yes, of course. Are you OK, Tariq? Any news on Millie?'

'The hospital consultant has put her on a higher dose of steroids, which isn't uncommon, he said.'

'I see. If you ever need to go to the hospital urgently, just let me know. I'll cover for you.

'Thanks, Sandra, I will. Thank you for offering.'

Tariq led Sandra to his desk. Since it was lunchtime most of the desks were empty, and no one was close by. He pulled open his top drawer and showed her the wrinkled document ledger he'd found next to the bin. He turned to page seven and displayed the same page on the Dell monitor. Sandra squinted at the screen and then at the paper copy.

Tariq asked her, 'Can you see anything different between them?'

Sandra studied the screen and cross-checked the paper copy. She looked confused and said, almost in disbelief, 'Documents 15,651 and 15,652 have had their designations changed. They're now Appendix documents instead of main case documents, which means they'll probably never be tabled in court.' She looked around nervously to see who was in sight. 'How can this happen?'

Tariq looked back at her, echoing her question.

Sandra continued, 'This means someone has gone back into the ledger after the formal review and changed it. I thought the ledger files are protected to stop this sort of thing?'

Tariq replied, 'All the case team have access. I don't think that Burton even knows what it is.' Tariq continued in hushed tones, 'Harper. I think it's him. He's trying to sabotage the case again to get me sacked so he can take my dead shoes.'

Sandra restrained a smile at Tariq's attempted English expression. 'Please Tariq, don't go around accusing everyone; it'll just make things worse. I would hide that sheet away, if I were you. If anyone sees it, they'll start asking questions. As you know, it's against company policy to keep copies of ledgers for security reasons.'

'Yes, of course,' said Tariq. He was about to return it to the drawer when Sandra intervened.

'Give it to me.' She looked around again as she folded it over and put it in her handbag, 'That's the safest place you can get you know, a woman's handbag.' Sandra was about to return to the kitchen but turned to Tariq. 'You know what you need to do? Go to the property room to find those two documents and see what's in them. What does the ledger say?'

They both examined the table on the screen to read the descriptions: *Marketing Policy 44 pages, Company Policy 39 pages.*

'Well, they should be Appendix documents anyway; you can burn those!' Tariq said.

'Yeah, you could be right,' Sandra agreed. 'Wait a minute, what does the paper copy say?' She retrieved it from her small, elegant blue leather handbag and unfolded it. With a stunned expression, she showed it to Tariq.

He slumped down on his swivel office chair, eyes wide, and muttered, 'Shit!'

On the paper sheet, both documents were listed as *Head Office Transactions: Rigs.* One was 67 pages and the other 48 pages. Both document types were the highest classification in the disclosure strategy list, and they were significant documents. Tariq took a note of the unique reference IDs so he could find them in the property room – if they were still there, that is.

After lunch, Tariq tried to remain as calm as he could in front of Nathan as they went down to the property room on the basement floor. Nathan was first, as usual, to scan his pass on the door security detector pad. In the property room, Tariq went about trying to find the two reclassified documents that he'd been looking at with Sandra. They weren't in the box where they should have been. He sat down at the PC on the centre table, held up his digital security fob on his keyring, and entered the six numbers on the fob at the login screen to access the ledger files. The master ledger screen showed them entered just as he'd reviewed with Sandra, *Marketing Policy 44 pages and Company Policy 39 pages.*

Nathan looked over his father's shoulder and pointed at the screen, saying, 'Those are Appendix documents as they've got an 'A' against them. They don't keep those here as there would be too many of them; that's what the man told me, anyway.'

'Which man? Who was it?'

'He was in the lift before lunch with a box of documents.'

'Never mind about that; what was his name?'

'I don't know his name. Stop asking me his name.'

'OK, sorry. If you see him again, can you point him out to me. That would be a big help.'

'Yes, alright then.'

***

The next day, just after 10:00am, Simon Beecham, one of the two deputy disclosure officers, joined them in the property room.

'Hi Tariq, I thought I would find you here. Man, we're going to be busy. Good job, by the way, Nathan, on the page progress rate stats at the team meeting. That told Bashford!'

Nathan said, 'I like putting data into graphs and tables because the numbers follow rules. They never lie.'

'Unlike people, heh, Nathan?'

'Yes, not like people.'

Tariq and Beecham discussed the recent documents

that had been reviewed. Sometime later, Tariq opened the master ledger on the PC in front of him and asked Beecham, 'I don't suppose it was you who reviewed these two policy documents?'

Beecham crouched closer to the screen. 'No, not me. Look, you can see who reviewed them. SH, Stuart Harper, in column G… and counter-initialled by JB, Jack Burton.'

Tariq checked the screen himself. 'Of course, of course, I should have looked. Thanks.'

'Why do you want to know? They are Appendix documents so they'll be sent to St Albans. Harper arranges all that.'

Nathan said, 'They've already been posted, then, because they're gone from the box.'

Beecham looked up at the box, 'That's odd, it's half empty. Stuart usually waits until after the review is signed off before labelling the boxes, as you never know how much stuff needs keeping. Anyway, better crack on.' Beecham took a pile of random files and documents from one of the side shelves and set them down on the table before him. He took the top one, an unlabelled hardback green book about half an inch thick, and started to flick through the pages.

'I can make up some boxes if you like,' Nathan offered.

'That would be great. Three will be enough for now. Thanks,' said Beecham.

Tariq also grabbed some documents from the shelf and started to review them.

It didn't take long for Nathan to make the cardboard boxes. 'Is there anything else I can do?' Nathan surveyed the deep shelves on the right-hand wall, crammed full with a random collection of papers and books of different sizes, colours and designs, in a mixture of boxes and bags. There were also numerous black sacks on the floor under the lower shelf. 'I can sort out all the messy documents if you like. I can put them in order. I don't like the mess, you know, it gives me a headache.'

Beecham looked up with interest. 'How would you do that, Nathan? I wouldn't know where to start, mate.'

'I'll put all the same green books together, and then I can look at the dates and put them in order. The newest first. Then I'll look at the files to see if the pages look the same.' Nathan figured he'd more chance of Beecham's approval than his father's.

Beecham replied, 'Nathan, that's an excellent suggestion. I can't see any harm in it, and it might help speed things along. Why don't you make a start? See how you get on. Just keep a record of which box or bag each document came from. Here are some labels.'

An hour and a half later, Nathan had assembled several piles of documents with similar features. The concentration of common document types was a revelation to Tariq and Beecham. Tariq remembered his undertaking at the team meeting to review the Bosnian files. 'Simon, do you know where the boxes of foreign files are?'

'There's only one new box by the way. It's just come in, so it's probably still in the post room...'

'Oh, I know where that is!' declared Nathan. 'I can get it for you if you like?'

Since Tariq didn't want to be interrupted from his analysis of a confusing chain of emails in one of the files, he assented to Nathan's offer.

Nathan exited the property room and turned left along

the corridor with blue floor carpet tiles to the other side of the building towards the post room. Footsteps approached.

'Hi, Nathan, remember me? Ajay, the security man? How's it going then?'

Nathan's keen ear picked up the mellow Indian tones in his voice, which complimented his friendly demeanour. 'Hello, Ajay. I'm helping my dad with all the things that he isn't the best at, and I'm now putting the files in order, you see. I'm good at working out when things are not the same.'

Nathan's comment grabbed Ajay's attention. 'Is that right? Do you know, Nathan, you could be just the person I need. Could you do me a bit of a favour? Can you come over to the security room and check out some circuit diagram drawings for me?'

'Drawings? Um, what kind of drawings? I would like to see them though anyway. Can I see your drawings?'

'I tell you what, Nathan; when you can, come down and see me, and I'll show them to you. They're driving me up the wall! I could do with a fresh pair of eyes on them, someone like you, young and keen, and someone who can spot when things aren't the same. That would be great.'

Nathan replied with glee, 'Yes, I'm young and keen. I'll come over tomorrow. Shall I knock on your door then?'

'Yes, do that, but after 10:30am as I'll be issuing building passes before then. Must go. See you tomorrow, yeah?'

Following his conversation with Ajay, Nathan continued down the corridor to the post room. A well-drilled post processing system was adhered to in order to keep track of the large volumes of incoming and outgoing letters and parcels coming through the post room on a daily basis. This included sensitive legal evidence and material, which was transported by specialist vetted courier companies. The motorbike couriers arrived around 5pm to pick up the mail, and a later courier kept on standby in case urgent deliveries needed to be made. The standby courier was Burton's initiative, which had helped speed up the more complex fraud cases, such as the Magnus Conan-Whittaker case, by transferring documents to legal and other partnership teams the same day rather than late-morning the next day.

Along the corridor between the property room and the post room were the lifts, and next to the lifts were the toilets. Nathan was pleased to have found the toilets on his second day as a safe place to retreat to when his senses got overloaded. Locating a safe place was something that the family therapist Charlotte had suggested to avoid a full meltdown, which was embarrassing at the least. The toilets were conveniently close to the lifts if he needed to get down quickly from any floor. The lift was usually empty and was itself a calming space, with its ordered green LED floor numbers. Above the lifts, on the fourth floor, the LED floor numbers were bright enough for Nathan to see them from his desk, and he enjoyed tracking them through the eleven floors, including the basement. The lower basement level could only be accessed by steps from the basement, or down the car park ramp. Nathan passed the lifts, then the toilets, and entered the post room to find the foreign file box. The younger of the two postmen in the room pointed out to Nathan a single box labelled *Foreign, Bosnian*.

Nathan was walking back past the lifts with the box when the lift dinged as it arrived at basement level. The unexpected arrival of the lift prompted a reflex action by

Nathan to step sideways to conceal himself behind one of the building columns. Two men exited the lift. Nathan realised he'd look stupid if he was seen, so he quietly stepped back towards the toilets. One of the men went into a small alcove opposite the lifts. There followed a noise so excruciating, angry and loud, that Nathan put down the box to cover his ears with his forearms, elbows pointing forwards. In desperation, he grabbed the box and darted into the toilet on the other side of the corridor. Inside the toilet, he locked himself in the far cubicle and put the box on the floor. He sat on top of the closed toilet seat with his feet up, and his head clamped between his raised knees. He inflated the soft ball that his mother had bought him and put it between his knees. He could then rest his head on it, which had proved to be a more comfortable arrangement. To calm himself further he started humming, simultaneously rocking slightly backwards and forwards to control his breathing.

With Nathan still trying to calm his brain, two men entered the toilet; he assumed the same men that had exited the lift. One walked over to Nathan's locked cubicle and crouched down to look under the door. Nathan stopped rocking and controlled his breathing to a near-silent murmur. Only the box was visible on the floor. 'Hello?' the man said. Nathan resisted responding. The man said to the second man, 'There's something on the floor in there; it looks like a box.'

The second man responded, 'Stop fussing about, will you. That one was out-of-order yesterday; the sign's fallen off. The box will have plumbing parts in it. The Maintenance Team have a special tool to lock the doors.'

It wasn't long before the men were shouting aggressively

at each other. Nathan cupped his hands over his ears to blot out their angry voices. One of the men walked over again to his cubicle. Nathan breathed louder than he expected but the sound was drowned out by the urinals as they spurted water down the pans. The man had now taken a few steps away from the cubicle, and Nathan was able to settle himself enough to remove his hands from his ears. The two men continued their angry exchanges. One of them threatened the other with words and phrases that Nathan had never heard before. To his relief, the toilet door closed suddenly, and the room fell silent.

Nathan emerged from the cubicle sometime later. He'd no idea how long he'd been there. The aftermath of one of his meltdowns was akin to concussion. He usually remembered what happened at the start and regaining control at the end, but not much in between. At least no one saw him; that was the main thing. He realised he'd forgotten the box and had to go back to retrieve it from the toilet cubicle, then returned to the property room.

'Nathan, where the hell have you been?'

'I got a headache so I had to rest on my own, but I'm alright now.'

Tariq knew it best not to pry any further and joked, 'Well, don't forget about us, will you, Nathan?'

'How could I do that? You're my dad.' Nathan suspected that his father was telling another of his silly jokes.

Beecham chipped in from behind a pile of old red hardback accounting books. 'Ha, ha! Of course he wouldn't, but you just wait until he's got his first girlfriend, like my son.'

Nathan said, 'I still wouldn't forget Dad because I might

want him to give me a lift in his car, then pay for a movie and fish and chips afterwards.'

'Sounds like my son all over! That's all I'm good for – money and transport. An occasional thank you would be nice. Is that too much to ask?'

Nathan felt his cranium swell again under the strain of deciphering Beecham's rhetorical questions. Nathan decided that it was best not to say anything when he felt like that, so he picked up the Bosnian box and gave it to his father as a gesture that he hadn't forgotten about him in the time he'd been gone.

'Thanks, Nathan. Only one box?'

'Yes, that's all there was.'

Tariq took the lid off the large box, 'Well, now, what do we have here?' he said, as he pulled out a wad of white A4 papers, held together with a large bulldog clip. There was a mixture of crisp new papers and older faded ones, not untypical of the random nature of material snatched by heavy-handed policemen on a night-time raid.

Tariq spent the next hour skim-reading the Bosnian text on the wad of papers. It was a strange feeling, understanding the text - but not remembering why. Amongst the bunce was a business case proposal referring to Magnus Conan-Whittaker's eye-watering investments in four fictitious offshore oil rigs. There were two new Bosnian names with UK addresses not yet known to the investigation on two embossed letterheads, signed by Karlo Mitchko, no less. Standard procedure dictated that surveillance operations would be put in place for these addresses. Even if the suspects were long gone, incriminating evidence could often be found, left behind in the rush to stay ahead of the authorities.

CHAPTER 11

At breakfast, Nathan polished off his bowl of two Weetabix as his father finished his instant coffee.

'Ten minutes, yeah? Don't make it a panic,' said Tariq.

'Yes, nearly ready, Dad. Could you pour me some banana milk, please?'

Tariq took a glass from the cupboard and duly poured some from the glass bottle they had delivered with the milk three times a week. If the milkman ever let them down, Nathan would sulk in his bedroom until his mother bought a replacement from the local Co-op shop. Nathan took his sandwich box from the fridge, put it in his worn black leather satchel, and secured its shabby leather straps. Every compartment and pocket of the satchel had a designated purpose. Persuading him to switch to the new satchel bought for him the previous Christmas had fallen on deaf ears, or on a stubborn brain, as his father put it. There were pens, pencils, tissues, coins, AA and AAA batteries, a small notebook, a magnifying glass, and other items squirrelled away in every compartment.

They left the house for the train station in good time. Tariq now allowed an extra five minutes to get Nathan out of the house. They boarded Nathan's preferred carriage on the 7:38am Charing Cross train, which usually had the same empty seats. Nathan sat by the window as the view eased his claustrophobia and prevented him from sitting between two strangers. It also curtailed Nathan's nonsensical questions and suppositions to his father, which was otherwise a relatively silent morning commute.

Nathan lifted his head from his word puzzle challenge book and asked, 'Dad, what is a black sheep? I mean, I've never seen one at all, not even in my dreams. Perhaps the other white sheep made it go last and then shut the gate on it, which is why I never got to see it. My friend Billy at school says that's sheepist because the black sheep was treated badly because of the colour of his wool.' A few amused expressions cracked on the faces of passengers in the carriage. 'And what exactly is a black male?'

The middle-aged black man opposite almost laughed out loud at Nathan's question and his father's embarrassed expression. Tariq looked back at the man opposite, grateful for his empathetic smile. Nathan followed his father's eyes, and seeing the chunky suited black man seated in front of him, realised that his question had been answered. Nathan said in a quieter tone, 'I heard someone in the office call someone a black male yesterday. Is that racist?'

Tariq replied equally softly, 'No, not really, it's just a description, maybe from a police statement or one of the security guards.'

'Nelson Mandela, then, would have been called that when the South African police locked him up in prison on Robben Island.'

'You could be right, Nathan. I'll tell you what, why don't you buy his autobiography and find out? They probably called him much worse!'

'OK, I'll buy the book. "Buy the book"; I heard that said yesterday as well.'

'I guess that's what the shop assistant said to you when you stayed in the bookshop too long?' said Tariq.

'Dad, I've never been in any bookshop too long, as there is no time limit, you know… So you must be joking, then.' Tariq smiled back. Nathan didn't pursue his father further on the topic as he often did when confronted with his jokes, most of which he didn't understand. Nathan continued studying his word puzzle.

To Tariq's relief, the remainder of the journey to the office went without a hitch. The bus arrived on time with free seats.

Nathan served himself a hot chocolate in the office kitchen, and Tariq had a white coffee. Sandra entered the kitchen, and after Nathan had returned to his desk, she said to Tariq, 'Cheryl phoned me yesterday; she sounded upset. She wanted to talk to me about what happened to her, but wanted to tell me privately, in person, and she wouldn't tell me where she was. I'm worried about her, Tariq. There's something wrong, I know there is. At least she's alive. Has she tried to contact you as well?'

'No, no she hasn't. Yes, that is strange. You should tell the police.'

Back at his desk, Tariq was responding to emails. Amongst them was a meeting invite from Lawrence Bashford, including Jack Burton and Mark Cooper from the International Liaison Team. The meeting was titled *Bosnia Interview*. Tariq had notified Bashford of the two Bosnian names he'd come across in the documents from the Bosnian box and assumed that the meeting had something to do with it.

While Tariq was still immersed in emails, Nathan went down to the ground floor to help Ajay, the security manager, with his drawings that were 'driving him up the wall'. He knocked on Ajay's door with no response, so he knocked again; this time the door opened. It was Ajay with a busy morning smile.

'Young Nathan, what a surprise!'

'Oh, shall I come back later then?'

'No, of course not. Now you're here, let's see what we can do. I'm just going to grab a coffee, OK? Sit yourself down there and I'll be back in a jiffy.'

Nathan looked blankly back at Ajay, considering the notion of him climbing into a huge Jiffy envelope. He then surveyed the security room. He recognised the building pass printing machine aside a small box of blank passes. There was a selection of lanyards hanging from some hooks on the far wall and a pile of building maintenance signs with notices like *Out of Order* and *Under Maintenance*. On the front wall hung a framed team photograph of Ajay with his work colleagues dressed in the SFO deep-blue security uniforms. Nathan looked through the windows of the main door and the side door leading to the control room. No one was nearby, so he sat down at Ajay's computer, which he hadn't locked, and started pressing a few keys.

About five minutes later, Ajay clumsily pushed the door open with his foot, holding a red Smarties mug of coffee. 'Sorry to keep you waiting, Nathan. Follow me.' Ajay pushed open the side door into the control room. Two security men in the far corner in the same dark-navy uniform looked up briefly then returned their attention to their monitors as their displays switched between camera feeds every ten seconds. The man with his back to Nathan said to his colleague on the other side of the large desk, 'Camera twelve.'

His white skinned, bearded colleague responded, 'What's the bugger doing? He can't park there. These delivery drivers are taking the piss.'

Ajay said, 'Sorry, Nathan. Ignore these renegades,' as he led him into a small back room off the main control room. Nathan was taken aback by the shelves, which were loaded with old security cameras and other electronic and mechanical equipment. On the side wall were two large paper drawings fixed to a grey noticeboard. 'Do you know what these drawings are, Nathan?' Nathan looked at each intently. The drawings had several coloured lines traversing in different directions between unidentified objects. Ajay explained, 'They're circuit diagrams, and look, this one is Revision A, and this one is Revision B, so they're supposed to be different. Can I see the difference? Can I hell! They look the same to me. I'm hoping that you're good at those spot-the-difference pictures.'

'Oh yes, I'm a whizz at those. I always finish those before my dad. He takes ages.'

One of the security guards poked his head around the door, 'Ajay, where's the vehicle registration book? There's a grey van waiting at the gate; I need to check it out.'

Ajay replied, 'Be with you in a minute. Nathan, take one of these highlighters, say the green one, and mark up on this drawing, Revision B, anything that's different. I need to sort this out today.'

'Right, the green one. Yes, OK, I'll try my best then.'

Ajay retrieved the grey vehicle registration book from a

shelf in the control room and gave it to the security guard. The van wasn't on the authorised list, so the guard left the room to go down to the gate to establish their credentials. Ajay went with him as he wanted to have a word with the guard at the gate about the shifts he'd claimed on his timesheet.

On Ajay's return to the security room, he checked Nathan's progress with the drawings. He asked, 'How are you getting on, Nathan?'

'Finished.' Nathan showed him the large A0 Revision B drawing marked in green highlighter.

Ajay unpinned the drawing from the noticeboard and lifted it high in the air as he walked into the control room to show his staff. 'John, Neil, take a look at this. See what Nathan's done for us! All the new cables are in green, and there's even a change in the specifications.' He turned to Nathan, 'Thanks Nathan, you're right, you are a bloody whizz.'

Nathan wasn't sure that was a good thing as he hated blood and the colour of blood. That's why he didn't eat tomatoes, and he didn't eat red peppers but was fine with the yellow and green ones and sometimes the orange ones. From Ajay's smile, Nathan could at least tell that he was pleased, which was the main thing. Nathan then made his way back to his desk on the fourth floor.

His father wasn't at his desk so he had another hot chocolate from the kitchen and then took the lift down to Property Room No.1. As he approached the room, he noticed that the door security sensor was flashing red as the door was held open by a half-full cardboard box. He pushed the door fully open.

'Nathan, for God's sake, where have you been? Blooming hell, I've been waiting an hour. Burton wants to see me, and I've been waiting for you to get back. Beecham's coming down here at 11:30am and he's forgotten his pass today, so somebody needs to be here for him.'

'I was helping Ajay with his drawings, like I said yesterday, so it isn't fair that you're getting angry with me. You're always getting angry, and I've done nothing wrong. Mum says that you're highly strung, so it's not just me. You can go now, then I can be alone and not get angry like you.'

'Alright, Nathan, you win. Sorry, it's just that I've got a lot on my plate with this case and everything else that's going on. I don't know who I can trust anymore.'

'What plate? You haven't even got a plate.'

'Please, Nathan, not now, son. Look, like I said, I need to go up to see Burton. Can you carry on sorting out the documents into types as you were doing yesterday?'

'Yes, I know what I'm doing, Dad.'

'Oh, and as I said, Beecham should be here soon. Keep the door open until he arrives,' said Tariq as he left the room, pacing towards the lift.

Burton greeted Tariq in the corridor as he approached his office on the ninth floor. 'Tariq, howdy brave-fella. Really enjoyed our little campfire heart-to-heart th'other day. Glad you've come up. Sorry to drag ya' away from all that important stuff ya' doing on the case. Come into ma office and si' ya'self down; we just need a few minutes of ya' time for a short briefing.' Burton was looking smarter than usual and was in a more formal mood, which put Tariq on edge. Was he in for a formal dressing-down?

As Tariq entered Burton's office, Nigel Pemberton, the

International Fraud Director, got up from his chair and said, 'Hello Tariq, jolly good to see you.' Standing next to Pemberton was Mark Cooper, who said plainly, 'Hi, Tariq.'

Pemberton said to Tariq, 'I'm sure that I've seen you around on the fourth floor, yah?'

Although not an aristocrat, Pemberton looked and spoke like one. The closest to his ilk Tariq had come across was Hugh Bonneville from the TV series *Downton Abbey*. Pemberton had a distinctive Scottish twang to his upper-class delivery, probably a result of attending a private school in Scotland in his youth.

'Yes, that's right,' replied Tariq, resisting calling him 'sir'.

'Good, good, thought so. Jack informs me that you've stumbled across a couple of Bosnian names with their fingers in the pie. Well done, fine work. Jack and I have agreed that we need to grab the bull by the horns by taking swift action – to strike while the iron's hot, so to speak. Both of them are resident in North London and I've filed a Section 2A application for a warrant for the arrest of these fraudsters so we have a police squad ready for a dawn raid at 05:00 hours tomorrow morning. All we need now is the nod from Judge Fullerton before midnight. He's a friend of the family so he'll rubber stamp it as soon as he can; Fullerton is a real brick.'

Tariq hid his surprise that Pemberton had sanctioned a raid before the usual extended period of surveillance. Also, having read the two emails from the Bosnians, he doubted there was sufficient evidence to issue warrants for their arrests.

Burton said, 'Isn't that what you wanted, Tariq? A

dawn raid to round 'em up and drag 'em into town to the sheriff's office? If, and when, we lasso these critters, you'll be called upon to interview them straight away, before they have time to concoct their alibis.'

Tariq responded, 'What I don't understand is why Bosnians would be involved in business dealings with Karlo Mitchko anyway. He's a Serb; they wouldn't deal with him.'

Burton replied curtly, 'Unless they wanted to double-cross him. They would enjoy doing that. The other way of thinking is that if there's millions to be made – they don't care!'

'Right, I see. I'll need to draft the Terms of Reference for the interview, which has to be signed off by—'

Burton cut in, 'The Director. That's right, my man; you know the process all too well. If you ask me, there's too much damn process! It just slows us down and gives 'em a head-start for the hills before we can gun 'em down. Anyway, that's why *he's* here,' Burton said, looking at Pemberton, who extended his hand towards Tariq, holding a few sheets of A4 paper. The title page had written on it *Interview Terms of Reference; Tariq Markovic (SFO) Interview; Theodore Sharisk, Kerim Hadzic.*

Pemberton said, 'We've got the interview booked for tomorrow at 11:00am after the police have done their checks; Room 10-08. One of the uniforms will stay with you for the interview. Sorry, that's all they could spare at short notice, and Mark here will be your scribe. I'm afraid we couldn't get an interpreter at short notice, so you'll have to do your best. Are you alright with that, Tariq?'

'Well, yes, I'll have to be. I didn't expect this so soon.

How do you know that they're still at the same addresses? They're probably long gone.'

Cooper explained, 'The police have already been carrying out surveillance at the premises, and they're occupied, a man in each – hence we're moving quickly.'

Tariq replied, 'OK, right then. Yes, I'll be ready at 11:00.' Tariq considered that if the interview went well, it wouldn't harm his case for being taken off probation.

'Great, thanks, Tariq. Good luck,' said Pemberton.

Nathan's desk was unoccupied when Tariq returned. Tariq checked his watch: 12:30pm. Nathan had probably already gone down to the canteen with his sandwiches for lunch, so Tariq made his way down to find him. In the canteen, Tariq opted for the lasagne with salad. He picked out Nathan on one of the long dining tables, halfway through his first sandwich.

'Hi, Dad. I've been going through all the files, but I need to show you because there are so many types, and some are nearly the same, so I don't know where they fit.'

'OK, Nathan. Show me after lunch, please; I've got a lot on my plate – not just lasagne, Nathan.' Tariq smiled at Nathan and added, 'I know what you're going to say next!'

'What?'

'*Salad.* Ha!'

'Funny, Dad. I looked it up on my phone, so I know what that expression means now.'

'Good, I'm glad. Do you know what I've got on my plate for tomorrow?'

'No, I don't know, and I don't even know if you are being serious now.'

'Well, I am being serious, Nathan, son, because I am interviewing two Bosnians tomorrow with Mark Cooper and a policeman. Remember Cooper? He was at the team meeting the other day. He does International liaison. He was wearing a stripy light-blue tie.'

'Oh yes, I remember that tie. It was actually blue and green stripes. I always remember ties.'

'Yes, that's him, Nathan, you've got him. Anyway, 11:00am tomorrow, I'll be doing my interrogation.'

After lunch when Tariq was on his own in the property room, he turned over the pages of the interview Terms of Reference (ToR) that Pemberton had handed him in Burton's office. Tariq said to himself, 'I don't believe this – this is a *joke*! They get a Section 2A warrant to arrest these guys and send them down to me to have a chat on their personal life in Bosnia and to establish their relationship with Karlo Mitchko. That's it? Absolutely no questions on the content of the emails. Bizarre!' Tariq concluded that Cooper was probably responsible, and that Pemberton couldn't have read the ToR; otherwise, he'd never have signed it off.

Nathan returned to the room to find his father with a scowl on his face. 'Do you want more on your plate, Dad?' said Nathan with a hint of humour.

'No thank you, Nathan, I'm not hungry.'

'Ha! Funny, Dad. I didn't think so.'

CHAPTER 12

Back at home, Tariq and Nathan had just finished their pizza with green salad for supper, when the phone rang in the hallway. Tariq answered it.

'Hello, darling, it's me. How did you get on today? How's Nathan coping with work?' It was Alice.

'Hi, darling. Yes, well, fine. Nathan's keeping busy, and no big meltdowns today, so that's a start.'

'Oh, that's good. I'm glad it's going well with Nathan... I'm grateful. I see Millie daily, and Mother is looking after me.' There was a pause. 'Tary, I'm ringing about Millie; she's got worse. Her white blood cell count is still going up. I'm scared: I'm scared we're going to lose her...' Alice was sobbing now. She gathered herself and continued, 'The thing is, the consultant told us about this new type of steroid just patented in America. It's performed well in pre-trials... but it's expensive.'

'How expensive?' Tariq asked.

'Well, four thousand pounds plus import duties and transit costs, so near five thousand.'

'That's crazy, why can't she get it on the NHS?'

'Because they can't sell it here until they've done the regulatory trials; why do you think I'm telling you this,

Tariq? Please. That's the whole point; it's not available on the NHS yet, and it could take years.'

'How are we going to find that kind of money?' Tariq replied, trying not to sound angry.

'Mother said she'd loan us a thousand, and I can put in a thousand, so the shortfall is three thousand. Please, Tary, can you go to the bank tomorrow? You can put it on the mortgage if that's the best way of doing it.'

Tariq sighed. 'God! OK then. I'll use up the holiday money and borrow the rest.'

'Can you go tomorrow?'

'Yes, I'll go at lunchtime. When do you need the money by?'

Alice said, 'Tomorrow, Friday. I've paid the thousand pounds deposit, and we need to pay the balance by Friday. Sorry, I didn't have time to talk to you about it.'

'Is that Mum on the phone, Dad?' Nathan asked.

'Yes, it's your mother,' he answered back to Nathan, then concluded speaking to his wife, 'Don't worry darling, see you soon. I'll hand you over to Nathan.'

Nathan was pleased to tell his mother all the exciting things he'd been up to in Dad's office. She didn't spoil his mood by mentioning Millie.

Nathan went up to his bedroom, and Tariq to the sitting room, where he turned on the TV to watch the news. A pretty black woman presented a news item reminding viewers that the London Olympics opening ceremony was due to start tomorrow evening. In the piece, she explained that the construction of the Olympic Park was the largest regeneration project in Europe, worked on by forty-six thousand people. She explained that the site has a hundred hectares of new parks, eight kilometres of new waterways and half a million new plants. Eight world-class venues had been constructed, requiring five miles of existing overhead power lines to be taken off pylons and re-routed through underground tunnels. The whole site was built on contaminated land, which was previously West Ham rubbish tip, and two hundred buildings had been demolished. The piece concluded with a sneak preview of the opening ceremony featuring the queen, Daniel Craig playing James Bond, and Rowan Atkinson as Mr Bean.

The next news item was the trial of Ratko Mladic at The International War Crimes Tribunal in The Hague for war crimes in the Bosnian War, which resulted in the break-up of the former Yugoslavia. The main hearings had just begun and there was some amateur film footage of a large group of Bosnian men being led away, who were allegedly later shot en masse. The charge of mass shootings was substantiated by the exhumation of mass graves, which the Serbian forces had moved on a large scale in an attempt to hide the evidence, according to the UN prosecution lawyers. The prosecution alleged that the Serbs hadn't been able to move the remainder of the bodies as they'd run out of time due to the unexpected early signing of the Dayton Peace Accord on 14th December 1995 by the President of Serbia, Slobodan Milosevic, and by the Presidents of Croatia and Bosnia & Herzegovina. Evidence of the original mass graves had been photographed by American spy planes that flew over the sites, probably called in by agents on the ground. The identity of these agents remained unknown and would probably never be revealed, it was explained. The then-US President, Bill Clinton, had always denied that they had any agents on the ground, and so the US was not culpable for failing to intervene earlier to stop the alleged genocide of Bosnian men and boys. Critics maintained that Clinton was desperate not to let anything take the shine off his achievement of brokering the Dayton Peace Accord.

There was a second film clip of the Srebrenica town sign with soldiers marching past towards the mountainous forests in the distance. General Mladic could be seen in uniform, talking to the doomed Bosniaks, surrounded by the more heavily armed Serb forces. Days later, thousands of Bosnian men would be dead, allegedly shot by the Serb army under Mladic's orders. Seeing the images made Tariq feel nauseous and he reached for the TV remote to turn it off, but hesitated when he recognised a face from one of his recurring dreams. With his finger poised on the remote, he stared at the man on the TV screen. He was casually dressed, wearing a polo-necked sweater. Who was he? Why was he there? More film footage ensued, and attention was then drawn to a senior-ranked Serbian soldier they wanted to trace, thought to be one of General Ratko Mladic's subordinates. Witnesses had testified that they had seen the soldier at several locations where massacres had allegedly occurred. It was their supposition that he was probably a local commander carrying out Mladic's orders. There were no clear photographs of this man. As a consequence, suspicions had been raised by the Bosnians of a cover-up by the Serbs. The handful of Bosnians that survived had observed that the man had a distinctive double-headed eagle tattoo on the back of his neck, probably representing the Serbian emblem. This man hadn't been seen since the end of the war, and the

Serbs claimed that he'd been assassinated by Bosniaks keen on revenge.

Tariq pressed the off switch, opened the drinks cabinet and poured himself a large whisky nightcap.

That night, in his dream, the man Tariq had seen on TV looked intently at him, holding out the loaded sack in front of him, saying forcefully, 'Take it and go, go *now*, you must go *now*, they're onto you. This is your last chance, move!'

Tariq awoke startled. He sat up in his bed, sweating and breathing heavily. Who was that man, and why was he at The Hague?

***

As they arrived at Eden Park station on their way to the office the next morning, it was announced on the tannoy that their train was cancelled. The next one to arrive was packed with twice as many passengers so Nathan refused to board as he'd done on the first day. To avoid another meltdown, Tariq took Nathan to the station café and bought him a hot chocolate, and a cappuccino for himself. Tariq had a conversation with the lady running the café about Team GB's chances of winning any gold medals at the Olympics. She complained about her numerous attempts to book tickets using the online ticket allocation system, which kept crashing. Tariq decided not to mention that he'd been lucky to get tickets from the SFO for the following Saturday.

Tariq and Nathan caught the 8:18am train, forty minutes later than their original service. Tariq was just relieved that Nathan was on the train this time. It wasn't as busy as the earlier peak time trains, and there were plenty of empty seats. On the journey, Tariq made notes in preparation for the interview with the Bosnians at 11:00am.

They approached the black stone flight of eleven steps up to the SFO office reception. Tariq noticed a red Ford Focus parked down the street, close enough to see the outlines of two men in the front seats. He noticed things like that; maybe it was his military training, he considered.

Mark Cooper, the International Liaison manager, caught up with Tariq in the kitchen on the fourth floor. 'Morning, Tariq. You OK for the interview at eleven?'

'Yes, sure, I'll be there.'

'I just wanted to give you this. It's the protocol that we have to follow, yeah. You need to read out to them the legislation and on what grounds we're interviewing them. It's all on these sheets here. We've also given you a list of questions if you need them. I've got to do something now, and I'll see you there ten minutes before the interview. We can make the final preparations then, yeah?'

'Yes Mark, fine. See you then,' said Tariq, unfussed. Cooper always tried to make out that the international side of investigations was somehow more high-profile than UK-based ones. In Tariq's experience, a lot of time could be wasted on red herrings when pursuing international lines of inquiry. Unless the SFO had immediate grounds to make arrests, the culprits often fled to their homeland, where it was near impossible to extradite them from. On large-scale frauds such as the Magnus Conan-Whittaker case, senior foreign government officials could be either involved or bribed to block extradition requests. At this stage, though, the SFO didn't yet have compelling evidence that the two Bosnians were complicit in the fraud.

Tariq asked Nathan to complete the ledger progress report at his desk and then to go down to the property room to continue collating the case documents. Tariq took a coffee up to Room 10-08 on the tenth floor for the interview as arranged. The room was next to Pemberton's office, which was permanently at his disposal, whereas other staff had to reserve rooms using the intranet Matrix booking system. The interview room already had a sign on the door: *Do not enter – Interview in progress*; probably Cooper's doing. A pair of brown padded chairs was positioned on either side of the table. On the table were a few clear plastic cups, a bottle of water, a writing pad, and some pens. Some interviewees from countries with extreme regimes were suspicious of any liquids they were offered to drink as they feared they could contain a truth serum of some kind, or worse. Unopened branded mineral water bottles were therefore used.

Mark Cooper entered the room purposefully and said to Tariq, 'Take a seat, mate. We've got the room for two hours, so plenty of time to get them to relax, for them to open up and spill the beans. The brief is fairly tight…'

Tariq interjected, 'Tight? More like useless, you mean. Our only remit is to ask them what their connection is with Mitchko; that's it! Have you actually read it, or did you write it yourself?'

'No, I didn't! Pemberton gave it to me already signed. You can ask him about it.'

'Nonsense. Pemberton doesn't have time to write interview briefs!'

'Usually, no, but he's getting desperate for a breakthrough on this case. The future funding of the SFO is riding on it. If you really want to know, he told me that he doesn't want to give the game away that we're onto them, so we keep them sweet and see if they let anything slip. If we go in heavy-handed they're just going to clam up, so drop it, Tariq. Pemberton knows what he's doing.'

Tariq didn't argue further; there was no point.

Cooper explained, 'I'll play bad cop and you can sympathise with them that they've been brought in unnecessarily, and can go home as soon as it's over; just get 'em talking. Pemberton has donated some Venchi chocolates from Harrods, claimed on expenses no doubt. He reckons they're the best chocolates in the world, so that's good enough for me.' Cooper then pointed at the black golf ball-looking object in the middle of the table. 'That's the microphone – it's already wired up to the recorder. I warn you, it's super sensitive; it'll pick up anything you say under your breath. It's designed to look low-tech so suspects assume they won't be heard if they whisper between themselves. We can play the tape back afterwards.'

Cooper went over to the small black box on a side table with a bank of switches and pressed the nearest one. 'A quick test – say something into the microphone. Start off loud, then quiet. I can adjust the sensitivity.'

'OK. Testing, testing, testing.' Tariq lowered his voice to be barely audible. 'Testing, testing, testing.'

Cooper adjusted a dial on the recorder. 'That's it, got it, thanks; we're good to go.'

A few minutes after 11:00am there was a knock on the interview room door. A young, well-groomed policeman leaned his head around the door, 'You guys ready? Shall we bring 'em in?'

Cooper turned to Tariq for confirmation; Tariq gave him the nod. 'Yes, we're ready.'

There was a short delay, followed by the scuffling of feet along the corridor. Two policemen guided two men in ill-fitting business suits to the two chairs facing Tariq and Mark Cooper. Tariq's gut reaction on seeing the men was that they looked more akin to roughneck farmers than businessmen; not the type who would have the nouse to make serious investments, even dodgy ones. They both appeared to be relaxed, rather than the usual anxious expressions. The man sitting on the left, with light-brown hair combed back, stared blankly at Tariq. The second Bosnian on the right was an older man, also unshaven, with thinning grey hair. The older man altered his gaze from examining the grain on the wooden table to glancing up at the ceiling.

The second policeman, a middle-aged sergeant, spoke with authority to the Bosnians. 'I need to advise both of you that you do not have to say anything, but it may harm your defence if you do not mention when questioned something which you later rely on in court. Anything you do say may be given in evidence. Is that clear?'

Tariq concluded that the policeman hadn't been properly briefed as the men were not yet even under caution, so he translated a different message to the Bosnians – that they'd been invited to the SFO office as part of routine enquiries; and they were not under official caution. The younger Bosnian shrugged his shoulders; a sign of blissful ignorance, or a bluff perhaps. Cooper requested that the junior policeman sitting next to the side table turn on the recording device.

Tariq spoke in Bosnian, reading out the Section 2A interview warrant on the table to his right. 'Before we start, can you confirm that you are Kerim Hadzic of 234 Fulham Avenue, Hammersmith and Fulham SW6 7DL, and that your date of birth is 14th February 1964."

'Yes, that is correct,' said the man to his left, in Bosnian.

'And can you confirm that you are Theodore Sharisk of 322 Bessemer Road, Welwyn Garden City AL7 3DR, date of birth 25th June 1955.'

'Yes, that is me,' said the man to his right, in Bosnian.

Tariq continued in Bosnian, 'You're being interviewed by me, Tariq Markovic, and Mark Cooper of the Serious Fraud Office.'

Amongst the Bosnian gibberish, Cooper at least recognised his name spoken by Tariq, and said, 'Hello,' to the two men, and then asked the Bosnians, 'Do you know why you are here?'

Tariq interpreted, '*Znate li zasto ste ovdje*?'

'*Ne.*'

'I didn't think so.' Tariq looked at them both in turn in the eye, as is polite custom in Bosnian culture, and then said to them in Bosnian, 'You may be aware that Karlo Mitchko, the ex-Serbian finance minister, is wanted in connection to the alleged Magnus Conan-Whittaker fraud. We have to ask you, what is your relationship with this man?'

'What do you mean, relationship?'

'How do you know him? Have you been in contact with him?'

'You're talking nonsense. He is a corrupt Serb, the Serbian finance minister before war broke out, and we are just innocent Bosnians, so we have nothing to do with this man.'

138

The scope of the interview was deliberately set to avoid any reference to the email evidence, so he didn't push them any further on their dealings with Mitchko. The formal interview soon ended, before the allotted time. The recording device was turned off, and Cooper left the room for a comfort break, leaving Tariq on his own with the Bosnians and the junior policeman, who was distracted with sending text messages on his phone.

After a pause, the older, more talkative man said, 'Tariq. You have a Serbian name, I think.'

'No, I'm Bosnian; that's all I know.'

'What do you mean, "that's all I know"?'

'I was in the war. I suffered a head injury; I don't remember anything.'

'Oh, that's terrible; that can happen in war. My friend Rodavan, he had memory loss, but he's recovering now. I had to help him; it took months. I went back with him to places he'd been to help him remember. He was exposed to some kind of nerve gas, they say, supplied to the Serbs by the Americans. So Tariq, is that right – you can't remember anything of the war?'

Tariq didn't expect to be discussing the Bosnian War but was somehow grateful that he could talk to these men in his mother tongue about things he'd blocked out of his mind for so long now he'd almost forgotten about this missing era of his life. 'I don't remember much. It was a bad time. I still have nightmares.'

'You see, Tariq, you're with your fellow Bosnians here; this could be an opportunity for you to remember.' He reached into his jacket pocket and pulled out some small postcards.

'Tariq, do you mind? Let me help you remember.'

He laid out the postcards in front of Tariq as DI Randall had done with the photographs of him and Cheryl. The postcards had scenes of mountains, lakes, streets and towns. Tariq scanned them all quickly and was drawn to a white stone multi-arched bridge spanning a wide green river. The apex of the arches were pointed medieval Gothic in style. He picked up the postcard and stared at it as if looking through a window back in time.

Tariq then spoke up in a trance-like state. 'Visegrad, this is Visegrad, and this is the Drina River. As a child, I walked over this bridge, the Mehmed Paša Sokolović Bridge. I swam in this river with my brothers.' The Bosnian men exchanged glances. Tariq wanted to weep for his lost family, but this wasn't the place. He wiped his eyes and reigned himself in. 'Thank you. Do you mind if I keep this?'

'Yes, please keep it. I can get another one.' He paused before saying, 'I was just thinking that your dialect sounds like you're from Visegrad.' He paused again before asking Tariq in a serious tone, 'Did you get out in time in 1992? Before the massacres?'

Tariq looked back at him, still with moist eyes. 'No, I didn't; I think I saw bad things, which is why I am not remembering Visegrad. OK, now you understand?'

The Bosnian hesitated to give Tariq time to compose himself. 'I hope you don't mind me asking, but are you Muslim or Christian?'

'My daughter, Millie, is a Christian. I go to church with her sometimes.'

The younger man changed the subject, asking Tariq, 'So, have you been watching the trial in The Hague of General Mladic?'

'Yes, I've seen some of it on TV.'

'That murdering bastard should hang for his war crimes. I lost family and friends because of him. The problem is getting enough evidence to convict him. That's why the prosecution is so keen to find the mystery man with the two-headed eagle tattoo on the back of his neck. Some say that Mladic is protecting him as he's a key witness, but do you know what is so strange about this man?'

Tariq shook his head.

'It seems that no Serbian ever saw his face, so no one knows who he is or what he looks like.'

'So why's that? How is that?' Tariq asked.

'Exactly. That's what we're all trying to find out. They know one thing about him, from people who heard him speak.'

'What's that?'

The man looked straight at Tariq. 'He was from Visegrad, just like you; so you probably know him. Visegrad was a close-knit community back then, so you should know him. Try to think hard, Tariq…'

Tariq suddenly stood up from his chair, knocking it over behind him. The policeman looked up from his phone. Tariq concluded, 'Well, I've never heard of him. I have nothing more to say. We're finished now, yes?'

Mark Cooper returned to the interview room, and the Bosnian men were escorted out of the room by the young policeman.

CHAPTER 13

Following the interview with the Bosnians, Tariq returned to his desk emotionally drained, trying to make sense of previously buried memories that had broken through into his consciousness. Raw flashbacks of the noise and smells of death pounded him like waves, threatening to overwhelm him. After taking deep breaths to calm himself down he went to the canteen with Nathan, who surprised his father by choosing the cod in batter with chips, as he'd usually refused anything in batter at home. Nathan explained that the batter in the canteen was yellow instead of orange like it was at home, so he wanted to try it. He didn't like anything too orange, but marmalade was OK. Tariq also had the cod and chips, with peas. At lunch, Nathan explained that while Tariq had been in the interview, he'd been in the property room creating a pile of matching files and documents, and Stuart Harper had been with him cataloguing the important ones. Nathan also mentioned that Sandra had been looking for him, but she'd said that it wasn't about anything urgent.

Tariq informed Nathan that he needed to go to the bank after lunch to discuss his account, and Nathan should continue collating the files in the property room while he was out. Tariq was resigned to borrowing more money on the mortgage for Millie's treatment. If it worked, it would, of course, be worth it. On the other side of the coin was the brutal outcome that if the drugs didn't work, Millie would be dead, and they'd be thousands of pounds worse off.

So Nathan wouldn't freak out later, Tariq informed him in advance of the all-staff meeting at 3:30pm. He also reminded him that their tickets for the Olympics were for a week on Saturday. Nathan was excited about the Olympics but complained that Millie couldn't come.

Tariq walked down the office front steps and up the short uphill section of Elm Street to Grays Inn Road, towards Lloyds bank. On the other side of the road he saw a red Ford Focus car, but he couldn't be sure it was the same one he saw parked outside earlier. He slowed down and examined the car in the reflection in a shop window, but there was too much glare to discern if the same men were in it. He would look again on his return from the bank.

In the bank, he sat and waited for about ten minutes until an over-friendly young man with a spotty complexion wearing a dark suit introduced himself to Tariq as one of the loan assessors, and escorted him into a compact glass-fronted office. The young man in the dark suit went through a list of menial questions about Tariq's family and work status. After waiting for his computer to process the data inputs, he said, 'Mr Markovic, it looks like there's a small problem with your credit rating. It's just below the threshold for the cheapest deal, but there's still plenty of options.'

'That can't be right; I've always had a good credit score. Does it say why I have a lower rating?'

'No, sorry, that information is not available.'

'What the hell?! That is ridiculous; I don't understand it. What is my rating?'

'It's seven hundred and fifty-five, and the cheapest deal has an eight hundred threshold. The next interest rate is 6.5%, which is only one percent higher than the best deal at 5.5%. Are you still happy to proceed, sir?'

Tariq sighed and responded, 'I have no choice. Yes, I am.'

Tariq walked back to the office mulling over his reduced credit rating. Surely this was an error? As he turned onto the main road, the Calthorpe Arms pub on the corner of Wren Street came into view. He crossed the road and entered the pub. Inside, three elderly men sat around a table in the far corner. Tariq considered that it was too early for Burton or Pemberton to be sneaking in for a drink after work. The Calthorpe Arms had a friendly, cosy feel to it, just what he needed right now. Underfoot was a bold tartan carpet. There were green leather bench seats matching the dark-green Edwardian woodwork decor. Tariq was soon staring into his second glass tumbler of double whisky and Coke, the ice melting in the heat of the day. He reminisced how his life was two weeks ago, before Millie's diagnosis. What he'd give to get those days back now! His life had gone down a crooked path into the dark woods – a place where nothing good happens. He was just about to take a final swig of his drink, now mostly melted ice, when his phone buzzed with a text message. It was Cheryl. Judging by the tone of her message, she was not in a good mood and wanted to see him soon. He reflected that he hadn't been entirely honest with the police about his relationship with Cheryl. He slammed his glass down on the table. The old men looked over at him. His thoughts churned over in his head. Who the hell had taken the photos of him with Cheryl and handed them over to the police? Where had she been the last four days?

Tariq left the pub less sure-footed than he'd entered and forgot his commitment to check on the red Ford Focus. He took extra care ascending the office steps, holding on to the handrail, and went straight to his desk. He drunk a glass of water and sucked on a strong mint from his desk drawer; always handy.

Simon Beecham, one of the deputy disclosure officers, was with Nathan in the property room sorting through the case files. Beecham was usually relaxed about everything and was easy-going company. As Tariq entered the room, Nathan asked, 'Hello, Dad. Did you have a good discussion with the bank?'

'Yes Nathan, it was a blast,' Tariq smirked.

'Now I know you're joking.'

Beecham looked up at him, which was Tariq's cue to ask, 'How are you, Simon? How's your love life, hey?'

'I've got a second date tomorrow, as a matter of fact.'

'Now we're talking. Who is she?'

'Her name is Jane, but her friends call her Janey.'

'So you're calling her Janey, then? You're in there, mate.'

'Like I said, it's only the second date so I don't want to get carried away.'

'Why? Strong, is she?'

'Ha! Right, funny. Yeah, she's an ex-wrestler.'

'Maybe you need a bodyguard. You can hire me.'

'You can stay well away. I'm sure you'd love to charm

her, like you did…' Beecham stopped himself, to Tariq's relief.

A couple of hours later, while they were all still in the property room sorting through the files, Tariq said, 'Hey, look at the time; it's nearly half past three. We need to get up to the staff meeting, guys – it's on the sixth floor today.'

The three exited the room, pulled the door to, and ascended the stairs to the sixth floor, as the lifts were always busy before a staff meeting. Tariq, Nathan and Beecham sat at one of the open-plan desks in the communal area. Nathan moved his chair next to his father near the window. Tariq's friend Stephen, who he'd spoken to at Sir Peter's presentation, was on the adjacent table. Tariq asked him, 'Hey Stephen, any news on the Nadir case then? What's the verdict?'

'No, it rumbles on. Do you know what the QC told us yesterday? He said that since the first case against Nadir seventeen years ago, eighteen witnesses, no less, have died. Can you believe that? Damned inconsiderate of them, I'd say!'

Nigel Pemberton, the International Fraud Director, approached with an elegant stride and took his place to face the gathered staff, about a hundred in number. He briefly surveyed his audience and spoke in his distinctive eloquent Scottish tones. 'Thank you, ladies and gentlemen, for your attention at this special staff meeting.' Murmurings were curtailed and silence descended on the assembled staff.

He continued, 'As Sir Peter previously announced, we've been fighting our corner to maintain our budget following the formation of the National Crime Agency. We think we've done pretty well; as well as we could. However, at just under forty million, we've been allocated four million pounds less than we've been asking for. This represents a ten percent cut in our funding, which, to be frank with you, is disappointing. So we need to cut our cloth accordingly, as Sir Peter alluded to.'

Tariq whispered to Stephen, 'Here it comes.'

'We will therefore be consulting on an organisational restructuring over the next few weeks. We need to reduce staffing levels in a few areas, but you'll be pleased to know that these should, for the most part, be accommodated by natural wastage rather than forced redundancies.'

Pemberton's announcement was like a tsunami wave rising on Tariq's horizon; not here yet, but inescapable. He asked himself, would he drown before it arrived? He had six weeks of probation remaining, and his present case wasn't going well. Unless he had proof that Stuart Harper was behind the failings of the last case and the present one, there would be no life raft to rescue him from the flood waters. There was no point making unsubstantiated accusations against Harper as it would smack of desperation. He had to get proof!

Nathan was, not surprisingly, oblivious to the significance of Pemberton's announcement; probably for the best, Tariq surmised. He noticed that Nathan was strangely attentive to Pemberton's speech but then realised that his son's gaze was focused above Pemberton. He realised that his son was in fact tracking the changing green LED floor numbers on the lift panel behind... 4, 3, 2, 1, G, B. The only reason for anyone to visit the basement was for the post room or Property Room No.1. This particular lift was located just along the corridor from the property room. Tariq scanned the faces of the assembled staff for Stuart Harper, but he couldn't see him. Was that him in the lift? The case document ledger was updated last Friday and was due to be re-scanned later today, so now would be an ideal time to alter it before scanning. Tariq glanced back at Nathan in acknowledgement of his observation of the lift and Nathan also caught his father's eye. Pemberton had just concluded his speech and was taking questions on the timescales of the restructuring, so Tariq took the opportunity to say quietly to Nathan, 'Follow me.'

Tariq stepped sideways behind the adjacent partition; Nathan followed and asked, 'Dad, where are we going? If we're going home, I need to get my coat and sandwich box from the fridge.'

'No, we're not going home, the property room; this way.' Tariq kept low until he was behind a side partition at the back of the room. On the way to the lifts, Nathan announced that he needed the toilet. Tariq bit his tongue and went with him: Nathan having a meltdown was the last thing he needed right now. After Nathan had finished in the toilet, they took the lift to the basement and walked along the corridor to the property room. Tariq opened the door. Someone was in the far corner of the room in a small alcove that led to the storeroom at the back. Tariq called out, 'Hello, who's that?'

'Hi Tariq, it's only me.'

'Sandra, hi. Sorry, I wasn't sure who it was.'

'I'm glad you're here, Tariq,' said Sandra with a worried look. 'I was thinking about coming up to get you. I couldn't stop him – he took the original ledger hard copies away with him. He said the assurance protocol was that the old hard copies should be destroyed as they were Sensitive. He said that Burton had told him that we must be careful to follow all the processes as set out in the disclosure strategy document…'

'Sensitive, why Sensitive? First I've heard of that. Who was it Sandra? Who?'

'It was Harper, Stuart Harper.'

'I knew it, I bloody knew it! Where did he go?'

'I think he went along the corridor to the shredder.'

Tariq bolted out of the door. He could hear the distinctive noise of the shredder down the corridor, emanating from a small alcove next to the far lift. He could see the back of a man standing in the alcove feeding documents into the shredder. He was about to confront Harper when he realised it wasn't him: it was Bashford, Lawrence Bashford, the Case Controller. Bashford saw Tariq coming.

'You alright, Tariq? You look a bit stressed.'

'Yeah, well, just working hard on the case. Did Harper go this way?'

'Yes, about five minutes ago.'

'Was he carrying any papers?'

'Uh, sorry Tariq, I wasn't really looking; he was walking quite fast and then caught the lift. Is there a problem?'

'No, no problem; I just wanted to speak to him about something, that's all.'

Back in the property room, Tariq asked Sandra and Nathan, 'Notice anything untoward on the ledger? Any gaps?'

Nathan started looking at the box files on the middle shelf on the side wall to check for missing documents.

'Nothing I can see, Dad.' Tariq then handed Nathan the

completed-to-date list of files and asked him to check each box. There were hundreds of documents to check, so it took Nathan nearly an hour.

The conclusion of Nathan's review was that the documents were all on the shelves as listed in the ledger. Tariq declared, 'Nothing appears to be missing on the shelves.'

Sandra was sat at the desk in the centre of the room in front of the computer screen and reported, 'And I can't find anything on the... Oh, that's...'

'What?' Tariq asked impatiently, crouching behind her to view the screen.

'It's just that there's a list of written correspondence from A to K, and E and F are missing. Why would you list them out and then jump from D to G?

Tariq said, 'Yes, you're right. Do we know what it is?'

'That's the thing, there's no description; they're just missing. If there's a gap like that, there should at least be a note on the ledger, saying *not used*.'

Tariq said, 'Have a look, Nathan. Are they in the box file?'

Nathan went through the pages, 'No, nothing.'

'Pass the file down to me, would you, Nathan?'

Tariq then went through each document in turn. 'Shit. I went through these myself only a few days ago. The two letters missing are from the Bosnians to Karlo Mitchko, the Bosnians I've just interviewed. What the hell is going on here? I had copies of those letters in the interview, but I gave everything to Cooper. I'll check with him the next time I see him.'

CHAPTER 14

Monday after work, Tariq and Nathan visited Millie at the hospital. They took their usual route, walking to Farringdon station from the office. It was a hot summer's day, and beer gardens were busy with conversations, and glasses amassing on outdoor tables. Tariq could only look on in envy.

From Farringdon, Nathan relaxed in the spacious, less crowded Thameslink trains which went via London Blackfriars to Denmark Hill station; a short walk from King's College Hospital. He had no feelings of claustrophobia on that train.

It had been arranged for Nathan to stay the night and the following day at his mother's, so he'd brought an overnight bag, carefully packed down to his favourite mug and cereal bowl. Nathan had therefore booked the next day off from work, as had his mother. When meeting in the hospital reception, his mother gave him the usual fist-pump greeting, and took his overnight bag from him. Alice gave Tariq a grateful hug, especially for his help in raising the capital for Millie's expensive American drug therapy. She whispered to him discreetly, 'Thank you,' and said no more about it; then said, 'Tariq, you need a haircut. I keep telling you that long hair doesn't suit you, and it's beginning to look a mess.'

'I'm not sure I want to look like a soldier again.'

'I keep telling you, Tary, that I prefer you looking like a soldier. Short hair suits you; it shows off your strong neck. You can cut it shorter at the back and keep it longer at the front.'

'Alright, alright, it's a deal; when Millie comes home, I'll get it cut, OK?'

Nathan added, 'Yes, me too, but I'm not getting it cut like Dad's.'

Millie was in the same bed at the end of the corridor. Alice greeted her first and then Tariq, who said, 'Hello, little darling. How are you feeling, my sweet?'

'Dad, you seem worried.'

Tariq leaned forward. 'I just want to see you better, that's all.'

'Hey, I was praying for you this morning.'

'You were praying for me?'

'Of course, as always, and a Bible verse came to me for you.'

'For me? Really? What verse?'

'Exodus chapter twenty-three, verse twenty.'

Tariq looked at her blankly, 'Sorry Millie, what was that again?'

'Dad, pay attention, and listen to what it says.'

Alice said, 'Please Tariq, Millie is obviously tired, don't test her patience.' Alice changed the subject, 'We've ordered the new drug from America. The early trials have been promising…'

'Thank you, Mum. Thank you, Dad. I hope it wasn't too expensive?'

Alice replied, 'Of course not, it's the least we can do. How are you getting on in here? How's the food?'

'Not too bad; I had bangers and mash yesterday with peas, but I'm not really that hungry these days.'

Nathan piped up, 'Are you reading your book, *The Hunger Games*?' You should read it as I know you like to read the book before seeing the film, so after you've read it, and when you're home again, we can watch the film together.'

Tariq turned away from the bed, fearing that this day would never come, wiping a tear from his eye.

'Thank you, Nathan,' responded Millie.

After leaving the ward, Nathan said a quick goodbye to his father, excited to be reunited with his mother. Tariq caught a 185 bus to Catford and then the mainline train to Eden Park station, enjoying the solitude after being with Nathan for the last fortnight. He wished, he dared to hope, that Millie's prayers would see him through. Something good had to happen soon, didn't it? Who would pray for him if she didn't make it? It was too much to think about.

After disembarking at Eden Park, he crossed the road to the Beluga fish and chip shop for a large cod and chips with mushy peas, and bought a half bottle of Jack Daniels and Diet Coke from the local Costcutter shop.

Back at home, he enjoyed his takeaway supper in front of the TV without interruption, slumped in his armchair with the half-empty bottle of whisky. Just before he could extricate himself from the chair, Ratko Mladic's trial was on the news again. There had been a delay to the start of the trial while the judge considered new submissions from senior lawyers from both sides. There was no mention of the missing man with the tattoo. *He's probably dead,* Tariq surmised.

***

The next morning, Tariq caught the earlier 7.07am train from Eden Park. He planned to get to the office early as he was taking the afternoon off to meet someone. Also, he'd a one-to-one meeting with Lawrence Bashford at 9.00am and wanted to make a start sifting through the piles of matching files that Nathan had previously sorted. He picked up a cappuccino and croissant from the office canteen on the ground floor and started perusing the files in the property room. He'd just finished cataloguing the first pile when Bashford entered the room.

'Tariq. Morning, comrade. I would have been here earlier, but Burton collared me, as he does. I've never known a head of department to get so obsessed with a case. He wanted to know if we were on track and kept repeating that I should speak to him directly if there were any problems with the case. He said the same to Stuart Harper the other day. He sees himself as a trouble-shooter. Personally, I think he's scared shitless that we're going to lose the Nadir case, and he can't stomach losing this one as well. Hell, if we lose, it's years of work and millions wasted. Rumour has it that Burton will be out the door if we lose the Nadir case. Sir Peter will be seething if we're seen to be throwing money down the pan just when our budget's been cut. As you know only too well, it would be his second big failure after what happened on the Frederick Rainsford Commodities case. Sorry, Tariq, for bringing that up; I know it's a sore point for you. Oh, and Burton was asking how the interview went with the Bosnians?'

'Yes, fine. We covered all the points on the terms of

reference for the interview; not set by me, by the way. Apparently, Pemberton set the interview brief as loose as possible to keep them relaxed, to catch them off-guard. He's planning to bust them in the next few days. When I see them next time, I look forward to seeing their reaction when I show them the email correspondence with Mitchko.'

Bashford was aware that Tariq's daughter was gravely ill and informed him that he would be allowed to take compassionate leave if he wanted, especially if Millie's condition deteriorated. He was supportive of having Nathan in the office, since he was making himself useful on the case. He also mentioned that Burton had granted Stuart Harper delegated power to sign off the weekly ledger as a substitute to Tariq, if he was out of the office.

Tariq latched onto this last point. 'What? That makes no sense! Harper is a deputy disclosure officer. Deputy disclosure officers shouldn't be signing off on behalf of senior officers.'

'Tariq, please, it's just in case you need to take time out of the office. He doesn't want any unnecessary delays.'

'Well, don't say I didn't warn you. You need to keep an eye on him. I tell you, I will be.'

At midday, Tariq walked to Farringdon station, as he'd done the day before with Nathan on the way to visit Millie, but this time catching a Circle Line train to King's Cross, where he crossed over to the Victoria Line. He looked behind him occasionally to check he wasn't being followed. He continued on to Finsbury Park station and walked through the park to Finsbury Park café. Tariq instinctively evaluated the park too open for someone to tail him without being seen, as the footpath tracks were straight, bordered by open grassed areas.

Cheryl was seated under the café canopy, overlooking a sloped green and a lake just beyond, shimmering in the midday sun. Tariq instantly recognised her smooth curved body and the perfect profile of her nose and cheekbones. She sipped her coffee and took a bite of her raspberry muffin, and turned to greet Tariq as he approached with a cream tea on a tray. He put the tray down on the table and kissed her on the cheek; she reciprocated. Her baby bump was clear to see.

Tariq said, 'Sorry I couldn't come sooner, it's just that…'

She interrupted, her natural strawberry-blonde hair catching the breeze. 'No need to explain, honey, I understand. What can I expect? How's Millie? Has she started the new treatment yet?'

'Tomorrow; it starts tomorrow.'

'I really hope it works, Tariq, for your and your family's sake. I can't imagine how I would cope with that.'

Tariq focused on her intense brown eyes. 'Yeah, thanks, it's costing enough; I hope so. It's a pioneering new drug, so it hasn't completed all the trials yet, but the reports from the States are promising.' Tariq stirred his tea, staring briefly at her radiant Eastern European face with rosy lips. He added, 'We'll know if the drug works in a few weeks' time.'

'How're Alice and Nathan?'

'Alice is anxious about Millie, as you might expect. She's staying at her mother's. Nathan has had his moments; he refused to get on the train on his first day to the office, but he's now making himself useful at work. He's picked up things that no one else would have noticed. He's surprised me. He's been a whizz, to use his own word.'

'Good to hear that Nathan is getting on OK. He needs to find his own way in the world.'

Tariq asked, 'How are you coping with the pregnancy and everything? How did the scans go last week?'

'Good, yeah, looks like a healthy baby; that's the main thing, isn't it? I felt a bit sick a few days after that, but I'm over the worst now. And before you ask – prawn cocktail crisps; that was my craving yesterday. Today I think it's raspberry muffins.' She smiled and took another bite.

'Ha! Well, mine's scones with cream and strawberry jam.'

After she'd finished her muffin, Tariq asked her, 'What happened to you? No one knew where you were for days. Your own mother and even your sister didn't know where you were. The police were looking for you.'

She looked down at the ground as she took a fresh tissue from her handbag and wiped the tears from her eyes.

Tariq reacted, 'Oh, sorry, sweetie, it's alright. I just want to know what happened. I was worried about you. We all were.'

Her voice was breaking with emotion. 'There were three of them. I went down to collect the package from the back room in the lower basement; someone drove up in a dark-coloured van, so I walked across the car park towards it. The next thing I knew, I was waking up in a hotel bed, Park Plaza Hotel across from St Thomas' Hospital.'

Tariq asked as plainly as he could without upsetting her further, 'Who were these men? What did they look like?'

'The man with the gun...'

'A gun! God, why didn't you tell me about this before?'

'Please, Tariq, I'm telling you now. The man with the gun had a thin beard… he threatened to kill me. They made me sign a non-disclosure agreement not to leak anything to do with the case, and they told me to stay in the hotel for two hours, and I wasn't to contact anyone until Monday. They'd be tracking my calls and watching me, so…' She was too upset to continue. Tariq went up to her and put his arm round her shoulder. She took a couple of deep breaths and continued. 'I told them everything, Tariq. I'm sorry, I'm so sorry…'

Tariq sat back in his seat, suddenly feeling vulnerable, and said, 'It's alright, Cheryl. What did you tell them?'

'That you're the father of the child… and you're working on the Magnus Conan-Whittaker case.' She paused again. 'Someone is tampering with the files, Tariq; documents have gone missing. Stuart Harper has been sniffing around. I don't know what he's up to.'

'It's OK, darling, there's no rush. Have a drink. Take your time, yeah. I'm here to help. Let's talk it through nice and slowly,' he said, and took a sip of tea from his porcelain cup. 'So how do you know documents have gone missing?'

'I just happened to pick up a diary referencing Karlo Mitchko. It was bright red. It looked important, but when I checked the ledger at the end of the week, there was no sign of it, as if it had never existed. The following week, it turned up again: Harper had found it.' Cheryl said in a more serious tone, 'Tariq, there's something else I need to tell you… they have photographs. Sorry, Tariq, I don't know how they got them…' She wiped away her tears.

'What photographs?' He didn't want to mention his

visit to the police station, as it would just exacerbate her fragile mental state.

'They're of us in the hotel room after the Christmas party. We're both naked on the bed.'

Tariq slumped back in his chair contemplating that these photos were even more incriminating than the ones the police had shown him at the station.

'There's more. They warned me not to mention the ledger to anyone; I'm to stay away from it. They would know if I'd made any corrections. Also, they said to warn you that if you interfere, they'll send the photographs to your wife...' said Cheryl, now sobbing into her handkerchief.

She got up from the table and walked down the bank towards the lake. Tariq followed her and embraced her. She rested her head on his shoulder. It seemed apparent that it was the same men who'd kidnapped Cheryl who had sent the first batch of photos to the police as a warning shot to keep him in line. He'd now put himself in a worse position with the police by denying that he'd had a relationship with her. He'd also denied point blank that he was being blackmailed. Well, he wasn't at the time, was he?

Cheryl composed herself. 'They said that if the Magnus Conan-Whittaker case goes in the SFO's favour they'll release the photographs.'

'Bastards! This is all my fault, Cheryl. I should have never...' He checked himself. Tariq then walked back up the bank to the restaurant to buy her another coffee and raspberry muffin, and he bought himself an IPA beer. He returned and placed the tray of drinks and muffin down on the grass between them.

'The thing is, Tariq, the baby is due in less than a month

and I'll have no income. I'm agency, not permanent staff. I'll end up homeless! What am I supposed to do?'

'Oh God, Cheryl. I didn't realise.'

As Tariq was saying goodbye to her, Cheryl gripped his forearm. 'Tariq, please be careful – they're probably watching you; they said they'd be watching me. You have to understand what these people are capable of – they're professionals, they're not playing games. Carry on as normal, and if anything goes wrong, blame it on Harper.'

After meeting Cheryl, he travelled on the tube to Victoria train station and then on a main line train to Herne Hill station to pick up Nathan from his grandmother's house. He stopped off for a couple of whiskys at The Half Moon pub across the junction from the station. At the pub Tariq's thoughts turned to Harper. He had to be the inside man, which would explain why documents had been hidden from him on his previous case. Since Harper had been working on the case from the start, he could have removed most of the credible evidence by now. Perhaps it would work out? He should let Harper continue to sabotage the case, and then nail him at the end. The SFO would lose the case, the photos of him with Cheryl wouldn't be released, and Harper would be sacked, not him.

As he was about to leave the pub, he thumbed through the *London Metro* newspaper until he came across an article on the Ratko Mladic trial. Halfway down the page was a grainy photograph of the Mehmed Paša Sokolović Bridge in Visegrad. Tariq leaned in on the picture, almost spilling his drink. The caption was 'Visegrad Bridge murders 1992'. Tariq wiped his brow across his red scar, and a drop of sweat landed on the page. He finished his drink, peered into the empty glass and whispered to himself in despair, 'Oh Millie, I need your prayers right now. Please pray for me. Please live, Millie. Oh God, let her live. If you're there, have mercy on me. I've reached the end of my rope.'

CHAPTER 15

From the pub Tariq walked up Herne Hill to his mother-in-law's house, across from Ruskin Park, to collect Nathan. His mother had taken him shopping for new clothes, which was best done on a less crowded weekday. Clothes shopping with his father usually didn't end well. The last time, Nathan had locked himself in one of the changing cubicles, refusing to come out. The highlight of Nathan's day with his mother had been a boat trip on the Thames from Westminster Bridge to Greenwich, a taste of freedom; the river glimmering and vast, out in the tranquil bay. Alice had then taken him to the Greenwich Planetarium. The blackness inside, with the stars joined in their constellations, was a calming balm for Nathan's overactive mind.

Back on Planet Earth, on the return train journey home, the challenge for Tariq was to listen patiently to Nathan's detailed recount of his boat trip and cosmic experience. A welcome distraction or exhausting concentration, Tariq wavered between the two states of mind. Nathan's mother had sent him home with his favourite food supplies, including his recent taste for cod in batter for tomorrow's evening meal. A small punnet of blueberries was also a new addition, probably because the berries looked nearly black, like liquorice, which he liked.

Thursday morning, Nathan read the *Metro* on the train journey into the office. Tariq assumed that he'd discovered the cartoon strips and puzzle pages. Tariq again mulled over what Cheryl had said to him in the park. How was he going to handle Harper? Could he help to throw the case and blame it on Harper? He would need irrefutable evidence against him. He had to involve Sandra – she would be his alibi; the only way to save his job. Was it too late to involve the police now?

Tariq and Nathan climbed the black stone steps up to the SFO office. 'Morning, Beryl,' said Tariq.

'Morning, Tariq, and morning, Nathan. How are you, Nathan? How's it going with your dad?'

'Hello Beryl. Yes, fine thank you. I was with my mum yesterday anyway, and I'm helping Dad today to sort out all the files in order.'

'Excellent, well done, Nathan. I tell you what; I bet you're being more useful than your dad ever was at your age,' quipped Beryl.

'Ha! Thanks, Beryl. Come on, Nathan, don't listen to her; let's go,' said Tariq, guiding him through the glass security gates.

Tariq and Nathan dropped their bags at their desks on the fourth floor and visited the kitchen for their usual hot beverages. Mark Cooper caught sight of Tariq and made a beeline for him.

'Tariq, good morning, good to see you. I need you to do something for me – Pemberton's idea; who am I to argue? He wants some documents collected.'

Tariq looked bemused. 'What documents? For the Conan-Whittaker case?'

'I don't know; Pemberton just said that a box of documents needs collecting from St Albans.'

'St Albans? You're kidding. That'll take all day! How am I supposed to get there?'

'Calm down, alright. He said that you can take the office car. It's in the basement; here are the keys.'

Tariq hesitated before taking the keys off him. *This is crazy!* Tariq fumed inwardly. He'd taken half a day's leave yesterday, and this fool's errand meant he wouldn't get much done today either, but as Cooper said, who'd argue with Pemberton?

Tariq explained the situation to Nathan. Nathan was unperturbed and informed his father that Ajay in the security room wanted him to help check some new drawings he'd just received because, as before, they were giving him a headache.

The office 'car' was in fact a black transit van with tinted windows. Tariq opened the back doors of the van to check inside. There were some flat-packed cardboard boxes and a few other stationery items. He entered the postcode into the TomTom satnav for the St Albans address. The estimated journey time was just over an hour; not as bad as he thought. He could be back for lunch. It occurred to Tariq that if anyone was planning on following him, he should make it easy for them by lowering the van windows, as bait to take them on a wild goose chase up and down the M1, to St Albans and back.

Back at the office, Nathan was informed by Ajay's security team that he'd have to wait until 10:30am to see him in his office, so he returned to the property room to find Simon Beecham and Stuart Harper both reviewing the files. Stuart Harper was inputting the catalogue coding on the PC for each reviewed document as they went. Nathan went through another box from the shelf and put the documents and files therein with the matching piles on the central desk. At 10:30am, he explained to Harper and Beecham that he was going to see Ajay in the security room on the ground floor.

Nathan knocked on Ajay's door.

'Come in. Oh, morning, Nathan. Good to see that you're still keen; take a seat. I need to process this building pass.' Nathan looked on as Ajay completed the data template on his PC, then took a small plastic card from the grey box of blank building passes with a green top bar – an all-areas access pass. He fed the card into the mini printer on the desk next to him, which churned away with a high-pitched grinding noise, the pass emerging out of the printer. Ajay said, 'Right, that's it. If you don't mind, young fella, I'm going to the kitchen for a coffee, so wait here for a couple of minutes and keep an eye on things.

Nathan was leaning over the mini printer when Ajay, coffee in hand, returned, stopping outside the door to speak to one of the other guards. Nathan sat back down as Ajay opened the door.

'Thanks for waiting, Nathan. I just needed my early dose of caffeine after a long morning sorting out everybody's problems.' He put his coffee on his desk and slid open his top drawer to put away some keys. 'OK, Nathan, follow me. More drawings to look at.'

Nathan then felt a brain overload coming; maybe it was the screeching sound of the mini printer that had had a delayed reaction in setting him off. Charlotte at the Child

Psychology Centre called it the 'rumble stage'. She said it was like a tsunami pressure wave coming – the only course of action was to find a safe place to hold up in until it had passed. He went to the back room, sat on the single chair by the wall and told Ajay that he had a headache and needed to rest for a minute.

'Sure, Nathan, I understand, mate. Take your time; tell me when you're ready.'

Halfway up the M1 with the hot sun beating down, Tariq closed the tinted windows. There was no sign of anyone tailing him. He took the slip road off to the Welcome Break service station, where he used the toilet facilities and ordered a black coffee and an egg McMuffin from McDonald's.

The satnav guided him to an industrial estate on the north side of St Albans. He had to stop briefly to read the address as the whole estate was under the same postcode. He approached a grey corrugated metal clad warehouse in the far corner of a large tarmacked courtyard adjacent to a wholesale paint supplier and other trade outlets. The grey warehouse had no signage to indicate what it was, or who owned it. Tariq surmised that it was SFO policy not to advertise their presence on the site. On the left side of the warehouse was a dark-grey heavy steel roller shutter door, and on the right, two small windows of an office room. Peering through one of the windows, it appeared that no one was in the office, so he pushed the buzzer on the wall as the sign instructed. A minute later, footsteps approached and the shutter suddenly clattered into life, moving up steadily, revealing countless rows of high metal racks extending to the back of the building filled with boxes of documents, each labelled with their relevant legal case.

'Hello mate,' said the white-haired tubby man in jeans and a black shirt standing in the opening. 'Are you Tariq?'

'Yeah, I've come from Elm Street to collect a box.' Tariq couldn't help himself staring up and into the distance at the array of floor-to-ceiling shelves filled with boxes and files as far as the eye could see. Judging by the condition of some of the boxes, they were decades old.

Tariq turned to address the man. 'Are all these ours then, like, SFOs? All these documents?'

'Oh yes, and this isn't all of them. This place is full up, so they've hired another self-storage warehouse in The Docklands, London. I know that as my mate lives down there, and he reckons it used to be a cannabis farm! Anyway, this is your box.' Tariq looked at the box he'd put on a low bench table. It had large printed red text stating *Unused Material – BAE Systems 2010,* together with a reference number. He said to the man in the black shirt, 'This case was dropped. Are you sure this is the right box?'

'That's the only one Pemberton told me to give you; that's all I know. While you're here – what's going on with you lot? I've never had so many documents sent to me on a case.'

'Would that be the Magnus Conan-Whittaker case?'

'Ugh, think so. They're just labelled *MCW,* so yes, it must be that one. Strange thing is, and don't tell anyone I told you, I've been given strict instructions that they all be stored in the Attorney General's private storeroom. I've never known anything like it.'

'Who's sending them, by the way?'

'S. Harper, that's what it says on the transfer sheets.'

Tariq loaded the box into the van. The man pressed a button and the shutter came clanking down again.

As Tariq was about to drive off, he leaned down to pick up the empty McDonald's breakfast muffin box from the footwell. As he did so, he felt a small plastic item on the floor. He instinctively latched onto it and picked it up. It was a purple lipstick cover. He recognised the design as the same as the one Nathan had found in the back room belonging to Cheryl. 'My God!' he whispered to himself. This was the same van that Cheryl had seen approaching in the basement. It hit Tariq that the lipstick lid would now have his fingerprints on it, not to mention all over the steering wheel and the door handles; the crime scene was now well and truly contaminated, and him incriminated. A thought occurred to him - was this the reason he'd been sent on this futile errand to St Albans? Was it Pemberton's idea or had he been acting on someone else's behalf?

Driving back to London on the M1, Tariq considered what the man at the warehouse had said about the documents. Why is Harper sending large amounts of documentation to St Albans to be stored in the Attorney General's private storeroom? Did the Attorney General even know that his storeroom was being used? Harper could have forged a letter to the warehouse; a perfect arrangement perhaps to get rid of the critical documentation. Also, was there any way of finding out who'd booked out the van the day Cheryl had been abducted? Pemberton was sure to have a record of all the bookings? He couldn't ask him directly, and there was no point asking SFO security since the vehicle was on the approved list, so they wouldn't care who's driving.

After twenty minutes of gentle rocking, Nathan's throbbing headache subsided.

Ajay re-entered the room. 'How are you doing, young man? Recovered? My sister used to get migraines that used to last for hours, so you're doing better than her.'

'I'm alright now, thanks. I'm just going to get some hot chocolate from the kitchen and I'll be back,' said Nathan in a subdued tone.

'Yeah, sure. When you get back I'll show you the new drawing I want you to look at. It's driving me up the wall.'

On his return, Ajay explained his frustration at not being able to tell the difference between the previous revision and the *Revision C* copy he'd received this morning. The drawing revision text box simply stated *wiring amended*. Nathan stared at both drawings on the raised table. He peeled off a yellow Post-it note with some writing on it stuck on the drawing.

'Ah, let me take that, Nathan, I shouldn't have left it there,' said Ajay.

A few minutes later Nathan had highlighted in yellow where two wires had been amended to a new connection terminal on Revision C.

'How the blazes am I supposed to find that? Nathan, you've done it again, mate. That's two pints I owe you!'

'Two pints of what?'

'Beer? Anything you want, Nathan.'

'I like Coca-Cola. Thanks.'

Ajay entered the control room holding up the highlighted drawing to his security staff as he'd done before. 'Hey, look boys, young Nathan here has cracked it again! Stevey, grab hold of this drawing for me, would you, while I switch some wires around.' About thirty incoming coloured cables came up from the cable tray behind the desk into a long black metal box with an array of red and green LED indicator lights. Ajay leant around the back of the box, peering up at the drawing. He said to himself for all to hear, 'So if I swap these cables over like this, then this box of tricks might actually work?' He manoeuvred a laptop connected to the black box closer towards him, and typed in the passcode with one finger, one digit at a time, as Nathan noticed older grown-ups do. 'Yes, it works!' exclaimed Ajay.

'Calm down, calm down,' said Stevey in an exaggerated Scouse accent.

'Have a look at this, Nathan,' said Ajay, pointing at the laptop screen. He explained, 'These here are all the cameras. If you click on this here you can access any camera and take control of it with these arrows here. Look, camera B7 is on screen now, and it moves like this... This is all Burton's idea by the way. He wants to be able to access the cameras remotely, from any office, or his laptop. He says that's what all the modern security systems are upgrading to now; apparently it's standard in the US. It means that he can log in to check on things when he's out of the office, and out of hours if he needs to. I don't get it myself. We have staff here twenty-four-seven, so I don't understand why he feels the need to stick his nose in, if you ask me. At least he should be happy now. Thanks again, matey – I was beginning to think that we'd never get it to work.'

Nathan said, 'I'm glad I could help, Ajay. I need to go to lunch now.'

CHAPTER 16

On his return from St Alban's, Tariq drove down the final stretch of Grays Inn Road towards the SFO office, passing the Calthorpe Arms. He would have stopped for a drink, but the double red lines meant he couldn't even stop for a quick double whisky without a traffic camera picking him up, resulting in a parking ticket. He soon approached the SFO yellow metal vehicle gate, which opened in front of him on its rollers in relentless industrial fashion. He drove to the rear of the office building, passed the parked cars, and to the top of the lower basement carpark ramp. Since his pass wasn't all-areas he had to show the security guard the written authorisation from Pemberton, who checked with control on his two-way radio. The basement roller shutters coiled upwards and Tariq drove down the ramp and parked up in one of the marked bays. Exiting the vehicle, he noticed a 2012-registration red Mercedes S-Class parked in one of the end bays; probably Pemberton's, as he was in the office today. It reminded Tariq that he needed to deliver the box of documents to him he'd collected from St Albans, so he took the lift up to the tenth floor. In the lift he looked down at the box and got that feeling again that he'd been sent on a fool's errand.

The lush, mottled blue and turquoise carpet on the tenth

floor was a thicker pile than the lower floors, reflecting the higher status of persons occupying the floor. Approaching Pemberton's generous-sized office, he knocked on his door, but there was no response. He peered through the patterned office glass wall. The room appeared unoccupied. He put the box down and opened the heavy glass door. Inside, his office was eerily quiet apart from the distant noise of machinery and labourers occasionally shouting to each other in the adjacent construction site. He placed the box on the crafted African mahogany desk with brown leather inlay. *They don't make them like that anymore,* he thought. He put the van keys on the desk next to the box, but then decided he should put them out of sight in one of Pemberton's desk drawers. The top drawer was locked. In the second drawer was a large black hardback 2012 diary with a handwritten title, *Pool Car,* on a plain white label. Tariq looked up to check the coast was clear, then lifted the diary onto the desk. He thumbed through the pages hurriedly to 13th July, the day of Cheryl's abduction. Tariq looked up again. Pemberton stood in the doorway looking straight at him! The thick hall carpet had masked his approach. 'Tariq, what the hell are you doing, man?' barked Pemberton with his unique Scottish intonation.

'Hello, Nigel. Yes, sir, sorry – I've just brought you the box from St Albans, and I wanted to put the keys away… and I found the booking diary, so I thought I would record what time I got back to the office.' Tariq shut the book as he glanced down at the diary entry for 13th July – *A.T-G.*

'Ah, right. Just leave it there, Tariq, I'll sort that out, and leave the keys on the desk. How was the journey – traffic not too bad?'

'Fine, no problems. I'll leave the box on the desk, shall I?'

'Yes, that's plum good. Thanks again, Tariq. Good job.'

As Tariq approached his own desk he observed Nathan editing a spreadsheet on his PC at the desk behind. 'Hello, Nathan. Keeping busy, I see. Good man. Lunchtime, yeah?'

'Yes, Dad. I'll get my sandwich from the fridge.'

Tariq followed his son to the fridge, and they caught the lift down to the canteen. Chicken fajita wraps were Tariq's choice for lunch. They sat opposite each other on one of the long, heavy, mock-pine dining tables. Before Tariq could ask him, Nathan volunteered a detailed account of his morning activities. Nathan explained, 'I was in Ajay's office helping him with a new drawing so he could get Burton's remote camera application working...' Nathan checked himself; he was going to mention something else but decided not to.

Tariq was curious. 'Burton's what? What is he doing with the cameras?'

'Oh, he is installing a web-based CCTV system so he can view all the camera feeds from another office or a laptop, from anywhere, you see.'

'Oh, really?' Tariq didn't want to debate with his son why Burton would be involved in installing a remote office monitoring system.

Nathan changed tack. 'Then I helped Stuart Harper in the property room with the documents. He said he was updating the table and took some documents away to copy.'

Tariq remembered the warning passed on by Cheryl for him not to interfere with the ledger, and could feel his anger rising. He asked Nathan plainly, 'Why was Harper copying documents?'

'I don't know, Dad. Why are you asking me? He didn't say. I assumed that is what you're supposed to do.'

'Yes, sorry, Nathan. I didn't mean to have a go at you.'

Tariq took another bite out of his wrap, flavoured with hot paprika. The taste reminded him of his youth. The smiling face of a woman serving him some food appeared in his mind. His mother?

Nathan broke in on his father's temporal vision. 'I nearly got a bad headache again when I walked past the noise box. That man in the first meeting was using it, wearing his purple tie – it was Stuart Harper. I jumped in the lift to escape it as quickly as possible.'

Tariq mused that Harper was probably playing music on his CD player, as he sometimes did to relieve the boredom of reviewing hundreds of documents every week. It was SFO policy to allow staff their own methods to keep their spirits up during tedious, drawn-out cases, as long as it didn't disturb anyone else.

Tariq asked, 'How's your sandwich? Why don't you have some of my fajitas? Try something different.'

'No thank you, Dad; I don't want to eat something that I can't see, inside a wrap.'

Tariq smiled, 'Alright, please yourself. Mum said that I should get you to try some new foods as it's good for you. Only little kids have the same sandwich every day, you know.'

Nathan looked sheepish. 'Yes, alright then. I'll try something different tomorrow, then.'

'Good. I'll hold you to that, you know.'

Nathan nodded nervously.

Tariq took a coffee, and Nathan a hot chocolate, down to Property Room No.1. No one else was in the room, which was unusual. Tariq reviewed his calendar to see if there was a team meeting he'd forgotten about, but there wasn't anything.

Nathan continued sorting the files according to their respective subject types: finance years, invoice ledgers, accountant instructions, etc. Only a couple more days' work, Tariq reckoned. The next stage would be to sort each pile in date order. An hour in, Tariq messaged Sandra to come down to see him if she had time. She arrived about ten minutes later, carefully shutting the door behind her. Tariq noticed that her hair was a touch dishevelled, not her usual smart, well-formed bob, and her expression was deadpan. She walked across to him, and before she spoke, Tariq lifted to her eyes a Post-it note on which he'd written *Room could be bugged – Burton has new surveillance*. She gave Tariq a surprised look and nodded. She motioned to Tariq to wait as she took her phone out of her bag and selected one of her Spotify playlists at full volume.

Nathan looked over with concern. 'Sorry, too loud, too loud; turn it off or I'm going... I'm going then.' He exited the room.

Nathan's impromptu departure was an unexpected bonus as they could now talk freely under the music of Lady Gaga's *Poker Face* echoing around the room. Tariq said to Sandra, 'I've spoken to Cheryl. She's been warned to back off as she was onto them.'

'Onto who? Who's threatened her?'

'I don't know, OK! I'm now more sure than ever that

Harper is in on it. I found out yesterday that he's been sending hundreds of documents to the storage facility in St Albans, using the Attorney General's private storeroom as cover. Sandra, you've got to help me – you're the only person I can trust. I'm at my wits' end!' I need your help to get Harper.'

Sandra replied, 'Harper was updating the ledger this morning. What are you expecting from me, exactly?'

Tariq grabbed her gently by the arm to draw her closer in. 'Listen to me – all you have to do is secretly copy the ledgers before Harper changes them on Fridays. You don't have to do anything with them, just file them. I will copy any incriminating documents before he can get rid of them. It's the only way we can build up enough evidence against him. Please, Sandra, I can't trust anyone else. Burton might be in on it as well. I don't know what he's up to, upgrading the surveillance system, and I can't get Beecham involved – it's too risky. He could be working with Harper...' Tariq stopped talking, pointing to a silhouette of a man approaching through the frosted door window. Tariq stepped away from Sandra and signalled to her to turn the music off. Perhaps he was just curious of the sound of Lady Gaga blaring out from the room. Tariq was now in the far corner of the room, and found himself peering through the storeroom window. Inside were shelves of cleaning equipment, mops and disinfectant. The man outside had gone, which was Sandra's cue to leave. She didn't look back.

After his tête-à-tête with Sandra, Tariq felt claustrophobic in the property room, so he walked along the corridor to the water dispenser to get a drink. On his return, Nathan was on the PC on the central desk. 'Hi

Nathan, you're back. I hope you haven't got a headache again?'

'No, I'm fine, thank you, Dad – because I left the room in time. Next time, can you warn me if you're going to play music? I don't like loud music, only if its classical; I've told you that.'

'Sorry about that, Nathan. I just needed something to raise my spirits, to keep me going on the document review. It can get boring at times. Anyway, what are you doing then?'

'I'm going through all the electronic files. I don't even know if we have hard copies of these files, so they all need to be checked. If you look at the file properties, you can see what file type they are and when they were created. Look at this one – it's a PDF, created 4th April 2010. Dad, I can already see that some files have been deleted, as I've matched the archived versions.'

Tariq hid his alarm that someone could also be deleting the electronic files, as he hadn't considered this before. Tariq said in a clear, assertive tone, 'OK, Nathan, they're probably just junk.'

'Well, look at this one, it looks quite important…'

Tariq interjected, 'Thank you, Nathan, I will look at them later.' He didn't want to send his son into a tailspin straight after he'd recovered from the loud music. Nathan went back to sorting the files.

Tariq started reading through a pile of financial reports that Nathan had collated. Most of them were irrelevant, but there was one reference to a payment made to lease out an oil tanker from Abu Dhabi, United Arab Emirates, which was worth keeping as a supporting document.

It was nearly 4:30pm. Tariq asked Nathan, 'Where's Harper got to? If you see him, tell him I need him down here now! Otherwise, we don't have any hope of catching up with the filing. Where is he, for God's sake?'

'Don't shout. It's not my fault! I don't know where he is. Maybe it's taking him longer to copy the documents than he thought. Two of them were quite big.'

It was often required to provide multiple copies of critical documents if different specialist law firms needed to review them, but as the senior disclosure officer, Tariq would usually be aware of such requests passed down from Bashford, who in turn would have received the request from the prosecutor, who ultimately decided which documents were presented in court as evidence. Tariq wasn't aware of any such requests, unless Bashford had gone straight to Harper for the extra copies. In any case, this should be recorded on the prosecutor's feedback list, which highlighted the most valuable documents, with supplementary notes requesting further supporting documentation if available. Documents not considered beneficial to the case were also mentioned, to avoid wasted effort by the SFO team in sending through similar items. It occurred to Tariq that he couldn't risk asking Bashford for the feedback list, as he might be working with Harper on the scam.

Nathan wanted to escape the property room for fear of another meltdown, so offered to look for Harper, starting on the fifth floor by the photocopier. Tariq later went up to the fourth-floor kitchen for a cup of tea. While still in the kitchen, he got a call on his mobile from Nathan, who sounded flustered.

'Dad, I've just seen Harper. I went all over, looking for him at the photocopying machines, but couldn't find him anywhere, so I went back to the property room. I'd just opened the door when I saw him come out of the cleaner's cupboard with a small red book under his arm. I saw it!'

'OK, Nathan. Where are you now?'

'I'm trying to speak quietly because I'm following him. Why is he taking that book? He shouldn't be taking anything out of the office, should he? Because that's office property, isn't it? That's why it's called the property room, isn't it? By the way, did you see my puzzle book? I think I left it in there.'

'Please, Nathan, we'll get your puzzle book later. You're right about not taking anything out of the office. You need to tell me where you are.'

'I'm in reception. He's just going down the office steps... oh, now he's turned left into the street.'

'Follow him, Nathan! Don't let him out of your sight, OK? I'm coming down now; I'll catch you up in a minute. Don't lose him.'

Tariq took a quick sip of his tea, tipped the rest down the sink, and made a dash for the stairs. On arriving on the ground floor, he walked calmly through the low-level glass automated security barriers and through reception; he didn't want to attract attention from the security guards.

'Bye, Beryl.'

'Bye, Tariq, have a nice eve—'

Tariq was already through the main doors.

He hurried down the black stone steps onto the pavement, then turned left and caught sight of Nathan as he disappeared into a side street. He ran down Elm

Street towards him; at least it was downhill. He reached the corner of Phoenix Place, where he last saw Nathan, and then spotted him ahead, entering a local park. Nathan turned round to his father and pointed where Harper was heading. Tariq waited a few seconds before jogging down the road into the park through another entrance, to catch up with Harper. Inside the park, he leaned against a wall to catch his breath. He scanned for snipers tracking him from high windows or rooftops, and stayed under the cover of the dense foliage and tree canopies. Leaves fluttered in the wind as if a helicopter was hovering above. A car misfiring sounding like a gunshot echoed down the street which caused Tariq to dive to the ground behind a sycamore tree. After recovering his composure, he looked across at Nathan and signalled to him to cross the park, but Nathan was too busy tracking Harper, who was now heading down the street beyond the park. Nathan poked his head around the park exit gate to see where Harper was going, but a refuse truck obscured his view. When it finally moved out of the way, Harper was in the distance, at the far end of the street, hailing a taxi. The taxi stopped and he jumped in.

'Damn! Shit! We've let him slip through our fingers,' Tariq exclaimed, as he wiped the sweat from his brow, his red scar visible. 'Hard luck, Nathan. It's not your fault, son. We nearly got him. I just wanted to see where he was taking the book, and to whom.' Tariq looked down the street that Harper had just gone down, and said, 'Do you know what, Nathan? There's a good pub halfway down there; it's called The Phoenix. We used to go there quite a lot before I changed teams. I need a drink! Come on, I'll buy you a Coke.'

Nathan wasn't so sure. 'I won't like it if it's too noisy. I don't want any more music, otherwise I'm going home.'

'It's a deal, Nathan – if it's too loud then we leave, OK?'

They walked towards the pub, passing elegant Regency-style houses. As Tariq pushed open the large panelled wooden doors of The Phoenix, he turned around to Nathan, giving him one of his ironic smiles (lost on Nathan). He mused that Nathan would never have agreed to come all this way to a pub if he had asked him first.

In the pub, they were immediately greeted by a familiar voice. 'Heh, Tariq, I didn't know you still came here. Come and join us.' To their right, Mark Cooper was sitting with Nigel Pemberton on a side table. Pemberton was as smart as ever in his dark-blue pinstripe suit. Cooper was more casual and had already taken his tie off.

Tariq responded in as upbeat a manner as he could. 'Hi, Mark. Hello, Nigel. What a surprise...'

'What are you having, Tariq? And you, Nathan?' Pemberton asked.

CHAPTER 17

Mark Cooper went to the bar to get the drinks, leaving Tariq and Nathan with Nigel Pemberton at the table.

'Tariq, I didn't expect to see you here, my man. This is my secret drinking hole,' said Pemberton, leaning back in his seat.

Tariq responded, 'Well, I used to come here a lot when I was working with Andy Shelley on the Silvermere Gold Investments case – we were in here twice a week. Working on that case was a crazy time. We won it, though. You've met Nathan, my son, haven't you?'

'Hello Nathan, good to see you. Nice to see that ya father's giving you the full tour of the neighbourhood and all the local facilities.'

'Yes, hello, I'm Nathan. It wasn't really a proper tour. We were following Mr Harper, you see, but we lost him. He caught a taxi,' said Nathan. Tariq hid his unease.

'Harper? What were ya doing following Harper?' enquired Pemberton.

Tariq interjected, 'Well, Nathan, that was my excuse to get you this far, to the pub.'

'Ya dad must have been craving a wee drink that badly to start making up stories, heh?'

Nathan looked hurt. 'It wasn't a—'

Tariq cut his son short, 'Let's not bore Mr Pemberton with how we got here.'

Cooper returned with the drinks. Tariq took his pint of pale ale from him and clinked his glass against Pemberton's malt whisky, Cooper's Guinness, and Nathan's Diet Coke.

Tariq made a toast, 'Thanks Mark; cheers! Here's to success for the Magnus Conan-Whittaker case.'

A pint downed, Tariq left the table for the toilet. Pemberton eyed up Nathan for a few seconds and asked him, 'So Nathan, why were you following Harper? I'm curious.'

'Oh, I saw him take a book from the office – it was a red book – and Dad said that we should see where he was going.'

'And did you?'

'No, he must have run really fast to catch a taxi at the end of the road.'

'Your father doesn't like Mr Harper much. But let's not talk about it anymore.'

Tariq returned to the table. Noticing the empty glasses, he said, 'OK guys, let me get the next round in. What's everyone having?'

'Tariq, you're a gentleman; Grouse for me, a double,' replied Pemberton.

'A pint of the black and white for me, Tariq, thanks,' responded Cooper.

Tariq added, 'I'll join you. Nathan – Coke?'

Nathan caught his father's eye. 'Can I have the black-and-white as well? I want to try it.'

Cooper jumped in, 'Of course you can, Nathan. Get the young man a proper drink.'

Tariq grimaced at Nathan. 'OK then. Don't tell ya mother.'

'No, of course not, Dad.'

On Tariq's return with the drinks, Pemberton said, 'So Tariq, I understand that you saw some action in the Bosnian conflict?'

Tariq paused, 'Yes… but I don't remember much about it now. Probably for the best.'

Nathan, already a third of the way through his Guinness, said, 'He only has dreams and nightmares about it now, but he doesn't like to talk about it, do you, Dad?'

Pemberton said, 'That's understandable, Nathan. The soldiers that came back from the First World War were the same, you know. My grandfather never said a word about what happened to him at the battle of Verdun before he got injured. I asked him several times, but he just clammed up – too painful, too depressing; and my grandma said that he had nightmares sometimes. The only nightmares I get are about my ex-wife!'

'I see. I didn't know that, Nigel,' said Tariq.

'The divorce came through about a year ago now. At least that's over with. She fleeced me, the wee bitch. The judge believed her pathetic sob story, and she got half the estate – bloody outrageous! I have the option of buying her out in twelve months; if I can raise the cash, that is. After that she can put the house on the market. It's been in the family for generations. Damn disgrace, if you ask me. I haven't given up on getting it back; the kids want to keep it, of course; it's their family home. Twenty acres in all. Sorry, that's enough from me on that nonsense.'

Tariq asked Pemberton, 'Going back to the war, I heard that you worked for NATO during the war in Kosovo?'

'Yes, that's right – logistics for the Kosovo force. We were bombed a few times by the Serbs, but I don't pretend to have seen any front-line action, not like you, Tariq. Are you following the Ratko Mladic trial? They're saying on TV that the soldier with the eagle tattoo on his neck is the key man who could nail Mladic, but no one knows who he is.'

'Well, he is probably dead, killed in the war.'

'What makes you think that?'

'Because if he were alive, they would have found him by now.'

'Apparently, he escaped from Bosnia and is living in London under a false identity. He could be under our very noses, and we wouldn't know it. Did you know, he came from Visegrad, the same village as you; perhaps he's an old friend of yours and been in touch with you?' Pemberton stared intently at Tariq, awaiting his response.

'How… How would you know that? I barely remember, I…'

'Sorry, Tariq, I read the transcript of the Bosnian interview. Mark gave it to me to sign off.'

'Oh right. Yes, I see, of course.'

'Relax, I'm just being curious. And thank you for stepping in at short notice as translator; much appreciated.'

Pemberton, noticing that Nathan had left the table, added, 'I know you wanted to get stuck into the Bosnians – put the boot in, so to speak – but we want to catch them off-guard with their kilts around their ankles, you see. We're playing the long game with those two. Please keep it to yourself, Tariq – but we've put a tail on both of them. It's unofficial, OK, so don't say a damned word to a soul on the subject, will ya now?'

Tariq nodded. 'Sure, of course not.'

Nathan returned to the table. Cooper said, 'So Nathan, I hear you're keeping yourself busy helping your dad in the office?'

'Yes, I've been busy doing jobs for Dad, and I've also been helping Ajay in the security room.'

'Security room? What were you doing in there?'

'They're installing a new remote-access CCTV camera monitoring system, and Ajay can't tell the difference between the drawings. He says that they should have clouds on them, but that seems silly to me! He's fed up with it, but he has to do it because Burton told him to.'

Pemberton, half listening, asked, 'What's that, Nathan? Burton's idea, did you say?' He glanced over at Cooper. 'Sorry, Nathan, I shouldn't be asking you all these questions about work. We're here to relax… So what do ya do in your spare time?'

'I go diving on Wednesdays, and I've just passed my confined space diving test so I can dive in open water, and I support Newcastle United.'

Pemberton said, 'I don't believe this; so does Mark here. Don't get him started!'

'Started with what?' Nathan asked.

'So, what do you think of last season then?' Cooper asked Nathan.

'I think fifth in the league is good because they qualified for the Europa League. We were unbeaten for the first ten games until we were beaten by Manchester City. If we hadn't been beaten by Tottenham five-nil and then lost a two-goal lead to Wolves, then they could have qualified for the Champions League because Newcastle finished with sixty-five points, only five points behind Arsenal.'

Cooper responded, 'Don't remind me, Nathan; that was painful. At least the new signings, Demba Ba and Papiss Cissé, came good. Between them, they scored most of our goals, especially Ba. Like you said, we should be grateful for a Europa League spot; it will be good practice for the Champions League next season.'

Nathan said enthusiastically, 'Demba Ba scored sixteen goals, and Papiss Cissé scored thirteen, so they scored more than half the total of fifty-five goals. I think Cissé was better than Ba because he scored thirteen goals in fourteen appearances. Ba scored sixteen goals in thirty-six appearances.'

Pemberton asked Nathan, 'Did you see any games this season?'

'No, I didn't go to see them play in a stadium.'

'Well, maybe Mark can get a ticket for you. You can go with him.'

'No, it's alright. I don't really like crowds; that would give me a headache.'

Cooper said, 'I haven't had the time recently, anyway, to go to any matches, as I've been too busy house-hunting.'

'Oh yes, how's that going?' Pemberton asked.

'We haven't found anything we both like yet. The one I thought would do us near Dulwich, my wife didn't take a shine to as the garden was too small, and the house she did like we couldn't afford. She needs to realise that we can't afford the perfect house. That's her problem; everything has to be perfect. Goodness knows how much she has run up on credit cards. She does my head in sometimes. You've got all this to come, Nathan. A good-looking young man like you must have a girlfriend?'

Nathan took another drink of his Guinness. 'There is a girl I quite like at school, but I'm not sure she wants to hang out with me. Maybe I could ask her out next term, but I will have to wait for my chance.'

'That's the spirit, Nathan. To tell you the truth, I was too scared to ask the girl I fancied in fifth form – that would be year eleven for you. I got my friend to ask her in the end. Didn't do me any good, though; some other boy had already asked her out. So, Nathan, don't be too slow like me and miss out. The first week of term, go up to her and ask her!'

Pemberton ribbed Cooper, 'Story of his life, you see, Nathan – too slow to see it coming.'

Cooper defended himself, 'Don't listen to him, Nathan; he was born with a silver spoon in his mouth. He was sent to the school of royals – Gordonstoun School, founded by Prince Philip's mentor, Kurt Hahn, no less. They say that he taught the prince how to think. So, Nathan, my friend Nigel here has had a head-start on the rest of us. Unfortunately, he can't afford to keep up with the royals, you see, but he can still enjoy looking down his nose at me.'

Pemberton countered, 'Ha! Don't listen to that stuff and nonsense, Nathan; he's speaking like the true pleb that he is.'

Cooper laughed, 'Hah! You see what I mean, Nathan? I know my place!'

Cooper offered to get another round in and queued up at the bar, which was starting to fill up.

Nathan returned from the toilet again, sat down and

promptly finished the last of his second pint of Guinness before Cooper delivered another round to the table. Tariq was surprised that Nathan was on his third pint, but was beyond caring. Pemberton asked Tariq and Nathan, 'Are you guys looking forward to the Olympics on Saturday? You're lucky to get tickets you know, in a VIP box. That's the best place to be.'

Tariq said, 'Oh yes, I know! Sandra told me. We're getting excited about that aren't we Nathan?'

Nathan asked, 'Will there be cheese sandwiches?'

'I'm sure we can run to that, Nathan, and we'll have plenty of your newly acquired favourite black-and-white drink.'

'Oh, thanks. I will be looking forward to that then. I know people think that I like funny things. I surprise people all the time because I have unique talents, you know. My mum says that sometimes people can be too surprised, but I can't help that. I like things that other people don't like, and I don't like other things that neurotypical people like. In the film *Temple Grandin*, she says that she's "different, not less". For example, I prefer the silver medals, not the gold medals. Everybody else is thinking about the gold medal, but that doesn't seem fair to me as the man who won the silver medal needs someone to tell him that the silver is "different, not less". I don't even like the look of the gold medal; I think the clean shine of the silver medal is even better than the gold. I know, of course, that it is better than the bronze. Did you know, so far, we've won two gold and two silver medals…'

Tariq interjected, 'Alright Nathan, don't go on too much.'

Pemberton said, 'No, Nathan, I love your take on it – but Mark and I are late for another engagement, so we need to vamoose. Great talking to you, Nathan, and Tariq. See you for roll call tomorrow at dawn.'

Cooper took a final swig of his drink and followed Pemberton out the door.

Nathan informed his father that it was time to leave. Tariq was now feeling the effects of the last double whisky Pemberton had bought him, on an empty stomach. He looked across the room and felt uneasy at the chorus of raised voices in the now nearly full pub, which triggered something in Tariq. He needed to escape the angry crowd before they realised that he was an imposter and turned on him. He went to stand up but his knees went from under him.

'Dad? Dad, what the hell are you doing?'

'Nathan, Nathan, "different not less". Do you mind helping me out, son? They can't know who I am. They'll take me alive – they'll interrogate me!'

Nathan leaned forward reluctantly to thread his arm under his father's and lifted him to his feet.

'There you go, son, you're stronger than you thought.' Nathan guided him across the pub to the exit door. A man in a yellow high-vis coat, saw their plight and opened the door as they approached. 'Thank you, kind sir, very grateful,' said Tariq. Out in the cool twilight air, Nathan caught sight of the main road in the distance where Stuart Harper had jumped into a taxi three hours before, so he headed in that direction. Nathan and his father meandered down the pavement, as Nathan supported him with each stride. 'Steady as you go, son. Nice and steady, now. What's your mother going to say about this then, Nathan? Hey? About you drinking too much Guinness…'

'Me? Now I know you're joking – when it's me helping you home. Fancy that, the autistic son rescues his war-veteran dad.'

'Yes, you're right, son; best not to tell ya mother. Mum's the word, or should I say *not* the word? Ha!'

They finally arrived at the main road, where Nathan slumped his father onto a bench on the footway facing the road. He bought two Ginsters cheese and onion pasties and two bottles of water from a late-night food store on the street. He offered his father a pasty and one of the drinks, and then hailed a taxi, as he'd seen his father do on the way to the office. He directed the taxi driver to take them to London Bridge station, and from there, they caught the train to Eden Park.

On the train, Tariq deteriorated into a semi-comatose state, so Nathan had to shout at him to wake him up as they approached their station. He then guided his father home and onto the sofa. He went into the kitchen to make him a cup of tea, but on his return, his father was already out for the count.

CHAPTER 18

Nathan was the first downstairs in the morning. He put two Yorkshire Tea teabags in the Orla Kiely teapot, half filled it with hot water from the kettle, and put two slices of bread in the toaster. He sat down on the kitchen table and looked at his watch: 7:24am. His father should be up by now. Nathan took a cup of tea up to his bedroom and knocked on the door. 'Dad?'

'Yeah? God, what time is it?'

'It's 7:26 now. We'll be late.'

'Bloody hell, Nathan! Why didn't you wake me up sooner, for God's sake?'

'I don't think God is that bothered with what time you get out of bed, to be honest with you – he's got more important things on his mind. I've brought you a cup of tea; shall I bring it in?'

'Yes please, bring it in.'

Tariq was now sitting up on his bed, head in hands. Nathan handed him the tea.

'Thanks, Nathan. I don't suppose you could get me a couple of ibuprofen? They're in the white box under the kitchen sink.' Nathan obliged, and Tariq swallowed them with the remainder of his tea. He then stumbled across the landing to the bathroom to freshen up and brush his teeth.

Nathan rescued his still-warm toast from the toaster and added his favourite morning toppings – Rose's lime marmalade and Cheddar cheese. He considered making a sandwich for lunch but remembered it was Friday, so they would be serving fish and chips for lunch in the office canteen. He decided that he now liked fish and chips.

He heard his father cursing as he came down the stairs, doing up the buttons on his white shirt.

'Nathan, are you ready, son? We can catch the 7:58am if we leave in five minutes.'

'It's cancelled. I looked it up on the National Rail train app. The next one is 8:18am,' said Nathan, holding his phone up.

'Bugger! Well, we can at least blame Southeastern trains for our lateness. Boil the kettle, would you, Nathan?'

'OK, Dad. Do you want any of my toast? You can have the last slice; I don't want it now.'

'Yes, thanks, Nathan. Let me guess – cheese and green marmalade?'

Nathan didn't respond, and Tariq sat down at the kitchen table. Nathan brought him a small mug of instant coffee. He joined his father with his cup of tea. Tariq looked up from his coffee at Nathan. 'What the hell happened last night? I didn't know Pemberton and Cooper were drinking mates. No wonder Cooper has that cushy job! He just skulks around, making himself busy organising foreign interviews and translators, while the likes of us run around doing the donkey work. I mean, what does that guy do all day?'

'Don't ask me, Dad. I've only been there three weeks, and I've only met him twice. He was friendly to me, anyway.'

Tariq, with an embarrassed expression, said to his son,

'Thanks for helping me home last night. I shouldn't have had that double whisky – big mistake. I didn't know you liked Guinness. How much did you have in the end?'

'Two and a half pints; I didn't finish the last one. I didn't even know that I would like Guinness, either. I have a bit of a headache, so please don't shout at me, OK? I don't want too much noise this morning.'

'Fine, suits me. I'm still thinking about what happened yesterday. How did Harper get away? He must have seen us tailing him and, while we were in the park, sprinted to the other end of the road for the taxi. Listen, Nathan, can I ask you a favour? I know you can't help it sometimes, but can you try not to mention to anyone in the office that we were following Stuart Harper last night; and especially don't mention to your mother that we got drunk, yeah? Or rather, I got drunk. It just looks bad.'

'Yes, Dad, I won't talk about it in the office or to Mum. Now you've asked me I won't do it, you see. I don't mind you explaining what not to say; in fact, I wish you would tell me more often what not to say. Then I wouldn't end up sounding like an idiot, or as Mr Pemberton says "*an Heid the baw*",' said Nathan, mimicking Pemberton's Scottish accent.

'Alright then, Nathan. Sorry, I'll try to remember to tell you, but I won't always be there. Come on, we need to go. Check the app again.'

'The 8:18 is on time, you'll be pleased to know,' said Nathan.

Tariq and Nathan arrived fifteen minutes late at the office, but no one on their case team was around to notice. Cooper had mentioned to Tariq in the pub that the transcript summary of the Bosnian interview was ready for collection from his office. Tariq sent Nathan down to the property room to work on the document collation while he went up to the eighth floor to find Cooper. Would he still be in a friendly mood or worse than ever? After exiting the lift, Tariq approached his office and became aware of raised voices coming from the conference room next to Cooper's office. As he got closer, he recognised the voices of Nigel Pemberton and Jack Burton. They were almost shouting at each other; Burton's deep booming Texan power versus Pemberton's cutting authoritarian Scottish tones preaching in righteous outrage. Tariq edged nearer along the corridor.

Pemberton was saying to Burton, '... and without my authorisation! This is completely reprehensible.'

Burton then walked away from Pemberton to the back of the room towards the large glass window, staring into the distance. He turned back around to face Pemberton, saying, 'The Attorney General has given me specific authority. You can ask him yourself.'

'I'll be seeing Dominic at the Olympics on Saturday, so believe me, I will be.'

Tariq was taken by surprise as the lift along the corridor bell dinged. Tariq had a second to move out of sight. The door to Cooper's adjacent office was open, so he darted inside, half expecting to face Cooper sitting behind his desk, but he wasn't there. The Bosnian interview transcript was on the edge of his desk, so he read all five pages of it. There was no mention of him coming from Visegrad.

Tariq returned to his desk, then made a coffee and went down to the property room. Nathan was sorting the final pile of documents from a green box he hadn't seen before. He was getting quicker at recognising the same design of notebooks, buff files, letterheads, and other similar types, and putting them in the appropriate labelled boxes.

'Hi, Dad. Are you alright?'

'I'm fine, Nathan. Never felt better. How's the headache?'

'Better, thank you. Look, I think I've finished going through all the files and boxes on the shelves so far. I've gone through the box that Simon Beecham brought in this morning. He told me that there was another box to collect from the post room. Shall I get it and start putting everything in date order?'

'Yes, thanks, Nathan; that would be great.'

Nathan walked along the basement corridor to the post room to collect the box. As he approached, he could hear that terrible screeching noise he'd heard before. He peered quickly around the corner of the room to see who was making the noise. He could tell by his purple tie that it was Stuart Harper. Nathan had that meltdown feeling and needed to quickly find a quiet, safe place. Behind him was a plain black metal door, which he pushed open to reveal a small room with piles of chairs and table tops without legs. It was a quiet space, which was all that mattered. He sat on one of the chairs and took some deep breaths.

Ten minutes later, Nathan emerged from the furniture storeroom and made his way to the post room. As he passed the kitchenette tucked in along the corridor, Ajay shouted across at him, 'Hey, Nathan! How are you, mate? What are you up to?'

'Hi, Ajay. I think I am alright now, thanks. I drank

too much Guinness last night, you see, and now I'm a bit sensitive because—'

'Ha! At least you're honest, which is what I like about you. Anyway, I was going to tell you that Pemberton came to see me this morning and told us to stop the roll-out of Burton's CCTV system. When I asked him why, he said there was a dispute with the software supplier, so we couldn't use it. He didn't look happy about it. I can't believe it – all that work, and he pulls the plug! Anyway, I thought I'd tell you in case you were wondering what was happening.'

'OK, Ajay, thank you for telling me then.'

Nathan collected the box from the post room and returned to the property room. Simon Beecham was helping Tariq catalogue the files.

'You alright, son? What took you so long?'

'I was going to the post room to start with, but Stuart Harper was there, standing at the noise box. I hate that noise box thing!'

'Nathan, you keep saying that. What is this noise box? I've no idea what you're talking about.'

Simon Beecham looked up from his pile of files. 'The only thing we have like that is a shredder; perhaps he's talking about the shredder?'

Tariq looked across at Nathan, eyes wide. 'Right. Nathan, come with me, show me.'

'No, I'm not going back there. You can go if you like.'

Tariq opened the door. The distinctive noise of the shredder filled the corridor. The shredder was in a small recessed alcove with a back door opening into the basement car park. Tariq walked down the corridor towards the alcove. The door was open, and cigarette smoke was in the air. As Tariq looked on, Harper fed another document into the shredder and blew his cigarette fumes through the open door.

'Harper, what are you doing?'

'Calm down, Tariq. What do you think I'm doing? Shredding old documents.'

'What documents?' Tariq grabbed a document from the pile next to the shredder.

'Spare irrelevant material, that's all. Please, Tariq, don't fuss. I know you like to fuss.'

'Don't bullshit me, Harper. You know, and I know, that you don't need to shred these; we mark them and they're taken away, so you'll have to do better than that. Answer the question: why are you shredding these documents? What have you done with the red book you took yesterday?'

'What are you talking about?'

'We followed you last night and saw you jump in a taxi with the book.'

'Tariq, what is the matter with you? I caught a taxi, yeah, so what? That's none of your business, so back off. Why were you following me anyway? What I do in my own time is private! I could complain about being harassed you know. I know you're still bitter about taking the rap for the Frederick Rainsford case. You were the senior disclosure officer, I wasn't; that's all there is to it – get over it!'

'You mis-filed documents on that case, and now you're destroying documents on this one – so it doesn't look good, does it, Harper?'

'Tariq, do you know why I'm really down here? I'll confess, if you like?'

'Yes, go on; I'm waiting.'

Harper squared up to Tariq. 'Because I fancied a smoke, and this is the only place in the building where I can have a puff, alright? So if you want to tell Burton, go ahead, fill ya boots. I have to warn you, though – I've seen Burton down here smoking the odd Habana cigar himself, so I don't think you'll get much sympathy from him.'

Tariq hesitated before again thumbing through the pile of documents Harper was shredding. He gave Harper a final stare and walked away back down the corridor. To make a point, Harper lit up a cigarette and looked across at Tariq as he walked off, and then fed another document into the shredder.

Deflated after his unfruitful encounter with Harper, Tariq went to the kitchen for a coffee. On his return to the property room, Mark Cooper was at the door on his way out.

'Ah, Tariq, I've just dropped off the Bosnian interview transcript. Nathan's got it.'

'Right. Thanks, Mark.' Tariq thought it best not to tell Cooper that he'd already read it in his office.

In the property room, Nathan was on the PC on the central desk. He said, 'Dad, I know I can sometimes tell you things you don't care about, but I've just noticed something about the email files. Can I tell you what it is?'

'Yes, Nathan, I don't mind you telling me, whatever it is.'

'Well, I've checked when these electronic files were first created. I know how to do it for any file or email, even if they are edited or saved at a later date. All the other emails I've looked at are at least two years old and match up with the dates on the emails themselves.'

'So what are you trying to tell me, Nathan?'

'The emails sent by the Bosnians you interviewed are only three weeks old.'

'No, that can't be. You can tell by the dates in the emails. Look, that one's dated 11th December 2009. That is over two years old, like you said.'

'Dad, believe me, this email file was first created 10th July 2012.' He pointed to a table of metadata that he'd generated. *First created 10/07/2012.*

Tariq slumped back in his chair. 'Maybe they've been copied and re-sent?'

'This is the original email, not a copy.'

Tariq sat back silently in his chair, trying to fathom why these emails had suddenly appeared. He had tried to explain to Pemberton and Burton that it was unlikely that Bosnians would collude with Serbians on high-stakes business deals. Had someone set them up? It would explain why they denied knowing Karlo Mitchko.

CHAPTER 19

In his home kitchen, Tariq sat at the table drinking the real coffee he'd just poured from the cafetière as he studied the two Olympics tickets Pemberton had given him earlier in the week. *Olympic Stadium Executive Box Sat 4 Aug 10:30am.* There was a handwritten note on the blank side: *11:30am.*

Nathan entered the kitchen. 'Morning, Dad. How are you today?'

'Hi, Nathan, good to see you bright and early.'

'Well, you're half right, I think.'

'Ha ha. Nathan, remind me. Did you say yesterday that we should catch the 9:50am train from Eden Park to get to the Olympics on time?'

'Yes, that's the one.'

Tariq looked up at his son. 'Sorry, Nathan, but you can't go like that.'

'Like what?'

'Wearing jeans and a T-shirt, that's what. We've got smart tickets, you know,' said Tariq, waving them in the air, 'so bloody well dress smart, would you? Like you're going to work.'

'Now you tell me. OK, OK. Toast first, please.'

'And there's no need to make a sandwich – you'll be

spoilt for choice for food and drink today. Pemberton will be offended if you bring sandwiches.'

Nathan went upstairs to change. The phone rang. Tariq answered. It was Alice.

Tariq said, 'Hello darling, sorry I missed your calls; Nathan and I have been working late. We need to go in twenty minutes to the Olympics, just to warn you.'

'Of course, that should be fun. Look out for Nathan, won't you? He doesn't like crowds; you know that, don't you?' Alice's tone turned more sombre. 'Tary, I'm worried about Millie. She's almost gone into a coma since taking the American drug. I've spoken to the consultant, Dr Freeman. He said that she's reacting to the stronger drug, and the next forty-eight hours are critical. I...' Alice broke down with emotion.

'Look, darling, you're going to have to give her time, OK? That's all we can do right now. I'll see you tomorrow at the hospital. Just be patient; that's all we can do.'

'This is serious. Do you get it, Tariq? She could die! I wonder sometimes if you're capable of facing reality. You're shutting it all out, as you've always done, ever since the Bosnian War ended. Please, Tariq, don't leave me to face this on my own. Don't close yourself off to Millie...'

'That's not fair. I love Millie, but the reality is that there's nothing you or I can do for her now. I wish there was, but there isn't! It's not fair to Nathan to have him sitting in the hospital every day. I'm really sorry, darling, but we've got to go now. We'll come to the hospital tomorrow as arranged.'

Nathan braved the journey to Stratford to the Olympic Park. He didn't like travelling into the unknown, and on a new route. He hoped Mr Pemberton had remembered his promise to provide him with his favourite black-and-white drink that would calm his nerves. He did a number puzzle in his puzzle book and looked up fun facts about the Olympic Park on his mobile phone.

They arrived at Stratford station just outside the Olympic Park with about half an hour to spare, so they took a closer look at the giant 'Candyfloss Orbit' structure, as Nathan called it.

A man wearing a blue casual denim jacket and jeans tailed them at a distance. He had a toned athletic profile, and was wearing sunglasses under an Olympic-branded purple baseball cap. He took a few high-resolution pictures of the Orbit with his camera phone with Tariq and Nathan in shot, which he enlarged and emailed to someone.

Nathan bent his neck skywards at the giant sculpture. 'Dad, do you know that this is Britain's highest piece of public art? Personally, I don't even think it is art, as it is more like an observation tower. They say you can see twenty miles, but that's probably with binoculars on a clear day.'

Tariq commented, 'They were talking about this on the TV recently. It was designed by the sculptor Anish Kapoor, who won the Turner Prize for something – I know not what.'

Nathan went on, 'It's made of five miles of steel tubes and weighs two thousand tonnes. It's one hundred and fourteen metres tall. I don't want to go up it, though, as there's probably too many people up there at once.'

'Come on, Nathan, we'd better make our way to the stadium; I think I saw a queue outside, so we might have to queue up.'

As they walked across the pedestrian bridge over the water channel towards the stadium, they were greeted by young, energetic Olympic Ambassadors clad with dark-pink tabards. 'Hello, thank you for coming to the stadium today. Can I see your tickets please? Thank you, please go straight through the left-hand entry point.' Tariq observed ahead the two Priority Tickets entrances at two light-green open gazebos. The entry points were marshalled by an army of pink tabards working in groups around the stadium like worker ants, each with a specific task. Tariq offered their tickets to the young marshal, the shiny gold and coloured Olympic ring graphics gleaming in the sunlight. The marshal smiled and raised his arm to signal permission to continue through to the other side of the tented gateway. The man with the purple baseball cap watched them keenly as they entered.

A hum of excitement exuded from the gathering crowd in the stadium as if the structure itself was coming alive just for this day. They passed through what looked like a wall of giant ribbons in Olympic colours into the perimeter canopy of the stadium. Tariq studied the ticket for the designated stairway code, H, up to the VIP box, about a third of the way round, walking clockwise. Nathan followed, head bowed, trying not to notice the increasing concentration of excited people milling around. Another checkpoint of pink worker ants examined their tickets at the foot of the wide walkways of rising stairs. There was yet another check of their tickets at the entrance to the high-level curved corridor to the executive boxes. The man with the baseball cap followed close behind, diverting into the general stadium seating before the VIP checkpoint. He found a secluded corner, put on a pink tabard and mingled with the other worker ants.

Tariq and Nathan walked down the sleek white corridor to find Pemberton's executive box. As Tariq knocked, he noticed the *Serious Fraud Office* sign on the door advertising *Frank Whitten Solicitors*. A cost-sharing deal negotiated by Pemberton, Tariq guessed. Pemberton opened the door with a half-full champagne flute in hand, dressed in an expensive grey suit with a tartan waistcoat.

'Tariq, Nathan, welcome! Come in, gentlemen. You're right on time. Fancy an aperitif?'

'Yes, well, why not? Thank you.'

'Nathan, hello again, I know what you'll be drinking. Help yourself to some Guinness or whatever you fancy, laddie.'

On their left, on a long table with a clean white linen tablecloth, were various plates of high-end nibbles – Kettle Chips, cocktail sticks with cheese and olives, tiny square crackers with a variety of bite-sized toppings. At the end of the table was a selection of wine, beer and champagne glasses. Straight ahead was a spectacular glassed panorama of the Olympic stadium, now about half full. It was an awesome sight, all the more enigmatic in the clean, opulent silence of the room itself. No wonder Pemberton was glowing in his den of luxury, looking out on the amassing crowds as if he were emperor. In centre-stage of the room was a rectangular dining table, laid out for five, on another white linen tablecloth. Silver cutlery, wine glasses and napkins, were all precisely arranged for each place setting. Nathan scanned the room with relief – it felt a safe place.

Mark Cooper emerged from a corner room, concluding

a phone call on his mobile. He turned round to face Tariq and Nathan. 'Hello guys; isn't this impressive?' he said, looking across the stadium. 'We could be in with a chance of a couple of gold medals later. Jessica Ennis is running this evening. Unless she's collapses on the track, she should get the gold, and Mo Farah has a good chance for a medal in the ten thousand metres; you've got to stay for that. Hey, did you hear that we won two golds this morning for the men's four rowing and the women's double sculls?' Cooper paused briefly and added, 'Sorry, nearly forgot to introduce you to Amar. Tariq, Nathan, this is Amar. He deals with all the surveillance operations and the police liaison for the dawn raids and the like. He's Bosnian, like you. We needed someone who could deal with Karlo Mitchko's associates, who are mostly Serbian or Bosnian.'

'Hello, Tariq, so pleased to meet you – and you, Nathan. I was especially looking forward to meeting you, Tariq, as I understand you are a Bosnian War veteran, but, like me, you probably don't like thinking about those times. A terrible time for our country at the hands of those murderous Serbs. I heard that at the interview with the Bosnians you remembered swimming with your family in the Danube, next to the beautiful Mehmed Paša Sokolović bridge of Visegrad, which must have been difficult for you. Anyway, I shouldn't be talking about such things on a special day as this.'

'Hello Amar, good to meet you,' said Tariq. Amar had a neatly cut, greying beard. His accent and rounded smiling face, with a hint of menace, confirmed to Tariq his Bosnian heritage. Jibing your fellow countryman was a national pastime, as you were honoured to be part of the national extended family. The best way to respond, thought Tariq, was to jibe straight back at him. 'Who told you about the interview? They're supposed to be confidential,' he said, glancing accusingly at Cooper, who looked concerned at Tariq's thinly veiled accusation, especially with Pemberton in earshot.

Amar saved Cooper's embarrassment. 'Of course they are, and the SFO would never break their confidence. I happened to be escorting the Bosnians back to the police station, and they mentioned in the car that they may have upset you with their conversation, but it was not intended.'

'I was fine with it. Interviews often throw up unexpected topics. It was just a routine interview.'

'More champagne?' intervened Pemberton, topping up Tariq's glass.

'Thank you for the Guinness,' said Nathan, having helped himself to one of the chilled cans in the fridge.

For lunch, there was a choice of prawn and ginger dumplings or a buffalo wings starter, brought in on a trolley by two smartly dressed young men, not long out of sixth form, Tariq considered. The main course was brown sliced chicken with caramelised onion and dates, followed by key lime pie and chocolate fondant. The Guinness had relaxed Nathan's senses, and the food was an education to his taste buds, especially the chocolate fondant – delicious. Nathan and Mark Cooper discussed the improvements needed for Newcastle Football Club to win next year's Premier League. Pemberton recounted memorable experiences in his youth at Gordonstoun boarding school, drawing on amusing tales from college masters about teaching Prince Charles years before he attended the school. Pemberton and Cooper left the dining table first, decanting to the white leather sofas facing each other at the far end of the room, sideways to the clear glass wall.

Amar, his eyes glazed over from too much rich food and a bottle of Sauvignon Blanc, moved over to the table opposite Tariq. 'So, Tariq, have you looked around the Olympic Park yet? You ought to, you know. There's so much to see and you need to make the most of it while you're here.'

Nathan said, as he got up from the table, 'We've already seen the Orbit structure, which is supposed to be artwork, but I don't think it is that great. It looks like it might fall down, if you ask me.'

'Ha! I agree, Nathan. This is the idea, you see – it's what makes you look at it even more.'

Nathan went to get another Guinness from the fridge, leaving Amar and Tariq on their own, facing each other. Amar's expression hardened, and he said to his fellow countryman, 'Do you know the full name of the Orbit, my friend? It is the ArcelorMittal Orbit. Do you know where the iron ore that went into the steel for the Orbit came from? I'll tell you: the Omarska mine at Prijedor. If you were a true Bosnian, you would know what happened there twenty years ago in 1992. Do you know what happened to our Bosnian countrymen there? Surely you can remember? Why can't you remember? Maybe you don't want to – now *that* I can understand.' Amar stared into Tariq's eyes, searching for a glimpse of a memory stirring within him. Tariq's expression remained unchanged. Amar gripped Tariq's left forearm and looked intently at him as if this was his only chance to appeal to Tariq, to retrieve his long-hidden memories – to find something of himself. 'Tariq, my friend – thousands of Bosnians were tortured, raped and murdered by the Serbs there in 1992.' He gripped Tariq's arm even harder. 'It was a concentration camp – worse than Auschwitz. In 2005, that son of a bitch of a company, ArcelorMittal, promised to put a memorial at the Omarska mine for all our fellow citizens who perished there, but where is it, Tariq? We're still waiting. Then the same company builds the Orbit right here, in the Olympic Park. That's why the Bosnian survivors call it "a memorial in exile".'

Tariq listened as he subdued the emotions that the name Omarska evoked deep within him. Amar sensed it meant something to him; he loosened his grip now. 'We're catching up with the perpetrators, Tariq; we're hunting them down to pay for their war crimes. Ratko Mladic is next; you know that, don't you? If it were me, I would just line him up against a wall and put a bullet in his head, and one for luck, like they did outside the White House at Omarska. That's justice for me, and for all of those who died at his hands, and by those following his orders. Do you know who we're looking for now? The unknown man who stood by at the mass shootings at Srebenica.'

Tariq responded, 'The man with the eagle tattoo on his neck?'

'Yes, Tariq. I'm impressed, you've heard. The net is closing in.' Amar paused before asking, 'Can you help us find him, Tariq?'

'Me? How can I help?'

'We know he was from Visegrad, as you are. It's a close-knit community. He was even seen swimming as a young man in the Danube River, just like you remembered at the interview, Tariq. Perhaps you can remember him? He would have been a Bosnian Serb, which is why he ended up under Mladic; most Bosnians remember who were the Serbs. You can never forget what they did.'

'No. I don't know. I can't remember him. I'm sorry, you're wasting your time with me!'

Pemberton, now standing up, said to them, 'Amar, Tariq, stop reminiscing about your homeland and join us for coffee.'

Amar replied, 'Of course. Tariq doesn't remember anything anyway. It's a tragedy really, what war can do to a man – he can lose his whole identity.'

Tariq looked blankly back at Amar. They joined Pemberton and Cooper on the sofas for coffee and mints, expressing their gratitude for the fine lunch cuisine. They then all went out onto the balcony overlooking the athletics track. Track and field heats were in progress, with orange LED sign boards occasionally flashing up times, distances jumped, or the distances that javelins, discuses or shotputs had been thrown, accompanied by muted cheers from dedicated fans. Tariq and Nathan informed Pemberton that they would be looking around the Olympic Park as Amar had suggested, and they would return for tea around 6:00pm.

As they exited the corridor down the stairway, a man in dark glasses and a purple cap on the top tier of spectator seats got up from his seat.

CHAPTER 20

On exiting the stadium, Tariq persuaded Nathan to visit the Aquatics Centre. Nathan commented that he thought that the Aquatics Centre was more of a work of art than the jumble of steelwork that was the giant Orbit. They walked along the Waterworks River canal running through the Olympic Park. Nathan appreciated the quiet and calming ambience. Families enjoyed picnics along the tiered banks, with children scampering up and down the grass-covered tiers. Nathan said he preferred to remain on the riverbank while Tariq looked around the park. Tariq agreed to his request, and they checked their mobile phones were on. Tariq walked up to the far northern end of the park, observing the industrial-sized sculptures along the way. He reviewed the exorbitant prices of souvenirs and food from the food stalls. Fish and chips was twelve pounds; it was lucky he wasn't hungry. Giant TV screens around the park screened live events; some sites were more popular than others. Near the end of his park tour, he walked across to an area of grey portacabin toilets. As he approached the toilet block entrance, two well-built, overweight men with cold eyes blocked his path. 'Tariq? Tariq Markovic?'

He instinctively mumbled, 'Yes.' The bigger man in jeans and a red-and-pink checked shirt put his hand on Tariq's right shoulder, digging his thumb into a soft pressure point next to the bone. The sharp, agonising pain disarmed him, paralysing his ability to shout out. The second man put his arm around Tariq's waist, twisting him to the side and through the open door of a green portacabin First Aid unit. To an onlooker, the two men appeared to be helping a sick man into the room to get treatment. They pushed Tariq in and closed the door quickly behind them, bolting it shut from the inside.

The other man, although shorter, had arms thick with muscle. He said to Tariq, 'Any noise from you and I'll break your face, got it? We have a few questions and I suggest you think very hard before you answer, yes? We can do this the easy way or the hard way, OK?'

Now seated at a small grey treatment table, Tariq looked up at the men, rubbing his shoulder as the pain subsided. 'Who are you? What do you want?'

'Some Bosnian friends of ours have informed us of some interesting things about you, Tariq, that we want to talk to you about.'

'What friends? The Bosnians from the interview?'

'That doesn't matter,' said the taller of the two men.

'Look, you've got the wrong man, I don't know anything! I wish I did. I can't help you!'

'Just to be really clear, so you don't die for nothing, we think that you know the man we're looking for: the man from Visegrad with the tattoo, one of Mladic's henchmen.'

'I don't know anybody from Visegrad, so why don't you both piss off.'

'Don't be so hasty now. I told you that you must think hard, right? You come from Visegrad; we know that you remember that much.'

'I remember swimming by the bridge, that's all!'

'Come, come, Tariq, I'm sure you can remember who you hung out with; you were there for most of your childhood. After all, it's a small town, so everybody knows everybody; somebody must know who he is. Why is it that there are no photographs of him? It smells like a conspiracy to me. All we want is to identify the man with the eagle tattoo on his neck. Think now, Tariq – you must have seen him around all the time. There wouldn't be many with a tattoo like that. Tariq, for the sake of the Bosnian people, you have to help us find this man. He was a witness to Mladic's war crimes. He deserves to go down with him. The Serbs say they don't know him. They have concocted a story that he was a Bosnian spy recruited by the UN or the CIA. We have it on good authority from the UN and the CIA that they didn't have any spies on the ground at the time of the Srebrenica massacres.'

'You have to believe me – I don't know who he is. He was Serb, I'm Bosnian, so why would I have anything to do with him?'

'Maybe you *were* a Serb, but you just can't remember? Anyway, Bosnians and Serbs got along just fine before the war, so don't give me that "Bosnians don't speak to Serbs" crap.' The man in the checked shirt put his hand on Tariq's shoulder and started to push his thumb into Tariq's already bruised flesh.

'Aaagghh! Please, I don't know…' There was a knock at the door.

The other man shouted, 'We're busy, we can't help you with first aid right now. Come back later.'

'I need antiseptic and a bandage please. Can you pass it

through, please? It's an emergency,' came the muffled reply. Tariq grimaced as the thumb of the first man dug into him. The second man found a wrapped bandage and a small plastic bottle of antiseptic from one of the side cupboards. He unbolted the door and held them out to the man waiting on the other side. It was the man with the purple Olympic baseball cap. At that moment, through the gap in the partially open door, a mini baseball bat arced upwards between the smaller Bosnian's legs, slamming into his unguarded testicles. He yelled out in pain, curling up into a ball on the floor in agony, holding his groin. The second man with the checked shirt released his grip on Tariq's shoulder and reached for the knife concealed in a waist-belt holster under his loose shirt. The man with the purple cap stepped forward into the cabin instantly, bringing the bat down firmly on his wrist, knocking the knife out of his hand. Checked shirt attempted to retrieve the knife from the floor. As he did so, baseball cap delivered a final blow to the back of his head, rendering him unconscious.

The man with the baseball cap said in an American accent, 'Tariq, quick, out. Follow me, please.' He left the bat behind in the portacabin with the two neutralised Bosnians. As he directed him out of the toilet block into the open public area, he shouted across at two policemen who had just walked past, 'I heard a fight in the First Aid room down there on the left. I think one of them had a baseball bat.'

'OK, sir, we'll deal with this; stay here, please, so we can get a statement from you,' said one of the policemen.

'Yeah, sure.' As the police approached the cabin, baseball cap said to Tariq, 'Time to leave, come with me.'

Out of sight of the policemen, Tariq asked baseball cap, 'What's going on? Can you please tell me what is going on? Who are you? Who were those men?'

'Tariq, calm down. It's the Bosnians; they're desperate to track down the missing man they think will send Mladic down for good.'

'The man the Serbs say was a spy?'

'That's what *they* say. I can't explain anything now. Take this phone; it's got a tracker. Call the speed dial treble-two nine if you get into trouble again. You don't have to say anything; we'll come for you. Be vigilant until the trial's over.'

'Who's "we"? What trial?'

'Mladic. Ratko Mladic, of course,' said baseball cap as he put his sunglasses back on. He added, 'Sorry, I can't be seen with you, Tariq. Go back to your son and enjoy the rest of your day. Those goons won't be bothering you again today.' He merged into the crowd as an ambulance quietly pulled up to the toilet block, blue lights flashing. Tariq massaged his tender right shoulder and left the scene before the police came back looking for him

Tariq was walking along the canal path when a plane flew high above, probably on its final approach to Heathrow Airport, fifteen miles west. The sound of the aircraft was enough to stop him in his tracks. He sat down on the bank, holding his face in his hands, memories flooding back. It sounded like a US reconnaissance plane he'd heard flying above him many times in the Bosnian War. He thought back for the first time in many years. He'd had something to do with those planes, hadn't he? He was on a special mission. The man with the eagle tattoo... *Yes, I remember that man! Oh God, I know that man, he was—*

'Are you alright, sir?'

Tariq looked up, initially blinded by the bright sky.

'St John's ambulance,' said one of the two men in St John's uniform.

'Oh, yes, thank you. I just needed to sit down for a bit.'

'It's hot, isn't it? Take one of these. You need to keep hydrated.' He handed Tariq a small bottle of mineral water.

'Thank you very much.' Tariq opened the bottle and drank half of it. The men left him.

Tariq considered leaving the venue after what had just happened. Who were those men? Who was the American in the baseball cap who'd rescued him? It seemed that his past was suddenly catching up with him. What was the point of running? Maybe he didn't want to run anymore? Where could he go to escape his past? Nowhere on this Earth.

Tariq approached Nathan, who was where he'd left him, on the bank next to the canal.

'Hi, Dad. Buy anything?'

'I nearly bought a T-shirt until I saw the price. I mean, twenty-six pounds for a T-shirt, that's ridiculous!'

'Yeah, I agree, you can buy eight pints of Guinness for that.'

'Not here, you can't, it's eight pounds a pint; that's only three pints! Come on, let's walk back to Pemberton and Cooper for tea – that's free!'

The crowds were building as the evening schedule of races drew closer. Nathan dodged the streams of fast-moving people in front of him, determined to get to the sanctuary of his safe space that was the executive box. As they made their way back, Tariq mulled over whether Pemberton, Cooper or their security man, Amar, had deliberately set him up with the Bosnian interview, which had led to his confrontation with the Bosnians in the First Aid room. Had this been their plan from the beginning, to pin him down in the Olympic Park?

'Tariq, Nathan, welcome back!' said Pemberton, putting on his well-practised professional smile as they entered the executive box. 'Take a seat; tea will be here any minute.' Mark Cooper and Amar had just donned their jackets and were making their way out of the door. Pemberton explained, 'Mark and Amar are just leaving to meet someone at the Orbit observation tower. That is, if Amar can overcome his political objections.'

Amar smiled back at Pemberton and shook Tariq's hand on his way out, 'Good to meet you, Tariq. I would have liked to have talked to you some more and maybe help you to recall some happy memories of Visegrad... next time!'

At high tea, as Pemberton called it, Pemberton was asking Tariq about the MCW case he was working on. Tariq swallowed the last of his mini smoked salmon sandwich. 'It's going to be very tight, especially with new boxes that keep coming in. If any more come in, I'll be asking for an extension of time.'

'Quite right, quite right, of course, you should if you need it. Overall, though, are you happy with the way the case is going? I mean, are the ledgers all in order as they should be? How are you getting on with Harper? I know you two have some history on the previous case.' Pemberton paused and leant forward on his sofa towards Tariq, saying in a quieter Scottish tone, 'Tariq, can I trust ya to keep a secret?'

Tariq's eyes widened, and he nodded back. 'Sure.'

'I'm on your side on this one. I trust you more than Harper and Burton, for that matter. Burton's been setting up some remote CCTV surveillance system behind my back. I'm grateful to Nathan, by the way, for bringing it to my attention in the pub. There may also be a third person involved. Can you help me, Tariq, to sort it out? If you see or hear anything, let me know, will you? No emails, please; it's not secure. If you find any evidence, put it on a memory stick and pass it on to me. Let me sort it out discreetly.' Nathan returned with more nibbles, prompting Pemberton to say in a normal voice, 'Thank you, Tariq, for all your help. Keep up the good work.'

Pemberton left the box soon after 7pm, to meet his old friend, the Attorney General, Dominic Choudhry, who had an executive box of his own, to discuss something. Tariq got comfortable on the sofa, reading the business section of the *Daily Telegraph*. He nodded off before he got to the end.

Pemberton's loud Scottish-accented voice, combined with Cooper laughing loudly as they approached down the corridor, awakened Tariq from his slumber. He got to his feet and walked shakily over to Nathan on the balcony. 'Nathan, do me a favour, would you? Go back in there and be polite to Pemberton and Cooper, would you? I'm half asleep. Ask them if you can have another Guinness.'

Nathan reluctantly agreed, and soon came back with a pint of Guinness. Pemberton and Cooper seemed happy enough discussing something or another, so Tariq thought it better not to interrupt them. The light was fading now, and banks of bright stadium lights lit up the athletics track and everything going on within. Sometime later, Tariq told Nathan, 'Get Pemberton and Cooper – Jessica Ennis is about to run the eight hundred metres. Quick, it's about to start.'

Pemberton and Cooper joined Tariq and Nathan on the balcony. The four looked out onto the oval track below as the starting pistol echoed around the stadium. The crowd roared into life. Ennis was ahead as the bell went for the final lap. Pemberton shouted to Tariq and Nathan, 'She's going to do it! She only needs to finish. It would be incredible if she could win it!' Ennis was third at the six hundred-metre mark and looked to be dropping back. At one hundred metres to go, the crowd hushed as she fell back to fourth, but she dug in and kicked again down the home straight. With sixty metres to go, the crowd roared her on again as she pushed on past Theisen, the Canadian, and Chernova, the Russian.

Cooper bellowed out, 'Yeah! Yeah! What a finish!' Nathan had had enough of the noise and retreated behind the glass wall, shutting the door behind him. To calm himself down, he helped himself to another Guinness from the fridge.

About twenty minutes later, Tariq banged on the glass door, 'Nathan, come out here, it's Greg Rutherford, he could be on for a medal in the long jump. He's getting ready for his second jump now; look, there he is.' The crowd started to clap him on in unison. Tariq explained, 'Look, he always follows the same routine to get himself psyched up. He slaps his left thigh twice, shakes his left fist, plants his right foot, looks down, leans forward, looks down the track, looks down again, wiggles the fingers, moves one step forward into a running stance, rocks forward, left leg goes back again, right foot points upwards on his heel, head down – he's off! Accelerating, accelerating, accelerating – take-off! Wow! That looks like a big one… eight point two one metres! He's top!'

After several jumps from other athletes, it came to the fourth round. Rutherford followed his set routine, charged down the runway, and took off, flying above the yellow Olympic sand. 'What a jump, Nathan! That's eight point three one metres; that's his best yet.' At that moment the starting pistol for the ten thousand metres went off. Mo Farah and twenty-eight other athletes set off at breakneck speed around the track. Three and a half laps into the race, Tariq announced to all, 'He's done it, he's done it – Rutherford's got the gold; that's one we never expected! Now, can Mo get another one? Where is he? Look, he's in the middle of the pack, there.' At the three thousand-metre mark, he was in eleventh place, keeping steady with metronome-like strides.

At the halfway point, the time was just over fourteen minutes. The commentator announced, 'It's on the slow side, so the pace will probably pick up in the second half of the race.' Mo was in seventh place but not too far behind. With ten laps to go, Mo Farah dropped back a couple of places, then with four laps to go he took the lead.

Tariq shouted out, 'Come on, Mo; you can do it!' With two laps to go, the runners were bunching up at the front, but Mo was holding his own in second place. The bell rang for the final lap; the crowd went wild as Mo edged in front. At two hundred metres, he was just ahead but was being chased down by the Bekele brothers from Ethiopia.

Coming up to the home straight, Mo opened up his stride and pushed ahead. 'Yes! Yes! Go on Mo... he's got the gold!' Tariq turned to Nathan. 'You won't forget today, will you, son? This could be the greatest day in GB's Olympic history ever! You probably won't see something like this again in your lifetime!'

CHAPTER 21

The following morning, a Sunday, Tariq sauntered down the stairs in odd socks and with a pink shirt hanging out, rubbing his eyes as he entered the kitchen.

'Morning, Dad. Did you sleep well?' said Nathan, eating a bowl of cornflakes on the kitchen table with a cup of weak tea.

'Great, thank you, Nathan,' said Tariq with a hint of sarcasm. 'You?'

'Yes. Like a snoring log.'

'What a day yesterday, hey? We'll never see the likes of that again in our lives. Two gold medals in the morning, and then three more within an hour right in front of our eyes. Incredible!'

'Six, actually, Dad. We won six gold medals yesterday. We missed the women's cycling team pursuit in the afternoon. So far, we've won fourteen gold medals, seven silver and eight bronze. I don't understand why we've got more gold medals than silver and bronze because they are supposed to be the harder ones to win. I think that the silver medals look better than the gold ones. How can an orangey colour be better than sparkly grey?'

'Well, gold is more expensive; everybody knows that, but I hadn't thought about Team GB winning more golds than silver and bronze. You're right – that is a bit strange, but it'll probably even itself out by the end. Anyway, it's even better to have more gold medals, regardless of what you think about the colours, I'm afraid, Nathan!'

Tariq phoned Alice to find out about Millie. He was relieved to hear that she had now stabilised, and was conscious. Mid-morning, Tariq and Nathan went into Bromley to shop for food and clothes, as the bigger shops were open on Sunday. Tariq left Nathan to take his time to look at jumpers and had a pub lunch with a couple of pints of pale ale. While Tariq was in the pub, a text came through from Cheryl saying how nauseous she was feeling with the pregnancy. She said she needed extra money for baby clothes, a cot, and a pram. 'Bloody hell!' Tariq exclaimed to himself. He replied that Millie's treatment was expensive, and his credit rating had already been affected as they'd missed a payment on the mortgage. He suggested that she ask her family to help out, then directed her not to contact him on this number again and to use his private Hotmail account. Cheryl replied that she'd already sent him three emails, but he hadn't responded. Tariq apologised that he'd had a lot on his mind recently.

Late afternoon, Tariq and Nathan drove to Camberwell to visit Millie at King's College Hospital, as arranged. Alice and her mother, Margaret, were already by her bed.

'Hello, darling; hello Millie, Margaret,' said Tariq. He exchanged brief hugs and kisses with his wife and his daughter, in her bed, and less enthusiastically with his mother-in-law. Millie gave Nathan a high five, the best she could in her tired state.

'How are you, Millie, my gorgeous?' said her father, holding her hand at the bedside.

'I'm feeling slightly better today. I've got my appetite back. Mum brought me some lamb stew in a flask; much better than the bland stuff they serve here,' Millie whispered so not to offend the other patients who didn't have such an option.

'That's great to hear, Millie. The medication is working.'

Tariq looked across at Alice, who was wiping a tear from her eye after four weeks of emotional exhaustion, followed by a brief smile of hope for Millie's recovery.

Millie said, 'The consultant told us that I should go home soon so I am in the comfort of my own home.'

Alice said, 'I'll be coming with her to look after her at home. I've told work that I'm taking some time off; they were very understanding.' Tariq inwardly grimaced as her taking time off would mean less money coming in; she, like Cheryl, was freelance with no holiday pay.

Nathan said, 'That would be much better. I've missed you, Millie, it's so much more fun when you're at home. You know me better than anyone.'

'Thank you, Nathan. I've missed you too.'

'I've bought the *Guess Who* game. Do you want to have a quick game?'

'Yes, go on, Nathan. Put it on the bed here, on the tray.'

Millie and Nathan each selected their mystery person and took it in turns to guess the characteristics of the other person's character with questions like, do they wear glasses, or a hat? Have blonde hair, or no hair? Are they male or female?

Nathan soon asked Millie excitedly, 'Is your mystery person Victor?'

'Yes, it is! You've got to admit, Nathan, that was a lucky guess, wasn't it?'

'Yes, well, that's all part of the game, isn't it?'

Tariq said to Nathan, 'Now, don't wear Millie out, will you? She needs to conserve her energy.'

Millie said in his defence, 'Dad, please; I need to have some fun in here. I'm lucky I've got Nathan to play with. It's dead boring for most of the day on my own.' Millie and Nathan promptly embarked on another game.

***

Monday morning, Tariq and Nathan caught the usual train from Eden Park. As they approached the office, a uniformed police officer with a moustache and menacing manner, flanked by a police sergeant, stepped out in front of Tariq and Nathan from their police car, blocking their path. The second officer said with cold authority, 'Morning, Tariq. We meet again. Did you enjoy the Olympics yesterday?'

'Hello, Randall. What do you want now? Can I please just get on with my life, for God's sake? I have things to do.'

'Yes Tariq, you can get on with your life as soon as you come with us to the police station. If you've got nothing to hide, you won't have a problem with that, will you?'

Tariq looked around briefly to see if anyone from the office was looking on; he couldn't see anybody. He said to Nathan, 'Sorry about this, son. I'll be back as soon as I've answered a few questions from these clowns. Can you carry on sorting the documents in the property room? If anyone asks where I am, tell them I've gone to the hospital on the way to work to drop off something for Millie. OK?'

Nathan looked confused. 'What clowns?'

'These two clowns dressed as policemen – it's a joke, Nathan, please!'

'Hilarious, I'm sure,' said DI Randall. The sergeant smirked.

Nathan asked, 'What were you dropping off to Millie? Someone might ask me.'

'Anything! A hot water bottle as she's cold in bed.'

The sergeant came round the back of the car. 'Get in please, sir – we have things to do as well, and it's not standing round here talking to jokers like you. I'm sure you don't want me to have to bundle you into the car outside the office.'

'OK, OK!' Tariq sat on the back seat, and the sergeant shut the door behind him.

On arriving at Bishopsgate Police Station, Tariq was relieved of his leather satchel man bag, the same bag he'd taken to the Olympics. He hadn't checked its contents since then. Tariq was left for a few minutes in the compact police kitchen to help himself to tea or coffee. He made a white instant coffee and was sipping it when DI Randall walked up to him, accompanied by the younger police sergeant.

'Follow me please, Tariq,' said Randall. He led the way down the stairs to the same basement room he'd been interviewed in the week before. Tariq flinched on entering the same damp concrete room, but at least he was familiar with it now. He steeled himself. He'd survived last time, and he'd do the same again today.

'Sorry to drag you down here again, Tariq; the redecorating upstairs is taking longer than we thought. Anyway, here we are again. Take a seat.' Randall informed him that the interview was being recorded and asked, 'Is this your bag, Tariq, this leather satchel bag?'

'Yes, of course it is. You know it is. Why are you asking stupid questions?'

'We've just found these inside your bag. Recognise these, Tariq?' Randall placed three A4-size, high-resolution colour photos of him and Cheryl in Finsbury Park café on the table. Tariq stared at the pictures in disbelief.

'I've never seen them before! This is just another set-up! Somebody is stalking me. Why don't you go after them? I need protection, that's what I need. Why am I being followed? Before you say the obvious, yes, she's pregnant; we met for a coffee on a sunny day. There's no law against that is there, for God's sake?'

'This is getting beyond a coincidence, isn't it, Tariq? Twice you've been here, and twice we've been looking at photos of you with the same woman. So why would someone go to all that trouble? There must be some reason, mustn't there? It seems that it's obvious to everyone, except you, Tariq.'

'Beats the hell out of me. I don't know what the hell is going on here. I have nothing to say to you.'

DI Randall put on his over-friendly tone. 'As I said to you the last time we spoke, if someone is blackmailing you, then you just have to be straight with us; we can give you all the help you need. So please, Tariq, this is your chance to come clean. To get a clean slate, as it were.'

Tariq looked back at Randall, considering his options. Was this the right juncture to feed him something? 'Look, I admit I'm worried about these photos. I love my wife and my family, and these could make it bad for me. At the same time, I've received no demands, no threats, nothing. If and when I do, I shall let you know, OK? But how did you even know those photos were in my bag? And why did you get the hotel photos instead of me? I'm asking myself. The simple answer is that someone wants you to believe that I'm being blackmailed, when I'm not. Have you considered that?'

'Oh, we consider everything Tariq, everything – bluff, double bluff, half-truths, lies, etcetera, etcetera. So why would someone want to make us think that? Enlighten me.'

'To put me in the frame for the Magnus Conan case when it goes bum-down, boobs-up, as we say in Bosnia. Or to get me kicked off the case to get me out of the way.'

Randall leant forward, closer to Tariq, and said, 'A little bird tells me that the Magnus Conan case you're working on is being sabotaged; documents have gone missing, the master ledger is being doctored. Ring any bells?'

'Who told you that? It's obvious; it's Harper, Stuart Harper, probably working for Burton. You should be talking to him, not me. Speak to Pemberton – he'll tell you what Burton's up to.'

'We will, Tariq. Rest assured, we will be. But we are talking to you today, so let's not get off-topic. Burton, you say? He's the Case Director, isn't he?'

'Yes, and he's also the Head of Investigations.'

'The problem is, Tariq, what we need is evidence. If you want to clear your name, get some evidence so we can get Harper.'

'I'm trying! It's not as easy as you think when all eyes are on you.'

'I suggest you try real hard, Tariq.'

'Right, yes, I will. Can I please get out of this room now? It gives me the creeps.'

'Not yet, Tariq. We haven't even got to the reason we brought you here in the first place.' The sergeant slid some official Home Office-headed papers across the table towards Tariq with his full name printed on them. Tariq thought this unusual, as he rarely used both middle names as written in full on his passport. The papers were dated January 1996 and titled *Asylum Application*.

Tariq looked up at the sergeant. 'What are these? Why are you showing me these?'

'Can you confirm that your full name, as stated on your asylum application, is Tariq Ivanovic Davud Markovic?'

'Yes, that's my full name – so what?'

'You were granted asylum from Bosnia in 1996, weren't you? And then UK citizenship in 2001, yeah?'

'Yes. So?'

'Do you know how many Bosnian refugees were granted asylum that quickly after the war? Only six. Your case was considered a special case because your family in Bosnia couldn't be traced, nor could you be traced on any database records. Considering you couldn't remember anything of your former life in Bosnia, it was considered inhumane to send you back there, and especially as you were suffering from PTSD. It was as if you'd never existed. Very odd, or you could say very smart, couldn't you, Taric?'

'Sod off! Do you think that I invented my memory loss? That's horse shit. You can speak to my doctor if you want. I have nightmares and flashbacks. I wish I could remember more. I really do.'

DI Randall walked back towards the interview table. 'So you could be anybody, couldn't you?'

'What do you mean?'

'You could be, say, Karlo Mitchko's long-lost cousin, who now conveniently works at the Serious Fraud Office. He's at the centre of the whole fraud case you're working on, is he not? It would be convenient if an insider working on his case could lose a few key documents to ensure that the fraud charges against him didn't stick, especially now that he's being extradited from Serbia. The noose is tightening around his neck, don't you think? He must be getting desperate by now.'

Tariq jolted upright, his chair falling backwards behind him. 'That's total bullshit! I don't remember Bosnia, but that doesn't mean you start making stuff up.'

'It's just another little coincidence, isn't it, Tariq? As I said, we consider *all* angles. That's our job.'

'Have you finished? This is plainly a stupid line of questioning. Can I go now, please?'

'Sit down! I haven't finished yet.'

'Please, what now?'

'It looks like we may have found your uncle, Dr Safan Bromisch. Does that name ring any bells?'

Tariq didn't expect this. 'No. No, I'm afraid it doesn't. This is getting more bizarre.'

DI Randall continued, 'And there's another coincidence – he's an associate of Karlo Mitchko. Fancy that.' Tariq sunk his head into his hands, his forehead damp with sweat; the scar on the left side of his forehead was redder than usual. DI Randall, now seated at the table, waited in silence for Tariq to... confess, perhaps?

Tariq spoke into his palms, his voice now trembling. 'Why is this happening to me? This can't be happening to me. This is another set-up! Who told you about this stooge, and why is he looking for me now, seventeen years later?'

'He probably thought you were dead with the rest of them. The Bosnian authorities made some enquiries and showed your picture around Visegrad. Dr Bromisch thinks that you could be his nephew. How do you know he's not your uncle when you can't remember anyone? I strongly recommend that you cooperate. Otherwise, I'll be tempted to detain you for forty-eight hours, for starters. We've already made arrangements for you to visit him in Montenegro. Some of my colleagues think I am too trusting, allowing you to leave the country, but I believe you and I have an understanding, don't we?'

Tariq dropped his hands from his face and said quietly, 'Yes, OK, I'll go. I'll have to clear the time off with the SFO.'

'No need for that, Tariq. You'll be going this Friday night, returning Sunday. We'll fly you out on Friday to Tivat, Montenegro, from Gatwick. Your uncle, as he claims, will be travelling over from Bosnia. Your police escort will give you the details en route. Be ready with an overnight bag on Friday at 10:30pm for a pick-up from your home. Failure to show up will be considered non-cooperation with the police, and we could start talking to the immigration authorities...'

'I said I'll go, damn it!'

'Good, good. Interview terminated.'

The police were discreet enough to drop Tariq off on a side street, out of view from the SFO office. He took a few deep breaths as he approached the office steps and straightened his tie. He considered that the police had nothing on him; why should he be worried?

'Morning, Beryl. Alright?'

'Good. I heard you had a good time at the Olympics. Three gold medals in less than an hour – that's why they're calling it super-Saturday. Nathan told me everything on his way in this morning. I hear Millie is cold in bed in the hospital.'

'Cold?'

'Yes, cold – that's why you took the hot water bottles to her this morning. All six of them.'

'Oh, of course; yes, the hot water bottles. I don't know why he said I'd taken six of them, though?'

'Well, he said Millie would need one under each leg and each arm, then one between her legs and one under her head so she would be warm all over.'

'Cooked all over, more like. I don't know where he gets his ideas from. I'll tell Millie that the next time we see her – that'll make her laugh. Anyway, see you later, Beryl.'

Tariq went up to his desk, made himself a coffee and went down to the property room. He was surprised to find Sandra there and not Nathan. She was collecting some of her personal effects and putting them into a cardboard box with her name on it. 'Hi, Sandra. What are you up to?' She turned to Tariq with a face like thunder.

'Hello, Tariq.' She then pointed upwards and said just above a whisper, 'Is this place bugged? I'll speak to you outside in a minute.' Sandra finished packing her box and left the room. Tariq followed her down the steps to the lower basement room with the skip. There were no cameras in the room, and it was unlikely there would be recording devices.

'What's up, Sandra?'

She said with emotion, 'I've been taken off the case, that's what.'

'Why, what for, who…?'

'Pemberton, that's who. He said he suspected somebody was tampering with the disclosure documentation. He couldn't tell me anything specific until he had concluded his investigations, but said it would be best that I was transferred to another case. For pity's sake, Tariq – you've been emailing me copy documents; how would I explain that? I've had to delete everything, and I suggest you do the same. What gets my goat is that he probably thinks that I'm colluding with you on the whole thing. You should have told him straight when you noticed something was wrong.'

'How could I? Without evidence, I can't go around accusing Harper or anybody else. That's what I was trying to do – collect evidence.'

'Well, it's too late now. I can't help you anymore, and I would be very careful if I were you. There's a lot of shit going around – first Cheryl and now me, and you'll be next. I shouldn't be seen with you like this; it just adds to everyone's suspicions. Before I go, I should tell you something about the property room.'

'What?'

Footsteps could be heard coming down the stairs a few flights up.

'I've got to go, Tariq. I can't be seen down here with you.'

'What is it? What about the property room?'

'The small corner room, the cleaners' storeroom. I saw…'

The footsteps were getting louder now.

'What, Sandra? What did you see?'

Sandra walked off briskly into the car park and out of sight. The footsteps above continued past, probably towards the post room on the other side of the corridor, leaving Tariq alone in silence. This was a setback. In shock with Sandra's departure, he leaned heavily against the half-full yellow skip, with orange elephant trunking hanging from the ceiling above.

CHAPTER 22

On the train home, Nathan smiled to himself. He was looking forward to Millie coming home soon. Playing the *Guess Who* game with her for the first time in the hospital had given him a glimmer of hope that normality could return with her recovery. Tariq didn't want to burst his bubble and just smiled back. It was a small mercy that she would be coming home on the Tuesday after his planned trip to Montenegro for the weekend to meet his phantom uncle. He didn't have a choice in the matter. Since they hadn't seen each other for at least seventeen years, would his uncle even recognise him? He'd had an army-regulation crew cut hairstyle back then. His hair was now a thick, unkempt, brown mane. He remembered his promise to his wife that he would get it cut when Millie came home.

Near their train stop at Eden Park, Nathan handed Tariq a small yellow square Post-it note with *No.78* written in blue biro. Tariq asked, 'Where did you find this?'

'It was stuck to the back of my puzzle book when I picked it up from the property room yesterday.'

Tariq surmised that it was a tag someone had made for one of the case documents, which had accidentally got stuck to the puzzle book. He put it in the bin when disembarking the train.

Tariq reheated the fish pie he'd made on Sunday with freshly boiled peas. Nathan ate his dinner while watching the *Phonejack* comedy TV programme, mimicking the comedic accents of the characters. Halfway through the show, he heard a scream of annoyance from his father in the study.

'Nathan, come in here now!' Nathan pressed the mute button on the TV remote and entered the study with dread at the cause of his father's rage. 'Nathan, what the hell have you done with my prize office team photograph?' he shouted at him, while holding up the now-blank photo frame in one hand and the *Guess Who* game in the other. Nathan had replaced the *Guess Who* game characters with real faces cut out from the photograph with name labels. Tariq added, 'That picture was irreplaceable; it will never happen again, do you understand me? And you've ruined it. Bloody hell, Nathan, what were you thinking?'

'I thought the game would be better if you could use real faces.' Nathan then went into defensive mode, saying, 'Not arguing; I'm not arguing. I'm going to my bedroom now.' He stomped up the stairs into his bedroom, shutting the door behind him. With Nathan gone, Tariq threw the *Guess Who* game across the room in anger, its pieces shattering over the wooden floor, some bouncing off the back wall.

He left the scattered mini-framed face tiles on the floor and went across the hallway into the kitchen. He reached for a glass from the cupboard, opened the freezer door, dropped in some ice, and filled it with whisky from the drinks cabinet in the sitting room. He slumped down on the padded armchair facing the TV, switching the programme over from *Phonejack* to the last episode of Series 1 of *Line of Duty* that he'd recorded on the Sky+ box. He swigged down half of the whisky and placed the glass on the casual table at the side of the chair, paused the TV, and put his head in his hands. Being abandoned by Sandra, his last confidant at work, when the police were breathing down his neck, was a body blow. He had earlier ignored yet another email from Cheryl asking again for money. His credit rating had gone down again, and his wife had stopped working at the very time they needed money to survive. If his wife found out about Cheryl, his marriage would be over anyway, and the Bosnians would still be looking for him.

'Oh God,' he mumbled into the now-empty glass. He thought back to Sandra. Pemberton had thrown her off the case and he would most likely be next. It occurred to him that this meant he had to move fast to find the evidence against Harper before it was too late. The changes to the ledgers were something tangible that he could use as evidence to prove his innocence to Pemberton and the police. He still had the original version Nathan had copied when he first arrived, and a few later copies that he'd emailed to Sandra. Nathan had shown him the metadata listings in the office, revealing who had accessed the files, and when. Stuart Harper's name appeared the most.

The *Line of Duty* programme ended. He returned to the study to pick up the pieces of the *Guess Who* game off the floor and put them in the box, which he took upstairs to Nathan's bedroom. The door was firmly locked.

'Nathan?'

'What is it?'

'Sorry, Nathan, for shouting. I've brought you the game

with the faces on it, just as you made it. You can keep it if you like?'

'Thank you, Dad. That's good of you. Leave it in the study for now. I don't want it now. Sorry for cutting up the photograph. I should have asked you first.'

'Don't worry about it then. I was going to take it down anyway. It's quite an old photograph, which is probably why I like it, because I look younger! I had short black hair back then. I've got a lot of things on my mind, you see.'

'Yes Dad, I understand as well. I won't say anything about the police, I promise.'

'Thanks, Nathan. Goodnight.'

'Goodnight, Dad.'

***

On the train journey the next morning, Tariq was reading the free London paper, the *Metro*. There was more coverage of the Olympics and an article with diagrams of the Mars rover Curiosity, which had just landed after an eight-month transit through space. It was designed to investigate Mars for its habitability in advance of a possible human mission. He mused frivolously that he should volunteer.

In the office, Tariq found a 1GB memory stick in his desk's top drawer. This amount of memory was more than enough to download the ledgers from the PC in the property room. Plugging anything into work PCs without approval from your head of department was forbidden, following a cyber-attack caused by a similar memory stick earlier in the year. Notwithstanding this, the PC USB ports were now locked down against transferring files. The downloaded malware virus had almost shut down all the SFO servers before it could be isolated. The potential large-scale loss of highly sensitive legal documents and prosecution evidence collected over many years would have severely embarrassed the SFO.

Nathan looked across at his father nervously; he was twiddling the silver memory stick in his hand. Nathan said quietly, 'Dad, you know those things are banned here, don't you? It was part of my office induction training, but I might have a way around it if you're really desperate.'

Burton approached from behind. 'Tariq, I hear you and Nathan had a swell time with Nigel at the Olympics on Saturday!' he bellowed. Tariq closed his hand over the memory stick, hiding it behind his back as naturally as he could as he turned round to face him. Burton paused and examined him. In that moment, Tariq feared that Burton's army training had sensed that his posture was that of someone concealing a weapon. Perhaps it was just a reflex that Burton couldn't help, even now. Burton continued, 'What a night, hey buddy, for UK sport! A great night, hey! Sorry to disturb your morning, buddy, but can you come over to my office now?'

'Of course, no problem.' Tariq threw the memory stick backwards into Nathan's lap as he walked away with Burton. Nathan put it in his bag.

On the way, Burton recounted some of the highlights of the Olympics. 'That Chris Hoy of yours is built for speed on a cycle, ain't he, by God! By heck – six gold medals! Now that's an impressive record for anyone.'

Once behind his desk, Burton's expression morphed into a serious mode. 'Do you know what, Tariq? I trust you.

I trust you, soldier, to level with me – man to man. You and I have been through a hell of a lot on the battlefield in our time. We've faced the worst and survived to tell the tale. We've both gone through it, haven't we, Tariq? And I want you to survive this case and come out smelling of roses.' Burton paused. 'Do you know what the sweetest smelling roses need to grow?'

'No.'

'You cover them in piles of rotten horse shit – that stuff reeks. I should know; I've seen and smelt enough of it on my ranch back in Texas, I can tell you. So, if you've got some shit to get off your chest, you go on and tell me right now, buddy.'

'What do you mean? I'm just doing my job. We're a bit behind with the document sifting, but that happens all the time.'

Burton fixed his eyes on Tariq, examining him for a twitch of hidden guilt. Tariq didn't give him any.

'Did you know that we've taken Sandra off the case?'

'Yes, I heard.'

'You heard? Who told you?'

'She did.'

'What did she tell you?'

'Just that she was needed in the St Albans office.'

Burton paused again, eyeballing Tariq. 'That's right, she's needed at St Albans…'

The phone rang. Burton took the call and waved Tariq out of his office.

On his way back to his desk, he considered what Pemberton had said to him at the Olympics about Burton's unauthorised initiative to set up the remote CCTV system.

If Burton was the mastermind undermining the Karlo Mitchko case, any evidence he provided to him would be destroyed or, worse still, pinned on himself. On the other hand, Burton would enjoy kicking his Limey arse if he found out that he hadn't been straight with him about the corrupted ledgers. Perhaps he'd bought himself some time to download the ledgers before they denied him access to the case files; and possibly shut down his work email account completely. Would he last the week?

Tariq made himself a coffee in the fourth-floor kitchen, which he took down to the property room. Only Nathan was in there. Tariq asked quietly, 'Nathan, I hoped to find you here. Have you got the memory stick?' Nathan reached for his bag and checked for activity in the corridor before handing it to him. 'Thanks. Please tell me, Nathan, how can I use this thing? You said you had a way around it. I'm desperate, son.'

'I can help you best if you remain calm and don't freak me out. It doesn't help me if you are in panic mode, OK?'

'Sorry, Nathan. Sorry, son, for all of this.' Tariq took a tissue from his pocket and wiped his sweat-laden forehead. His scar was a brighter red. Nathan walked over to one of the metal cupboards on the far side of the room and brought out an old laptop with a few leads. He said, 'I tried this laptop last week, and it works. Look – it has a network and a USB socket. This is an old one; it hasn't even got an SFO asset number sticker. I doubt it's been configured with the USB port locked. The IT department probably don't know it's here.'

'So can we set it up?'

'I've thought about this. It's no good plugging it in

on the desk here as you wouldn't have time to hide if you heard someone coming down the corridor. It's best to put it in the drawer here; it just fits. You can feed the network cable from the back of the drawer under the table into the intranet port at floor level. How long would you need the laptop for, Dad?'

'About forty minutes. I need to go through my emails to find the temporary ledger files and match them up with the final versions, and check the timelines on the files.'

'Forty minutes! That's way too long. Ajay, the security guy, told me that unless a PC or laptop's IP address is registered on the SFO main server, it will shut it down when it refreshes the IP address scan every eight minutes. The problem is we wouldn't know when it will refresh, so we won't know how much time we'll have before we're locked out. To save time, you should copy the files onto your personal drive on the main PC here and download the whole directory in one go. By the way, Dad, they'll know which port it's plugged into in the building. They might come up here looking for the laptop, so you would have to get out pretty quick.'

The lift dinged down the corridor: Nathan grabbed the laptop with the bundle of cables and slid it onto the upper shelf of the cupboard where he'd found it. He attempted to shut the metal door, but one of the cables snagged in it, so the door re-opened slightly, with a loop of black cable hanging out. Simon Beecham entered the room and looked straight at Nathan beside the cupboard door. Tariq said to Nathan, 'There's nothing in there, Nathan; just shut the door, will you, please?' Then he turned towards the door. 'Hello, Simon, how's it going? Glad you're here as we're still behind with cataloguing this lot.'

'Yeah, I know, that's why I'm here. I'm going to try to finish off a box today.'

'Great, thanks. Appreciated.'

Nathan asked, 'What shall I do, Dad?'

Tariq walked over to the open shelves on the opposite side of the room, grabbed a black sack and emptied its contents on the table in front of him. 'Can you group this lot together like you've done for the boxes? It's a dirty job, Nathan, but someone's got to do it.'

'You're not wrong, Dad. There's dust all over everything.'

Simon smiled at Nathan and joked, 'Is your dad giving you all the dirty jobs to do? I know exactly how you feel, Nathan.' He smiled at Tariq.

The rest of the morning was spent in the property room, progressing the case filing. After lunch, Beecham completed logging a large box of documents. There were now about fifteen boxes on the Relevant Material shelf. Tariq sorted another box of files, although most were obviously irrelevant – mainly lists of Magnus Conan-Whittaker staff receipts, including taxi fares and hotel stays. Nathan created several piles of common document types from the contents of the black sack. Tariq couldn't help thinking that regardless of the day's good progress, he would still be unceremoniously dumped off the case and given his marching orders, unless he had some definitive evidence to support his innocence. The police were bound to say something to Pemberton soon about Cheryl and the suspected blackmail, if they hadn't already.

CHAPTER 23

Tariq didn't say much on the train on the way home. He asked Nathan if he knew how to break the code on the keypad door lock for the cleaners' storeroom, or if he could ask his friend Ajay in security. The answer was 'no' on both counts.

Tariq cooked up bangers and mash with peas for dinner. Nathan went upstairs to his bedroom, and Tariq watched the Olympic highlights of the day in the lounge. Alistair Brownlee had won the gold in the triathlon, it was gold in team dressage, and also for Chris Hoy and Laura Trot in the cycling. He poured himself another whisky. There was no Coke left, so he drank it neat with ice. He stared into the glass and asked his reliable liquid gold friend Jack D, 'Any ideas? Any bright ideas? I could get a gun and hold Pemberton hostage until someone got a copy of the ledgers to prove that Harper set me up. Then they'd believe me, wouldn't they? I would make him confess to sabotaging the Magnus Conan case. I would be vindicated and live happily ever after, wouldn't I?'

Nathan was walking past the sitting room at the time. 'Dad, are you talking to yourself? Mum says that's annoying.'

'Hey Nathan, sonny boy. Now I'm talking to you. This

is a bit late for you, isn't it? It's ten thirty; have all your clocks stopped?'

'No, they're all working, thank you, so you don't need to worry about that.'

'Glad to hear it, Nathan. I won't worry about your clocks, then; that is a great relief to me.'

'I think you're drunk. It doesn't help anything. You know that, don't you?'

Tariq looked down again at his near-empty cut-glass tumbler. 'Did you hear that, Jack? He doesn't appreciate all the help you've given me in the biggest shitstorm of my life.'

'Dad, please, listen to me; I've had an idea. You need to listen, OK? It's important.'

'Nathan, I'm all ears and no brain in between! Shoot!'

'You know the problem with the SFO computer network servers blocking the unregistered laptop when the scan refreshes every eight minutes? I've worked out a way of knowing when it refreshes. You'll then have eight minutes to log in and download the files onto the memory stick. That should be enough. I've got a better memory stick I can give you which will allow you to download the files quicker.'

Tariq put his glass down carefully on the occasional table. 'How could you possibly know when it refreshes, Nathan? How?'

'I'll take my laptop to the office tomorrow, log in, and when it locks me out, then we'll know. There's a network socket extension in the lower basement room; I can connect from there, and unplug it as soon as it detects my location. I'll ring you, and you can start your log in – yeah? I'm going to bed now. We can talk about it in the morning.'

'Do you know what, Nathan? You're not just an ugly face, you know. That could work... that could work.'

'I think the expression is "pretty face", actually.'

'Well, in your case...'

'Funny, Dad. I see you're in joke mode; I should have known. Goodnight.' Nathan ascended the stairs.

***

Tariq asked Nathan on the train in, 'Did you bring your laptop?'

'Yes, Dad, I've brought it; it's here,' Nathan said, as he lifted his laptop out from his bag.

'Oh, OK, thanks.'

'Well, I figured that you don't have another option.'

Tariq half smiled back, thinking that Pemberton could have already taken him off the case and blocked his access to the SFO servers.

Beryl wasn't at the reception desk, which was a rare occasion; a sign, perhaps, Tariq thought, that today wouldn't be a typical day. He caught a fleeting glimpse of Stuart Harper's bright purple tie as he entered the lift. Tariq could feel an involuntary release of adrenalin into his system, increasing his heartbeat by a notch.

On the fourth floor, Tariq put his briefcase under his desk and walked across to the kitchen. Nathan followed him and dispensed a hot chocolate into his Cadbury's mug. Tariq had a strong coffee.

Someone said from across the kitchen, 'Hi, Tariq, how's it going?'

'Stephen, hi. Yes, fine. What're you doing here? A meeting? You look smarter than usual.'

'Pemberton's summoned me to his office.' By the way, did you hear? Nadir was found guilty! I can't tell you how relieved I am. I've been on that case for three years now. The thing is, Tariq, Pemberton mentioned to me a few weeks back that when the Nadir case is over, he wants me to help you out on the Magnus Conan-Whittaker case. That's why I wanted to speak to you first. He was talking about me taking over the senior disclosure officer role, or at least some aspects of it. That's your position, as far as I know, isn't it? So I don't understand what Pemberton has in mind.' Stephen continued, 'I can see by the look on your face, Tariq, that Pemberton's told you bugger-all, as is his style. He wants me to start Monday, but I'll tell you something, Tariq – I need a rest. In the words of Arnie, "I need a vacation".'

'You're right, Stephen; I'm the last to know what's going on in my own case. That would just be too easy, wouldn't it? I would appreciate it if you could push it back for a couple of weeks. I need time to tidy a few things up, but don't tell him that.'

'Oh, sure; suits me, mate, believe me.'

'Thanks.'

'No worries, Tariq. Must go. Maybe I'll see you at the staff meeting at two o'clock.'

'Oh yeah, the staff meeting. They're holding them almost weekly now, aren't they?'

Tariq, Nathan and Simon Beecham spent most of the morning in the property room, sifting through separate boxes of documents. Beecham was excited to find an email sent directly from Karlo Mitchko requesting a direct transfer of funds from one of the Magnus Conan business accounts into an account in Serbia, supposedly to cover a sizeable invoice from one of the oil rig maintenance companies. If this account could be linked to Mitchko, it would be a clear piece of evidence of the fraud that he continued to deny any personal knowledge of. It certainly debunked his declarations that he wasn't aware of the bank transfers. This document was therefore classified in the Very Relevant category and filed on the top shelf. Tariq considered that at least Beecham witnessed this document's existence if it later disappeared. It also occurred to Tariq that Beecham wouldn't have made a fuss about the Mitchko email if he was the one removing key evidence; if he was the culprit, he would have quietly destroyed the email. Tariq then copied the email before Harper could get his dirty hands on it. Tariq knew that he was in a cleft stick, with the threat of the photos of him and Cheryl being released if the SFO won the case.

Beecham left the property room just before eleven o'clock for a meeting unconnected to the case. Tariq was on the central square desk PC and asked Nathan, 'Do you know how this file audit tab works?'

'Dad, I can see you haven't read or understood any of the training information on the caseload software system. You can use it to trace the history of any file or document.'

'Really? Can you show me, then?'

'Look, Dad, if you select this file here, for example, you can see that you scanned it in on 5th May 2012, S Beecham viewed the file on 7th May, and S Harper copied it on 8th May.'

'Copied it? Why would he want to do that?'

'No idea, don't ask me; I wasn't even here! If you sort

the files into categories with VR at the top, you can see...'
Nathan looked at the data on the screen before him and
paused in silent contemplation.

'What? Nathan!'

'Please don't shout at me, Dad, when it's not my fault,
like you do most of the time. S Harper has copied all the VR
files – literally *all* of them. Also, there is something strange
going on with the audit data as right at the bottom of the list
there are about twenty files with a note: *Unknown, Deleted.
No data available.*'

'So... what does that mean, Nathan?'

'I don't know for sure, but someone has deleted the
original file, and the audit trail file.'

'So we'll never know, then, what those files were, or
what happened to them?'

Nathan explained, 'Wait... let me see if I can recover
them. I can run a search for the last month to see what I can
find in the computer's recycle bin.' Nathan then pressed a
few keys and waited for the search to finish.

Tariq grew impatient, 'Any luck?'

'Got 'em! Would you believe it? There are sixteen
deleted document files and seven audit files. I can select
these and undelete them. I'll save them in the directory,
ready for you to download... Someone's coming, Dad.'

Tariq stepped back and turned to face the shelves
behind him as Mark Cooper entered the room.

'Hi, Tariq.'

'Hi, Mark. Come to help out?'

Nathan shut down the ledger on the PC and went back
to sorting a pile of papers he'd previously arranged on the
side of the table. Cooper asked Tariq if he'd found any more

foreign correspondence that would need translating. Tariq replied in the negative, and Cooper promptly left the room. Tariq sat down and took a deep breath, mainly in relief that it had been Cooper instead of Harper.

SFO staff started to gather on the sixth floor in the breakout area for the staff meeting, which was due to start shortly at two o'clock. Tariq had arranged with Nathan to take advantage of most people being at the staff meeting to sneak away to log in with their laptops to download the original case ledger files. Pemberton would probably be first up, followed by Burton. Tariq wanted to create a semblance of an alibi by being seen by both Pemberton and Burton at their presentations, so they would wait until Burton had started his speech, before sloping off down to the property room. Pemberton kicked off as predicted – delighted to announce that Asil Nadir had been found guilty of ten counts of theft to the tune of thirty million pounds. The office in-joke was that the total value of missing funds was near one hundred and fifty million – so who'd made off with the other one hundred and twenty million? Pemberton remarked that Nadir would have to swap his twenty thousand-a-week rented house for much smaller shared accommodation at Her Majesty's pleasure. The food wouldn't be quite so good either. Sentencing was due in three days, and rumour had it that he could get up to twelve years.

Burton then followed on by reminding everybody of the restructuring plans with as much empathy as he could muster, saying, 'It might be a bucking bronco ride for some of you over the next few weeks. The restructuring is designed to make the organisation better equipped at tackling evolving work streams, and has nothing to do with getting rid of staff.' Judging by the wary expressions around the room, Tariq concluded that no one believed him. Ten minutes into Burton's presentation he was tailing off into business clichés and platitudes. Tariq stepped sideways, away from the assembled group, as did Nathan, both disappearing from view behind the tall, dark-blue padded partitions. Nathan retrieved his bag with the laptop he'd hidden in a cardboard storage box, and they both went quietly down the stairs rather than be seen using the lift.

Down in the lower basement room, Nathan located the network socket on the side wall behind the half-full yellow skip under a low-level metal shelf. He plugged in his laptop and logged in with a username and password. He used a dummy account that he'd printed off from a list in the security office while Ajay was out making a coffee. This way, security couldn't identify Nathan as using the laptop. Unfortunately, Tariq couldn't do the same, as he would have to use his name and password to access the ledger files and documents. SFO security would only be able to identify the laptop, so it was vital that he secreted it back in the cabinet if they came looking.

As Nathan reached the basement, Tariq entered the property room and shut the door. There was no separate door lock on the inside. He then removed the old laptop from the metal cabinet on the back wall and plugged in the network cable. He loaded the start-up screen and typed in his login details in readiness for Nathan's call. Three minutes later, he was still waiting; it was five minutes now. Then Nathan called on the mobile. 'Dad, go! You've got eight minutes.'

Tariq hit enter on his keyboard and waited patiently for the programmes and files to load up, which seemed to take an age. Two minutes in, he heard someone approaching. Tariq attempted to put the laptop back in the cupboard but the network cable was too short. He was about to pull the cable out of the back of the laptop when he heard Nathan's voice outside. 'Dad, it's me.'

Three minutes now gone, he was nearly ready to download the files onto the memory stick.

Nathan came over to his father's laptop. 'Let me do it, Dad, I'm quicker.' Nathan highlighted the files to copy and said, 'There are two hundred and eighteen files – this could take longer than I thought, although the audit files are quite small.' The LED green light above the memory stick flashed as the files transferred. A minute later a message came up: *96 of 218 files copied.*

Tariq said, 'Come on, come on; why is it taking so long, God damn it!'

'Some are bigger files, Dad! It just takes that long.' Nathan looked at his watch. 'Two minutes left.'

A minute later, a message came up: *164 of 218 files copied.*

'This is bloody ridiculous, Nathan.'

Nathan stated plainly, 'Forty-five seconds left.'

The scar on Tariq's forehead reddened as he wiped off the sweat. *207 of 218 files copied.* Nathan was ready to grab the memory stick as soon as the *download complete* message popped up, and Tariq was poised to pull out the network and power cables and put the laptop back in the cupboard. They needed every second of the time before the server shut them out. Nathan noted that it was now over eight minutes. He concluded that the refresh period may vary depending on the server. *Download complete.*

Without warning, the door to the property room opened before Nathan could remove the memory stick from the side of the computer. Tariq and Nathan turned to face the door and froze in shock; it was too late to hide the laptop and the memory stick was still flashing green. Standing there was Mark Cooper, the International Investigation Lead, and Ajay, Head of Security. Cooper moved calmly towards the laptop, and before Tariq could react, he removed the silver *SanDisk 3* memory stick.

'I'll be taking that, if you don't mind, Tariq. One minute, you were at the staff meeting; the next, you'd vanished. When I couldn't find you at your desk, I thought I might find you hiding in the basement, so I decided to try the property room – and here you are. Pemberton told me to keep an eye on you – for good reason, it seems.'

Ajay said, 'You must know what happened last time, Tariq, when a virus nearly corrupted the SFO database; I nearly got the sack for that. That's why I'm now paranoid when the system flags up an unauthorised device, so I came to the basement straight away.' Nathan hadn't thought of that – that security got a warning as soon as an unauthorised device is plugged into the system. Nathan sensed a meltdown coming, so he exited the room without a word, passing the men standing in the doorway. He hid in the same toilet cubicle where he'd witnessed the two men's altercation on his third day in the office. He inflated his comfort ball and sandwiched it between his legs.

In the property room, Cooper added to Ajay's comment. 'Everybody knows that, Tariq, including you, so don't bother making excuses. I will obviously be informing Nigel Pemberton of this incident, which, by the way, has been witnessed by security.' Ajay looked at Tariq disapprovingly.

'Mark, please, listen for a minute. If you look at what's on that memory stick, you'll see that Stuart Harper has copied all the ledgers after deleting some of the original master ledgers and scanned documents. It's all there, so why don't you start looking for him before you jump to conclusions, for once?'

'You can't keep trying to palm everything off onto Harper because of what happened on the Frederick Rainsford case that got you put on probation – which you've clearly contravened, I might add. Save your breath for Pemberton, Tariq; it's his decision now whether you'll work on this case again, or even work for the SFO ever again. And don't think that we don't know the police have already questioned you; people talk. It wouldn't surprise me one bit if you were in cahoots with your fellow Serb Karlo Mitchko to help him clear his name. I hope he's paying you enough.'

'Piss off! I'm not a Serb, I'm Bosnian.'

'Yeah, whatever, Tariq. In any case, Mitchko was a Bosnian Serb, and you can be sure he's a Bosniak when he wants to be.'

CHAPTER 24

Tariq couldn't bring himself to read the paper on the train home. He just stared out of the window. Nathan had recovered to normality after sitting on top of the toilet seat with his head between his legs for fifteen minutes. He encouraged his father by saying that he'd done the right thing in attempting to copy the original ledger files, despite being caught. Tariq was still stewing at the injustice of the day's events. He said, more to himself than to his son, 'I'm going to get that bastard Harper and nail him to the wall until he confesses everything.'

Nathan replied quietly, 'I don't even know if you're joking now, Dad, as that isn't even possible.'

'There's a first time for everything, isn't there, Nathan? I'm going to need my hammer from the shed... or would an axe be better?'

'I'm not talking to you, Dad, you're not making any sense.' Nathan went back to reading the *Metro*.

Tariq thought again on what Sandra was trying to tell him about the cleaners' storeroom. Harper was up to something in there. Finding out could be the key to proving his innocence by exposing Harper's devious antics.

Upon opening the house door, he stumbled upon three letters lying on the doormat. Two were junk mail, the third an official letter from Nationwide Building Society. Tariq took a sharp knife from the kitchen and cut the letter open. The letter gave notice that they had missed another month's mortgage payment. It stated that unless resolved in seven days, further charges would be billed, which would further affect the addressee's credit rating and may result in repossession proceedings.

Tariq sat on the sofa in the sitting room and called Alice on his mobile. 'This is ridiculous!' he muttered to himself.

'Hello, darling. Is everything alright?' she asked her husband.

'Not really. I'm facing the sack at work, and then I find out that the mortgage hasn't been paid again. That's why I give you five hundred pounds a month, isn't it, Alice – isn't it?'

'Please, Tariq, I don't need this right now. You know how expensive Millie's medicines are, and I'm taking a few weeks off; what am I supposed to do? I don't care about the house or a stupid credit rating – I just want to save Millie. Does that make any sense to you, or have you just shut it all out as you usually do? I'm at my wit's end; I don't give a damn about anything anymore except Millie. I just hoped you felt the same.'

'Now that's not fair, and you know it. I'm sorry, OK, I don't want to have a go at you, darling. I wish you'd let me know first, before I got a letter through the letterbox. It was a shock, that's all.'

'Yes, I should have told you; I just didn't feel like talking about it. So, what is happening at work? You getting the sack is the last thing we need right now. Is it serious, or just the regular stuff and nonsense?'

'This could be serious. The SFO have had their budget cut, and they need to make redundancies.'

'But you'll be interviewed for your job, and you have as good a chance as anybody, don't you? You told me once that they like you there.'

'Some like me, others don't. Don't forget that I'm on probation so I'm probably the first in the firing line.'

'Oh, I forgot about that. Oh God, that's not good then, is it? Oh Tariq, I'm worried about you now.'

'Let's not worry about it now. Like you said, let's concentrate on Millie getting better. I'll sort things out in the office once and for all.'

'What do you mean by that? Don't do anything stupid, will you?'

'Oh, I'm long past that stage already... Anyway, there's something else I need to tell you.'

'Yes, what?'

'The police have contacted me. The immigration authorities say they've found someone who claims to be my uncle, so I'm flying to Montenegro Friday evening. They're going to pick me up from the house.'

'That's wonderful, Tariq, isn't it? I always hoped you would be reunited with your family again. It's the first step in helping you to remember – to find your true identity. It could be a turning point for you.'

'The thing is, I don't even remember having an uncle. It's probably a wild goose chase.'

'That's as well, but you must go, Tariq, to be sure. Please go.'

'Yes, agreed. So you need to collect Nathan after work on Friday.'

'Yes, that's alright, but it'll have to be early though, say four o'clock, as I've got a friend coming for dinner at seven, and I need to get everything ready.'

'Yeah sure, that's fine. I'll tell him. Thanks. Can you then take him to work on Monday morning? I'm coming back Sunday evening.'

'Yes, of course. Don't forget that Millie's coming home Tuesday, so can you tidy up the house up and get her bed ready?'

'Sure.'

'Thanks. Bye, love.'

'Bye.'

Tariq went into the study, sat on the office swivel chair, and poured himself a whisky and Coke.

***

For breakfast, Tariq served himself two boiled eggs with buttered toast. He felt like a man on death row, enjoying his last meal of choice. Tariq explained to Nathan that he was going away for the weekend and his mother would collect him from work early. Nathan was grateful at the prospect of spending the weekend with his less-stressed mother and seeing his sister again.

Nathan spent the entire train commute to work completing puzzles Nos. 65 and 66 in his puzzle book to avoid any awkward conversations with his father, especially in regard to yesterday's events. Tariq pondered that Mark Cooper had snatched the evidence from their grasp, which, ironically, was now being used to push him out of the SFO for good. He considered that if he found Harper with his hands in the till, he would enjoy carrying out a Muslim-type amputation as due punishment. Just think – Harper would never misfile a document, enter false information, or delete files again; except with his tongue. Only fair, Tariq considered, since he now faced the equivalent of the guillotine on his career and reputation.

Tariq used the stairs rather than risking getting stuck in a lift with the enemy, as he saw Harper, and now Cooper. He approached his desk with a tinge of relief that his office belongings weren't already in black sacks. It seemed all quiet on the Western Front. Perhaps everything would work out? He mulled over whether to take a proactive approach by talking to Pemberton, Burton, or both of them, in a pre-emptive strike to explain his actions with the memory stick. He could at least try to convince them that his motives were honourable by saving the ledger files onto the memory stick before all the evidence was lost. The elephant in the room was Harper – he needed to confront him soon, but without evidence he would be embarrassed again, as he had been at their last encounter. What had he done with Mitchko's red diary after he jumped into the taxi the night they'd met Cooper and Pemberton in the pub? He had some explaining to do. Tariq needed to catch him alone, without witnesses. Today had to be the day.

Tariq's ruminations at his desk were rudely interrupted by Pemberton's sharp Scottish tone as he approached. 'Tariq, could you come up to my office now, please?' The seriousness of his voice was enough to turn a few heads and raise eyebrows within earshot. Tariq didn't try to converse with Pemberton in the lift to the tenth floor or along to his office. Pemberton was walking at pace and was sat at his desk by the time Tariq entered the room. Mark Cooper was already sitting on the other side of the desk, and looked up sheepishly at Tariq as he sat down.

'You can probably guess why you are here, Tariq. Mark has explained to me what happened yesterday with the memory stick. Mark Cooper held up the silver SanDisk memory stick for all to see.

'Yes, that is the device I was using to download the ledger files yesterday that I was going to hand over to you to check for irregularities.'

Cooper reacted, 'That's bullshit. I had to take it from you.'

'I intended to hand it over, then you decided to grab it, completely unnecessarily.'

Pemberton cut in, 'Gentlemen, gentlemen. Do you know what? I don't care. Tariq, you must know that using external devices is a disciplinary offence after all the trouble we had with the virus last time. I take it that you didn't have permission to use it?'

'No, I couldn't afford the delay.'

'Well, that's too bad, isn't it? Because as of now, you are suspended from the case. I expected better from you. You're already on probation, which was your chance to show you're up to the job, and then you go and do something stupid like this. What were you thinking, man?'

'I'll tell you what I am thinking…' Tariq paused and said to Pemberton, 'Do you mind if I speak to you alone?' Pemberton motioned to Cooper to leave the room. Tariq said, 'With respect, sir, I suspect someone is tampering with the ledger. Documents have gone missing, and the ledger changed before it'd been officially registered. My money is on Stuart Harper. He was working on my previous case, which also had issues, for which I was held responsible as the senior disclosure officer, as you know. Don't throw me under the bus until you've looked at it first, please!'

'If you'd come to me at the time with all this, I might have had some sympathy, but not now that you've been caught breaking strict office protocol. I've heard enough, to be honest with you. I've got better things to do. As from now, you are suspended from the case, and I will speak to Sir Peter over the weekend whether more serious disciplinary action needs to be taken. I will inform you of my decision on Tuesday, as I'm out of the office on Monday. I suggest you go home early today rather than skulking around the office.'

Tariq realised that there was nothing more he could say to change Pemberton's mind, so he got up from his chair and left the room.

On his return to his desk, Tariq found Nathan doing one of the SFO online courses on the roles and responsibilities of the different personnel in a case under investigation. 'That looks interesting, Nathan – roles and responsibilities, hey.' Tariq noticed a prompt on the screen to find out the Attorney General's role. It stated: *The Attorney General has overall responsibility for the work of the Serious Fraud Office (SFO). He has the power to organise, from time to time, external audits of the SFO operations and staff, with the agreement of the SFO Director, to ensure good practice is being adhered to and to expose any corrupt activity.* 'Sorry son, for disturbing your course… I must admit, I didn't know that about the Attorney General. Interesting. You should send him an anonymous email tipping him off on what is going on around here, and say that Harper should be investigated. Maybe he'll take an interest and take it up with Pemberton. Problem is, though, that Pemberton and the Attorney General are mates, so who am I trying to kid?'

'I don't have his email, Dad.'

'Shame. Look it up.'

Tariq spent the morning catching up with emails. At half past twelve, they both went down to the canteen. Nathan copied his father's choice of shepherd's pie with salad for lunch; he picked out all the red tomatoes, of course. Tariq made a point of sitting on a table with an inward-facing outlook so he could spot Harper if he showed up. He could then follow him down to the basement, where he usually went after lunch for a smoke.

Tariq said, 'Your favourite, Nathan – shepherd's pie. You'll enjoy that.'

'I feel a bit of a fraud though, as I'm not even a shepherd.'

'Well, Nathan, you've done a good job helping round up the dodgy files. I think that qualifies.'

'Yes, we rounded up all the ledger files, didn't we, Dad? Onto that memory stick, until Mr Cooper took it. I saw him put it in his drawer, by the way, but he locked it.'

Tariq's expression turned more serious. 'Yeah, we sure tried, didn't we?'

'Millie told me once that only Jesus is the good shepherd; Cooper, on the other hand, is not a good shepherd. He doesn't care about the truth or what happens to you, Dad. I think that you're more like the good shepherd because you care about rounding up the files.'

'Thanks, Nathan; that sounded like a compliment. I wonder how far a good shepherd would go to save his sheep?'

'Oh, that's easy to answer – the good shepherd lays down his life for his sheep. That's what Millie said, anyway.'

Tariq finished his lunch and said to Nathan, 'I've arranged for your mother to collect you at three o'clock, an hour earlier than originally planned. I've got to sort something out at work. As I told you on the train, I'm going away for the weekend, so your mother will bring you to work on Monday morning.'

'Oh, OK then. Do you think I could see Millie today? I forgot to tell you that Mum thinks she is going through a critical stage.'

'Oh God, no. Oh my goodness. I don't know, son. You'll have to ask your mother.'

Alice arrived on time in her navy Saab, 2006 registration. She turned on her elegant female charm to persuade the security guard to let her park outside the vehicle entrance gates for a few minutes. Tariq brought Nathan down to her. They waved to each other briefly before she drove off, Nathan smiling in the front seat.

As Tariq waited in the lift lobby, he caught sight of Stuart Harper exiting the far lift and descending the stairs to the basement. He looked shifty, but he always did when sneaking into the basement for a smoke. Tariq walked purposely across the lift atrium floor and down the same stairs, first checking that Harper was out of sight at the bottom of the stairwell. He could feel his army combat instincts kicking in and his adrenaline level and heart rate rising sharply. He moved with light feet, slowly and steadily down the steel staircase. On emerging at the basement level at the foot of the stairs, he could see the property room door ajar, so he stepped quietly along the corridor, cocked his pistol and peered in. Strangely, the room appeared empty, but he could hear some activity coming from within. A noise like whirring helicopter blades descended behind him along the corridor, and voices emanated from the pine forest beyond. Tariq wiped the sweat from his brow, his red scar like a diagonal stripe across his forehead. Surveying the terrain ahead, he saw the outline of a man walking past the storeroom on the far edge of the clearing. He stooped down low and moved stealthily around the side of the room, where he crouched under the table.

The man walked around the other side of the room. Tariq nestled into the long green grass under the table to get some cover. The grass swished gently in the breeze, smelling of wet mud and congealed blood. His target would probably be armed, including short-pull grenades, so he needed to take him out with lethal force. Other enemy soldiers could be nearby, so the target had to be quietly executed. Without looking, he screwed the silencer onto his gun barrel. The figure continued to walk around the room on the other side of the desk. He took something from a box on the wall shelves and turned around.

As he suspected, it was Harper; he was now sliding a grey document into a large manila envelope, to be posted out to the Attorney General's private storage room in St Albans no doubt. All the more reason to take him down before he could get to the post room. As Harper walked around the table, towards the main door, Tariq set himself to make his move. He'd been in similar situations many times before. To disable him in a single manoeuvre it called for a forearm around the neck, pulling up the free arm behind his back, then slamming a right boot into the back of the knees to knock them firmly down into the ground. The contents of the envelope would be the evidence he needed to justify the assault to his commander. He was at the point of springing forward to bring him down before he reached the exit door, when he heard voices coming down the corridor. There was no way of knowing if they were friend or foe. The door was now half open, so any move on Harper would be seen by the approaching patrol, possibly resulting in an escalating combat scenario, and he wasn't wearing a bullet-proof vest. Harper left the room and the voices soon went quiet, so Tariq opened the main door to see which direction he was heading in: to the post room as Tariq had predicted. Tariq stepped quietly down the carpet-lined corridor towards the post room. Through the quarter-open door, he could see Harper, now in civilian clothes, handing the sealed manila envelope to an army motorbike courier, who dropped it into his side pannier.

Harper then turned around towards him, walking towards the post room door. Behind him, Tariq heard the same voices exit the men's toilets, so he instinctively ascended the stairs to the fourth floor, then rested on the landing. The threat had gone, for now; his adrenalin rush subsided and his breathing slowed. He wiped the sweat off his brow across his fading red scar, now aware that he was also back in civilian clothes, in urban terrain. Tariq held his head in his hands, ruing the missed opportunity to nail Harper. Would he get another chance to confront him again? He just needed one more chance. It was easier to get the truth out of a man who feared death, which is why Harper would confess.

CHAPTER 25

With Nathan gone, Tariq felt more alone in the office than he'd expected, with no one to share his turmoil or to humour him in his dark corner. Pemberton had given him licence to leave the office early, so he tidied his desk and made his way to the Calthorpe Arms. Out on the street, he stopped behind a bus shelter and looked back to check if anyone was following him. As a routine, he scanned any open windows and rooftops of overlooking buildings for snipers. He continued, occasionally glancing behind him until he entered the Calthorpe Arms. The colourful red-and-green tartan carpet welcomed him as before. He looked to his left and was pleased to see that the same green leather Chippendale seat he'd sat in on his return from the bank was free. He reserved the seat with his bag and coat and approached the bar. Tariq and the barman recognised each other. 'Two pints of Shepherd Neame, a double whisky, and a packet of cheese and onion crisps please John,' requested Tariq.

The barman totted up the prices on the till and said, 'that'll be ten pounds, fourteen pence please.'

Tariq was only half listening, as he was thinking about how close he'd just been to exposing Harper as the mole. 'What was that, John, ten-fourteen?'

'Yes Tariq. You have ears, but fail to hear.'

'Oh, sorry about that. I've got a lot on my mind at the moment.'

Tariq paid in cash and sat down on the firm green leather bench seat. He stared across the room, recalling the last time he was here after his trip to the bank – three thousand pounds worse off and with his credit rating in freefall. Judging by Nathan's comment, passed on by his mother, that Millie was going through a critical stage, it was the final roll of the dice for the so-called American wonder-drug. Had they been fools to think they could buy Millie's life with an expensive lottery ticket? It was all based on blind hope, and now they had to face the stark reality. Would the Grim Reaper have his day? He remembered his wife's comment that she would give anything to save her. Why was he even thinking about the cost? What price would a man, or woman, pay to save their child? Would the good shepherd really lay down his life for just one of his sheep? Tariq then thought of the other failed gamble – to copy the original ledger files. Why did Cooper come looking for him? Perhaps he had something to hide? He was all too keen to rush up to Pemberton to show him the memory stick. Was it just a ruse to deflect attention away from himself? Was he working with Harper? Pemberton had bought it, that was for sure. Meanwhile, that rat Harper was getting away with murder – the murder of his career. He had seen him with his own eyes in the post room, passing the envelope to the courier. He had been that close to taking a clean shot at him. 'I could have nailed the bastard!' he said to himself, facing across the room.

'Sorry mate, did you say something?' said the barman with a disapproving scowl.

'Nothing. Another pint of bitter, please – Neame. Cheers.'

'Of course, coming right up.'

Four pints of Neame bitter and a second double whisky later, Tariq was contemplating how he could find his way through the maze of his past, present and future. Maybe the only way through was to smash through the walls to find salvation. Did his past hold the key? He'd caught glimpses of memories of a happy life as a child with his brothers and his father in Bosnia. How could he forget his brothers, laughing and swimming in the Danube together under the Visegrad bridge? There was joy, wasn't there? Tariq's emotions welled up as he cried out to himself, 'Father, I so want to see your face again, to hug you again. Sorry, Father, for running away – I was scared. The Serb devils came with guns. The missile shell hit the house; my brothers, your sons, were gone – I couldn't save them… *Oče, žao mi je, žao mi je. Volim te Oče. Molim te oprosti mi!*' Tariq wiped the tears from his eyes.

'I think you've had enough, matey. Haven't you got a home to go to?'

Tariq looked up at the barman nonchalantly. '*Da, Da, idem sada!*'

'Yes, whatever, mate.'

Tariq swigged the rest of his whisky and brushed past him towards the toilets, shouting back, '*Idem da pišam!*' On his way out of the pub, he shouted, '*Zbogom svinje!*'

'And the same to you mate!' returned the barman.

Tariq had already made up his mind to see Millie before his enforced visit to Montenegro. Chances were, either or both of them could be dead in a few days – Millie from natural causes, him from an unnatural one by the hands of the Bosnians and Serbs hunting him down. He had to see her, now or never.

He walked in the direction of Farringdon station, heading north on Grays Inn Road, dodging the lamp posts as they tried to block his path. No taxi would pick up a man staggering from side to side along the pavement. He bought a small bottle of Jack Daniels on the way, which he'd drunk by the time he reached King's College Hospital. He climbed the hospital stairs, clinging to the bannisters, up to the Davidson Haematology Ward on the second floor.

It was just past 9:00pm, well outside visiting hours, so he couldn't just walk in. As he approached the ward, he noticed a disposable surgeon's apron and mask discarded in a bin in the corridor. He retrieved the pale green apron from the bin, slung the hooped strap over his neck and knotted the string tiebacks behind his back. He then put the mask straps around his ears. As he did so, the ward doors were pushed open by two porters hurriedly pushing an elderly man on a wheeled stretcher. Tariq grabbed some abandoned forms on a side table and pretended to study them as if they were patient's notes as he tailgated the porters through the double doors. He kept the same posture all the way to Millie's bed and rotated the visitor's chair on the side of her bed to face away from the ward sister sat at her desk in the far corner.

He looked straight at Millie. She was obviously confused with the unidentified medic now at her bedside. A number of consultants and doctors came and went in the wards, so his presence wasn't unprecedented. Tariq pulled down his mask.

'Dad!' Millie said with restraint. The nurse sister looked

up briefly from her desk and went back to some paperwork. Millie stilled her voice. 'Dad, what are you doing here? Like the disguise, by the way. You should have been a spy.'

'Millie, Millie! How are you darling? How are you feeling?' He slumped over the bed to give her the best hug he could. 'I just had to see you before I go.'

'Go where? You smell of drink, Dad. Are you drunk?'

'Not drunk, Millie, just happy to see you, that's all. How are you feeling?'

'Dad, you've asked me that already. I feel a bit better, thanks.'

'You mean everything to me. You know that, Millie, don't you?'

'Thank you, Dad. It's good to see you.'

Millie held his hand and looked into his glazed eyes. 'So, where are you going?'

'Apparently to visit my long-lost uncle in Montenegro.' Tariq took a tissue from his pocket to wipe the tears from his eyes. 'The thing is, Millie, I don't care about my uncle, but I have to find my father, you see, and my brothers, if they're still alive. I don't know what happened to them…' He wiped more tears from his eyes. I need to know who I am. They're coming for me, Millie. They're looking for the man with the eagle tattoo, you see – here.' Tariq pointed to the back of his neck. 'Maybe I do know him. I remembered his face, you see, but I can't remember his name.' He slumped forward onto her bed again. It was her turn to put her arms on his shoulders. Tariq pulled himself up off the bed as he heard multiple footsteps behind him.

The ward sister said in a stern voice, matching her face, 'Excuse me, who are you? Can I see your ID please?'

'Sishter, please, I haven't got any ID because I'm her father... and I just wanted to speak to my precious daughter.'

'Well, you've spoken to her, and you now need to leave as this is not in visiting hours, and you're disturbing the other patients.'

'Can't a father see his own daughter?! A good father would do anything to spend time with his child... he would give his life to save his child, like the good shepherd.' By this time, a security guard had joined the ward sister and her assistant. Tariq rolled his eyes. 'OK, OK, I'm going.' He hugged Millie a final time in her bed.

The security guard grabbed him around the waist, 'OK, sir, we need to help you out of here.'

The guard and the assistant nurse escorted him out of the ward, along two long corridors, and through the main hospital automatic sliding doors. Out on the street, Tariq stood up straight long enough to hail a taxi.

Back in the house, Tariq made a cup of tea and reheated half a quiche with new potatoes in the microwave, which he ate with coleslaw. On leaving the kitchen, he noticed that the study light was on. He looked up at the kitchen clock: 10:15pm. The police were due to pick him up at 10:30pm to take him to Gatwick Airport, so he'd only quarter of an hour to freshen up. He'd already packed his weekend bag.

He used the downstairs toilet, and then went into the study to turn the desk lamp off. The door closed behind him. Startled, he swung around. A man stood in front of the now-closed door, pointing a pistol at him. Tariq knew by the way the man held the gun that he knew how to use it. The man was wearing jeans and a black sweatshirt. He sat down in a deliberate, slow action on the upholstered chair to the side of the door, all the while keeping the gun pointed at him. He said in an Eastern European-sounding accent, 'Turn the desk light around to face you and sit down in the chair.'

Tariq did as directed, thinking that he recognised the accent as Serb, not Bosnian this time. He didn't know how he knew; he just knew. Tariq sat down and looked up at the intruder, who was now stepping towards him, gun still pointing at his skull.

'Bend forward. Put your head between your knees.'

Tariq hesitated at the strange request.

'Just do it!'

In the half-light of the study, the man combed his fingers through Tariq's hair, pushing clumps back and forth around the back of his head and neck. He gave up looking for whatever he hoped to see and sat back down.

'You should get your hair cut. I've never seen such thick hair on a man your age. With hair like that and brown eyes, you look more like a Serb than a Bosniak.'

'Who are you? Why are you here? What do you want?'

'I've got my orders from my compatriots in The Hague. Let's just say that I'm assisting Ratko Mladic's defence team to challenge the jumped-up charges brought against him; so I'm a loyal Serb. My job is to gather evidence and witnesses wherever they might be hiding, and I believe you can help me to find someone.'

'The man with the eagle tattoo?'

'Yes, Tariq, how did you know? The double-headed eagle tattoo, to be precise, is symbolic to both the Serbs and the Bosniaks, so unfortunately, we are none the wiser about his nationality. He was with Mladic on the battlefield, but it appears that no one saw enough of his face to recognise him, as he always wore his military cap and dark glasses. Mladic was informed that Slobodan Milosevic, the Serbian President, had sent him. I knew Slobodan before he died in 2006, and he told me himself that he hadn't sent him, so who was this man, Tariq? Probably a double-crossing spy, that's who. We do know that there was only one tattoo parlour in Yugoslavia which did that tattoo.' He reached into a black case by his side to retrieve a colour photograph of the tattoo on the back of a man's neck, extending to the base of his head. 'There you go; look at the detail on that; the distinctive-shaped yellow eyes and red-and-white shaded wing tips. That tattoo parlour was in Visegrad, and we now know that the tattoo artist tattooed two men at the same visit with that design before he fled the massacres in 1992. Only these two men had the tattoo. One of them is believed to have been killed in the war, but no one really knows.'

Tariq, still half inebriated, stood up in defiance and stepped towards the man.

'And what do you want from me?!'

The man in black lifted the gun and said firmly, 'Sit down or I'll kill you.'

Tariq stood there for a few seconds, swaying slightly on his feet, and then opened his arms wide and said, 'Make it a clean shot; I haven't got much left to live for, so go ahead.' He felt his legs go from under him. He stepped back and slumped back in his chair before he fell over.

'Now let's not get melodramatic, Tariq, please. I can

see that the war was a trauma for you; it has been for a lot of us. So, let's sit down and talk about what happened out there. I sense that deep down, you desperately want to know, so I can help you, Tariq. I can help you bring to the surface the things you've chosen to forget. Forgive me, I've already found your whisky,' he said as he picked up the bottle from the floor and poured another measure into a glass on a side table. 'I would offer you one, Tariq, but I can see that you've probably had enough already. I don't want you falling asleep on me now.' The Serb took a swig of whisky and leant back into his chair, the gun held firmly in his other hand. He hesitated and looked straight at Tariq, asking, 'So, Tariq, you come from Visegrad and you swam in the Drina River: is that right?'

'Who told you that?'

'I have contacts. I know a lot more than you think. We know that, like you, the tattooed man often swam in the Drina River with his friends and family,' the man leaned forward towards Tariq, 'and I'll tell you something else we know.' He paused.

'What?'

'There was only one Tariq Markovic living in Visegrad, and there's a marked grave there with his name on it. So who are you, Tariq?'

Tariq held his head in his hands and said in a muffled voice, 'I don't know who I am.'

'I told you – you look more like a Serb than a Bosniak, and it makes you wonder, doesn't it – who is this uncle you're visiting in Montenegro?'

'How do you know about that?'

The man with the gun just touched the side of his nose

with his free left hand. He continued, 'So, Tariq, or whatever your name is, you lived in Visegrad all your young life; surely you know who the tattooed man was? If someone had a tattoo like that from the only tattoo parlour in town, the whole town would know about it, wouldn't they? Especially someone like you, of similar age, who swam in the river every summer. You would notice something like that, wouldn't you?'

Still with his head in his hands, Tariq opened his palms to speak. 'I don't know who he was.'

'Let me refresh your memory of what happened in June 1992. The Bosniaks say that hundreds of their countrymen were rounded up by the Serbs and taken onto the Mehmed Paša Sokolović Bridge, lined up, shot or hacked to death, and then thrown over the parapet.'

Tariq was rocking backwards and forwards slightly in his chair, with his hands still covering his face, and tears seeping through his fingers onto the floor. The Serb offered him his half-full glass of whisky. Tariq drunk it and spoke.

'Хвала... please, I don't want to remember that – it was terrible, so terrible. I didn't want to be a part of that.'

'Now we're making progress. We think the other man felt the same, and was recruited as a spy.'

'I don't know anything about that.'

'He was probably recruited by Jovica Stanisic, otherwise known as the Ice Man. Have you heard of him?'

'Yes, I've heard of him. He was mentioned on the TV in the Mladic trial. They say he was the mastermind of Slobodan Milosevic's regime, the Serbian President at the time. They say that he was the first to term the phrase "ethnic cleansing".'

'That doesn't matter. The real issue is, was he a loyal Serb or was he a traitor? Let me tell you what happened at Stanisic's trial in 2009. The CIA submitted a sealed dossier to the court describing how he had helped the United Nations to end the war, which led to the signing of the Dayton Peace Agreement. Do you know who took most of the credit for that agreement? I'll tell you. The President of the United States, Bill Clinton, no less. Behind the scenes, it was agreed that the United States government would provide a significant financial package to rebuild the Balkans, but there were conditions, and one of them was that no mention was ever to be made of the CIA's involvement in the war.'

Tariq asked, 'What was the problem with that?'

'Because the CIA declared to the UN at the time that they had no men on the ground to justify why they couldn't have intervened earlier to stop the so-called Srebrenica massacres when eight thousand men were allegedly killed. What we now know is that somebody on the ground passed detailed information to the UN of the locations of the original mass grave sites, and the locations of NATO hostages. The identity of this man is the key to exposing the guilty parties to everything that happened. The judge at Mladic's trial now in session at The Hague has got wind of the fact that Americans could be withholding key information in regard to their intelligence-gathering activities. If we can prove the CIA were manipulating events, the presiding Judge at The Hague would have to throw out the case and drop the charges against Ratko; so now you understand why we need to find this spy.'

Tariq responded, 'I'm not sure I believe a word you say. I can't help you find this spy.'

The Serb declined to respond, poured himself another half glass of whisky, and took a couple of sips. He sat there in contemplation, 'Do you know what, Tariq? I'm tired of chasing this man. I don't care anymore whether he was a Serb, a Bosniak or a CIA agent: I just want to know the truth; that's all. Be warned, my friend, there are many who would enjoy torturing you if they thought you could lead them to him. So why don't you tell me who you remember growing up with in Visegrad for all those years?'

Tariq was somehow more alert now, following his macabre flashbacks of what had happened on Mehmed Paša Sokolović Bridge. 'There was my best friend; his name was…'

Ding-dong, ding-dong. The doorbell rang.

The Serb stood up, opened the study door, and looked across the hall towards the front door.

'Are you expecting any visitors?'

'It's the police. You'd better leave.'

'You're lying. Don't move.' The Serb went over to the window and pulled back the curtains a few inches. 'Shit!' He then came back through the study and headed for the back door. 'I'll be seeing you again, Tariq; I can promise you that. I can help you remember before it's too late, my friend.'

CHAPTER 26

On the journey to Gatwick Airport the three uniformed policemen chatted among themselves about the frustrations of their current investigations and the indiscretions of their colleagues. They briefed Tariq on the arrangements in Montenegro; who he was to meet, when, and where. One of the policemen handed him a bottle of water and a ham sandwich. Halfway through his sandwich, he glanced at the car dashboard. He recognised the Jaguar logo on the steering wheel; the speedometer registered 93mph. The exit sign on the M23 to Gatwick Airport came into view. The police driver weaved around slower cars onto the slip road.

At the airport, they parked up in a priority layby in the drop-off area adjacent to a VIP-type entrance. An armed policewoman stood guard. She flashed her pass across the security door sensor and stood aside as the Gatwick terminal door opened for the three policemen and Tariq. They then entered a private lounge. In the far corner were two light-brown sofas facing each other with a glass table in between, on which was a scattering of used Met Police mugs. A middle-aged, well built, plain-clothed man approached Tariq.

'Tariq M...?'

'Yes, that's me.'

'Can you fill out this form, please? Do you have any medical conditions? You're not afraid of flying, are you?'

'No, nothing medical. I'm usually OK with flying, but I've never travelled like this before.'

The man smiled. 'Coffee or something stronger?'

'Whisky and Coke?'

The man smirked again, took a few steps back, and opened a low cupboard door, revealing several liquor bottles of varying colours and sizes. Without leaving the cabinet, he mixed the drinks and returned with a filled white plastic cup in one hand and a pen in the other, 'There you go. Don't forget to fill out the form.'

As he was signing the form, two policemen manhandled a short, rugged-faced Japanese man through the door from the main airport concourse and into a side room. He heard one of the uniformed policemen say to the man, 'Calm down, we just want to ask you some questions.' The Japanese man looked across at Tariq for help as the door was closed by one of the policemen and locked. A flashback of an interrogation in the Bosnian War hit him unexpectedly; he closed his mind to it and downed his drink in one go from the plastic cup.

Sky News was on a large flat screen TV on the wall. The Sky reporter was at The Hague, announcing that the judge had suspended the Ratko Mladic trial due to procedural irregularities in the presentation of the prosecution evidence. The news report then brought up a headshot of a man called Jovica Stanisic, also known as the Ice Man. A policeman in the room behind him, enjoying some banter with his friends, let out a howl of laughter, which drowned out the reporter's explanation of the Ice Man's relevance to the trial's proceedings. Tariq recalled what the Serb had told him back at the house. Was he telling the truth about CIA involvement in the Bosnian War and why they needed to find this unidentified agent? This was the first time he had seen a clear picture of Jovica Stanisic on the TV. Tariq felt a cold chill running down his spine. He mouthed to himself, *I know this man.*

Tariq scanned behind him and around the room. No one was paying him any attention, so he went over to the drinks' cupboard, poured himself another whisky, and sat back down with his half-full plastic cup. Repressed memories were seeping back into his consciousness. The Ratko Mladic trial had opened old wounds in him and in others who would do anything to get the justice they craved. Some of them saw him as the key to unlocking the truth. His encounter with the Serbian man in the house had stirred up something in him that was long forgotten – a brief glimpse of his past and why he'd closed the door on it. The whisky calmed his nerves.

The policeman who'd sat next to him in the car stood in front of the departures screen and announced that they had fifteen minutes to get to the departure lounge for the EasyJet flight to Tivat leaving at 1:10am. Two uniformed officers directed Tariq to bring his bag and to follow them closely. Tariq struggled to keep up as the officers moved quickly across the airport concourse. He'd hoped for a private police buggy, but no such luck. He was at least grateful that they were fast-tracked through the security checks and waved straight onto the plane upon arrival at the departure lounge. Only one of the policemen accompanied Tariq onto the plane. Twenty minutes later, they were airborne.

The M23 motorway street lights snaked beneath them with the dual white beams of car headlights travelling silently on opposing carriageways.

Less than an hour into the flight, the air stewards moved steadily down the aisle with trollies serving a choice of sandwiches and snacks; Tariq also had a beer. He was tired and fell into a deep sleep.

In his dream he sat at a table in a restaurant on a side street somewhere in Bosnia. Sat opposite him was an American and a Serb. A third man, who he hadn't met before, joined them at the table. He said to Tariq, 'You've survived many dangers so far on this mission, but you will soon face a choice of life or death. Call on me and I will rescue you.' This man addressed him by a name he hadn't been called since the War. If only he could remember what it was.

***

Tariq was awakened by a prod on his shoulder, 'Sorry to disturb you, sir, but you need to put on your seatbelt as we're coming into land now,' said an angelic-looking female air stewardess leaning over him.

'Yes, of course. Sorry.'

'No problem, sir. Enjoy the rest of your flight.' She continued down the aisle to the back of the plane, checking right to left for seatbelts fastened. Tariq saw below him a vast expanse of water rippling in the moonlight, which came into focus as they descended to Tivat Airport; the approach runway lights now visible in the distance as the plane banked for the final approach. A minute later came a *bump*, *bump*, followed by the roar of reverse thrust from both engines, flaps full; they were safely down.

The Tivat Airport terminal looked like a converted aircraft hangar with airport facilities shoe-horned in as an afterthought. Typically, arrival passengers descended the boarding stairs and walked a hundred yards across an open concrete concourse to the terminal building and straight to passport control.

Tariq thought momentarily that he'd lost his police escort but realised that the policeman had changed on the plane into civilian clothes. There were no fast-track procedures through passport control or security checks this time. Tariq got the impression that the officer wanted to appear as normal as possible so as not to alert the Montenegrin authorities that they were on official police business.

Through the airport glass back wall, a brown Ford Galaxy people carrier vehicle could be seen pulling up at the airport pickup point. On exiting the airport, they were greeted by a portly, well-tanned, grey-haired driver, smiling at them confidently.

'Mr Wilson, yes? I take you to the Tivat Airport Hotel, and in the morning to Fanfani Resort.'

'I am Mr Wilson, yes, thank you,' said the officer.

'You have suitcases?'

'No, just our bags. No suitcases.'

'OK. You get in, please.'

Tariq and PC Wilson checked into the Tivat Airport Hotel. They shared a twin room.

After breakfast, the same brown Ford Galaxy pulled up outside the hotel. The driver walked into the hotel lobby at 10:00am, as arranged. Wilson directed Tariq onto the back seat next to him. The car drove off, and they secured their seatbelts. Tariq stared into the distance out of the car window, his thoughts returning to Millie and her precarious hold on life. Alice and Nathan would be visiting her in the hospital today, Saturday, and he felt a pang of guilt that he wasn't there with them, but took some solace that he had spoken to Millie the night before in the hospital. Also, Alice and Millie had both encouraged him to take the trip to Montenegro to meet his uncle… if he existed.

Tariq cast his gaze across the blue sea of the Bay of Kotor as they drove along the coastal road, which hugged the edge of the mountainous terrain, occasionally passing through long, well-lit tunnels. Within an hour they joined the queue for the ferry at Lepetane, the eastern ferry port. The taxi driver walked over to the kiosk to buy the tickets. Judging by the extended conversation and expressive body language exchanged with the man in the ticket booth, they probably knew each other. The driver bought some cigarettes and vodka from the general store on the other side of the street and strolled back to the car as vehicles disembarked from the ferry that had just arrived from the other side of the bay.

PC Wilson asked Tariq with a twinkle in his eye, 'Can you swim?'

'Yes, I can swim. Why do you ask?'

'Firstly, if you fall in, I won't need to worry that you'll drown, and secondly, so I can keep a special eye on you in case you fancy diving in at some point.'

'Ha! I'm not that good a swimmer.'

The driver returned to the car and drove them up the

ramp onto the ferry and parked up. Tariq and PC Wilson disembarked, and then the driver, who locked it. Tariq and PC Wilson walked up to the front of the ferry for a better view.

It only took ten minutes for the small ferry terminal town of Kamenari on the western side of the bay to come into view. As the ferry manoeuvred into the terminal, the taxi driver shouted at them in broken English from the higher deck to return to the vehicle. The ferry crew threw mooring ropes from the front of the ferry to waiting port hands on either side of a wide concrete ramp, who promptly wrapped the ropes around large rusted steel marine bollards. Only five other cars were in front of them, so they were soon off the ferry and back on the coastal road heading west. PC Wilson asked the driver, 'How long to the Fanfani complex?'

'Fifteen minutes,' replied the driver calmly.

They pulled into a layby with the Adriatic Sea glimmering brightly from behind a waist-high stone wall. The beach was narrow, with a grid-like arrangement of white plastic sun loungers with tied-back parasols. The Fanfani Hotel was on the other side of the road, which had classic Mediterranean red-terracotta roof tiles, with a hardwood framed glassed restaurant extending along the side of the main hotel building. A grey stoned pathway led up from the road to the hotel. To the right of the path was a square-cut hedge, and on the other side, a well-established pergola with interwoven mature vines. The taxi drove off behind them as Tariq and the officer climbed the stone steps to the reception desk. Behind the desk was an elderly man with a happy, wrinkled face, wearing a short-sleeved shirt with a palm-tree print. His smile revealed a missing tooth.

'*Zdrah-voh, Dobro Jutro,*' he said with warm enthusiasm. After a short pause, he switched to poorly pronounced English, 'Hello, I welcome you to our hotel. Name, please?' PC Wilson produced his passport, which described him as Mr Martin Gordon Wilson. 'Ah, yes, your chalets ready for you. You go through door, your rooms are at back, on left.' He pointed towards a glass door to their right. 'You have suitcases?'

PC Wilson replied, 'No, no suitcases, just hand luggage.'

'OK. Here your keys; Wilson number 13 and Markovic number 11.'

PC Wilson handed Tariq his key.

'Lunch one o'clock. Please enjoy your stay, yes?'

Tariq responded, 'Thanks,' as they walked through the side door. In front of them were several stone paths weaving through a semi-wild area of plants, shrubs, and more palm trees. Carved wooden signs indicated the chalet numbers. They both followed the path to the far side, as the man at the front desk had explained.

'Ah, there's mine,' PC Wilson pointed to chalet 13, 'and there's yours over there. I can't watch you all day, but if you leave your chalet, let me know – this is for your own safety. And in case I forget to mention it later, breakfast is at eight o'clock; don't be late. The rendezvous is tomorrow.'

Tariq tried his key in the door of No.11, but it wasn't a good fit and was obviously the wrong key. Tariq returned to the front desk with his key, but the hotelier was nowhere to be seen. He was about to shout for somebody when he noticed that the number on the key fob looked more like 17 than 11. Tariq shrugged and walked off to find No.17, just behind No.13, further away from the beach. The key turned the lock, and he entered his chalet, which consisted of a shower room with a toilet and a bedroom with a standard double bed with matching wooden bedside cabinets on either side. On the wall opposite the bed was a narrow black table with a kettle and a few sachets of coffee and tea. Tariq made a cup of tea and unpacked his overnight bag.

After hiring sun loungers, Tariq and Wilson had a fish dinner with white wine at a restaurant on the seafront, a short distance from the hotel. They returned early to their chalets, feeling tired after the overnight flight. In his chalet, Tariq scanned the TV channels from his bed with the remote control, and fell asleep.

***

Bang, smash, bang! Tariq stirred from his sleep. It was now dark, and he went over to the thick green curtains and parted them slightly to determine the source of the disturbance. The door of chalet No.11 was open. Two men were inside; their silhouettes could be seen moving urgently around the bedroom. One of the men turned on the light, revealing the second man pointing a gun towards the bed. Since there wasn't anybody in the bed, the man with the weapon stooped down to look under the bed frame. He then turned towards the window and closed the curtains in a single violent movement.

Tariq looked at his watch: 5:08 am. Tariq panicked with the thought that it wouldn't take long for the men to work out that he was in No.17. He changed quickly, grabbed his bag and threw in his clothes and belongings. He turned his light off and exited his chalet, crouching behind the low-level, white-washed stone dividing wall. He scurried as low as he could to Wilson in chalet 13, and knocked on the side glass door; no response. He knocked harder, trying not to alert the intruders. The side curtains opened. Wilson pointed his pistol directly at him. 'It's me! Let me in!' Wilson opened the door. Tariq put his finger to his mouth to warn Wilson to keep quiet. Tariq explained, 'Two men – they've broken into chalet 11, where I was supposed to be; they're armed!'

'OK, we need to go!' Wilson frantically changed in the near dark, emerging soon after from the bathroom with his travel bag. 'Follow me!'

Wilson climbed over the low stone wall onto the coast road, directing Tariq towards a black Range Rover parked in a layby up the road. Wilson unlocked the doors with the key fob as he approached, jumped in the driver's seat, and dropped his bag behind him onto the back seat. Tariq opened the nearside door and climbed into the passenger seat. Wilson put the car into drive gear and pushed down delicately on the accelerator pedal. Glancing back across the courtyard as they passed, Tariq saw the two men in reception, studying the hotel room guest book by torch light.

CHAPTER 27

An hour down the coastal road from the Fanfani Hotel, travelling west, PC Wilson took a sharp left turn into a forest track and parked up out of sight in the woods. He said to Tariq, 'Stay here. I need to make a call.' He returned to the car a few minutes later with a severe expression. He said nothing to Tariq, roared up the engine and did a rapid U-turn back up the track, then turned left onto the main road to resume their journey. After another hour, PC Wilson pulled over at a roadside café, parking the Range Rover behind a high stone wall in the adjacent car park. 'Come on, I'm hungry,' Wilson said to Tariq.

They both ordered the full English style breakfast with coffee. With his hunger relieved, Wilson looked up at Tariq and asked, 'What's going on, Tariq? Don't you think it would help if you levelled with me?'

'Sorry, you've lost me; maybe it's too early in the morning. Level with you about what?'

'Back there, at Fanfani, there was a Bosnian-registered car. I noticed it when we drove off; I made a note of the plate.'

'So what? There are lots of Bosnian cars around here. It's a popular holiday resort.'

'I got Interpol to trace the plate.'

'And?'

'It's registered to Karlo Mitchko – the man at the centre of the case you're working on, yes? So why would he want to track you down? Why would they come looking for you? Are you in too deep, and you don't want to admit it? It looks like they knew you were coming. How do you explain that?'

'I can't explain it. I can't explain any of it! Anyway, you wouldn't understand.'

'Try me. Help me understand, Tariq.'

'It's nothing to do with the case; they are looking for a man, a key witness, in the Ratko Mladic trial.'

'Sorry – who's "they"?'

'The Serbs, the Bosnians. I don't know who they are!'

'And what has this got to do with you?'

'They have it in their heads that I can lead them to this witness of the genocide; he comes from Visegrad like me, so they're convinced I would know him. He has a double-headed eagle tattoo on his neck. They'll do anything to find him...' Tariq held his head in his hands. 'I nearly remembered him... Please, I don't even know who I am anymore!'

Wilson dropped his questioning.

As they continued their journey to meet his so-called uncle, Tariq reflected on the men he'd seen briefly at the Fanfani complex breaking into the chalet opposite. He had heard them speak in Serbian. The Serbian man that accosted him in his home knew he was going to visit his uncle in Montenegro, so he shouldn't be surprised that they knew he was coming.

PC Wilson suddenly braked. An old rusty tractor blocked the road in front of them. Tariq muttered, 'Typical farmers, they do this deliberately to the tourists.'

PC Wilson wasn't listening. In a super-alert state, eyes wide, he grabbed the radio from the holster on the dashboard. 'Possible ambush, I repeat, possible ambush.' He returned the radio to the holster and selected reverse gear, immediately accelerating backwards, away from the tractor. It was too late; a dirty blue transit van now blocked the road behind them. Two men, one from each side, bounded out of the van towards them. Wilson pressed the call button on the radio. 'Ambush, ambush…'

A man wearing a worn brown leather jacket with grey hair pointed his gun at Wilson, 'Open door now, or I shoot.' The English was basic, but enough for Wilson to get the gist. He lifted his hands in the air. The second, younger, shorter, stocky man pulled open the driver's car door, took hold of the radio from the dashboard, smashed it down on the road, and then stamped on it, splintering broken plastic pieces across the road. The older, silver-haired man directed them both to get out of the car with their hands on their heads and to lie face down on the road. A third man, with a loose yellow T-shirt, pushed Tariq down to the ground and frisked him. The second, shorter man came over to Tariq and half dragged him into the back of the blue van. Wilson lay face down on the tarmac as instructed, helpless, as the van doors slammed behind him; it then reversed at speed back up the road. The van backed into a field entrance, clattering into a metal gate, then sped off, tyres screeching. PC Wilson returned to the driver's seat to pursue the van, but the keys were gone.

Tariq, now recovered from the initial shock of the hijack, ripped off his blindfold and threw it forward at the windscreen; it landed on the dashboard. The younger man, wearing an army camouflage jacket, with a cold expression, lifted his gun and pointed it at Tariq. 'Put it on or I kill you.'

Tariq leant forward towards the man in defiance, saying back to him, 'That's OK, soldier, I prefer to be killed with my eyes open. I prefer to be looking straight at you when you shoot; not with you behind my back, yes? But first, you should introduce yourself. It's rude not to explain why you have abducted me, and maybe you should apologise for spoiling my day.' The assailant turned to his colleague and shrugged his shoulders. He put his gun back in his holster. Tariq put out his hand, 'Tariq Markovic, pleased to meet you. What is your name? How are you today?'

The man retreated into the corner of the van and said in good English, 'You don't need to know who I am. We're doing this for all the Bosnian people who suffered and died at the hands of Ratko Mladic at Srebrenica. We owe it to them. This is for them. We want justice for our people, that's all. Mladic is guilty, everybody knows that.'

'Yes, I agree he's guilty – yes, guilty. I'm Bosnian; I'm on your side. What do you want from me?'

'We'll find out who you really are soon enough, and then you can tell us who the man with the eagle tattoo is.'

Tariq said plainly, 'I don't know anything. I keep telling you people – I can't help you.'

'Don't worry; we will help you to remember, the easy way or the hard way. I think that it will be the hard way for you.'

The van slowed and turned into a badly potholed side lane. Once parked up, the driver walked around to the back of the vehicle and opened the rear doors.

'Out!' said the man with the yellow T-shirt. Free of his

blindfold, Tariq looked around at the terrain and the layout of the farm buildings to get his bearings as they took him down a rough slate path to a small stone building behind a barn half full of hay bales. The room inside was dark; the window shutters were closed.

As the door to the building opened, a solid wooden table came into view in the middle of the room, with loose white ropes laid out across it. Tariq flinched backwards, turned and tried to run back up the path. He could face down a gun, but not this, oh God, not this! Two of the gang grabbed hold of him and wrestled him down onto the slate stone patio. They then lifted him off the ground and locked his arms backwards to manoeuvre him forward through the open door. Tariq kicked his flailing legs behind him with no effect. A fourth man with a white T-shirt was already in the room with the ropes ready. They lifted him onto the table and tied the ropes securely around his wrists, legs and torso. They also tied his neck down. The ropes were then threaded under the heavy table and secured to the metal under-shelf, pinning Tariq onto the table above. Tariq was forcing himself to take deep breaths to relieve the fear enveloping his body. He hoped that he would awake from the nightmare. New memories flashed through his mind of the torture he'd received in the Bosnian War. He wanted to remember now; it would be the quickest way out of here. He struggled against the ropes.

Tariq exclaimed, 'What do you want?! I can't help you! You have the wrong person. You're wasting your time!'

One of the men wrapped a pillowcase around Tariq's head and tied it up around his neck. The cloth bulged up and down as he tried to suck in oxygen. Tariq shook his head violently, prompting two of the men to hold his head still. Using a white enamelled milk jug, a third man poured water into the pillowcase covering Tariq's mouth. Tariq's body jolted, his arms and legs pulling at the ropes; his neck tensed up and his lungs heaved as he spluttered the water back upwards to stop it flowing down his throat into his lungs. He recovered his breath, so the stocky man with the hardened army demeanour repeated the process. Tariq's body, lungs and throat convulsed as they had done before. He drew a small desperate breath and the man again poured the water from the jug onto the tight fabric covering Tariq's mouth: Tariq spluttered out the fluid less efficiently this time, choking uncontrollably, his lungs burning with the build-up of carbon dioxide. The man reached again for the jug of water and began to pour; Tariq looked back at his outline through the pillowcase, fearing that he wouldn't survive this round, but all of a sudden, the man stopped pouring and, with his other hand, untied the pillowcase.

The older, silver-haired man facing him at the far end of the table near his feet said, in an insincere friendly tone, 'Unless you want some more, you remember now and answer questions, yes?'

'Yes! You bastard. Yes! Ask me the question.'

'OK, let's see if you answer questions. Name?'

'Tariq Markovic.'

'Real name?'

'Tariq Markovic.'

The man asked the question again with a more aggressive tone now.

'Real name?!'

'Tariq Markovic – this is the name they found on me.'

'Who found you?'

'The UN peacekeepers. They took me to the hospital.'

'What UN peacekeepers? You tell me, who were these people?'

'I don't know who they were… There were Americans in the hospital, that's all I know, God damn it!

'So how did they know who you were?'

'ID, I had ID; they found my passport; they showed me my passport – that's how I know who I am, OK?'

'I see. Help me understand – they gave you a passport and say "look, this is who you are"?'

Tariq now hesitated, as he realised his interrogator had exposed something he should have questioned many years ago. Had he been given a false identity in the hospital, or had there been some mistake? At this point it dawned on him that he had since built his life on this identity, and chosen not to rewind his memories before this reference point. The second older man said, 'I think you remember now, yes? The man with the eagle tattoo in Visegrad; what was his name?'

Tariq lay there recovering his breath, trying desperately to regain his memories.

'You have had time enough, my friend,' said the older man. He continued, 'So you tell us what we want to know, or do we help you remember again? Yes? Or we die trying, or rather - you die trying. That is English expression, yes?'

'No, please, no, you don't need to do this – give me time, for God's sake.'

'Like seventeen years more, you think? We haven't got time, my friend. The trial will be over soon. I hope, for your sake, that you remember this time.'

Tariq struggled, straining his muscles, his head again shaking from side to side. He then started to self-calm, taking deep breaths as if some memory of army survival training had kicked in. A voice in his head said, *The best way through this is to start off as calm as possible.* Time had run out. They tied the pillowcase around his neck as they'd done before. The man with white T-shirt poured water from the enamelled jug through the cloth down his throat. Tariq started choking, gurgling the water in an attempt to keep it out of his lungs. The man poured more water into the fabric. Tariq convulsed violently this time, struggling to breathe, his lungs desperate for more oxygen, the cloth bulging up and down as he fought for breath. The shorter man said, 'You tell us now. You tell us about the man with the eagle tattoo. We know he was there; we know you know him from Visegrad; you know who he is. Was he part of Mladic's command? You will remember now: *Zaboga!*' He shouted in Tariq's face.

The silver-haired man moved the shorter man out of the way so he could speak to Tariq in a controlled tone. 'The sooner you tell us, the sooner we can stop all this, and we all go home. Yes?'

Sensing that he could be on the edge of his mortal life, he said a short prayer and opened the doors of his mind into his previous life. 'I have something. I can remember something.' The gang of four fell silent for a moment, listening intently.

'My best friend, my childhood friend. We used to swim together in the Drina River. He was a Serb. I know his name.'

The gang glanced at each other in the hope they would get the name they'd been pursuing for the past fifteen years.

Tariq continued, 'When we were young, we went to the tattoo parlour together… I watched them do it.'

'Watched them do what?'

'The tattoo, the eagle tattoo on the back of his neck. I remember now – it was his birthday!' The men leaning over him were getting tired of the trivial detail.

'What was his name?'

What Tariq said next surprised even himself; it came out of his deep subconscious. 'Stefan Avramov.'

The gang looked at each other with relief, sharing their breakthrough moment.

The older man asked as plainly as he could, to keep the momentum going, 'So, well done. Now, what is your name?'

Tariq recalled his dream on the plane and tried to remember the name the third man sitting at the table had called him. As a revelation, the name came to him, 'Stefan used to call me *Bo*, but my full name is Bogdan Tanović.' Tariq repeated the name slowly to himself, determined not to let it go. A blinding light then hit his eyes. A fifth man had opened the front door into the kitchen, letting in the sunlight, so bright that he couldn't make out his face, but he seemed to have a reassuring demeanour.

Just before Tariq passed out, the man addressed him by his revealed name, 'Bogdan, the door is open. Come with me.'

CHAPTER 28

'Come with me. Wake up, wake up! We haven't got much time,' said the man on his knees next to him in a quiet but urgent American tone, as Tariq awoke from his dream on the threadbare horsehair mattress bed on the stone floor.

'Who are you? I'm not going in there again. Please, I can't remember any more.'

'Ssshh, don't talk, I'm here to spring you out of here. Calm down. Follow me, quick.'

Tariq turned over on his side to mobilise his strained muscles and sat up. The American helped Tariq to his feet and supported him under his arm as he led him towards the door, which opened onto the corridor and back towards the kitchen, the torture room. The American peeped around the half-open solid farmhouse door. Muffled voices could be heard from the kitchen. The American, walking in socks, holding his shoes in one hand, pointed at Tariq's feet, directing him to do the same. In the corridor, the American shut the door quietly, and slid the bolt back across, as he'd found it. He walked cautiously down the corridor towards the voices and beckoned Tariq to follow. Halfway down on the left was a door that opened into a side room. The American went through it and stopped to allow Tariq to catch up. The kitchen door was suddenly opened by one of the gang. Their voices echoed down the corridor; another door closed. One of the Bosnian gang had gone into the toilet. The American stepped quickly across the side room towards the exit door; Tariq followed. He opened the latch and pushed gently on the door. The hinges were stiff, and the door creaked as it opened and he ceased pushing it any further so as not to alert the gang. He signalled to Tariq to wait quietly. The toilet flushed, and at that moment, he pushed the door open and closed it behind him. Now both outside, they put their shoes back on and ran down the farm track to where the American had parked his white VW Golf on the main road. He opened the passenger door for Tariq and pushed it shut as quietly as possible. He did the same for the driver's door from the inside. Tariq expected the American liberator to start the engine and accelerate away, but instead, he calmly released the handbrake; the car then quietly gained speed down the hill. A hundred yards down the slope, the driver said to Tariq, 'Ready for a rolling start?' He let the clutch out and the engine fired up.

Now up to 60mph, the American explained, 'We need to get the next ferry in thirty-six minutes before they realise you've gone AWOL.' Tariq noticed the TomTom satellite navigation screen fixed to the inside of the windscreen showing the route with a journey time to the ferry at Kamenari of thirty-four minutes.

Tariq looked across at the driver, studying his face closely for the first time. 'I've seen you before, haven't I? You saved me from those crazed Bosnians at the Olympic Park. You're not wearing your baseball cap this time.'

'Yes, I've dropped my disguise.'

'How did you find me?'

'The phone, remember? It has a tracker.'

'It can't be; it's been dead for days now. I forgot to take it out of my coat.'

'Reserve power mode. It sends out a blip every minute for a week – not your average phone. That reminds me, there's a plug in here to charge it up. What happened in there, by the way?'

'I nearly died in there, that's what happened.'

'Real sorry, buddy, that I couldn't get you out earlier – I had to bide my time.'

Tariq asked, 'Did you see the man who appeared through the door? Was that you?'

'Not me. I was outside the whole time: I didn't see anybody; you were probably hallucinating. That's what happens when you're asphyxiated.'

'But he knew my real name, Bogdan Tanović.'

The American's expression turned angry. 'What? God damn it!' What else did they get out of you?'

'The man with the double-headed eagle tattoo on the back of his neck. I remembered his name – Stefan Avramov. I remembered going with him to the tattoo parlour to get it done.'

'Shit! This is bad. I'm going to have to report this, buddy. They won't like it one bit.'

'Like what?' asked Tariq.

'Let's just get to the ferry, OK?'

With the ferry in sight in the bay below, Tariq said, 'You haven't told me your name.'

'Frank, just call me Frank. The youngsters call me

Uncle Frank, but I don't think that applies to you; no offence.'

'What is your part in this, Frank? Why are you following me? I'm guessing you work for an American agency.'

'Tariq, that's classified, and I strongly recommend, for your own safety, that you forget the name Bogdan Tanović, if you know what's good for you.'

'Why, Frank, have you been following me half the way across Europe? And why should I stick to my old name?' Tariq paused and asked, 'Has Jovica Stanisic got something to do with this? I remember dealing with him.' Frank slammed on the brakes, bringing the VW to a standstill, their seatbelts locking them into the seats. Tariq asked, in shock, 'I thought we were in a hurry?'

Frank turned towards Tariq and said, wide-eyed, 'We are, but if you want to stay alive, you don't know Stanisic, and you don't know Avramov! Got it? Because of you, Avramov is a dead man! Keep it that way until the Mladic trial is over. Got it!?'

'Now the Bosnians have the name of the man with the tattoo; they should leave me alone.'

'Wrong, Tariq! Every Bosnian will now be out looking for him, and they won't rest until both you and him are brought to The Hague as key witnesses to the genocide, and every Serb will be trying to stop that from happening.'

Tariq asked, 'Why me? I don't remember anything... well, I didn't until today.'

'Because you're the only person who can identify Avramov... Time's up.' Frank put the car into gear, accelerating fast, screeching the tyres, catapulting them to 70mph, then braking heavily at the blind bend. Tariq braced himself.

After the bend, Tariq said, 'The trial could go on for months, years even. Where does that leave me?' The American didn't respond and continued at speed along the coastal road, descending towards the ferry terminal. They were the last car on the ferry. Once on board, Frank didn't let Tariq out of his sight. Tariq went to the toilet, and Frank waited outside. The American's mood had turned more serious since their conversation in the car. Tariq was concerned as his American guardian angel seemed to be suddenly turning against him.

On the ferry, now halfway across the harbour, Tariq and Frank saw two cars drive down to the ferry terminal they'd just departed from. Four men got out of the car and stared intently at the ferry near half a mile away, with their hands on their hips. Tariq couldn't make out their faces, but he recognised their hair and clothing – it was the Bosnians.

Frank took a call and walked along the deck to get some privacy. From the body language Tariq could tell that it was a difficult conversation. A few minutes later, he returned and said to Tariq, 'They want me to take you in.'

'Kiss my ass! You understand that expression, don't you?'

'We need to take you in for your own safety, or do you want to be tortured again? Like you said, the trial could go on for months or longer. Surely you can appreciate that you need protection?'

'I want to keep my freedom; that's what I appreciate the most.'

'We can do this the easy way or the hard way. Do you

know what these are?' He brought out of his side bag two boxes of medical tablets.

'What?! Where did you get those? That's the medication that Millie's taking. I don't understand – what are you doing with those?'

'That's right. Millie needs them. We know that only too well. We also know that they're flown in from the US. It's an experimental drug, not licensed for sale outside the US, so we can put a stop to your supply just like that, which would be a shame, wouldn't it? Especially as she is making such good progress.'

Tariq replied in a subdued tone, 'I thought you were with the good guys. How could you sink so low?'

'Not my decision, buddy. This one goes way above me – right to the top. Look, calm down; this is for your own good.'

'Tell your people to come over here and speak to me. I'll meet them in London.'

'No can do, sorry. My orders are to bring you to the US so you can't come to any harm, and to give you a thorough de-briefing.'

'I don't have to listen to this crap. I still don't know who you are.'

Frank reached down and took out a plain folded black wallet from a sleeved pouch strapped to his stomach under his red and yellow floral polo shirt. *CIA* was embossed discreetly on its slender spine. He then opened it, placing his thumb over his agent number. The face was his, and the quality and detailing were on a par with a UK passport. On one of the open pages was a square hologram of an American bald eagle on a blue circular background. There was text curved above within the blue circle in white capitals, *CENTRAL INTELLIGENCE AGENCY*, and below, *UNITED STATES OF AMERICA* in red capitals on a yellow banner.

Agent Frank dropped the car off at the hire firm and then walked across the Tivat Airport car park. He told Tariq to get behind a large black van for cover and said, 'Put these on.' He handed him a red baseball cap with the Montenegrin emblem on it and then some dark glasses; also a white T-shirt with *MONTENEGRO* written on it and the Montenegrin emblem underneath. The emblem was of a yellow-coloured eagle with two heads looking in opposite directions, intertwined with other symbols.

Thud! An empty wine bottle arced firmly down on the back of Agent Frank's skull. It was a controlled impact, enough to knock him unconscious without a sound. Tariq turned around to see who had delivered the blow. PC Wilson cushioned the agent's fall to the ground with his arms threaded under the agent's, then laid him flat behind the black van. Tariq exclaimed, 'Wilson? What the hell!' Wilson searched the agent's bag and his pockets, taking out two mobile phones. Tariq took his chance to retrieve the two boxes of medical tablets from the agent for Millie.

Wilson said with urgency. 'Come on, we haven't got long before he comes round. I've organised a priority boarding, but they'll still want to scan your bag. Wilson guided Tariq to the Turkish Airlines check-in, which was now deserted as passengers were already boarding. He had to shout for one of the staff to attend the desk, 'Police, police, emergency check-in.' A young woman with the deep-red tailored steward's uniform appeared from behind the screen and scanned the policeman's passport. Tariq then presented his passport, which she also scanned. Looking back through the large glass airport sidewall, Wilson noticed a man making a phone call as he approached the black van.

Wilson flashed his police badge at the airport security desk and dropped his bag onto the mini-conveyor belt. The scan revealed nothing, but the archway detector beeped as Tariq passed through. He pulled his trouser belt off and re-entered the detector, successfully this time. They then walked briskly towards the departure lounges. It wasn't obvious which desk was Turkish Airlines', so Wilson had to double back to view a departure gate display screen.

'Gate 12,' he said. 'It's at the far end of the departure lounge.'

A male attendant in the same deep-red uniform blocked their path, 'I'm sorry, sir, but the departure check-in is now closed.'

Wilson could see passengers climbing the boarding steps into the plane less than a hundred yards away. Noticing that an adjacent terminal departure door was open, he grabbed Tariq's arm and pulled him through the open door. He turned briefly to the attendant, showing his badge, 'Police!' They sprinted towards the plane to outrun security personnel looking in their direction and talking into their radios. At the top of the boarding stairs, an air stewardess had almost closed the plane door when she caught sight of PC Wilson and Tariq climbing up the steps and she re-opened it to allow them on board.

CHAPTER 29

Fifteen minutes into the flight, they were at thirty thousand feet, looking down at a thick layer of white cloud. The Turkish Airlines flight attendants progressed methodically down the aisle, serving a choice of chicken and cheese rolls, drinks and snacks. Tariq asked PC Wilson to get him a couple of whisky and Cokes to calm his nerves. Tariq turned to Wilson. 'Thanks for rescuing me back there. It was getting heavy.'

'Yeah, those Bosnians are bloody brutal. You don't mess about with them. It had to be a clean hit. Sorry if I startled you.'

'That's OK. You're right – the Bosnians are brutal. I need to recover from that gang.'

Wilson looked confused, 'Gang? I only saw that one guy. The guy I took out.'

'Ah, yes, uh… the other three had just driven off,' Tariq lied.

A few minutes before the descent to Gatwick Airport, Wilson said to Tariq, 'I'm authorised to inform you that we're monitoring the Elm Street SFO office.'

'Monitoring for what?'

'External emails. Mobile phone calls.'

'What for? Why?'

'It came from high level, so don't ask too many questions. We believe there's evidence of criminal activity in the SFO Karlo Mitchko case investigations. He's got a lot to lose if he goes down for fraud; his reputation and at least fifteen years in the slammer. DI Randall has told me to put it to you that the offer is still on the table if you want it; now's the time for a plea bargain. All you need to do is to come in and give us the evidence against your accomplices. We know the Bosnian gang are on your case – I can vouch for that. If they've a blackmail screw on you for your affair with Cheryl, or getting to Millie, that's not your fault; we get it. We're on your side, Tariq.'

'Wilson – sorry, I don't even know your first name.'

'Wilson will do.'

'Wilson, OK. I admit that the Bosnians have threatened me to lose the case, or they'll release the photographs of Cheryl and me – but it's not me that's sabotaging the case. I'm not the one taking documents out of the office and sending them to the warehouse in St Albans; Stuart Harper is. You need to go after him and Burton – tell DI Randall that. They're trying to set me up as a scapegoat for the whole thing. Why can't you police people get it? Why can't you help me for once?!'

PC Wilson changed tack. 'Do you know what we discovered on the first day of the stake-out at the SFO?'

Tariq was obliged to ask, 'What?'

'Encrypted calls with very specific encryption signatures.'

Tariq looked at him quizzically. 'You've lost me; specific to what, or who?'

'The CIA. Only the CIA use that type of encryption. It's easily recognisable, to our guys at least.'

The plane landed at Gatwick Airport just after 4pm. Tariq and Wilson were unloading their bags from the overhead lockers when Wilson's phone beeped loudly three times as if it were an alarm warning. Wilson looked at the message on his phone screen: *Encrypted device code #55.*

'My God,' he said to himself. Tariq looked confused to why PC Wilson looked dumbfounded. He said to Tariq, 'Sit down, please.'

Wilson sat down next to Tariq and told him to wait until all the passengers had left the plane. He showed the stewardess his police badge and requested that he be allowed five minutes to interview the passenger next to him. She smiled back at his request. 'Of course, sir.' Wilson held his phone against Tariq's bag to see if he could recreate the alarm signal, but nothing happened. He then retrieved a second handheld scanning device, primed it, and scanned Tariq's bag again. The device emitted a high-pitched buzz. Wilson looked incredulous. He homed in on the source as the buzz got louder and retrieved the Nokia phone Agent Frank had given Tariq at the Olympics. The scanner displayed a code that caused Wilson to stare in almost disbelief. 'CIA. Holy crap, you're one of them – you're CIA! You guys are good. I mean, *really* good. I would never have thought…'

'I'm not CIA! The guy I was with was CIA. The guy you knocked unconscious.'

'So why did you tell me you were being handled by the Bosnian gang? Too late to change your tune now.'

'The CIA want to bring me in for some reason – I didn't think it was worth explaining, as I don't understand what they are panicking about. I was just trying to keep it simple.'

'Simple, as in – you're not CIA? Sure, I get it, and you just happen to have a CIA encrypted phone in your bag? I wouldn't have put you down as one of them, but now it makes a whole lot of sense with all those encrypted calls. Like I said, you guys are good.' Wilson then made a call. 'Carol, I bet you haven't done this for a while, but can you run a CIA registration check on a Tariq Markovic; that's T-A-R-I-Q M-A-R-K-O-V-I-C.' Wilson glanced across at Tariq and waited for the response, 'OK, then. Yes, I'm ready, Carol. Right… what? I see…' Wilson glanced across again at Tariq. 'What does that mean, Carol?… No, nor do I.' The officer ended the call and stared at Tariq, before asking, 'Who are you, Tariq? Why are you on the CIA list as Highly Classified?'

Tariq said plainly, 'I've told you – I am *not* CIA!'

Wilson sighed, 'This is way above my head. My job is to deliver my report to DI Randall; it's his problem then.'

After getting through the Gatwick Airport terminal, Wilson and Tariq were picked up in a marked police car. The driver explained that it was less hassle with airport security if they use a marked car as it saves showing IDs to six different security guards. They made their way across to the M23 and drove north towards Croydon. Tariq's phone rang as they were approaching the end of the motorway.

'Hello, Alice, darling. I was going to call you; I've just got off the plane.'

'Yes, of course… I'll meet you and Nathan at the office tomorrow morning at 8:30am.'

Alice asked him about his trip.

'No, sorry, I didn't find out anything. I don't want to talk about it right now. I'm tired and I'm in the police car;

can we talk about it when you get back to the house with Millie?' Tariq had almost forgotten the original purpose of the trip: to meet his uncle. It didn't seem to matter now. Tariq concluded, 'OK, great; can't wait to see Millie back at home again. Bye then.'

They approached Tariq's house in Beckenham a few minutes past 7:00pm. As they approached the house, Tariq suddenly felt nervous and requested that PC Wilson escort him into the house and stay with him while he checked every room, including the garage and shed. Wilson gave Tariq his personal number if he needed to call him in an emergency, but if he didn't answer, he was to call 999.

After PC Wilson left, Tariq went into the kitchen. He twisted his left arm around and rolled up his sleeve to reveal the names he had written in blue biro soon after his revelation under torture in Montenegro, *Bogan Tanović* and *Stefan Avramov – man with tattoo.* He remembered Agent Frank's warning not to reveal these names until the Ratko Mladic trial ended. Tariq thought of Agent Frank recovering from a sore head, and probably feeling enraged that he had failed to carry out his order to deliver him to the US authorities from Montenegro. Now that he was back in the UK, they would need an extradition request to take him to the US, wouldn't they?

CHAPTER 30

On Monday morning, Tariq's alarm went off at 6:30am. He rubbed his eyes and walked across the room towards the window with the curtains drawn closed. His trip to Montenegro immediately returned to the forefront of his mind. Too much had changed for him to return to the status quo. He couldn't turn back the clock. He stopped himself at the last second from throwing open the curtains as he had initially intended. He moved to the side of the window to peer down the street. His eyes focused on a red Ford Focus under a semi-mature London plane tree. He recognised the car as the one he'd seen parked down the road from the Elm Street SFO office before interviewing the Bosnians. The fluttering reflection of the tree branches on the windscreen made it impossible to see clearly the two men in the front seats. It looked like one had a beard. Tariq drew back from the window; he didn't want to alert them that he'd seen them. He thought about ringing PC Wilson on his mobile, but decided that this wasn't an emergency; not yet.

Tariq got dressed behind the still-closed curtains while considering if the men in the car were Bosnians, Serbs, CIA, or even the police. Either way, none of them had his welfare at heart, so he'd best avoid them as long as he could. He decided to risk going into the kitchen for some coffee and toast. He went straight in and scanned down the garden for any surveillance operatives seeking cover. There was no movement outside except next door's black cat, Dora, walking along the top of the garage roof. Dora would have stopped and stared down at anyone hiding behind the fence, but she continued to amble across the roof and jumped onto the shed roof as usual. Tariq maintained his surveillance of the garden as he bit into his buttered toast. He suddenly wished that Nathan was with him. He usually had an alternative solution when facing a problem.

Tariq took his chances using the rear exit via the back gate and then down the track to the road behind. He phoned Wilson, but it went to voicemail. He left a message informing him of the two men in the red Ford Focus, and said that he was leaving the house. At least the police would have some clue as to his movements if he were abducted, but it was probably a wasted call. He took the longer route to the next train station, Elmers End, as they would have been expecting him at Eden Park station. He caught the train at Elmers End station without incident.

Tariq caught the No.17 Bus from London Bridge station to the SFO Elm House office, arriving just after 8:30am. Alice was waiting in the car with Nathan, a short distance from the office. Nathan jumped out of the car to greet his father. 'Hello, Dad, we've just got here. I had a good time with Mum yesterday – she took me swimming and to the diving club, and we had a takeaway Chinese meal. I tried the sweet and sour chicken and I liked it, even though the sauce was orange. I don't usually like orange.'

Alice gave Tariq a brief hug and said, 'I'm sorry, darling, that the trip to Montenegro was a waste of time.

You can tell me all about it when I'm home with Millie tomorrow.' She paused. 'Tariq, I'm worried; the consultant told me this morning that the American drug supplier has run out of stock, and she's about two weeks short of finishing the course.' She wiped a few tears from her eyes. Tariq unclasped the strap of his man bag and pulled out the two boxes of tablets that he'd retrieved from Uncle Frank just after officer Wilson had clubbed him from behind with the bottle. Alice took them and read the label, then stared intently at Tariq, saying, 'What? How? Where did you get these?'

'I got them off this American guy on the plane. We got talking, and it so happened that his seven-year-old son had just recovered from leukaemia using the same drug, so he had some spare boxes.' Alice spotted a traffic enforcement officer walking towards the car, which was parked on a double yellow line, so she gave Tariq another hug and a kiss on the cheek and jumped in the car to drive off, not before holding up the tablets and mouthing, 'Thank you.'

Tariq made a coffee and Nathan a hot chocolate in the office fourth-floor kitchen. Tariq logged on at his desk computer and replied to a few emails on the case. One of them was from Stuart Harper, who requested electronic copies of the last six weeks' document ledgers as part of an audit ordered by Pemberton. Tariq whispered to himself, 'What a cheek; that con artist has probably already doctored the ledgers, which will no doubt incriminate me.' Tariq thought back to the red Mitchko diary Nathan had seen Harper leave the office with, then taking the taxi before they could catch up with him. As Wilson had mentioned to him on the plane, the police needed hard evidence to make an arrest. Pemberton was due back in the office tomorrow, when Tariq could face a permanent office suspension while they decided on their next course of action.

Today could be his last chance to secure the hard evidence he needed. Since Pemberton had suspended him from the case, neither he nor Nathan were permitted entry into the property room. After a couple of hours of looking at emails on his PC, Tariq was restless, and decided to take the lift down to the basement, just to walk around. When in the basement, the lift bell dinged down the corridor. Out of curiosity he looked to see who'd exited the lift. It was Harper! He walked out of the lift, down the corridor, away from Tariq, towards the post room. He was carrying a large brown envelope, and entered the post room through the half-open green door. Tariq strode up to the door and peered inside the post room. Harper had his back to the door and used the SFO post stamp to stamp the envelope he was carrying, which the SFO used in lieu of stamps. Tariq scanned the room. No one else was in there. Harper then walked back towards the door to place the envelope in the outgoing grey post bag. Tariq had missed his chance to get him last time; not this time – it had to be now. As Harper approached the post bag, Tariq manoeuvred quickly around the door, grabbing the envelope with one hand and Harper with the other. He twisted Harper's arm up his back and thrust him out of the post room into the corridor.

Harper screeched in pain and shock, 'Aaaagghh! Get off me; you're hurting me, you madman.'

'Shut up, Harper; just shut it, will you!'

Tariq man-handled Harper down the corridor and into the men's changing room, used mainly by male cyclists and staff who went to the gym at lunchtime. Tariq kicked the door shut behind him and continued their forward momentum as he pushed Harper across the room, slamming him back-first against a row of lockers on the opposite wall. The impact shook the lockers, causing some cycle helmets and bike shoes balancing on top to crash to the ground. The impact of hitting the lockers left Harper sitting limply on the concrete floor, moaning in shock. Tariq grabbed him by the throat and pushed him back against the steel lockers.

Harper, stunned, croaked, 'You'll never work here again, Markovic; this is assault.'

'You're right, Stuart; if I don't get some evidence today, Pemberton will probably kick me out tomorrow. Oh, and by the way, there are no cameras in here. What assault?'

Harper was wearing a red tie for a change. Tariq twisted it in his hand, tightening it around Harper's neck like a noose. Harper was struggling to breathe. As a man fights for his life, any logical resistance gives way to survival mode. Tariq lifted the brown envelope in front of Harper, 'Because of you, Harper, my career is shot, and I could be going to prison, so you'd better give me some answers, or I might do something to you that we both regret. I'll do time for you! Do you hear me?!' Tariq lifted the heavy brown envelope and waved it in front of Harper's face and shouted at him, 'What is this then!? *Why* are you posting documents out of the office?' Tariq noted the St Alban's address on the envelope; the warehouse that he'd visited two weeks ago. He ripped open the envelope. 'Let's have a look, shall we? What is this? *End of Year Account: Mitchko instructions to chief accountant Oct 2011 Doc. No. 7158.* This looks like a relevant document, wouldn't you say? Explain to me why you are posting it. Who are you sending it to?' Tariq tightened the red tie around his neck.

Harper, still fighting for air, replied almost in a whisper, 'Burton... Burton told me to copy it and send off duplicate copies of key documents.'

'Duplicates?'

'Burton wants key documents copied; he knows they're going missing...' Harper hesitated before continuing, 'He thinks that an insider is sabotaging the case, and he thinks it's you.'

'Me? Why me?'

'He reckons that you're probably a Serb underneath, and you had close bonds with Mitchko during the Bosnian War, so he thinks you're working for him; either that or he's blackmailing you. Why don't you admit it, Tariq?'

Tariq tightened the tie around Harper's neck in barely controlled anger. 'Serbian! Bullshit! The Serbs are after me, you know, as are the Bosnians and the CIA, not to mention the police. I am being fitted up, Harper; that's what is happening here, and you're in on it – so why don't *you* admit it!' Tariq slightly released the tension in Harper's tie and took a few slow breaths to slow his racing heartbeat. He then addressed Harper in a more measured tone. 'Has it occurred to you that Burton is using your meddling as a smoke screen to cover up what he's up to? It's all part of his plan to pin everything on me: I can see that now. For God's sake, Harper – don't be so bloody naive. He'll put you in the frame; he won't spare you. I tell you something; if Burton suspects you're onto him, I'd watch your back if I were you. There's a lot at stake here – Mitchko would pay millions to avoid jail, and he can afford it. Mitchko and Burton know how to get rid of people, you know. I'm a kitten compared to Burton. He's a Vietnam vet. Killing people is probably therapy for him.' Voices echoed down the corridor. Tariq got up to leave the changing room, not before tightening his grip on Harper's neck again. 'And what are you up to in the cleaners' storeroom, hey?'

'Cleaners' storeroom? I don't know what…'

'Don't lie to me, Harper. Nathan saw you coming out of the room last week. What are you up to in there?' Tariq didn't wait for Harper's response and exited the room as the voices grew louder. To avoid being seen walking back down the corridor, he descended the stairs into the lower basement room, passing the nearly full skip, and then into the adjacent car parking area. From the lower basement car park, Tariq used a different staircase to return to the fourth floor.

Nathan was still at his desk, 'Hi Nathan, sorry to leave you. I had to discuss something with Stuart Harper. I think he understood me in the end, but I don't expect any thanks for it. I didn't punch him or anything – I only tried to strangle him.'

'Dad, I know that's one of your expressions, but I'm not going to ask you what it means. I went down to the property room to get my puzzle book that I'd left in there.'

'Property room – I thought our passes had been de-activated?'

Nathan looked embarrassed.

'What's up, Nathan? I won't mind. How did you get in the property room?'

Nathan looked around to check if anyone was close by,

'I printed one off in the security room when Ajay went out for coffee; I saw how he did it, and he didn't lock his PC. I wanted a spare one, so I made an all-areas pass, that's all.'

'Nathan, as I said, I don't mind. In fact, I'm glad you did. You've given me an idea, and we'll need your friend Ajay's help.'

At lunchtime, Nathan went to the security room to find Ajay. Five minutes later, Nathan and Ajay approached the property room. Tariq was waiting just around the corner, trying to stay out of sight and to check that the coast was clear. Tariq gambled that Ajay wouldn't yet be aware that his authorisation to access the property room had been withdrawn by Pemberton. Ajay said, 'Hello, Tariq. Nathan tells me that some papers slid under the door of the cleaners' store.'

'Yes, that's right. I would appreciate it if you could open the door for us.'

'Yes, sure. I'll open it up and leave you to it; please close the door on your way out, yeah?'

'Yes, of course. Thanks, Ajay.'

Ajay pushed in the numbers on the number lock and opened the door. Tariq and Nathan entered the small room, and Ajay departed.

On the front shelf was the cleaning equipment and chemicals he'd seen earlier through the door. At the back of the room were black metal shelves. Tariq looked at what was on the back shelves in disbelief – documents; important case documents. Tariq noticed one in particular and picked it up – Document *7158*; the one he'd caught Harper with earlier in the post room. Tariq thought to himself, *What is going on?*

Nathan then looked across at him, eyes wide, 'Look at this, Dad – this is amazing!' Nathan was leaning over the bottom shelf, beckoning his father to come over.

Tariq positioned himself behind Nathan to see what he was looking at. Tariq exclaimed, 'My God!' Fixed to the bottom shelf were several orange trunking tube sections feeding into the basement skip below. Documents and the like could be dropped discreetly straight down into the skip. Tariq had seen the trunk hanging down from the ceiling so many times, but without a second thought as to where it was coming from or its purpose. Tariq said quietly to himself, 'This is how Harper was disposing of the documents!' He mused that the arrangement was brutally efficient, and beautifully simple. There was no way that Harper could have set this up on his own. Only a senior manager could have organised something like this – someone like Burton. He now had some evidence – the document 7158 that he'd caught Harper trying to mail in the post room, which matched the one he'd just found in the cleaners' room. At least he could show these to Pemberton tomorrow to back up his story, and Harper had confessed that he was working for Burton. Pemberton was already on Burton's case for setting up the CCTV web-based surveillance system without his permission. Peering down the trunking again, it was apparent that the skip was topped with a thick layer of broken concrete, put there by workmen carrying out some works in the car park. A new, empty skip would have to be brought in before Harper could dispose of any more documents down the trunking. Perhaps that was why Harper had taken the Mitchko diary out of the office that day – the skip had been full?

Tariq persuaded Nathan to leave early for a drink in the Calthorpe Arms, with a bribe to buy him a pint of his new favourite black-and-white drink, Guinness.

Two pints of Guinness and three of London Pride later, Tariq said to Nathan, 'I'm proud of you, Nathan. If it weren't for you, maybe I wouldn't have ever noticed what Harper was up to with the ledgers. It was you that spotted him taking Mitchko's diary that day and saw him coming out of the cleaners' storeroom.' Tariq finished his drink and said to Nathan, 'In case anything happens to me, I want you to know that… you're special to me, Nathan. I've come to realise that now.'

'Dad, are you joking with me? Why would anything happen to you?'

'I don't know, Nathan, I really don't know, but it could. You know I went to Montenegro over the weekend?'

'Yes, but you didn't say why.'

'I can only tell you this, Nathan – I remembered terrible things, terrible…' Tariq wiped away the tears forming in his eyes. 'But do you know what? I saw for the first time in my mind's eye, after seventeen years, the faces of my father and younger brother.' Tariq paused again and said, 'If anything happens to me, tell your mother that I love her and Millie. I've made mistakes, I know; I've been stubborn, I've run away from the past, I've been a coward. I hope you can forgive me, Nathan… I hope that I can find redemption for going down the wrong path.'

'Yes, I forgive you, Dad. Can we go home now, please?'

The question prompted Tariq to realise that it was too risky to go home. The men in the red car, or others, would either intercept him on the commute back or be lying in wait for him at home. He would have to risk it tomorrow to see Millie, but not today. Being denied seeing Millie perhaps one last time would be too much to bear. 'Nathan, I know you don't like surprises, but we're going to have to stay at a Travelodge tonight – the one at the end of the road. And before you panic, we'll go to the big Marks and Spencer and I'll buy you some new pyjamas, a toothbrush, and everything you need. You can take your time – it will be fun.'

Perhaps helped by the Guinness, Nathan went along with his father's proposal to spend the night at Travelodge without complaint, especially as he was promised new black-and-white pyjamas. They exited the pub through the beer garden and out through a side door onto a backstreet.

At the Travelodge, after Nathan had gone to sleep, Tariq received a WhatsApp message from Cheryl. He opened it to see a photograph of a beautiful sleeping baby with Cheryl looking over it, tired but elated. He gazed at the picture again, seeing himself in the baby's face. Tariq considered how long it would be before Cheryl asked for money for a baby's cot, pram, and everything else. He would end up being hated by all sides.

CHAPTER 31

Walking down Elm Street from the Travelodge towards the office the following morning, Tariq and Nathan noticed three marked police cars parked outside the steps. Tariq froze and turned around to walk back up the street but was intercepted by two police officers behind him, blocking his path. Tariq didn't recognise the policemen but spotted DI Randall looking across at him from a car on the other side of the road. One of the officers asked, 'Tariq Markovic?'

'Yes. What is—'

'Can you identify yourself, please?'

Tariq showed the policeman his SFO building pass. Nathan asked his father with a panicked expression, 'What's happening, Dad? Why are there so many policemen at the office? I don't like it. Why didn't they tell you they were coming? What do they want?'

'I don't know, Nathan. Maybe this policeman will tell me. Don't tell me Stuart Harper has made a complaint after he slipped over in the changing room? I grabbed his tie to help him breathe – he was half unconscious and delirious...'

'Save your breath, Mr Markovic – we'll explain everything down at the station. I take it that this is your son? He can come with us.'

In the car, the three policemen were not forthcoming

as to why he was being taken in for questioning, so he gave up asking. Inside the station, Tariq was separated from Nathan and taken into the same basement room he'd been questioned in on his previous visits. He was told to sit down and wait for the senior officer to join them in the interview room. A tall, stony-faced, plain-clothed senior-looking policeman entered the room.

'Hello, I'm Chief Inspector Jonathan Mills,' he paused. 'I know who you are.' He closed the door behind him and looked dispassionately at Tariq. He directed one of the junior officers to activate the recording equipment. He sat opposite Tariq and waited for the red light of the recording device to come on. 'This is the interview of Tariq Markovic at Bishopsgate Police Station in room B3 on Tuesday 14th August 2012, 10:19am. The lead interviewer is myself, Chief Inspector Jonathan Mills, and with me in the room are DI Randall and PC Hitchens. Can you identify yourself, please?' he said, focusing on Tariq.

'I'm Tariq Markovic.'

'Address?'

'234 Cherry Orchard Avenue, Beckenham.'

'You do not have to say anything but it may harm your defence if you do not mention something when questioned that you later rely on in court.'

Tariq shuffled nervously on his chair. 'Can someone please tell me what this is all about?'

'Can you identify this person please? I am showing Mr Markovic a photograph of the person relevant to this investigation.'

Tariq took the photograph from Chief Inspector Mills for a closer look. 'It's Burton, Jack Burton.'

'How do you know this person?'

'He's my head of department at the SFO. So what about him? Why are we talking about him?'

CI Mills hesitated, not so much out of concern, but to read Tariq's body language. 'Jack Burton was killed last night in an RTA – a road traffic accident. His car mounted the pavement, broke through a pedestrian barrier and entered the river. Police divers are still at the scene to retrieve his body, if it's still in the vehicle. An eyewitness reported that there were no other vehicles involved. The present hypothesis is suicide, but naturally, we will also be investigating whether the vehicle was sabotaged in any way. If we find the body, we will also be testing for alcohol and drugs in his bloodstream. The Thames River has strong tidal currents. The tide was going out at the time, so his body could already be in the Thames Estuary somewhere, as far as we know. We're also trying to trace a small boat close to the scene as a potential key eyewitness to the accident.'

Tariq responded, 'I can't believe it; I don't believe it. How could this happen?'

'Maybe Burton knew that we were on to him. He was facing the prospect of a long prison sentence. Pemberton informed us that he was going to confront him on a number of issues, but Burton left the building in a hurry with his laptop – perhaps not surprising. He was last seen speaking to Stuart Harper, probably his accomplice, and now Harper's gone missing; probably on the run.' CI Mills paused, 'Tariq, are you aware if Burton had any enemies that would have wished him harm?'

'No, I can't help you; I have no idea, God damn it.' Tariq buried his head in his hands.

'I hear Burton was giving you a hard time on the Magnus Conan-Whittaker case.'

'So? That doesn't mean I wanted to kill him.'

'Do you have any idea why he would want to install a remote online-access CCTV surveillance application when the existing system was perfectly adequate? I should inform you that the Attorney General denied granting Burton special clearance for the new system, as Burton claimed. If he had control of the system, he could delete surveillance files, couldn't he?' CI Mills paused and continued, 'The popular theory is that Burton decided, in a fit of panic, to go down, literally, with his laptop to the bottom of the river, the incriminating evidence so destroyed, sparing the embarrassment for his family and ensuring they benefit from his generous pension allowance. Very considerate of him, don't you think?'

The Chief Inspector stared at Tariq before asking, 'So Tariq, have you taken a bribe from the Bosnian Serbs, or is it blackmail?'

'This is nonsense. This has nothing to do with me!'

'Tariq, please...' CI Mills got off his chair, walked away a few steps and returned, leaning towards Tariq, speaking in a slower, more measured tone. 'Tariq, we know you're being blackmailed for your affair with Cheryl Blackmore, and you've had to pay for expensive medical treatment for your daughter Millie. How can you explain ten thousand pounds sterling paid into your savings account?'

'What? I've no idea! I can't explain it because I know nothing about it! I haven't bothered to check it. I've said to you people before that this is one big set-up. You should be chasing them, not me!'

'So, some generous people gave you ten thousand pounds for fun, did they? I suggest that's very unlikely, don't you?'

'Please trace the source account because it will lead you to the gang trying to frame me,' said Tariq as he wiped the sweat off his brow with a tissue, his scar reddening.

Mills continued his questioning. 'Hot in here, isn't it? If you don't want to stay in a room like this for a long time, then you need to tell me what's going on. I want names – who's behind this? Start talking and we can get somewhere, can't we?' CI Mills squared up to Tariq and almost shouted in his face, 'Stop wasting my time, Mr Markovic, before I lose all sympathy for you! You understand? You're only making it worse for yourself! If I find out you're holding back, I can guarantee that I will make life very difficult for you right up to the time you're sentenced for a long stretch. After that you're fair game in the scrubs, and I'll make sure you'll be in with a serious bunch of renegades. Oh, and by the way, despite your status being CIA – highly classified, as filed in PC Wilson's report, I've checked that you're not an agent, so don't think for a minute that that would save you.'

Tariq replied, 'Look, I've already told PC Wilson that I'm not CIA. I really want to help you find out who's behind it, but I'm sorry, it's not me you want; you've got the wrong guy. You need to…'

'Which guy should we be looking for? Tariq Markovic, or someone else?'

'What do you mean?'

'We've been in contact with the Bosnian authorities. According to them, Tariq Markovic was killed in the war. He has a gravestone in the Srebrenica war cemetery. Your immigration documentation says that you were under the custody of an American division of NATO, so we've also lodged an inquiry with them, and we're expecting a reply soon.' DI Mills leaned forward. 'So who are you, Tariq Markovic? Do you know who I think you are? You're part of Karlo Mitchko's clan; his extended family, or one of his inner circle of friends. Why else would you risk everything to scupper the case? What happened in Montenegro? Did the Serbian mafia get to you, sponsored by Mitchko? Are they behind this? I can't protect you unless you tell us, Tariq, or whoever you are! So, why don't you level with us, save all of us a lot of time? You'll get a much lighter sentence if you testify against Burton and Harper and the rest of them. So how about it?'

Tariq replied, 'I'd be happy to tell you all about Harper's involvement in this, because he's your man, *not me*!'

CI Mills got up from his chair and motioned to the junior officer to stop recording. He told Tariq, 'Don't think this is the end of it. I've got a feeling that the key to unlocking this riddle is finding out who you really are, and believe me, I'm going to find out.'

Tariq and Nathan were driven back from the police station by the same policeman. Close to the office, Tariq said to the police driver, 'Heh, I'd rather not go back straight to the office. I can't face it. Can you drop us down that road over there so we can get some lunch first?' The policeman obliged, and Tariq and Nathan disembarked.

'Where are we going, Dad?'

'Calthorpe Arms. It's nearly lunchtime. I'll buy you fish and chips and a Guinness.'

'Oh, yes; that would be good.'

Tariq mulled over the tragic demise of Burton, and of Harper on the run. At least the culprits were out of the way, but it left him carrying the can of suspicion. The food and drinks arrived, and halfway through his meal, Tariq said to Nathan, 'Do you know what, Nathan? I think I know why Harper took that red diary out of the office.'

'Why then?'

'There was no skip that day.'

Nathan stopped eating and reached for his laptop. 'Do you know what day it was?'

'It was the Wednesday before the super Saturday August... so that would have been 1st August.'

Nathan opened his laptop on the cushioned bench seat next to him. 'Dad, please don't get excited or mad at me, please. I helped Ajay set up the remote surveillance system, so I downloaded it onto my laptop, and Ajay needed to tell me the password to test it out.'

'But Pemberton's shut it down, hasn't he?'

'Yes, on the SFO system, but I still have it on my laptop. Do you want me to look for CCTV footage on 1st August?'

'Of course, yes, if you can.'

'The lower basement room doesn't have a camera, but I can do a search on the car park camera. The cameras are set to sleep mode until they pick up movement to save on memory and to avoid hours of dead footage being created.' Nathan pressed a few keys and continued to press the space bar as he scrolled through the footage. He commented on each event, 'Car, car, person walking up the ramp, car, car... skip lorry!'

'Can I have a look?'

'There, that's the skip lorry taking out the full skip.'

'Wow, Nathan, you amaze me sometimes. So we definitely know now that's why Harper couldn't have chucked it into the skip. What time was that by the way?'

'1st August, 4:26pm.'

Tariq leaned across to view the video footage. 'What was that, Nathan? Why did that video clip come up?'

'Oh, it was probably the door moving slightly; sometimes you can't see anything.'

'Zoom in on the door.' There was a rectangular hole cut out in the door panel above the door itself, where a service duct used to be.

Tariq said, 'Look, it's Harper; he's standing on a chair behind the skip. Look at that! He's reached into the skip and brought out a black file. He's now taking it away. Perhaps he didn't want to risk someone seeing important documents in the skip? When was that, Nathan?'

'3:09pm, the same day the skip was taken away. Dad, I need to shut it down now before they notice someone is accessing the cameras from an external channel.'

'Oh really? Yes, Nathan, shut it down now. Thanks.'

Still in the Calthorpe Arms, Nathan had finished his fish and chips and was sipping his Guinness when he said, 'Dad, I noticed something in the police station.'

'What do you mean, Nathan? What?'

'Well, while the other police were talking to you, I saw a policeman with a see-through bag marked *Tariq Markovic evidence bag No.3.*'

'Oh my God. They have three bags already do they!?'

Nathan responded, 'I wasn't thinking about that. I noticed the memory stick in the bag was a SanDisk 2.'

'So, what about it?

'We used a SanDisk 3 memory stick. I chose the SanDisk 3 as it has a quicker download speed.'

Tariq's eyes widened. 'So the police don't have the original memory stick – Cooper still has it?'

'Yes, I saw it on his desk, and then he put it in his drawer.'

'Cooper... why doesn't that surprise me? He must be in on it. God, how many more?'

Nathan looked at his father, uncertain whether that was a serious question, but Tariq answered his own question, 'Cooper set up the interview with the Bosnians and then leaked the transcript, probably under Mitcho's direction, and it explains why he was so keen to take the memory stick off me in the property room. Now he's given the police his own memory stick, he has the perfect alibi.' Tariq considered that by now, Cooper would have ensured that the files in the property room matched the doctored ledger master ledger, and furthermore, the evidence would point the finger at Tariq.

'Nathan, we've got to get that memory stick off Cooper – *today*. It could be our last chance.'

On the way back from the pub to the office, Tariq took Nathan along the side streets, through a side entrance into the SFO car park, and called a service lift to the fourth floor. He wanted to avoid any awkward office conversations about Burton's apparent suicide. The atmosphere in the office was understandably dire. There was an eerie silence with occasional subdued social interactions Tariq didn't want it to look like he'd something to hide so he returned to his desk as normal to continue working on the case handover report. He'd rather turn up and be asked to leave, as at least then he would be sent home on full pay until the matter was resolved or he was convicted and incarcerated. In any case, he had to get into Cooper's office to retrieve the memory stick somehow. He would need Nathan's help now more than ever.

Tariq said to Nathan, sitting at the desk behind him, 'Nathan, we have to get into Cooper's office to retrieve the memory stick. It's my last chance, you've got to help me. We need your *access all-areas* pass.'

Nathan looked alarmed but agreed to his father's request. He figured that he had to do everything he could to help his father prove his innocence.

They went up to Cooper's office on the eighth floor and were in the corridor when the lift door dinged. Tariq and Nathan stepped back quickly into the stairwell. Cooper exited the lift with two policemen, who he escorted into his office. It appeared that the policemen were writing down statements from Cooper. Ten minutes later, the policemen left the office, as did Cooper.

'Right, Nathan. Give me your pass please. Why don't you go back to your desk? If anyone asks where I am, just say that I've gone out to get some fresh air. They'll understand, and won't come looking for me.' Nathan handed over the pass and made his way down the stairs. Tariq walked over to Cooper's office, his heart beating like a drum, and used the pass to open the door. He heard footsteps coming down the corridor, so he closed the door and knelt on a chair so his legs couldn't be seen through the lower band of clear glass, the wider central glass panel being opaque. The footsteps passed, heading towards the lifts, so he went around to the front of Cooper's desk and opened his drawers in search of the memory stick. The first drawer was full of pens, stationery items, and miscellaneous knick-knacks.

'Where did you put it, Cooper? Come on – it must be here somewhere,' Tariq muttered to himself as he rummaged through each drawer in turn. After five minutes Tariq was getting desperate. He tipped the entire contents of the top drawer onto the carpet, but there was no stick. He opened the next drawer and tipped out its contents onto the floor in a similar fashion. He figured that the stick could be hidden in a small container right at the back of the drawer, so tipping out the contents was the quickest and most efficient way to find it. He did the same for the following three drawers. Cooper's office was beginning to look like squatters had trashed it. As Tariq had just finished spreading the contents across the floor in an arc of his hand to expose every item, he heard an urgent stampede of footsteps coming up the stairwell and then along the corridor. Cooper, DI Randall and a second policeman approached Cooper's office. Tariq stepped quickly across the room and locked the door.

Cooper then tried to force open the door and shouted, 'Tariq, the police are here. What are you doing in my office?!' He now stooped down to look through the clear bottom glass panel, and was shocked to see his desk drawers and their contents scattered all over the floor. This inflamed Cooper, and he banged on the door with the base of his fists. He then lifted his foot and attempted to kick the door open. The senior policeman, DI Randall, intervened, 'Mr Cooper, sir, please, there's no need for that – you'll damage yourself and property.' He spoke into his radio, 'Hi

Ajay, it's DI Randall. Can you bring up the spare key for room 805, Mark Cooper's room… Yeah, thanks. Quick as you can, please.'

Cooper exclaimed, 'Open the door now! You're done for, Markovic!'

Tariq estimated that he had two minutes, tops before Ajay arrived with the keys. In his rush he hadn't noticed before that there was another smaller side drawer, but it was locked. Tariq shouted out from the room, 'Where is it, Cooper?! Where is the memory stick with the ledger files? What have you got to hide? Why is the drawer locked?'

'I don't know what you're talking about. You've lost the plot, Tariq, admit it. You're going down for this and you know it.' Tariq was now crouching on his knees looking over the contents of Cooper's drawers strewn over the green carpet. He retrieved from the debris a silver-plated metal letter opener, which he then jammed into the lock of the locked drawer. He levered it upwards but it snapped off into the lock. 'Bugger!' Tariq crouched down again, desperately scrabbling through each pile of items from the drawers to find something else to get the locked drawer open. He found a screwdriver.

Cooper shouted at the policemen behind him, 'Where is he? Where's Ajay?'

'He'll be here any minute, Mr Cooper; just relax, please. We've got him covered; he's going nowhere.' Cooper started to take a run-up to kick the door open but thought better of it, twisting around in impatient frustration. The lift dinged, and Ajay walked quickly and calmly down the corridor towards them, holding an all-areas pass key and a bunch of master keys. Tariq knew his time had run out.

He grabbed the red-handled screwdriver and jammed it violently into the top of the locked drawer. This time the drawer sprung open.

The security guard tried his all-areas card pass but nothing happened. Ajay explained calmly, 'The sensor can disable the card lock if it detects severe vibration. It's an anti-break-in feature.'

DI Randall glanced over at Cooper, who looked embarrassed.

Tariq pulled open the side drawer. Its only contents were a bottle of Bell's whisky and a lead glass tumbler. Still on his knees, Tariq, almost in a reflex action, unscrewed the lid of the whisky bottle and poured himself half a glass. He held his drink high in the air towards Cooper, who was looking back through the glass, 'Cheers, Cooper – here's to nailing the fraudsters!' He then drank its contents in two gulps. At that moment Ajay found the right master key and opened the door. Tariq got to his feet, accidentally tipping the damaged sixth drawer upside down.

As Ajay and the two policemen approached him, Pemberton appeared in the doorway, 'What the blazes is going on, Tariq?! For God's sake, man – why can't you just go home quietly? There's no need for all this bloody mess!'

Tariq looked back at him, crestfallen, with his shirt hanging out, hair hanging messily over his fringe, holding the bottle of whisky in one hand and the now-empty tumbler in the other. Tariq didn't care for Cooper's respect, but he did for Pemberton's. 'Yes, sir. I was looking for something in his desk that you need to have...' Tariq happened to look down again at the upside-down drawer at his feet. There it was, taped to the bottom of the drawer

– the SanDisk 3 memory stick! Tariq bent down and tore the tape away to retrieve the memory stick. He walked over to Pemberton and concluded his sentence. 'You need to have something like this.' He planted the memory stick in the palm of Pemberton's hand. Tariq explained, 'That, sir, has the original case ledgers before they were removed by Harper and Cooper, who've then tried to frame me for their actions.'

Pemberton, lost for words, clasped the memory stick in his hand and looked across at Cooper on the opposite side of the desk. Cooper was the one who now looked crestfallen.

Pemberton said to Tariq in a magnanimous Scottish tone. 'Tariq, you've been under a lot of stress recently. Go home for a few weeks and get some rest. I hear your daughter is in hospital, gravely ill, so take some time out to be with her; she needs you, OK? We'll sort things out here. Just go home. We'll be in touch.'

That was DI Randall's cue to escort Tariq to his desk to retrieve his personal belongings and then escort him out of the building, confiscating his building pass. Nathan was waiting for him in the reception foyer, and they left together down the office steps, each with a black sack in hand. Randall escorted them up to the main road.

As Tariq and Nathan walked down Grays Inn Road towards the bus stop holding their black sacks, someone called from behind. 'Tariq!'

He turned around to see Stuart Harper. He looked tired and dishevelled, a shadow of the man he'd seen a few days ago. Half his shirt buttons were undone and his shirt tail was hanging out. He had a concerned expression and an anxious manner, scanning around as if he was being stalked. 'Tariq, please, you've got to listen to me! You're the only person left I can talk to.'

Tariq replied with suspicion, 'What do you want, Harper?'

'Not here. This way.'

They followed Harper into a pop-up craft beer bar down a nearby side road. Inside, it was furnished with vintage wood stools and tables. The bar frontage was made from odd-shaped reclaimed beach wooden planks. Harper led the way to a free table in the back room. He returned to the bar to buy Tariq a bottle of BrewDog craft ale and a Guinness for Nathan. Harper's was a pint of cider. Tariq said, 'This better be good, Harper.'

Harper dabbed his brow with a tissue, 'There's something bad going on, Tariq. A man followed me home on the train last night – I recognised him. He started to tail me down my road to my house, but I lost him. He had a gun, Tariq; I saw the holster strap when he walked past. I've seen him before, at the Elm House SFO office.'

Nathan left the table to go to the toilet to avoid the intense conversation. Harper wiped his brow with his sleeve. 'When have you seen him?' asked Tariq.

'I don't know – I've just seen him, maybe with Burton, or Pemberton, or both; I can't remember. Tariq, they've got Burton already. I know Burton – I know the guy, Tariq; really well. I've worked with him for two years. He's not the suicidal type. No way; no way! I'm telling you – it makes no sense, Tariq; you must see that. Don't trust anyone, Tariq, anyone! They're going after me next. If I go missing, you'll go to the police, won't you?' Harper hesitated before saying, 'You're army trained, aren't you? If you kill him, I'll give you an alibi.'

Tariq looked around the room and back at Harper in disbelief. 'I'm out of practice, I'm afraid. I'll look out for him.'

Harper was spooked by a face he saw across the street through the window. He exited the pub through the beer garden rear door before Tariq had a chance to persuade him to report everything to the police. Harper's statement would at least detract attention away from himself.

Harper never made it home.

CHAPTER 32

On the train back home Nathan was doing a puzzle in his book to calm his frayed emotions, when he said in an angry voice, 'Ruined! Someone's started the puzzle. Was that you, Dad?'

'No. Let me have a look.' Tariq took the puzzle book from his son and looked at the defaced page. It was puzzle No.78, the number Nathan had found written on a Post-it note a week before. The theme of the puzzle was *Craftsman,* and someone had underlined the clue *repairs wooden barrels or tubs*; the answer in the word matrix was also marked out in biro – *Cooper.* Tariq now realised that this was a clue left by Sandra, and just wished he'd taken notice of it when he'd first found it. It could have saved a lot of trouble.

Still on the train, now pulling away from New Beckenham station, Tariq considered whether the Bosnians would have tracked down Avramov by now. Following his near-fatal interrogation, Tariq could now remember his face and the expressions he used to pull, and he had some fleeting childhood memories of them playing and swimming in Visegrad... and that he was a Serb. Bosnians and Serbs enjoyed many friendships before the war, but it was the exception rather than the rule. Tariq asked himself if that made him a Serb? He felt a pang of guilt that he'd betrayed his friend by revealing his name from deep within his subconscious, which had bubbled to the surface under extreme torture. Tariq then considered – had they already killed him? Both nations wanted him dead: for the Bosnians, because he was one of Mladic's henchmen; for the Serbs, as he was a spy and a traitor, who'd passed on information to the CIA.

Tariq reminisced that Alice had told him once that she liked his hair short as it reminded her of the brave young army soldier she'd fallen in love with when she'd first met him in his hospital bed in Cyprus. Her company had sent her to audit the hospital accounts, which required an assessment of the condition of the hospital's main asset – its buildings. What she hadn't bargained for was meeting a strong but vulnerable, clean-cut soldier who'd just come out of a coma. Conversations ensued, which resulted in a blossoming romance. After his discharge from the hospital, they'd married six months later at her family church in Sanderstead, south Croydon.

Tariq said to Nathan, 'We should get off at Clock House station. They won't be expecting me to get off there, and there's a barber just down the road. I'm going to get my hair cut. I'm telling you this now so you won't be shocked when I come out. I made a promise to your mother that when Millie comes home, I'd get my hair cut – *army* short, get it?'

'Well, I guess if it's terrible, it'll grow back again. Maybe you should buy a wig just in case it goes wrong.'

'Ha! I'll tell you what, Nathan. I reckon you also need a trim because your hair looks a bit untidy these days. At least get it cut for Millie.'

Nathan grimaced, looked at the floor at the challenge, and then looked up again, 'Well, if that would help Millie get better, then alright then, I'll come with you. You have to get yours cut first, though.'

'You have a deal, Nathan.'

Tariq felt a glimmer of hope that Pemberton now had the memory stick with the original ledger files, which should expose Harper and Cooper's attempts at manipulating the case files, but would it be enough to clear his name?

Still on the train, Tariq received a WhatsApp message from Cheryl with another photo, this time of the baby asleep on the mother's chest. He responded with a thumbs-up and a red heart emoji, then deleted the messages.

As Tariq exited the train at Clock House station he had a flashback of Harper's fearful state in the bar, and discreetly scanned the carriage for anyone tailing him.

At the barbers, Tariq studied his new haircut in the mirror. As he had requested, his hair was Action Man short, 3mm thick, just above the ears all around, extending around the back of his head. This was the style in his division in Bosnia. It distinguished the Bosnian soldiers from the British and American soldiers stationed with them. The shorter the haircut, the more dedicated the soldier, was the mantra of his senior officer. Nathan, alarmed at his father's extreme sheared hair, had to be persuaded by the gentleman barber that he wouldn't receive the same treatment. Nathan insisted upon having a mirror to check the length of his hair at the back throughout his haircut. The end result was a layered style, which enhanced his understated handsome features, with well-proportioned ears and nose. Even his father was impressed. He'd never seen Nathan so well-groomed. It prompted Tariq to reflect on how his son had applied his unique brand of personal skills to help him at the SFO. Nathan had faced his weaknesses and brought to bear his unique perceptive thinking to the case. Maybe Nathan could thrive in the world, in a way he'd never thought possible. Pity, Tariq thought, that he'd probably never work at the SFO again after trashing Cooper's office. He was on probation, and Pemberton would have the nouse to terminate his employment with no comeback. Following his encounter with Harper, who, weirdly, was now asking him for help, Tariq judged that he wouldn't be pressing assault charges as he'd threatened in the changing room. Harper now feared for his life. Who was the armed man who'd followed him home, and who did he work for?

With their new short haircuts, Tariq and Nathan caught a taxi from Clock House, which pulled up outside the family home. Tariq paid the driver and walked with Nathan faster than usual down the front path to the house, double-locking the front door behind him. He retrieved his old Smith and Wesson army pistol from a locked box in the study. Although not loaded, it was a deterrent enough. He went through every room in the house, checking for intruders. Nathan followed behind him with instructions to phone PC Wilson on his mobile if he didn't come out of each room after twenty seconds. Tariq drew the curtains closed and checked every window was locked. He used his binoculars to scan the street and behind the garages. The red Ford Focus had gone.

Tariq and Nathan tidied up the house the best they could in preparation for Millie's return. Tariq had a quick double whisky to help him along.

Sometime after eight o'clock, Alice's navy Saab approached and parked outside on the street. Tariq told Nathan to calm down before he ran up the garden path to greet his beloved sister and mother. On reaching the car, Nathan said excitedly, 'Millie, Millie, you're home; I'm so glad you're home again. Let me carry your bag.'

'Thank you, Nathan. Wow! Like your hair; very stylish. What do you think, Mum?'

'I was just going to say, Nathan – I told you you're a handsome young man.'

Nathan responded, 'Oh, you should see Dad. His hair is really short, like *army*-short.'

Alice could now see that for herself as her husband approached on the garden path.'

Tariq hugged his wife, 'Hello, darling, good to see you.' She kissed him on the cheek, which he reciprocated. He then turned to Millie, gave her a gentle hug and kiss due to her fragile state, and carried his wife's large Louis Vuitton holdall bag back into the house. Alice took Millie upstairs to her bedroom to make sure she got some rest before dinner and that she took her medication.

Tariq, an average cook, made macaroni cheese with fried finely chopped bacon and onions, served with Italian leaf salad for dinner. At least he knew Nathan would eat it, except for the leaves. They all sat down around the dinner table in the kitchen. Tariq brought out the macaroni cheese, still piping hot, with his *The Simpsons* oven gloves – Nathan's Christmas present to him the previous year.

Millie entered the kitchen lethargically. Her mother asked, 'How are you feeling, little darling? Did you have a good rest?'

'Yes, well, OK, thanks Mum. Not too much for me please, Dad. I'm not that hungry.'

'Of course, Millie, there you go, just a couple of spoonfuls.'

'Thanks, Dad. It's the medication: it affects my appetite.' Millie took her plate and used the metal tongs to help herself to some lettuce. She asked, 'Dad, is it true what Nathan told me about you having to leave the office after you'd collected your belongings?'

Tariq looked at Nathan briefly with an air of disapproval, 'Well, yes, but it is just routine when the police are brought in on a case so that no one can tamper with the evidence, that's all.'

Millie redirected the conversation, 'I forgot to ask you, Dad – how was your trip to Montenegro?'

Nathan was poised to reply for him but following another cold stare from his father he thought better of it.

Tariq answered, 'It was a wild goose chase. It was a case of mistaken identity as I didn't find out anything, I'm afraid. Let's not talk about it: that's not important right now.' His wife looked at him, unconvinced that he'd told the whole story.

Near the end of the meal, Alice asked Tariq, 'Why has the *Guess Who* game in the study have faces glued on it with their names from your work photo, when Pemberton took you all clay pigeon shooting?' Nathan looked embarrassed as his father glanced across at him.

Millie said, 'Dad, why do you think Charlotte gave

him the *Guess Who* game in the family therapy session in the first place? This is the problem, Dad – you missed the first two sessions, didn't you? You missed talking about Nathan's autism.'

'What about his autism?'

'He has prosopagnosia.'

'Prosopag... what?'

'Prosopagnosia – face blindness. He doesn't recognise faces very well, so he has to look at other things, like whether they wear glasses, have a nose stud, or the colour of their hair; that kind of thing. That's why he plays the *Guess Who* game – it helps him spot other differences. He doesn't like to talk about it as he has his own way of working out who it is. Sorry, Nathan, but I had to say.'

Tariq looked stunned; 'I see. Right. Nathan, I didn't know. I didn't...'

Millie said, 'I notice that one of the faces on the game is still missing.'

Tariq replied, 'Oh yes; I tidied everything up quickly in the study but couldn't find the last one.'

After dinner, when Millie and Alice had gone upstairs, Tariq grabbed a scotch and invited Nathan into the study. 'Nathan, I want to thank you for all your help in the office, and I'm really sorry that we had to leave the office today so quickly with our black sacks. Quite awkward, wasn't it?' Tariq put his drink down on the low table and said, 'I need to ask you about something at the office. It's important, so just think carefully.'

'OK Dad, I'm ready. You can ask me.'

'How did you recognise Harper that day when he took the diary out of the office?'

'Purple tie. Harper always wears a purple tie.'

'And the second time, when you saw him coming out of the cleaners' cupboard in the property room.'

'Same; purple tie.'

'Thank you, Nathan. That's all, then.'

Tariq returned to the sitting room's drinks cabinet, topped up his drink, and slumped back on the sofa. He closed his eyes and recalled his confrontation with Harper after he had caught him posting the document in the post room. He remembered twisting his tie around his neck. It was red, not purple. Harper had been wearing a new red tie recently, and Cooper by chance had been wearing a purple tie. Recalling what happened that day when Nathan had seen Harper exiting the cleaner's room with Mitchko's red diary and they had pursued him through the park, it seemed obvious now – the man they'd seen in the distance catching the taxi *wasn't* Harper. This explained how he'd got to the end of the road so quickly to catch the taxi, as it wasn't him: it was just someone in the distance wearing a similar dark suit and purple tie, and it explained why they'd found Cooper in The Phoenix pub with Pemberton. It wasn't Harper with the diary – it was *Cooper*! Unusually, Cooper wore a purple tie that day, which he'd taken off by the time they saw him in the pub. For the first time it occurred to Tariq that Harper could have been telling the truth – that he was following Burton's directions to copy the primary case documents. He concurred with Harper that Burton wasn't the type to run away from anything in life, especially by driving his car into the Thames. He could understand now why Harper was in fear of his life now that Burton had been eliminated.

CHAPTER 33

On Sunday morning, Millie and Nathan were first down for breakfast. Tariq could hear the excited tone of Nathan's voice from upstairs as he crossed the landing to the bathroom. By the time Tariq went down to the kitchen, Nathan had finished his breakfast and was already in the bathroom. Tariq made a cafetière of coffee and sat at the kitchen table, sipping his coffee. Everything seemed normal for that moment. A fleeting moment to savour Tariq mused. Even the bathroom was free for Nathan, so no tantrums – before breakfast, at least.

Tariq was on his second slice of toast when Alice joined him in the kitchen wearing her favourite light-blue vintage Liberty paisley cotton dressing gown. Tariq smiled at her, taking in her curvaceous beauty and elegance. He realised then that he'd missed her more than he'd thought. He asked her, 'Cup of Char? There's some in the pot. I'll pour you some.'

'Yes, thanks. Where are Nathan and Millie?'

'Both upstairs; Nathan is in the bathroom.'

'It's so good to see them both at home again. Nathan would be devastated if she…'

Tariq gave her a couple of kitchen roll sheets to wipe the tears from her eyes.

Tariq said, 'She's home now, OK, so let's enjoy the time we have with her.'

Tariq leaned towards her across the table, between two used cereal bowls, and clasped her hands in his, as she dabbed the tears from her eyes.

Alice said through damp eyes, 'I can see that Nathan enjoyed spending time with you and helping you with your case at work. It can't have been easy. I know he can be demanding at times, especially at work.'

'Do you know what? He was, in the end, quite helpful; some of the guys in the office told me that. He was always thorough and picked up on things no one else did.'

Alice said, 'I'm sure everything will work out for you at the SFO. They'll sort out who's behind it all, and welcome you back with open arms. I just hope that Director of yours has the courage to sack the real culprits. It needs someone to make a stand. Are you listening, darling? Why are you staring out of the window?'

'Oh, just looking out for wildlife; it's a jungle out there.'

'Yes, you need to cut the grass this weekend… but not as short as your hair, mind. I don't think I've ever seen so much of your neck before! I'm impressed – you remembered your promise.'

Tariq turned round with a smirk on the side of his face. 'Glad you like it. You said you preferred it short as it suited my face and makes me look in control, just like when you first met me.'

'Love it, darling. Thank you for making an effort. I need to get dressed.'

Millie and Nathan were now in the study. To be friendly, Tariq knocked and opened the door; he wanted

346

to see what they were up to. He was surprised to find that they had reconstructed the work photograph that Nathan had cut up for the *Guess Who* game. There was a gap in the photograph as one of the faces was still missing. Tariq was about to start looking for the missing piece in the study somewhere, when Millie went to leave the room and asked, 'Dad, are you coming to church with me? You promised you would if you could.'

'Did I? Millie, please, I haven't been in years. It's not really my scene. The front door is locked, by the way.'

Tariq followed her into the hallway. Millie took the keys and opened the front door. Tariq was temporarily blinded by the low morning sun. 'Dad, the door is open. Come with me.'

The words seemed familiar, as if it wasn't just Millie speaking to him, which prompted him to change his mind, 'OK, then; I'll come with you.'

The church was an unspectacular 1930's building with high plain brown ceiling panels; no grand vaulting, just plain arcade arches. There were a few basic stained-glass windows and other religious touches, just enough to give it an air of otherworld ambience: a sanctuary for some, irrelevant to others.

Tariq was introduced to a myriad of Millie's friends, some young, some old, embracing her as if she were family. They eventually took their seats, which were modern upholstered chairs. The previous progressive vicar had removed the solid oak pews some years ago.

Tariq was surprised that the man who wore the loudest green-and-orange-patterned shirt turned out to be the vicar, as he stood behind a low wooden pulpit. The vicar, Reverend Rob Jones, was in his late forties. He had a small, trimmed brown beard and friendly eyes. With a restrained smile he addressed the congregation, 'Let us give thanks to God for bringing Millie back to us at this time.' Looking at Millie, he said, 'I appreciate that your treatment hasn't finished yet, Millie, so thank you for making the effort to be here with us this morning. If we knew you were coming, we would have arranged something special for you.' Millie half smiled back.

After a few worship songs, most of which Tariq didn't know, nor could sing with the same enthusiasm as those around him – the bearded vicar announced that his sermon would be on the Prodigal Son. Tariq considered that the vicar's friendly, relaxed demeanour wasn't conducive to the delivery of an earth-shattering sermon. Still, he would try to listen for Millie's sake.

The vicar prayed that the message would be used by God and said, 'So to remind you all about the story of the Prodigal Son – there was a man who had two sons. The younger one said to his father, "Father, give me my share of the estate." So he divided his property between them. Not long after that, the younger son got together all he had, set off for a distant country where he eventually squandered his wealth on wild living. After he had spent his inheritance, there was a severe famine across the land, and he got so desperate for food that he hired himself out to a farmer to feed his pigs. He longed to fill his stomach with what the pigs were eating, but no one gave him anything. He then came to his senses and said to himself, "How many of my father's hired servants have food to spare, and here I am starving to death!" I will set out and go back to my father and say to him, "Father, I have done wrong against heaven and against you. I am no longer worthy to be called your son; make me like one of your hired servants," so he got up and set off back to his father's house. While the wayward son was still a long way off, his father saw him and was filled with compassion for him; he ran to him, threw his arms around him and kissed him. The father said to his servants, "Quick! Dress him in my best robe and put a ring on his finger and sandals on his feet. Bring the fattened calf and kill it, and let's have a feast and celebrate – for this son of mine was dead and is alive again; he was lost and now is found." So they began to celebrate. Now the older son, who had been with his father the whole time, got angry and resentful so…'

Tariq soon lost concentration as he mulled over what had happened to him over the last few weeks. The tsunami of disastrous events and revelations threatened to overwhelm him.

The Reverend paused in his sermon, turned, and looked straight at Tariq saying, 'Do you know who you really are? To those who have ears to hear, let them hear – listen carefully. There is an even more important question, and it is this – do you want to know who you really are? To admit that *you* are that Prodigal Son? If you want to know your real identity then you need to get on your knees and say honestly to God your father, "I've squandered everything; I am not worthy to be your son; have mercy on me." You need to choose to come out of the forest of confusion, pursued by your enemies, to face the truth. Humble yourself, and you will know the truth, and the truth will set you free…'

On the walk home from the church, Tariq said to Millie in a serious tone, 'I guess you've told him everything about me?'

'What do you mean?'

'That sermon – it was just for me. Admit it!'

'Dad, that's ridiculous; he didn't even know I was coming today, let alone that you'd come with me.'

'Sorry Millie, but how did he…? Why was he talking just to me?'

'That's how it is sometimes.'

'I'm losing it, Millie. I'm…'

Tariq couldn't talk anymore without breaking down. Millie put her arm around her father as they walked home together.

When they got home, Millie went up to her bedroom. After checking that his wife wasn't around, Tariq collected his thoughts with the help of a Jack Daniels. He was halfway through his drink when an argument flared up upstairs between Millie and Nathan. Millie had locked herself in the bathroom, and Nathan was shouting at her through the door that he should be allowed to go first because he was much quicker. Tariq was making his way upstairs to try to calm Nathan down. As he did so, Millie said through the locked bathroom door, 'Now listen, Nathan, I'm not negotiating with you on this; you'll just have to get used to the idea.'

Nathan replied in a rage, 'That's blackmail, Cooper! Blackmail, do you hear? We're in this together, and you know it!'

Millie responded, 'What? Who's Cooper? You're making no sense, Nathan.'

Tariq stopped where he was in shock at what he'd

just heard Nathan blurt out. He sat halfway up the stairs, holding his head in his hands, as the significance of what Nathan had said sunk in. Nathan had a habit of borrowing phrases that he'd heard somewhere, like advertising slogans, and repeating them out of context. It wasn't only what Nathan had said, but that it was a perfect imitation of Pemberton's clipped Scottish accent. Tariq recalled the first few days in the office when Nathan questioned him on the train after work. It wasn't *black male* that he'd heard; it was *blackmail*. Another phrase that Nathan had said at that time also came to mind, something like *buy the book*. Pemberton had probably told Cooper to play out the scam *by the book*.

Tariq sat on the stairs for a few minutes, finishing his drink, as it dawned on him that he'd missed so many obvious signs that Pemberton was working with Cooper, and now he'd handed over the original memory stick to Pemberton, so he was back to square one. The Monopoly game phrase came to mind – *Go to jail, go directly to jail,* .... He was in a deadly game. Was there one last throw of the dice?

Tariq stepped back down the stairs to the drinks cabinet and poured himself a top-up of whisky. He then went across to the study and slumped down in the green leather padded desk armchair next to the door – the same chair the Serb war veteran had sat on with his pistol pointed at him. As he slumped in the chair, he looked across the room to spy a small item under the ornamental cabinet in the far corner of the room. He crossed the room and extended his hand to slide out the strange object under the cabinet. It was the missing face tile from the *Guess Who* game. He hadn't noticed before – but it was a younger Amar, the man he'd met at the Olympics with Pemberton and Cooper. His full name was on the bottom of his photograph – *Amar Tarnik-Genar,* A.T-G. It was him who'd booked the van the day Cheryl was abducted. He was their hit man. Tariq sat back in the chair, sipping his whisky. Amar was probably the man Harper had seen following him home armed with a pistol. The photograph with the missing square was on the side table next to him, so Tariq leant over and placed the photo of the man into the gap to complete the picture: Pemberton, Cooper and Amar were huddled together smiling into the camera, each holding their double-barrelled shotguns at the clay pigeon shoot.

After Nathan had gained access to the bathroom after Millie and calmed down, he entered the study, sat on the black swivel chair, and faced his father. 'Was church alright, Dad? What are you doing in here?'

'I was with Millie; that was the main thing. We sang a few songs, and the vicar gave a sermon as if he knew everything about me... I don't want to talk about it right now, Nathan.'

'What's up then? Why are you in here...' Nathan then continued in a quieter tone so his mother wouldn't hear, '... drinking whisky?'

'Nathan. I'm glad you're sitting down because I need to talk to you.'

'About what?'

'It's more about *who* – Pemberton, the Director.'

'He's the Scottish-sounding one isn't he? What about him?'

'Yes, that's him. I know now he's working with Cooper to sabotage the case. I know that for sure. I've made a big mistake, Nathan. I've taken the memory stick off Cooper and given it to Pemberton, so I'm back to square one. I'm finished, Nathan!' Tariq stared down into his near-empty glass.

'So, Dad, we need to get back into the office again to get it off him. It's probably still in his desk drawer, like it was for Mark Cooper.'

'Too late, Nathan, too late. We've returned our building passes.'

'I've still got my all-areas pass, Dad. I couldn't hand it in because they didn't know I had it in the first place.'

'Nathan, forget it! As you told me once; they've got thirty-seven cameras in that building – we won't stand a chance.'

'We will if I bring my laptop. I have the remote app to control the cameras, remember? I'll have to come with you, Dad.'

Tariq took a deep breath and swigged down the remainder of his whisky, 'OK, Nathan – what have I got to lose, hey?' Tariq looked at his watch. 'Let's leave at nine o'clock.'

Tariq and Alice went for a walk together in the afternoon and stopped for a coffee at the Kelsey Park café. Tariq wished and prayed that life could return to normal; and they could be together as a family again. Nathan stayed in the house with Millie, playing some board games together.

For dinner they sat together in the kitchen using up the leftovers of a risotto that Alice had made the day before.

It had been a hot day, so Tariq decided to have a quick shower before leaving with Nathan. He usually had warm baths, but there was no time. In the shower, Tariq hadn't noticed that Nathan had left the water temperature set on a hot setting, and before he could turn it down, the water scorched the back of his head and neck, which was especially painful as the skin on the back of his neck was now exposed after his short haircut. Tariq exclaimed in pain, 'Aaagghh!', then jumped out of the shower, landing on his knees on the towel mat outside. Steam continued to rise from the shower cubicle, filling the bathroom. He eventually reached in and turned the shower off. Tariq returned to his knees as the words of the sermon – *Humble yourself, and you will know the truth, and the truth will set you free* – enveloped his mind. All the burdens of the last few weeks and the last seventeen years weighed heavily on him, pinning him to the floor. He stayed kneeling for several minutes, weeping. He then said out loud, quietly but sincerely, 'I am not worthy to be your son. Have mercy on me.'

At that moment he felt something in him change. He then looked up in front of him at a square dressing mirror on the low table. Tariq concluded it was probably Millie's, that she'd brought back from the hospital. The dressing mirror was pointing at another large wall mirror behind him. By now the steam was beginning to clear, and he realised that he could see the back of his neck in the dressing mirror reflecting from the large mirror behind him. The image in the mirror started to come into focus as the steam evaporated. What he saw in the mirror was so shocking to him that he couldn't believe it; he *wouldn't* believe it.

As the air cleared further and the condensation thinned on the mirror, Tariq exclaimed to himself, 'No! No! This can't be, it just can't be! Oh God – no! How can this be?! This isn't possible. Nooooo!' In the mirror, he saw the clear profile on the back of his neck, in red inflamed skin, of a double-headed eagle. He wrapped a towel around him quickly and returned from his bedroom with the photograph of the tattoo the Serbian had left behind. 'Oh God!' The profile of his red skin matched that of the tattoo on the postcard exactly. The original tattoo had been carefully removed, probably by laser treatment, leaving the skin more sensitive to heat. He'd never had his hair cut so short since the war, and had never had a hot shower, let alone with the mirrors being there in alignment.

Tariq stayed on his knees with the realisation and conviction that it wasn't Avramov who was the spy – it was *him*! Like the steam in the room, the fog cleared in his mind. He now knew who he was; it had come back to him as if opening a page of a closed book after many years; seventeen years. He was a Serb, Bogdan Tanović. He remembered vividly going to the tattoo parlour with his childhood friend Stefan Avramov on his eighteenth birthday. They were like brothers, which is why they both got matching tattoos in the parlour. A year later, he was appalled by what his own people, the Serbs, had done to the Bosnians at Visegrad. Many that he'd seen killed close up on the Mehmed Paša Sokolović bridge by his countrymen were his friends. They were like family, and he'd witnessed them being cut to pieces and thrown into the Drina River like slaughtered animals. He wanted to do something, to bring justice for the Bosnians, which is why he'd agreed

355

to be an informer for the CIA, the only informer on the ground they had.

A sharp thought pricked him – Avramov would tell the Bosnians and the Serbs that it was him they should be after. How long would it take for them to catch up with him?

CHAPTER 34

Nathan came downstairs with his laptop at nine o'clock, as arranged. Tariq informed Alice that they needed to get something from the office before the morning so they had to go tonight. Since there was no sign of the red Ford Focus he decided to risk going out the front door, and walked with Nathan directly to Eden Park station. Besides, he didn't want to alarm Alice and Millie by sneaking through the back garden and leaving through the back gate. It was just after sunset and the western sky was a deep blood red. Tariq didn't want to dwell on the sight. A man in the twilight followed them at a distance. Two men in a silver Mercedes drove on slowly behind and into the train station car park, and tracked them as they entered the station. One of them made a call on his mobile. The man following boarded the train's rear carriage just before the doors shut.

Tariq and Nathan exited London Bridge train station and took a taxi to the SFO Elm Street office. A man in a loose, dark-blue casual suit followed behind in a cab. Tariq asked the taxi driver to drop them off down the road from the SFO office. There was a single security guard behind the reception desk. Tariq directed Nathan to sit down in the bus shelter just along the road from the office. Using the shelter wouldn't provoke any suspicion. From there,

Nathan logged in to the CCTV surveillance system on his laptop. A side entrance led to the ground-level bicycle racks, and from there, they could gain access into the SFO compound through a security gate operated by a staff pass. Tariq and Nathan agreed that this was the best way in. A camera covered the footway approach to the side entrance, and a second camera covered the bicycle racks. There were a few bikes locked to the racks, some of which had been abandoned for some time, judging by the extensive rust.

Nathan waited until there were no moving cars or pedestrians on camera before he froze the view, making it undetectable by the security guard monitoring the screens. Seconds later, Nathan used his building pass to open the side gate and enter the forecourt the other side of the bike racks. 'Dad, stop! Come back.' Tariq quickly stepped back. 'There's another camera; you're in shot. I need to freeze it. I'll have to keep both of them locked until we're inside as the outside camera also picks up the plant room door.' Nathan had to work out which camera inside the building to freeze next. There was a side door down some steps into the basement level labelled *PLANT ROOM*. The problem was that there were three similar Plant Rooms on the laptop display screen. Nathan suggested to his father that he push his white handkerchief slowly through the window grill in the door. 'Got it! I can see it. Take it out Dad – it's *PLANT ROOM 1*.' Nathan froze the display and they entered the building through the plant room door. Nathan was glad he'd added the option *Plant, Service Rooms and Staff Offices – Authorised Service Engineers only* to his building pass permissions when Ajay had left him at his desk for his morning coffee. He then unfroze the two outside cameras.

Tariq and Nathan again studied the laptop display screen, which switched between cameras every ten seconds. To save time working out the coverage of each camera further into the building, Nathan simultaneously locked the stairwell and floor camera displays, twelve in all. The security guard wouldn't be expecting anything going on in any case. They went up the stairs to Pemberton's office on the tenth floor using Nathan's pass to open the door.

A black Range Rover reversed up to the high-security fence adjacent to the bike racks, obscuring the full view of the surveillance camera. A man got out of the driver's door on the camera's blind side. He placed a mini-jack between the vertical metal fence railings and turned the handle rapidly around. About a minute later, the jack had bent the fence uprights outwards, wide enough for the man to pass through. He went through the gap and jumped down out of sight behind one of the locked bikes. He moved across the forecourt under the camera view, then edged along the wall and in through the same plant room door Tariq and Nathan had gone through. He also had a building pass for all doors. As the plant room closed slowly behind, a second man used the same gap in the fence to gain access into the SFO compound.

At the same time the men were accessing the side plant room, two men ran up the office front steps into the foyer. The security guard recognised them, and let them pass into the building.

The blinds in Pemberton's room were closed, so Tariq took the risk of turning the office light on. Inside his office, Tariq checked the desk drawers, to find them unlocked. Nathan opened each drawer in turn from the top, left-hand side, and Tariq, the right-hand drawers. Tariq said, 'Yes!' as he held up the memory stick to show Nathan. They closed the drawers as they had found them, exited the office and made their way down the stairs. As they approached the ground floor Nathan stopped on the landing to lock down the *PLANT ROOM 1* camera display. He couldn't believe what he saw – a man in a blue suit was approaching Tariq from down the corridor. He opened his mouth to shout a warning to his father but it was too late.

'Don't move. Put your hands up, Tariq! Hands on your head. Fancy finding you here. Where's your son? I thought he was with you.'

'I left him in the pub. I bought him a Guinness as a treat for keeping me company.'

The man took a few steps forward to look up the stair well towards the landing, but Nathan had already crept back up the stairs out of sight. He said, 'Yes, I remember – your son loves his black-and-white Guinness, doesn't he? Now, move! Down the stairs to the basement, now!'

Tariq stood his ground, 'Hello, Amar Tarnik-Genar. Good to meet you again. I thought we were getting along.'

'Well done, Tariq, you know my name, but it doesn't matter who I am. That won't help you now.'

'I know exactly who you are, Amar, and I know you're working with Pemberton and Cooper on the Magnus Conan-Whittaker scam. I hope that Mitchko's paying you well. I wouldn't trust Pemberton, by the way – he'd love to cut you out if he could; not to mention Cooper. You won't get away with it you know.'

'You don't know shit, my friend.' He pushed Tariq, with his hands still on his head, along the corridor and down the steps into the lower basement room. 'Against the wall! Spread your legs!' Amar then searched Tariq's jacket pockets. He found the memory stick. 'Thank you, Tariq, I'll be taking that. That's all we need to finish this job as clean as you like.' Amar stepped back and aimed his pistol at Tariq's head, saying, 'I thought you said that we wouldn't get away with it. You broke into Pemberton's office to retrieve the memory stick. I followed you into the basement; there was a scuffle; you came at me with a metal bar, and I shot you in self-defence.'

A shot rang out in the enclosed basement like a pressure wave – the distinctive sound of a pistol with a silencer.

Amar fell to the ground. A second shot killed him. Tariq turned around. Why was Amar dead and not him? 'I always had your back, didn't I, Bogdan? My tattoo brother, Bogdan Tanović. We were told you were killed in the war, along with your father and surviving brother. I can't believe that you're still alive. I've missed you, man We go back a long way. We enjoyed many summers together, didn't we, swimming in the Drina River in Visegrad?'

'Stefan, Stefan Avramov. I've only just got my memory back, Stefan. Otherwise I would have come looking for you.'

'Bogdan, my friend, I know that only too well, my friend, because all of a sudden, the Bosnian gangs are all looking for me. But I'll tell you something, Bogdan – I've still got my memory, and I've still got this.' He turned round and unfurled his pale yellow scarf to reveal a double-headed eagle tattoo on the back of his neck. 'That was a good birthday, wasn't it, Bogdan? We were blood brothers weren't we, with our matching tattoos.'

'Yes, I remember it well now, and before you ask – I didn't choose to get mine removed. I woke up in hospital and it was gone.'

'Let me guess – by the CIA?'

Stefan heard steps approaching the door. The door opened slowly. He kept talking and waited before kicking the heavy door backwards, which slammed into the man behind the door, making him cry out in pain. Stefan then yanked the door open to find a man lying on the ground nursing his hand, with his gun on the floor. Stefan slid the man's gun away from him with his foot. He then realised that the man on the floor had fallen back onto a second man behind him, who was now reaching across his chest for his firearm.

'Don't even think about it, big man. Throw it on the floor. Now! Inside!'

Embarrassed by how easily they'd been subdued, the two men moved into the basement room as instructed.

Tariq said, 'Burton! We all thought you were dead, drowned in the river.'

'Hi Tariq, good buddy. Yes, that was the general idea. Amar sabotaged the car, so we decided to go along with it to flush him and his cronies out into the open, and it was working, until now that is.'

Tariq said to the second man, 'Frank. What's going on? Look, I'm sorry for what happened at Tivat Airport. It was the British police… '

Stefan held his gun up towards them, saying, 'I'm glad you guys are acquainted, but can you kindly tell me who they are?'

Tariq answered, 'Frank is CIA, and Burton is the

SFO...' Burton produced his CIA ID card from his top pocket. Tariq exclaimed, 'What?! Burton, you're CIA?'

Burton asked, 'And you, sir, pointing the gun? Who are you?'

'Stefan.'

'Good to meet you, Stefan. Now you just relax, cowboy; we're here to look after Tariq over there. We've no quarrel with you, unless you have a quarrel with Tariq, that is.' Burton looked across to the far corner of the room to see Amar lying dead, his blood seeping across the concrete floor. Burton said, 'I see you've saved us a job by dealing with that bastard assassin Amar.'

'That's because I'm an old and loyal friend of Bogdan, as you know full well is his real name.'

Burton said, 'Right, sir. You're *that* Stefan.'

'Yes, *that* Stefan. My friend here needs to do the right thing and turn himself in to The Hague. He needs to tell the world that he was the one recruited by you lot to spy on Mladic – not *me*! And he needs to do it quickly before the Bosnians or the Serbs catch up with me.' Why should I have to die because you removed his tattoo, and I've still got mine?' Stefan twisted his neck around briefly to show his tattoo.

Agent Frank, still nursing his bruised hand where the door had slammed on him, said, 'Stefan. I'm sorry to burst your bubble – that's just not going to happen. There's no way that the CIA will let your friend here anywhere near The Hague, so let's try to work something out shall we, heh?'

Stefan gripped his gun and pointed at Agent Frank. 'You don't understand – unless he testifies that he was the informer, either the Bosnians or the Serbs will track me

363

down. The Bosnians will take me to The Hague to testify against Mladic, or the Serbs will kill me. He *has* to go.'

Agent Frank lifted his hands, 'OK, OK, Stefan, let's slow down heh, and let us talk for a minute about the problem here. First, let me tell you straight – if we don't report back from this office tonight, our men will track you down well before any Bosnians or Serbs get to you; I can guarantee you of that.' Stefan relaxed his grip, tilted his gun downwards at the floor and sat on the chair behind him.

Stefan said, 'OK, you have one minute, then, to talk about the problem.'

'If you've been following it on TV, you'll know that Mladic's trial is now suspended, and I'll tell you why. Someone, probably a Serb, has leaked to the trial judge that we – the US, that is – had an agent in the field who had provided much of the key evidence against Mladic. The judge has ruled that if there was such an agent, he must be cross-examined in court. Our president has recently issued a statement that the US had no prior knowledge of the massacres; otherwise this intel would have been shared with the UN and airstrikes would have been called in earlier.'

Stefan said, 'So the US president knows the CIA had an agent in close proximity to Mladic?'

'No comment. He doesn't have to know, because there was *no* agent.'

Tariq said to Frank, 'Unless I testify, that is. All I was doing was sending through the coordinates of the grave sites. Let me testify – that was my only remit.'

Agent Frank continued, 'Tariq, your intel was vital, son. Without it, maybe there wouldn't even be a trial, but I'm afraid that's as far as it goes. You're not going to The

Hague because "there were no US agents on the ground" – got it!?'

No one heard the footsteps coming this time. The door sprung open. Stefan, still sitting down, was slow to react. He got to his feet and turned his gun towards the door, but too late; the man at the door fired three shots. Stefan stumbled and fell backwards, his head thumping into the concrete wall behind him.

The gunmen, dressed in jeans and a black leather jacket, surveyed the room.

'Everybody very still, please. Try anything, and I kill you,' he said in basic English with a Serbian accent. He walked over to Stefan, who was lying on the ground on his side. The man rolled Stefan's body over with his foot, twisting him face down, revealing the double-headed eagle tattoo on the back of his neck. 'Finally, we find you – traitor to the Serbs. We look for you a long time. We don't worry anymore about you making up stories in The Hague against Ratko, do we?'

Agent Frank said to the man, 'Nice shooting, whoever you are,' as he looked down at Stefan.

The Serb answered back, 'Tell me, please – who are you?'

'CIA. We're CIA,' said Burton, opening his wallet to show his ID. Agent Frank judged this a mistake. The Serbs still hated the CIA for their role in bringing Mladic to trial. The Serb said to the Americans, 'And we've also been looking for you. You bastards recruited him. Isn't that right?'

Agent Frank responded, with a twitch of nerves, 'You're barking up the wrong tree there, fella. We've been looking for him, just like you. We're just following orders to bring him in.'

The Serb was standing in the same spot where the skip had been, and pointed his gun at Agent Frank, 'You're a Goddamn liar…'

Before he could pull the trigger, Tariq shouted, 'Drop it, Nathan! Drop it!'

The Serb responded, 'Nathan? Who's Nathan?'

A heavy hardback book fell at speed out of the overhead orange elephant trunking from the property room above, hitting the Serb's hand, breaking two of his fingers, and knocking the gun to the ground across the room. He yelped in pain and fell to his knees. Agent Frank picked up the gun and aimed it at the Serb, while Burton went behind him and handcuffed him.

The basement was soon swarming with police, Special Branch, and MI6 officials speaking to Burton and Agent Frank, while police paramedics examined the two dead men. After taking their statements, Tariq and Nathan were driven to the police station, where they were kept overnight in one of the police cells.

CHAPTER 35

Tariq managed to calm Nathan down in the police cell to get a few hours' sleep. They were awakened early and escorted into the staff canteen, where they had a cooked breakfast.

A police constable (PC) took Tariq up to the newly refurbished first-floor interview room. One of the female PCs stayed with Nathan and made him a hot chocolate, as he requested.

Agent Frank and DI Randall were waiting for them in the interview room. DI Randall directed the junior officer to leave the room and shut the door behind him. He offered Tariq a seat.

Agent Frank asked, 'Sleep OK?'

Tariq responded, 'Not bad considering.'

'The canteen breakfast isn't too bad, is it?'

'Yes, it was good, thanks.'

'Are you OK to talk after last night's shooting at the OK Coral?'

'You forget, I've seen worse shootings, but I would appreciate a debrief.'

Agent Frank replied in a serious tone, 'That's good, Tariq; that's why we're here, so I want you to listen carefully. Just to mention, Pemberton and Cooper have been arrested, but that's not your concern.'

Tariq asked, 'Who was the Serb you arrested last night by the way? What are you going to do about him? He saw everything.'

'Not everything. I'll come to that in a minute. The deceased Amar was Bosnian, but what he didn't tell you was that he was employed by Karlo Mitchko. He set up the bribe for Pemberton and Cooper – one and a half million each. Pemberton already knew Mitchko from his time with NATO in Kosovo. He's going through an expensive divorce, and Cooper can't afford the new house his wife has set her heart on, so they both accepted the offer.'

'So what about Harper and Burton; how are they mixed up in all of this?'

'Please, Tariq, let me explain, will you? Burton was appointed directly by the Attorney General...' Frank hesitated, '... because of you, Tariq.'

'Me?! Burton was appointed because of *me*?'

Agent Frank continued, 'The Attorney General didn't know about Amar then, none of us did. They suspected that you were the insider, working for Mitchko, as he was probably blackmailing you for your affair with Cheryl. What we weren't counting on was the Bosnians turning up, brought in by Pemberton under the direction of Mitchko.' Agent Frank sighed, moved his chair closer to the desk, and took out some typed notes. He looked back at Tariq and asked, 'How much to you remember about what happened in Srebrenica when you got out?'

'Something happened to me yesterday – my mind has been transformed. I remember everything now. I activated the GPS tracker at the mass shooting sites, as briefed by Jovica Stanisic and Bill Fonlerg at the café when it all started. I recognised Stanisic at The Hague on TV.'

'Tariq, those are people you need to forget ever knowing, quickly.' Agent Frank paused. 'The US government has a proposal for you, which I hope you accept, for your sake; but we'll come on to that in a bit. Firstly, we're sorry for what happened out there at the end of the war. Somehow, your cover was blown, so we had to get you out real quick. By chance a Bosnian soldier had been killed a few days earlier – Tariq Markovic; his uniform was intact and your size. Not even the UN knew the CIA had recruited you, so we had to smuggle you out as a Bosnian soldier. During your evacuation you were exposed to BZ Gas.'

'BZ Gas – what's that?'

'It is a chemical weapon, made in the US. It affects the nervous system, causing hallucinations and memory loss. What happened to you in Srebrenica was aggravated by PTSD and a blow to the head, which left you unconscious. When you came round we couldn't release you directly to the UN until we could be sure that you wouldn't reveal your recruitment by the CIA under interrogation. We gave you a real hard time for five days in that cold damp concrete basement. We regret that we had to test you, but it had to be done. You passed the test so we handed you over to the UN hospital in Cyprus.' Agent Frank paused. 'We look after our agents, Tariq, and after discovering your memory loss, a diplomatic arrangement was made between the US and UK authorities for the UK immigration office to fast-track your asylum application to the UK with your new identity.' Agent Frank took a sip of his coffee and continued, 'As you know, the other man killed last night was your old friend Stefan Avramov. We appreciate that you're probably still in shock at his death.'

Tariq said, 'I hadn't seen him for eighteen years, and he'd changed. He had a kind of madness in his eyes. He wasn't the person I thought I knew. I won't miss him to be honest.'

Agent Frank took another sip of his coffee, 'You see, Tariq, what happened to Stefan last night has given us an unexpected, but perfect opportunity, to put this problem to bed, for keeps. As far as the Serb is concerned – he killed the spy with the eagle tattoo they've been looking for ever since the war ended. He'll be a hero to Serbs for killing the Serb traitor, and to the Bosnians, for killing Mladic's henchman. He'll be released as part of a diplomatic exchange, or allowed to escape. It won't be long before word will spread among the Serbs and Bosnians, that the man with the tattoo is dead, so neither of them will be looking for him anymore. As I said, it's too good an opportunity to miss, and in order to take advantage of this opportunity, we need your cooperation. I'd like to think that when you hear the generous offer on the table, you'll agree that it's a good deal for all parties.'

Agent Frank finished his coffee and focused intently on Tariq. 'The deal is this – the American government require that you forget that the CIA ever recruited you and that you ever saw the massacres of the Bosnian men. You say nothing to your family, the SFO, your friends, anyone – got it? We also need you to propagate the story that the late Stefan Avramov was the spy with the eagle tattoo. One other thing; you're not to talk to anyone about the gas that took you out in the woods. Parties in the know will soon work out that your symptoms were consistent with BZ Gas, which could be traced to the US. We've agreed with the Serbs to keep its use out of the evidence at the trial at The Hague.' Agent Frank interrupted his briefing and said to DI Randall, 'I'm sorry; would you mind leaving us for a few minutes, as this is purely US business, authorised by the top man himself.'

DI Randall scowled and left the room.

With just two of them in the room, Agent Frank addressed Tariq in a clear American tone. 'To encourage you to accept this deal, I'm authorised to transfer into an account of your choosing two million dollars, tax-free, and to your family in Bosnia – half a million dollars.'

Tariq replied, 'My family? I don't even know if my father and brother are alive.'

'They're alive – we've traced them in Bosnia.'

Tariq trembled with joy. 'My father and brother *are alive*?'

'I was about to mention – that is part of the deal; we'll re-unite you with your family. As I said, you need to tell them about Avramov. The whole of Visegrad and Bosnia will soon know he was the spy; and believe me, Tariq, we'll be watching and listening to ensure that you stick to your side of the deal.'

Tariq struggled to contain himself as he wiped the moisture from his eyes, and said, 'I have an additional demand.'

'Oh? I have to tell you that I can't guarantee anything more than the offer on the table.'

'I want half a million dollars for Cheryl, tax-free.'

Frank looked back at Tariq for a few seconds, and said, 'Right, well, I'm authorised to go to three million, but's that's it. Good; we have a deal then.'

Agent Frank bent down to his side and took out two sheets of typed paper from his briefcase and placed them on the table. He produced a pen and wrote on the neatly typed contract, and on two blank cheques. He slid the two cheques across the table towards Tariq: one for $2,000,000 made out to Tariq Markovic, the second for $500,000 made out to Cheryl Bedford, and the contract, which Tariq duly signed. Agent Frank explained, 'You don't get a copy. That's the way it works with us, I'm afraid. I've already sorted things out with your family, but I warn you, Tariq, if you or your family break the deal, you'll all be extradited and incarcerated in the United States for a long time. But we don't need to worry about that, do we?' He leant over the table to shake Tariq's hand. Tariq obliged with a big smile. Agent Frank left the room promptly, and DI Randall took over.

At the end of Tariq's debriefing, Randall said to Tariq, 'Agent Frank asked me to give you these,' He handed him a brown paper bag. Tariq opened it. There were four small boxes of tablets; the ones that Millie was taking, and a small white card with a message written on it: *For Millie. I hope she recovers. Say thank you to Nathan for dropping the book; he's a real hero. If you're reading this – we have a deal, and never need to see each other again. Good luck. Agent F.'*

DI Randall said into his radio, 'You can bring them in now.'

The door opened, and there stood his father and

brother. They approached each other, first in disbelief, then embracing, weeping together with a shared joy they daren't believe they could ever feel again.

CHAPTER 36

Two months later, Tariq, Alice, Nathan and Millie were at the Melanie Klein Child Psychology Centre for their final family therapy session. Charlotte, the therapist, was concluding the meeting.

'It's so sad that this is the last time I'm going to see you guys. I'm especially pleased to see you looking so well, Millie, after all you've been through, and well done Nathan for getting the apprenticeship at the Serious Fraud Office in the same department as your father, now he's been reinstated as a senior disclosure officer. Alice, you did an incredible job to keep the family together while all this was happening, and Tariq, what an amazing story to hear that you've been reunited with your father and brother from Bosnia.

As the family left the building, Tariq said to Charlotte privately, 'Thank you for taking the time to listen to my story – it means a lot to me.'

'No problem, it was a pleasure. I can tell that you've changed; you know who you are now. I can see it in your eyes. What was the Bible verse you mentioned?'

'John chapter one, verse twelve; it is the greatest identity, and it's free, a gift to all who would seek it. Look it up if you like.'

ABOUT THE AUTHOR

Peter Carroll has four grown-up children and lives with his wife in Beckenham, South London.

As a Christian and Chartered Civil Engineer, he has drawn on his personal and professional life to craft a meticulously researched novel, grounded on real events.

From experiences gained from his traumatic childhood, and friendships with neurodiverse individuals on the autistic spectrum, he has written a highly engaging psychological thriller with twists and turns until the very last page.